Loretta was born in Perth, the eldest of four girls. She enjoyed writing from a very early age and was just eleven years old when she had her first short story published in *The West Australian* newspaper.

Having graduated with a degree in Civil Engineering and another in Commerce, she was hired by a major Western Australian engineering company and worked for a number of years on many outback projects. She drew upon her experiences of larrikins, red dust and steel-capped boots for her bestselling novels *The Girl in Steel-Capped Boots*, *The Girl in the Hard Hat* and *The Girl in the Yellow Vest*. *The Maxwell Sisters* is her fourth novel.

She lives in Perth with her husband and four children.

**Also by Loretta Hill**

Novels
*The Girl in Steel-Capped Boots*
*The Girl in the Hard Hat*
*The Girl in the Yellow Vest*

Novellas (available as ebooks)
*Kiss and Tell*
*One Little White Lie*
*Operation Valentine*

# The Maxwell Sisters

LORETTA
HILL

BANTAM
SYDNEY AUCKLAND TORONTO NEW YORK LONDON

A Bantam book
Published by Random House Australia Pty Ltd
Level 3, 100 Pacific Highway, N
www.randomhouse.com.au

First published by Bantam in 20



Addresses for companies within the Random House Group can be found at
www.randomhouse.com.au/offices

National Library of Australia
Cataloguing-in-Publication Entry

Hill, Loretta, author.
The Maxwell sisters / Loretta Hill.

ISBN 978 0 85798 429 6 (paperback)

Sisters–Australia–Fiction.
Wineries–Western Australia–Margaret River Region–Fiction.
Margaret River Region (WA)–Fiction.

A823.4
Cover images: women © Jake Olson/Trevillion Images;
background © Janelle Lugge/Shutterstock.com
Cover design by Christabella Designs
Internal design and typesetting by Midland Typesetters, Australia
Printed in Australia by Griffin Press, an accredited ISO AS/NZS 14001:2004
Environmental Management System printer

Random House Australia uses papers that are natural, renewable and
recyclable products and made from wood grown in sustainable forests.
The logging and manufacturing processes are expected to conform to
the environmental regulations of the country of origin.

*For my sisters,*
*Jacenta, Angela and Marlena*
*There is not a moment in my life where I cannot turn around and see you cheering me on from the sidelines or offering me a shoulder to cry on.*
*You always know where I'm coming from because you were there too. Life without you would be so lonely.*
*Incredibly less funny.*
*And with not much to eat.*
*Love you.*

*Patricia and Graeme Fitzwilliam*

*along with*

*Johnathan and Anita Maxwell*

*Cordially invite you to the wedding of their children*

*Phoebe and Christopher*

*On the 15th March*

*At 2pm*

*Tawny Brooks Winery*

*Rickety Twigg Rd, Yallingup*

*RSVP 10th Feb*

*Tawnybrookswedding@weddingbook.com*

# Chapter 1

Most recipients of the gold-gilded invitation were pleased and excited to receive it. A wedding in the heart of the Margaret River wine region. How decadent! They RSVP'd promptly, marked the date on their calendars and boasted about the upcoming event to their friends.

No one thought for a moment that such a welcome proposal would cause anyone to fly into a blind panic, least of all the sisters of the bride, who would no doubt be taking prominent places in the wedding party. But this was exactly how both women felt upon drawing the impressive card from its white satin envelope.

Fear.

Horror.

And more than a little desperation.

Natasha Maxwell received her invitation first. At thirty years old, she was the eldest of the Maxwell sisters and currently unemployed. She was home when the postman pulled up outside her house in suburban Sydney. At the sound of his motor bike, she hauled herself up onto her elbows from a lying position on the couch and watched him through a large bay window. This gorgeous piece of architecture had been designed and constructed, like the rest of the house, by the building company that employed her husband, a man she had not seen or spoken to in seven months. She peered across her flawlessly manicured lawn to where a terribly clichéd house-shaped letterbox was being stuffed with an oversized card. It wasn't her birthday and she had no expectations of parties in her future . . . except one. She stiffened.

*Oh no! It's here.*

*Already!*

Natasha pushed the gossip magazine off her chest, where it fell, forgotten, onto the floor amongst myriad other discarded items that had been lying there for weeks. Chocolate bar wrappers, overdue rental DVDs and library books. The television was on and the usual daytime talk show nattered away in the background. She wasn't watching it. She just liked a bit of white noise playing because it made her feel less lonely. Her laptop was open on the coffee table so that she could hear and respond immediately to any job interview requests that might come through. Not that there had been any that day, or even recently. The market, along with her career, had taken a turn for the worse with no sign of recovery.

Swinging her legs off the couch, she sprinted to the front door. In a moment she was through, running across the lawn, hoping to be proved wrong. Surely Phoebe intended to be engaged for just a little bit longer. It had only been three months since she'd called with the news. She remembered clutching the phone in fear as her sister's excitement filtered through.

'Engaged! Can you believe it, Tash? I never thought this would happen to me.'

Natasha had tried to be supportive and animated by the news. After all, what were big sisters for? Phoebe had been there for her when she got married, a gorgeous bridesmaid in dark green satin. Thinking back on that day, Natasha flinched. Everything was different now.

Her marriage was over.

But Phoebe didn't know that.

Natasha had made the deliberate decision not to tell anyone about it until she'd healed a little. Maybe once she'd got a job and a few new achievable life goals. *Then*, when she did reveal what she had been through this past year to her family, she wouldn't look like such a basket case. Because if there was one thing Natasha Maxwell couldn't be, it was vulnerable. Of all the Maxwells, she prided herself on being the one with her head firmly on her shoulders. The one who made the right decisions – always. She was a smart, dependable high-achiever who had it all.

At least she had been.

It had actually been quite easy to keep the change in her circumstances quiet. The rest of her family lived in Western Australia. So keeping up appearances was a matter of only a couple of vague phone calls a month. One to Phoebe and the other to her over-anxious Greek mum, who could make a drama out of anything, and often did.

In fact, her secret had been quite safe . . . until Phoebe's announcement.

'Can you imagine it?' her sister had gushed over the phone. 'A wedding. The whole family together again. Mum's going mental. It's been too long, Tash! I miss you guys.'

'I miss you too.' The answer was mechanical, almost wishful.

Phoebe didn't notice. 'We're going to have heaps of fun. I can't wait.'

Natasha had to smile at her little sister's characteristic child-like wonder. She was the bubbliest, most optimistic person Natasha knew. Even as a child, she remembered Phoebe's school teachers remarking on how happy she was all the time. She was such a hopeful spirit. All she ever wanted was for everyone around her to enjoy life as much as she did.

'So how's your fiancé taking all this?' Natasha asked.

'Oh, you know, he's just his usual fantastic self. Happy to let me make all the big decisions – about venue, time, theme. He just wants to get married as soon as possible. I'm thinking March.'

'Really? So soon?' She hoped Phoebe hadn't heard the tremor in her voice. After all, seven months was enough time to safely secure another job and get her head screwed on straight again.

*Are you sure?*

She'd already been at it for over four months with no such luck.

Natasha bit her lip nervously as Phoebe's voice became breathless. 'I know it's fast, but we're just too excited, you know? I mean, this must be how you felt when you and Heath got engaged.'

Regret coiled like a snake in her belly and for a second she was robbed of words.

Luckily, Phoebe filled in the blanks. 'When you meet the right person, you just don't want to wait.'

Natasha knew exactly what her sister meant. When Heath had proposed to her seven years ago, she had been light-headed with joy. One starlit night on a deserted beach, he'd whispered, 'I can't see my future without you, Tash. Be my wife, will you?'

It had been the best day of her life.

She quickly shifted her thoughts away from Heath and said lightly, 'You're right, tie the knot quick before he finds out about the Maxwell "crazy" gene.'

There was a knowing giggle on the other end of the line. 'Somehow I think he already knows about that.'

It had been a long-standing joke between the sisters, and indeed the entire town of Yallingup, that everyone in the Maxwell family tree had a little bit of crazy in them – some personal idiosyncrasy or fanatical obsession that would set them apart from the norm. It usually manifested itself in their passions, making them go that one step further than any sane person would usually venture. Some Maxwells had destroyed their lives on a deranged punt while others had become amazingly successful.

Take their father, for instance. The owner and founder of Tawny Brooks Wines – a worldwide success story. Johnathan Maxwell had always been crazy about grapes. His winemaking neighbours said he was as mad as a cut snake because he refused to use tried and true modern methods. No insecticides or machine harvesting. He believed that plant growth and fertility was irrevocably connected to the rhythm of the cosmos. He played music to his vines and let the moon be his guide. As far as the neighbours were concerned, the man was clearly unhinged but no one could doubt his methods worked amazingly well.

'So I was thinking . . .' Phoebe's voice broke through Natasha's thoughts. 'Will you be one of my bridesmaids?'

Natasha licked her lips nervously. 'I guess so.' She didn't want to jump headfirst into this pool without a life jacket, but couldn't see another option.

There was a groan. 'Is it my imagination or do you sound about as enthusiastic as a vegetarian in front of a steak?'

'Sorry, I didn't mean it to come out like that. Of course I'm thrilled. I'm just a little distracted right now.'

'Really? With what?'

With the fact that the last thing she wanted to attend was a family event where every move she made and word she spoke would be scrutinised, especially by her over-protective mother. She had wanted more time to deal with her situation before allowing her family to wade in, and wade in they would whether she liked it or not. She knew they simply wouldn't be able to keep their opinions or recommendations to themselves.

'Is this about Eve?' Phoebe asked Tash, reminding her of the long-standing argument between herself and the middle

Maxwell sister. An argument that now seemed so insignificant compared with everything else that was going on in her life.

'No, this is not about Eve.'

'Because,' Phoebe said sternly, 'in case you're wondering, I have asked her to be my bridesmaid as well and I expect you two to get along.'

'Really?' Natasha returned lightly. 'But she hates the limelight.'

'Well, I don't want anyone else,' Phoebe said firmly. 'I want both my sisters standing by my side when I marry the man of my dreams.'

Natasha's mouth curled. 'What did Eve say to that?'

Phoebe gave a defensive sounding snort. 'Well –' she hedged.

'She said she didn't want to, didn't she?'

'Eve saying no?' Phoebe scoffed. 'Don't be ridiculous. She said . . . she said she'd rather bake the wedding cake instead.'

Eve was a sous chef at a top restaurant in Perth – so this offer wasn't exactly ungenerous. In fact, Natasha was rather impressed with this clever move because Eve had always been a 'yes' girl. She didn't know how to say 'no' to anyone. For her to make even the slightest hesitation must mean she really wanted out. A dull ache entered Natasha's already battered heart. Was the rift between them really as bad as all that?

'So did you take her up on it?' she asked Phoebe tentatively.

'I said she could do both.'

Natasha's jaw dropped open. '*Phoebe!*'

'Well, I'm sick and tired of you two carrying on like this. It's high time you girls were forced to do something together so you can sort out your issues. I don't want to play piggy-in-the-middle any more.'

'Do you really want to risk your wedding on that?'

'That's exactly what I'm going to do,' Phoebe announced passionately, making Natasha both smile and cringe. *The ruthless optimist strikes again.* Phoebe definitely wanted 'happy'. And if she couldn't get it any other way she was going to get it by force.

'I just feel like if I can get the two of you in the same room again then maybe I can have my sisters back.' Phoebe's voice was small but hopeful. 'Even without the terrible argument you guys had, we haven't been as close in recent years. Eve and I seem to have lost that bond we used to have. Do you remember how we were as kids, Tash? Nothing could separate us.'

'I know,' Natasha said sadly.

'Dad used to say we were his best blend.'

'I remember.'

They'd always been so tight. When one sister was in trouble they'd all get together to nut out the problem. They were a bank of secrets. A book of adventures. A catalogue for embarrassing moments. They even had a secret phrase: 'Club members only'.

She closed her eyes as Phoebe's soft voice sounded in her ears again. 'So why are you holding on to a fight you had nearly a year ago?'

Natasha sighed. It was really all about timing. Right after her massive argument with Eve, all the upheaval in her own life had started, including the complete and utter breakdown of her marriage. By the time she realised she was no longer talking to Eve, months had already ticked by and the chess-board pieces were all in different places. Anger had become silence. Silence had become habit. And now that it was so ingrained she didn't know where to start.

She cleared her throat. 'I was kinda hoping Eve might make the first move.'

'Come on, Tash,' Phoebe replied crossly. 'You were the one making all the accusations at the time. You can't expect her not to have some pride.'

Natasha bit her lip. It was true, of course. She had told Eve she was a selfish coward who should face up to her responsibilities, not run away and hide from them. Now looking at her own life, she had to snort in derision. Talk about the pot calling the kettle black! 'I . . . I guess I do owe Eve an apology.'

'That's the spirit,' Phoebe encouraged her. 'Maybe when you and Heath fly to WA for the wedding, you can talk to Eve about it.'

The mention of her estranged husband brought reality screeching in like a train.

'How is he, by the way?'

'Who?' Natasha muttered distractedly as the squealing in her ears diminished.

Phoebe giggled. 'Heath, of course.'

'Er . . .' She swallowed. 'Busy.'

She didn't know this for a fact but it was a good guess. When Heath's boss had suggested the transfer to Melbourne where there was more work, it had seemed like a good opportunity for a trial separation. And it had been working well. They weren't fighting any more . . . at least.

However, if she were truly honest with herself, it felt like the guts of her life had been ripped out. Natasha spent most of her days reliving scenes from her past. Old arguments they'd had when she either regretted saying something or wished she hadn't said so much. Her distraction had not gone unnoticed by the managing director of Gunnings Food Group, a confectionery company where she'd headed up the marketing department. 'As much as I like you, Natasha, I can't afford to continue to pay you if you can't get any work done.'

So she'd started making promises. Promises she couldn't keep. Poor concentration and a lacklustre campaign had eventually cost her her job. Now she was surviving on savings but telling all her friends she was too busy to catch up with them.

'Tash, is something going on with you?' Her sister's voice was in her ear again like an annoying fly. 'I feel like you're not listening to a word I'm saying.'

'Of course I'm listening.' Natasha tried to inject a little indignation into her tone.

'Then what did I just say?'

'Um . . .'

'I rest my case.' Phoebe was unimpressed. 'Mum said you were acting a little distant with her last week too when she called.'

Natasha rubbed her temple. 'You know Mum, she calls at completely the wrong time and tells you some weird trivia that you really just don't care about. Last time she wanted to know if I knew pineapples were in season.'

'Well, do you?' Phoebe demanded, but she could hear the smile in her sister's tone.

'Not till she told me.'

'But they're so good for your immune system and metabolism,' Phoebe responded in mock protest.

'I see you got the phone call too.' Natasha grinned.

'Yes,' Phoebe returned. 'She is adamant that I pass solids regularly.'

Natasha laughed. 'So can you blame me for being vague?'

'I guess not. Mum does worry far too much.' To Natasha's relief her sister dropped the subject and they talked more on other less touchy topics before she rang off.

Since that day most of Phoebe's phone calls had been about how stressed she was. And Natasha had harboured the slight hope that the wedding planning, in all its overwhelming and time-consuming glory, had made Phoebe's idea of a short engagement wither and die. But now she was staring at this white card, realising that she had four months to come clean or invent a story.

She chewed nervously on her lower lip, trying to imagine an out.

Perhaps she *could* go home. She could just slip her wedding ring back on and say Heath was too busy in Melbourne and he couldn't get away. Then there would be no awkward questions. She wouldn't have to provide any difficult answers. And she'd get a break from all this – walking round and round in circles wishing her life was something other than it was. She could just enjoy being a big sister. Maybe she and Eve could even reconnect.

It would be a relief.

A single tear drew a wet path down her cheek. Could she lie to her family?

What sort of coward behaved like that?

Resolutely, Natasha put the invitation on the coffee table. She needed some time to think about this.

Because once she started lying . . . it would be very hard to go back.

# Chapter 2

Eve Maxwell had a lot on her plate.

Tender scallops and smoked trout picked from the bones were scattered on a bed of pasta, infused with baby spinach leaves, dill and shallots. Glossy with olive oil and generously seasoned with sea salt and cracked pepper. The warm buttery smell of seafood filled the air. She had always thought this dish would work better with marron instead of scallops but unfortunately her father's dam, more commonly termed 'Crazy Man's Lake', was not on hand as a source. At least some of Tawny Brooks' oak-matured chardonnay would be. It was one of the reasons she'd applied for work as sous chef at this restaurant – they kept a cellar full of her father's wine. She had reasoned this was at least one way she could give back after everything she'd taken from him. It was also perhaps the only good reason she kept on at Margareta's.

The owner, May, was a bitch. And the head chef, Sam, took all the credit for Eve's work. Even now as the plates went out she could hear them talking by the double door exit to the kitchen.

'Wow, Sam! How did you come up with this combination? It's brilliant – our most popular addition to the menu yet. Subtle but elegant. Simple but delicious. Scrumptious but minimalistic. You're a genius.'

Sam only nodded. His bald sweaty head was shiny under the bright kitchen lights. He didn't even cast a cautious glance in her direction to make sure she wasn't listening but said, 'Thank you,' with all the graciousness of a bona fide artist.

*And why shouldn't he?* her inner voice demanded. *It's not like you give him a reason to respect you. You never stand up for yourself. You never tell him where to shove it.*

She ignored her inner voice and pushed a dishcloth across the stainless steel bench. That was the voice of the woman who had put her father's restaurant out of business.

*I told you you weren't ready for a responsibility like that!* And that was the voice of her older sister, Natasha. A university-educated, startlingly successful executive marketer and the only person who had warned her not to dream too big.

Failure sucked. Living with failure sucked even more. Because you couldn't trust your first instinct with anything.

'I can't wait to see what you come up with next,' May continued to coo, her flirtatious smile resting briefly on Sam before shifting across to where Eve stood, observing them.

'See?' the owner smirked. 'Even Eve's looking to you for inspiration.' Her gaze shifted to the apprentice chef, Peter, who was laying out plates and wisely keeping his back to them. 'But we don't have time for slacking off, do we?'

Heat filled Eve's cheeks. Neither she nor Peter were slacking off, having both participated in every single dish plated tonight while Sam swanned about the room flirting with the wait staff. Eve was now taking a meagre second to catch her breath between courses.

It was at times like this that she wished she smoked. What a great excuse to go outside and regroup. As May's eyes returned to her, her right eyebrow arched menacingly and Eve swallowed. She realised that she was actually expected to respond to the accusation.

Eve hated confrontation in all its forms and wished she'd had the good sense, like Peter, to keep her eyes averted. By general rule she practised avoidance or withdrawal at any cost. She had only had one serious fight in her life, the results of which continued to exact revenge on her even to this day.

'Er . . . sorry,' she mumbled quickly to May and turned back to the bench where Lisa, the dessert chef de partie, was bringing all their prep from earlier in the day over from the walk-in fridge to add the finishing touches.

*Gutless wonder, you are*, her inner voice lashed out.

*Better safe than fired*, she responded and firmly shut the door on anything else her conscience had to say. She needed to focus on providing guidance for the dessert tasting plate. Besides, there was no use arguing with herself or with May, especially when the purpose of having this job was just to keep herself horrendously busy for the next few years so she had no time to think of anything else. Her gaze took in the unfinished crème brûlée, passionfruit sorbet, chocolate soufflé and mango crumble presented in four shot glasses on a white tray – another bright idea of hers she was yet to receive credit for. She breathed in the sweet and tangy combination of aromas deeply. Dessert always calmed her down. It was her favourite course, both to eat and to make.

As she directed Lisa to get the blow torch for the crème brûlée, she felt Clive, the chef de partie who did entrées and starters, looming behind her.

Not again.

She already knew what he was going to ask even before he opened his mouth.

'Eve, can you work tomorrow? I'm looking to swap my shift with someone.'

She sighed. Tomorrow was her first full day off in over a week. She had agreed to meet her sister briefly at a bridal shop in the city to give her a second opinion on a couple of dresses. But otherwise, she was hoping for a little bit of time to herself.

She quickly seized upon her appointment with Phoebe. 'I'm meeting my sister in the morning to help her with wedding shopping.'

'That's okay,' he nodded. 'It's an afternoon and evening shift. You see, my wife has bought tickets to a show at the Crown for our anniversary.' He gave her a wink. 'I feel like I should play along and pretend like I remembered.'

She laughed, if somewhat nervously. *Say no, say no, say no.*

But he put his serious expression back on. 'Sam has already said he can't.'

*Of course.*

'And neither can Lisa or any of the other chefs. I mean,' his face dropped, 'I suppose I could cancel on my wife but she'll be gutted. Is there any way –'

'Okay, okay. I'll do it.'

'Great, Eve!' he beamed at her. 'I know I can always count on you.'

*Sucker.*

The dinner rush passed as it always did – in a mad panic. And Eve went home exhausted.

She woke around nine the next morning and was having a lazy breakfast of her favourite cheese and chive omelette on toast when a text message came through on her phone. She hoped it was Phoebe cancelling. But it wasn't. It was her best friend, Spider. The man she'd secretly been in love with for the last eight years.

Her belly did a little somersault before resettling. She pushed her plate away from her.

She and Spider had gone through TAFE together. They worked as apprentices together at that quiet restaurant in Northbridge called The Grove. She still remembered the day they first met. He'd walked in, tall and gangly, and banged his head on a pot dangling from a hook above his head. As he'd rubbed his temple and stepped out of danger, he'd thrown her a big goofy smile. 'Is it just me,' he winked, 'or should this bench be higher?'

Given she was a mere five foot three, in her view the bench could be a few inches lower. She smiled wryly as he took the offending pan off its hook. 'I don't think I'm the best person to ask.'

'And you are?' He held out his hand.

'Eve.' She shook it shyly.

'Call me Spider.'

She returned his cheeky grin. 'That's a rather odd name.'

'Not if you're all arms and legs.'

Their friendship had grown from there. Being in exactly the same boat in almost every aspect of life, it was difficult not to relate. They covered for each other at work, studied together, exchanged shifts and notes all the time. He was so easygoing. So easy to talk to and confide in. She had known all along that she was falling in love with him and took no precautions to protect her heart. In fact, she was almost certain that he felt the same. He had dated other people but the relationships had been so fleeting that she had actually taken heart from his lack of commitment to them. Sometimes when he looked at her she thought she could see something there, like he was on the cusp of declaring himself. Every time they spoke, it was like being suspended over a giant glass of champagne. She felt fizzy with the force of her feelings. In her mind, it was only a matter of time before he stopped being the perfect gentleman and made a move. They were just so perfectly matched. They'd laughed together, stressed out together, even dreamed of owning their own restaurant together.

She remembered sitting in a café with him one night when he had urged her to take the plunge. He'd grabbed her hand. 'Come on, Eve, I know we can do this. Don't be afraid. I'll be right there with you.'

She would have given him anything.

He had made her feel so confident – with him by her side, the world was her oyster. For the first time in her life she'd campaigned strongly for something, begged her father to give them a chance. And he had. It was insane. Two barely qualified apprentices and he'd given them Tawny Brooks restaurant to cut their teeth on.

*The stupidity. The faith!*

It was a mad Maxwell move for sure.

Her bones ached with the memories. But the disillusion was mostly her own. While she had lost all confidence when their venture failed, Spider had branched out. He wrote books now. Recipes. He even had his own cooking show. He was practically a celebrity. Not that she begrudged him his success, which he had often tried to share with her – asking her to contribute a recipe or guest star on the show with him. But everything had changed.

*Everything.*

They were never going to be a couple. She was twenty-seven years old, in the prime of life. She had to stop hoping. Stop moping. Put some real distance between them. If only he wasn't making it well nigh impossible for her to do so. Although he no longer lived in Perth, he came to town often to do a radio spot, interview or presentation. And he always insisted on catching up. Every meeting was like sweet, gratifying torture.

She opened the message he had sent her. It included a photo – a succulent image of a lamb shank on a bed of potatoes, asparagus, carrots and chickpeas covered in a gorgeous chunky-looking gravy. The text read, 'I think I finally got the gravy right. Can't wait for you to taste it.'

She both recoiled and revelled in his need for her opinion. It would be great if she could just cut all connection with him. That at least would give her some head room and maybe even a chance to find someone else. But it was impossible. So she hurriedly texted him back, keeping up the pretence. 'No worries. Would love to. Was it the tomato? Too much, too little?'

She put her phone in her handbag and went to get dressed. She had to leave soon if she was going to make that appointment with her sister.

The car ride to the bridal boutique was short and unplagued by peak-hour traffic. She was a little early and waited on one of the stylish lounges right next door to the generous-sized change rooms, which weren't very soundproof.

'Oh my goodness, you're tiny! I've never seen such a minuscule waist.'

'Really?' responded the insecure bride.

'I swear it on my mother's grave,' the sales assistant assured her. 'You're the smallest girl I've seen today. That dress looks great on you!'

When the curtain was pulled back, a pleased bride-to-be stepped out to show the floor-length satin number to her teary mother. Eve squinted suspiciously at her waist, which looked about the same size as her own.

While she was mentally trying to measure it, someone pressed a kiss to her cheek. 'What are you thinking about so seriously?'

She glanced up to find her flawlessly stunning sister smiling down at her. Phoebe was dressed in a silk sleeveless dress that gathered at a low waist. Her glossy black hair, very similar to their other sister's, Natasha, was falling immaculately across her shoulders. Natasha and Phoebe had never suffered the fuzz that constantly framed Eve's face – the only Maxwell sister blessed, or should she say cursed, with curls.

Also, unlike her sisters, Eve had not inherited her father's metabolism. While she wouldn't call herself fat, she definitely had the more fuller figure of the three girls. Unlike her sisters, who carried off their slim perfection like *Cosmpolitan models,* she spent hours at the mirror agonising over which dress made her boobs look smaller or her hips and bum not quite so generous.

'Sorry I'm late.' Phoebe grimaced as she sat down beside her, holding out one of the two glasses of champagne she had received upon arrival for her appointment. She whispered, 'Not as good as Dad's but drinkable, I suppose.'

'Thanks.' Eve's lips twitched as she took the glass.

Phoebe blew her fringe out of her eyes. 'Anyway, the reason I'm late is I got bailed up by my future *M.I.L.*' She mouthed the initials as though they represented a covert operation she was handling.

Eve squinted. 'Are you talking about your mother-in-law?'

'Patricia Fitzwilliam.' Phoebe sighed, fortifying herself with champagne. 'She wants to be involved with the wedding planning. As in *fully* involved. This morning she wouldn't let me leave the breakfast table without discussing the bomboniers first.'

Phoebe and her fiancé lived in Dunsborough, a town not too far from the Maxwell winery in Yallingup. But they were in Perth for the week and staying with his parents for the visit.

Eve smiled. 'Just the other day you were complaining to me about how you wished you had more help with the wedding planning.'

'From *my bridesmaids*, from *my fiancé*. Not from her,' Phoebe retorted, making Eve instantly wish she'd held her tongue.

'Explain to me, will you?' Phoebe demanded. 'Why is it that I'm getting more help from my mother-in-law than my own sister? Come on, Eve. I thought you'd be right into this.'

'I *am* right into this,' Eve protested, trying to inject as much colour into her voice as possible.

'I'm not dumb.' Her sister folded her arms. 'You've been almost as silent as Tash these past few months. Is everything okay at work?'

Eve coughed, trying to squash the sudden ache in her heart. She needed a believable excuse and work seemed as good as any. 'I don't really get on with the owner . . . or the head chef. I've been thinking lately maybe I should apply for a job somewhere else.'

'Maybe you should. Although,' Phoebe rolled her eyes, 'I don't know why you don't just go home. I would if I could.

The last five days in Perth have been enough.' She sliced the air with her hand as she said it. 'Do you know what Patricia suggested would make the perfect take-home gift?'

Eve smiled. 'I'm afraid to ask.'

'A silver love-heart key ring with our photo on the front and our names and wedding date inscribed on the back.' Eve giggled as Phoebe put a hand to her forehead. 'Can you imagine it?'

'We-ll,' Eve drew out the word, trying to find something positive to say, 'it's definitely commemorative. I'd put it on my car keys.'

'Yes, because you're sweet,' Phoebe groaned. 'And possibly our mother would as well. But I think everyone else would think it's a bit presumptuous, don't you? I mean, I wouldn't want to hang someone else's wedding photo on my car keys.'

'They don't have to hang it on their car keys,' Eve shrugged. 'They could just keep it.'

'Then why make it a key ring at all?' Phoebe shrugged. 'Personally I'd rather go with something a little more traditional, like wedding cake in a nice box or even sugared almonds wrapped up in lace.'

Eve stuck out her tongue. 'Those things are disgusting.'

'Aren't they though?' Phoebe giggled.

'Well, I really don't see what the problem is,' Eve said. 'Just tell her you don't want them.'

Phoebe laughed. 'This coming from the girl who can't say no.'

Eve blushed but Phoebe didn't tease her further. 'The thing is, I'm supposed to be doing the whole bonding thing with her. You know, like trying to get to know her and win her approval, so to speak,' she winced. 'And I am trying. I just didn't think it would be this much work. I mean, it's supposed to be our wedding, but I feel like I'm jumping through hoops just trying to please her.'

'So what did you tell her about the bombonieres?'

'I said I'd like to keep my options open for now.'

'And what did she say?'

'She said if it's about the cost, she'd pay for it.'

'But didn't you tell her it wasn't about the cost?'

'Of course, so then she asked whether it was about the photo. Because if we didn't have a suitable one she could hire a professional photographer. The conversation just kept going. It literally would not end. In fact, I think we're still having it. It's just on pause at the moment.'

Eve chuckled.

'I'm sure Tash's mother-in-law was never this involved at her wedding.'

At the mention of her older sister's name, Eve felt a slight prick of guilt. She lifted her flute to her lips, waiting for the moment to pass.

She could feel Phoebe's eyes on her. 'Aren't you in the least bit curious as to how she's going? Surely you care a little bit.'

Eve slowly lowered her glass. 'All right. How's she doing?'

Phoebe frowned. 'Actually, I have absolutely no idea.'

'What do you mean?'

'She's been very hard to get hold of these last few months and when I do speak to her she's distracted as hell.' Phoebe bit her lip. 'I think something's going on, Eve. I think she needs us.'

Eve put her glass down on the coffee table next to the couch. 'The day Tash needs me will be the day hell freezes over.'

'You're so wrong.' Phoebe shook her head. 'She misses you. She regrets what she said. I know she does.'

'She hasn't contacted me,' Eve shrugged.

'She hasn't contacted *anyone*. In fact, I've been trying to ring her the last few days and it keeps going to voicemail.'

'Don't worry,' Eve assured her, 'Tash is as tough as an ox. She's probably just busy at work.' If there was anyone who could hold their own, it was her older sister, the corporate bad-arse of the eastern states. Eve grinned to herself. She had never known Tash to show a moment's weakness . . . Her grin faded. Or a moment's patience either. 'Let's not talk about Tash.' Eve glanced about the boutique. 'I want to focus on you. You and this wedding.'

*Even if it bloody kills me.*

'The attendant is getting the dresses I wanted your opinion on,' Phoebe nodded. 'In the meantime, I need to give you something.' She put her champagne down and reached into her handbag to draw out a white satin envelope.

'Is that –' Eve's trembling fingers turned it over and drew out the card.

'The invitation,' Phoebe finished for her. 'Yes, they've all gone out. I kept yours so I could give it to you in person. Do you like it?'

Eve hardly took in the aesthetics as her eyes scanned the words and she lost the ability to breathe. 'You're having it at home?' she asked, her eyes widening in shock. 'We never talked about that.'

Phoebe blinked. 'Were we supposed to?'

'Well, I just don't understand. I mean, whereabouts in Tawny Brooks are you going to have the reception?'

'In the restaurant.'

'But you can't,' she gasped.

'I not only can, but I will. And you're going to help me.'

Eve choked. 'How?'

'We're going to fix it.'

'What? How?'

'You, me, Spider, Heath and Tash. We're all going to go home a month before the wedding and get everything shipshape.'

It was her worst nightmare. 'Impossible.' Her voice was barely a whisper.

Phoebe frowned. 'Damn it. Spider said you might have a problem with this.'

Eve looked up quickly. 'He did?'

Phoebe put a hand on her shoulder. 'Honey, he's been your friend for ages. He knows you almost as well as I do. He knows how much that restaurant meant to you. He was just as disappointed when you both lost it. This is hard for him too.'

'Then why are you making us do it?'

Phoebe shook her head. 'Because the restaurant was special to me and Spider too. It's where we met, after all. Having our wedding anywhere else just wouldn't seem right. Besides, I think you need this.'

Phoebe was so off base Eve thought she'd need a plane to get back.

'I'm not suggesting you reopen if that's not what you wish to do,' Phoebe quickly assured her, reaching across and putting her hand over hers. 'But it's time to face your fears, Eve, and realise that you didn't fail. Life just happened and will continue to happen. It's not your fault.'

Eve's fingers clenched tightly together in her lap. Her fears didn't just concern the restaurant but she couldn't explain that to Phoebe. 'Phee, I don't think I can get a whole month off work.'

Phoebe pouted. 'Why not? Spider said you've been working yourself like a dog at Margareta's and you've got heaps of leave up your sleeve.'

'They need me there.' Eve's voice came out strangled. 'And I don't want to put any noses out of joint.'

Phoebe's mouth pulled into a hard line. 'Am I missing something here? Because a minute ago you said you were thinking of leaving. Eve, what have I done to offend you?'

'Nothing.'

'Then be there for me,' Phoebe pleaded. 'I'm getting married, for goodness sake.'

'Of course, of course.' Something very close to hysteria was bubbling in Eve and it was only by keeping her head down and her eyes to the floor that she somehow managed to get it under control.

'I need you, Eve. Much more than you know.'

She looked up into Phoebe's eyes, which were glistening with tears. 'Okay, all right,' she whispered, not knowing whether to be grateful or insulted that Phoebe never thought for a moment that her reluctance to be too involved, too present, too near to this wedding and all it entailed was anything more than just her lack of confidence.

By lucky chance, the sales assistant finally appeared with a dress on each arm. One was a lace creation, the other, satin. 'Here they are! I've found them at last,' the woman said as Phoebe stood up. 'Shall we try them on?'

Phoebe gave Eve's arm one last squeeze before she followed the staff member into the change room.

Eve dabbed at the wetness forming in the corners of her eyes.

*You can do this.*

*You should do it.*

Her sister and her best friend deserved her support. Not only that, they expected it. Perhaps she needed this to cure herself of her feelings for Spider. What other choice did she have?

She could hear Phoebe's attendant speaking from behind the curtain.

'Wow! You're absolutely tiny. Look at that waist. I think you must be the smallest bride I've seen today.'

'You're joking,' Phoebe's voice sounded flustered.

'I swear it on my mother's grave.'

*Her poor mother must be getting very uncomfortable in there by now.*

The curtain flung open and Phoebe came out, ethereally beautiful in lace. 'That dress looks fantastic on you,' the sales assistant gushed behind her. 'Are you sure you want to try on the satin one?'

'What do you think, Eve?' her sister asked. 'You always know what looks best on me.'

It wasn't a false compliment. As teenagers, Eve, Phee and Tash had loved exchanging clothes and dressing up together. They were always swapping accessories and doing each other's make-up. They'd had so much practice, you could say they were experts on what looked best on each other. Their wardrobes at Tawny Brooks had almost been completely interchangeable. So much so that it became difficult to identify what belonged to who any more. Their female friends used to marvel at the diversity of their clothes because they would all add things to the wardrobe that was their own particular style. The Maxwell sisters were never at a loss for any occasion.

'How can we get access?' their girlfriends had always asked.

Eve and her sisters would just exchange a look and laugh. 'Club members only.'

The memories caused a rush of warmth. 'I think you look wonderful, Phee. But we'll try on the other just to be sure. I wouldn't want to give my sister an uninformed opinion.' She paused before adding lightly, 'Speaking of opinions, I guess I should be there to renovate the restaurant with you guys as well. I wouldn't want to miss the opportunity to contribute my two cents' worth.'

Phoebe's eyes lit up. 'Seriously?'

She nodded and Phoebe rushed forward, throwing her arms about her. 'That's brilliant, Eve! Thank you so much. You won't be sorry you did.'

Eve smiled sadly over her shoulder. *Oh, I very much fear I will.*

# Chapter 3

Phoebe Maxwell had a secret.

A truly awful secret that wasn't hers to share. If it was, she would have moved permanently to Tawny Brooks and shifted heaven and earth to find the appropriate professional help. Instead, she had to be content to watch from afar and suffer her own helplessness.

She had sworn that she wouldn't tell a single soul.

Including her fiancé.

That was a test of willpower on its own. She told Spider everything. He was by far the sweetest, most giving person she knew and would have stayed up all night holding her hand to keep her from crying herself to sleep. But she couldn't tell him. So instead she stifled her tears in her pillow. During the day, she managed to fill her mind with activities to stop herself from thinking about it.

Eight-thirty to three she focused all her energy on her students at Busselton Primary, a school thirty minutes from her home in the neighbouring town of Dunsborough. After school, she helped Spider with the television show called *Spider's Kitchen* that he filmed locally and sold to the Channel Nine network.

In her meagre spare time, she threw herself into wedding planning. Keeping busy kept her positive. And of all the Maxwell sisters, this was definitely Phoebe's greatest skill.

When she'd broken her leg at age seven she'd covered it in glow-in-the-dark fairy stickers and become the envy of all her friends. After university when she hadn't been able to score a job in Perth she'd come home and met Spider – the love of her life. When Eve and Tash had fallen out months ago, leaving her the piggy-in-the-middle, she'd taken the opportunity to get closer to both sisters. And that had worked beautifully until recently.

Whatever the case, perhaps this was the reason why she'd been permitted to know the secret in the first place. She was the only Maxwell capable of finding a way to put a positive spin on it.

*If* that was even possible.

How could she mask a future that was going to rip her family apart? And then she realised something. Her family was already broken.

Once so tightly knit, the Maxwells were now distant at best. She barely spoke to, let alone saw much of her sisters any more. Where had all that closeness gone? Whatever happened to 'Club members only'?

Surely their different geographic locations wasn't the only thing to blame for their lack of communication. Phones, email, texting, Skype, Facetime, Facebook, Twitter. Did they really have an excuse not to stay in touch regularly? The only person to make an effort, in fact, was her mother. Though, Phoebe realised guiltily, how often she groaned when she received that call. Small and vibrant with dark Greek features only slightly fading with age, Anita Maxwell did not have the 'crazy gene' but made up for it with her tendency to worry about anything and everything.

In any event, it was because of this complete and utter family breakdown that Phoebe had come to a decision one night.

'We should have the wedding at Tawny Brooks.'

Spider, who had been reading a book on the couch opposite hers, looked up and smiled. 'You're speaking your thoughts out loud again, love.'

'Am I?' She looked across at him, marvelling again that he was hers. He had a smile that could melt steel, a floppy brown fringe that often fell in his laughing eyes. Tall and gangly, he was a far cry from the kind of man she used to think was her type. Spider's look was more intellectual than brawny, more boyish than manly, more sincere than smooth. And yet one look from him made her heart race faster than a Japanese bullet train. He was perfect for her and she could not have been more happy or satisfied that in just six months' time they would be husband and wife.

'My family needs some time together.' At last she had something to aim for, something that made her feel better about the dreadful knowledge she carried around inside of her.

'I think your family will come together wherever we have the wedding.' Spider's brow furrowed.

'No,' Phoebe had shaken her head, 'I don't just mean in the same room. I mean, close again. It has to be at home with all our memories.'

'Even the bad ones?' Spider grimaced.

She nodded. 'Especially those. There are some things we Maxwells have swept under the rug for far too long. Do you mind, darl? Do you mind if we get married at Tawny Brooks?'

He raised his eyebrows, a wry, resigned smile twisting his mouth. 'Are you sure your father would want that?'

It was a known fact that, for some reason, John Maxwell wasn't all too fond of his future son-in-law. His manner towards him was often abrupt and rather dismissive. Phoebe had tried many times to ascertain the cause of her father's rudeness but could not put it down to anything beyond her father being a cantankerous old man with a dislike for any male who dared lay a finger on his daughter. It was that attitude that had kept her from visiting Tawny Brooks more often. And in hindsight, she realised, there was a lot she had missed.

Her mouth hardened. 'He's going to have to like it. He can't keep carrying on like a toddler because he doesn't get his way.'

It was Spider's turn to frown. 'That's what I worry about, Phee. You can't force people to behave a certain way just because you think they should.'

'I know,' Phoebe grinned mischievously. 'But I can try. It's no fun having two sisters who won't speak to each other, a father who won't accept my fiancé and a mother who's going crazy because of it all. I just want things to go back to normal.'

'Are you sure there is a normal?'

'If we get everyone together, we might be able to find out. Besides, don't you think it'll be special? Tawny Brooks is where we first met.'

'How could I forget? You bowled me over. *Literally*.'

'That's right, I ran you over with my car, didn't I?' Her eyes twinkled at the memory. 'Forgot to look before reversing in the restaurant car park.'

'You say it with so much remorse.'

'Well, you did look rather cute on the ground covered in cake.'

'Eve was extremely upset about that cake. It was for a function. We had to improvise really quickly.'

'And I helped, didn't I?' she protested. 'I was in the kitchen with you guys all night so you could catch up.'

'And my fate was sealed.' He gazed fondly at her.

'There you see,' she sobered as her thoughts returned to their wedding plans, 'that's where it all began. Let's get married at Tawny Brooks, Spider. What do you say?'

He had studied her for a long moment in that way that was only his. He was reading her, weighing up her need against his own. And, as she knew he would, he put hers first.

'All right,' he agreed with a wry smile, 'it's not like my mother won't be over the moon. She's been hankering for an invitation to Tawny Brooks ever since we got engaged.'

With all her own emotional upheaval in the background, she had completely forgotten about Spider's mother. But Patricia Fitzwilliam had definitely not forgotten about her. In fact, her future mother-in-law was probably even more dedicated to her son's wedding than Phoebe was. She called her incessantly, wanting to be in on every detail.

'How are things going with her?' Spider asked. 'Are you guys getting along?'

How did you tell your future husband that you wished his mother would back off a bit, *especially* after you just asked him to have his wedding at your family home?

'Y-yes, she's lovely.'

'Do I detect a note of hesitancy?'

Phoebe racked her brain for an excuse she could use. 'It's just a little hard discussing things over the phone, you know.'

His eyes lit up. 'I'm so glad you mentioned that because I was just thinking we could go up to Perth for a week to get a few things organised. I mean, with you having taken two school terms off work to make things easier. Why not? You and Mum could bond.'

She hoped the smile on her face did not look too fake. She really didn't want to become the stereotypical daughter-in-law who couldn't get along with her husband's mother. So she'd put on her most enthusiastic teacher voice, one she always whipped out for these sorts of occasions.

'That sounds like a great idea. Why don't you go ahead and book it in? In the meantime, I'll make the trek over to Tawny Brooks. Gotta ask Mum and Dad if we can have the wedding at their place.'

'Yes,' he beamed back, 'that would probably be a good idea. Do you want me to come?'

'No, it's okay. I think I can handle it.'

The truth was, she hadn't wanted anything to turn her fiancé off getting married at her childhood home, least of all her moody father, whom she was absolutely determined to keep an eye on.

Since she'd moved out last year, she hadn't paid much attention to her parents. It had been too easy to get lost in her own life and schedule with Spider. Now she wished she had visited home more often. In the last few months there had been some big changes at Tawny Brooks, amongst other things.

For starters, her father had retired 'too early' in her mother's opinion. Having all that time off had certainly brought out more 'crazy' in him. By all accounts, he'd gone off the rails. And for 'Mad Maxwell', that was definitely saying something.

'I think it's a midlife crisis,' her mother had told her the previous week. 'Why else would he buy a new car totally unsuitable for rural living or want to go bungee jumping in the middle of the afternoon? I knew he shouldn't have retired just yet. He has too much energy.'

Phoebe shook her head sadly over the matter. She thought her father was looking much frailer of late. The other day when she'd dropped in unannounced she'd caught him sleeping in the sitting room. Her mother had said it was because he'd been up partying all night with his cronies. In particular, with one Horace Franklin who owned the winery next door. This in itself was strange as the Franklins and the Maxwells had been mortal enemies from day one, especially when it came to wine.

To allow for her father's retirement and daytime shenanigans, they had employed a winemaker named Adam Carter to run Tawny Brooks. Adam was nice enough, but she did feel that for a person who was not a member of the family, he was around far too much. Her parents allowed him to live on the property. Even when Spider was working at the restaurant fulltime he had kept a unit in Dunsborough.

She imagined it was because her mother needed someone to call when her father went off on another of his mystery jaunts, which he did at least a couple of times a week. He was certainly nowhere to be found the day Phoebe dropped by to ask permission to hold the wedding at Tawny Brooks.

The front door to the Maxwell residence was always unlocked, so she just walked straight into the large timber and stone house built to enjoy panoramic views of the surrounding vineyard.

She found her mother cooking in a large seventies style kitchen, with a broad kitchen counter and exposed brick walls. 'Hey, Mum!'

'Darling!' Her mother left her mound of chocolate chip cookie dough on the bench and came round to hug her. 'I was just about to call you. Would you like a drink?'

She went to the fridge and drew out a jug of cold water, which she poured in a tall glass before Phoebe could answer. 'You know I saw on the news the other day that three people were rushed to hospital with dehydration because they had not had enough fluids.'

Phoebe picked up the water and took a tentative sip. 'Weren't they sun baking on the beach or something?'

Anita's dark eyes glinted. 'Oh, so you saw it too. That's good. Then you know how important it is to drink water.'

'Mum, I can assure you, I get plenty of fluids during the day.'

'I just worry, sweetheart, what with everything that's going on in your life, you forget.'

She sighed. 'I don't forget, Mum. When I'm thirsty I drink.'

'But eight glasses? That's supposed to be the daily intake. Although it's rather ambiguous, don't you think, because who knows what size glass most people have in their pantry? I mean, what if you have really small cups in your cupboard. In that case, wouldn't you then need to drink extra to make up the quota?'

'Er . . . I guess so.'

'What size are your glasses, sweetheart? Are you still using those squat little tumblers I saw in your cupboard the last time

I visited? You really should throw those out, you know. Get some new ones. Do you want me to get some for you?'

'No, that's okay, Mum,' Phoebe said quickly. 'Don't worry about it.'

'Are you sure because I'm happy to go out and buy some for you.'

'No, I don't want you to go to any trouble.'

Her mother tapped her chin. 'In fact, come to think of it, I have some lovely glasses in a box in the roof that I never put in our cupboard because there wasn't enough room. Perfectly good glasses, brand new too. Why don't I get them and you can pop them in the boot of your car before you go?'

'No thanks, Mum.'

'Don't be silly. They're just going to waste up there. Your father and I don't need that many glasses in our kitchen cupboards.'

'Mum,' she grabbed her arm as though trying to shake her out of a stupor, '*I've got enough glasses*.'

'Oh, all right.' Her mother hunched her shoulders. 'But if you're going to use those dreadful tumblers for water, make sure you drink nine glasses not eight, won't you?'

Phoebe had no idea how many glasses of water she drank per day and had no intention of starting to keep track, but she knew it was easier to agree and move on than to protest.

'Okay sure, nine glasses it is.'

Her mother sighed and bit her lip apologetically. 'I'm annoying you, aren't I? I can hear it in your voice.'

Obviously, it was a trick question. If she agreed, she would risk hurting her mother's feelings and thus be stuck talking about nothing for another half an hour so that she could soothe them. If she denied it, her mother would extend the lecture on the merits of water drinking further to fully satisfy her interest. It was a lose–lose situation. So she decided to try to change the subject instead and said brightly, 'I have news!'

'Really,' Anita beamed. 'Why didn't you say so?'

*I've been trying to.*

'Spider and I have decided where we want to have the wedding.'

'Really? Where?'

'Here, if that's okay.'

Her mother gave a shout of glee and flung her arms around her again.

Phoebe winced as her mother squeezed her ribcage tightly. 'Okay, okay. I take it you're fine with it.'

'Of course I'm fine with it, this is just what I need!' Anita cried. 'All my daughters home again, even if it's just for one day.'

'What about Dad?'

'Don't worry about him, he'll love the idea.' Her mother patted her arm as she stepped back. 'He misses you girls terribly.'

Phoebe hung her head. 'I know. Where is he anyway?'

'Out.' Her mother waved her hand over her shoulder dismissively and stepped back around the counter to continue cutting shapes into cookie dough.

Phoebe groaned. 'Where to this time?'

'I don't know,' Anita frowned. 'He doesn't confide in me. He just goes.'

'I'll have a chat to him.'

Anita looked up sadly. 'No, don't. You might make it worse. He keeps telling me he retired to spend more time with me. And for the most part he has, but then he gets this vacant look in his eyes and just takes off for hours.'

Phoebe held her breath. 'You're not worried?'

'I think perhaps retirement is not as easy as he thought,' she shrugged. 'There is definitely something playing on his mind. I know your father. He will tell me eventually.' She seemed to inwardly pep herself up and lifted her eyes eagerly. 'Let's talk more about your wedding plans. We've got so much to figure out. Tell me what I can do.'

It was at this point that Phoebe realised that she had another big problem on her hands. Her mother wanted to be as involved in the wedding as Patricia Fitzwilliam. How was she going to split up the jobs without making either one feel passed over? At the time, she had foolishly avoided talking about the subject in too much depth. After all, she'd just promised her mother a wedding at Tawny Brooks; surely Anita would be satisfied with that for now.

What she hadn't expected was to be completely ambushed by Patricia when she and Spider went to stay in Perth. The woman could have been a professional wedding planner in another life. She had a list of 'to do' items long enough to make Phoebe's head spin. By the time she brought out the invitation sample she'd had designed, Phoebe had been relieved to have something to delegate to her without worry. After all, the details of the wedding had already been worked out at Tawny Brooks with her parents. How could her mother take offence at not being involved in putting that on paper?

To give Patricia credit, the design she picked was also very tasteful. So Phoebe gave her the go ahead to print and post them all. That had at least kept Patricia off her back for a few days, while she shopped for wedding gowns, caught up with her city friends and then, lastly, with Eve.

Quiet, shy and usually a homebody at heart, she had never thought that Eve would be so difficult to pin down. Spider had wanted to catch up with her too, maybe for dinner one night, but Eve had been suspiciously busy for the rest of the evenings they were in town. Phoebe was beginning to wonder if Tash was the only one she should be worried about. Eve had been so distant at the dress fitting and not at all enthusiastic about helping with the wedding. She'd had to practically beg her to come home a month before the wedding.

It made her worry about what her chances with Tash might be. Her older sister had been MIA for weeks now. She would have thought she'd at least get a call when she received the invitation. But the silence from Sydney was deafening. The person she did get a call from after her morning at the bridalwear shop, however, was her mother.

'I received the invitation yesterday, darling. And it's very nice. Very elegant, of course.'

*But.*

'I just wondered why Patricia and Graeme got first mention.'

'First mention?'

'Yes, their names are first on the invitation. For some reason they've been given seniority and I was just wondering casually why that was.'

Phoebe's brow wrinkled in worry. 'They haven't been given seniority, Mum. It's just one of those things.'

'Are you sure?' Her mother's voice trembled a little. 'I thought perhaps it might be because they're putting in more money than we are.'

Her parents weren't, in fact, putting any money towards the wedding. They had said they would contribute by supplying food, wine and the venue instead.

'Mum, it's nothing to do with money.'

'Because, you know, giving you full use of our property is a very big gift.'

'I know.'

'And food and wine, I mean, that's half the cost.'

'It is, and I'm really grateful.'

'Plus with vintage going on at the same time this whole function in our backyard is very inconvenient to us.'

'Are you having second thoughts about us having our wedding at Tawny Brooks?'

'*Of course not!*' Anita was adamant. 'That's not what I was getting at. I just think, given our contribution, it seems odd that you would choose Spider's parents as the leading party.'

'They're not the leading party, and I didn't choose to write them first. In fact, I didn't word the invitation. Spider's mum organised it all.'

'Is that so?' replied Anita, the cynical inflection in her voice indicating that all was becoming clear to her now.

Phoebe quickly switched to damage control. 'Mum, it's not like that. It's just one of those things. It doesn't matter whose name is first on the invitation. Nobody is going to notice.'

Anita snorted. 'If that's the case, then why did Patricia put her name first?'

'She probably didn't even think about it.'

'I think you're being naive there, darling. If she had a shred of humility she would have done the right thing and honoured our contribution.' When she heard Phoebe's sigh she quickly added, 'Not that I'm trying to make a big deal out of this. That's the last thing I want to do.'

*Really?*

'I have no desire to stress you out about the wedding. I know how much you've got on your mind.'

'Thank you.'

'But I do think if you'd just let me handle the invitations this never would have happened.'

As surely as Napoleon leading an army into battle, her mother was declaring war. Phoebe shut her eyes. Was she going to be the referee at Patricia and Anita's boxing match?

'In any event,' her mother went on to say, 'you'll have to give me the contact details of the printer she used as I have a few more invitations to send out myself.'

This made Phoebe pause. Here was the catch for having the wedding on her parents' property. 'Mum, we were kind of hoping for a small wedding. Not too many people.'

'I know.'

'Just family and a few of our close friends.'

'I wouldn't *dream* of inviting anyone who wasn't family,' her mother said airily.

Phoebe's brows furrowed. *Don't panic. Stay calm.* 'Then who else were you going to invite?'

'Well, my cousin Athena, for instance.'

'I've never heard of her.'

'Probably because I haven't seen her in five years.'

'Then why invite her to my wedding?'

'Darling, Athena is my first cousin. I couldn't have a wedding in the family without inviting her.'

'Mum, how many cousins do you have?'

'About twenty.'

'Twenty!'

'They all came to Tash's wedding,' her mother declared defensively.

*How do I not remember that?*

'Don't worry, darling,' her mother said, 'I don't intend to invite their children. But the spouses must be welcome, of course.'

'Right,' Phoebe agreed, faintly wondering how she was going to break it to Spider that they were going to have forty-plus strangers at their wedding.

In the end, she decided to put it off and give Tash a call instead.

But her sister, predictably, did not pick up. She left a voicemail message that remained unanswered for a couple of days. By then, it was time for Phoebe and Spider to leave Perth and return home. She didn't try Tash again till she was safely back in Dunsborough. This time, however, she tried Tash's office number instead. If her sister wouldn't pick up her mobile or her home line, then perhaps she would answer her work phone. It came as a complete surprise when the receptionist there told her that 'Natasha Maxwell no longer works here'.

'Then where does she work?' Phoebe demanded more to herself than to the woman on the other end of the line.

'I'm sorry, she didn't leave a forwarding number.'

Phoebe hung up, her fingernails madly tapping on her palm. Worry was definitely beginning to set in. What was going on with Tash? Where was she? She decided to call Heath to find out. He was probably at work too but she had his mobile.

Unfortunately, her call to him also went straight to voicemail so she left a message. 'Hi, Heath, it's me, Phoebe. How are you? Sorry it's been so long since we last spoke.' She took a deep breath. Leaving messages was always harder than you envisaged. Particularly keeping it short and concise with so much whirling around in your head. 'Look, I'm calling because I was wondering if you and Tash got the invitation to my wedding on the 15th of March and if you'll be able to come to Tawny Brooks a month early to help out. There's heaps of work to be done on the restaurant so I could really use your expertise.' She bit her lip. 'I've been trying to get hold of Tash but she doesn't appear to be picking up her phone. I also just heard she's no longer working at Gunnings Food Group. Is everything okay? Call me, all right?'

She put the phone down and was startled when it rang back almost immediately.

'Phee, it's me.'

'Tash! Oh, thank God. I was starting to worry. Why haven't you returned any of my calls? I even tried calling your work. Why didn't you tell me you'd moved on?'

'Because I haven't really,' Natasha replied. 'I'm still looking for work.'

'Any luck?'

'Not really. The market is pretty slow right now.'

'So then why did you quit? I thought you liked it there.'

There was a pause. 'I did. And I didn't quit. They let me go.'

'Oh.' Understanding dawned on Phoebe. Her sister had always been such a high flyer and this would have been a blow. Maybe this was why she had been so distant lately. *Say something positive*. 'Don't worry, Tash, with your reputation you'll get a job again in no time.'

Her sister was uncharacteristically silent so she tried another tack.

'Why don't you just take a break for a while? Do something fun. I mean, money isn't an issue, is it? Heath still has his job, right?'

'Y-yes.'

'Well, there you go,' she finished brightly. 'Speaking of fun. Did you get the invitation to our wedding?'

'I . . . we did,' Tash's voice seemed firmer. 'Actually, that's why I rang.'

'You are coming, right?' Phoebe tried to lighten the mood with a jokey tone. 'You're in the bridal party, remember.'

Her lightheartedness was lost on her sister. 'Of course I remember,' Tash replied seriously.

'I actually have another favour to ask you,' Phoebe began tentatively. 'Could you and Heath come down to Tawny Brooks a month early?'

'A month early?' Her sister hedged. 'Why?'

'Because the restaurant is a mess and I need your help. But especially Heath's, him being the engineer and all.'

There was a rather long pause. 'I don't think Heath will be able to come.'

'Why?' Phoebe couldn't help feel slightly hurt by Tash's response. She hadn't even said she'd ask him. 'Why?'

'He's just really busy at work right now. Huge project on. They just can't let him go. Not for a whole month.'

'Oh.' Phoebe was genuinely disappointed.

'I mean,' Tash rushed on, 'I'll be there, of course. I just don't want Heath to tick off his boss by taking all that time off. Especially since I've already lost my job.'

*Fair call.*

Phoebe's heart lightened. 'No, I wouldn't want that for you guys. Don't worry, I'll try and get someone else.'

'Thanks, Phee.'

'Besides, it's not like he's not coming to the wedding.'

Tash cleared her throat. 'We'll just see how it goes, okay? Of course he'll try his best to make it. In any event, I'm really looking forward to coming home. It's been ages and this is exactly what I need right now.'

Was it just her, or had her sister cunningly changed the subject?

'I'll see you in a few months, all right?' Tash added.

'Er . . . all right,' Phoebe responded, still trying to process her sister's words.

'Bye, Phee.'

'Tash –' But the dial tone was already beeping at her.

Phoebe stared at her phone for a long time. *Something is off.*

'Expecting a call?' Spider asked as he walked into the room and placed a box on the coffee table.

'No,' Phoebe shook her head, 'just finished one. What's that?'

'I don't know,' he shrugged, dropping his body on the couch beside her. 'Your mum dropped it off while you were at school. She said you'd understand.'

Phoebe leaned forward and flipped the lid open. There were eight tall glasses inside. She shook her head.

'Why do we need glasses?' Her fiancé peered over her shoulder.

'I'd rather not get into it. But it does put me in mind of something else.'

'What's that?'

'How do you feel about having forty strangers at our wedding?'

Spider wasn't particularly happy about it but given her parents were providing the venue, food and wine, he supposed he could concede the imposition. Phoebe was relieved. At least that was one worry off her hands. Organising a wedding, she was beginning to realise, was all about juggling.

*While hopping on one foot. And patting your head.*

She smiled to herself as she went to cook their dinner for the evening. Just as she was setting some pasta on the stove, her phone rang again.

'Hello?'

'Hi, Phee, it's Heath.'

'Oh, hi! How are you?' Her eyes widened in pleasure. 'It's been a while.'

'Yes, it has. You sound well. I know it's late but congratulations on your engagement.'

She laughed. 'Thanks. Look I'm sorry I made you call back. I did end up getting hold of Tash and she said you were very busy with a big project on.'

'Oh, she told you that, did she? Did she say anything else?'

Phoebe frowned at the weird inflection in his tone and that earlier feeling of unease gripped her again. 'Like what? Is something going on between you two?'

'No.' He gave a ghost of a laugh. 'Absolutely nothing.'

Phoebe bit her lip at this inadequate reply. 'She did sound really depressed.'

'Well, you said you knew she lost her job.'

That had to be it. There was no other explanation. 'Yeah. What she needs is some cheering up and that's exactly what I'm going to give her when she comes down to Tawny Brooks in a few months. It's a real bummer you can't make it to the winery early too, Heath. I could have used the extra set of hands.'

He coughed, cleared his throat and then said slowly, 'Well actually, Phee, turns out that project I'm on is winding down.'

She blinked. 'What! Really?'

'Yep, the government's run out of money. So they're dropping phase two.'

'Oh, well that's a shame.'

'Not if you consider that I'm free now to come and help out at Tawny Brooks.'

Phoebe grinned. 'Of course. But are you sure? Tash seemed pretty adamant that your boss wouldn't let you go.'

'Tash doesn't know anything,' Heath offered with a cheerfully conspiratorial tone. 'Let me surprise her with this, won't you?'

'Sure,' Phoebe smiled. 'I won't say a word.'

# Chapter 4

*Three months later.*

Phoebe was excited.

Today was the day everyone was due to arrive at Tawny Brooks for the start of wedding preparations and Operation: Fixing a Broken Family. In keeping with her plan, she and Spider had also decided to move into her parents' home in the month leading up to the big day. She couldn't see why she shouldn't participate in and perhaps guide her sisters' reunion and reconciliation. Plus, with Spider's parents staying there too, she knew her fiancé would want to keep an eye on them. His mother, in particular, was a loose cannon who needed to be handled with care.

They arrived Saturday morning and unpacked their things in one of the guest bedrooms. While Spider was catching up with her parents, she went down to the restaurant to do a little more reconnaissance. She wanted to make sure there wasn't any further damage she had not taken into account.

The restaurant could be reached via a single-lane dirt track that ran from her parents' home to the back of a public car park that serviced the restaurant, the garden and the Tawny Brooks cellar door. The cellar door was a large building of stone and timber made in the same style as the residence. Two large dark wooden frames with huge jarrah rafters formed apexes above a generous double glass entrance. A couple of old oak barrels cut in half made great pots for some deep red proteas. Behind the cellar door was the restaurant, which could be accessed by patrons who followed the limestone path through the surrounding gardens. These were tended lovingly by her mother and a fulltime gardener.

The garden was definitely one of Tawny Brooks' visitor attractions. All organically grown, it was literally buzzing with bees and birds of all varieties. Tall karri trees provided shade and that element of secrecy to lure in the curious traveller. By the tree roots, strategically planted along the limestone path, was a delicate mix of native and foreign flora. The main colours were red and orange, which was not unsurprising, given her mother always said, 'Gardens are about creating warmth.'

The gardener, Eric, usually kept a set of keys on his belt so she went looking for him first. She'd nearly forgotten how pretty it was in there. Different varieties of kangaroo paw, bottle brush bushes and proteas surrounded the rocky path that cut through. Rosebushes grew here too. They were not uncommon in vineyards as they were disease indicators when planted at the end of vineyard rows. In this garden, however, they were added for beauty only. Eric was clearing weeds beneath them when she found him. He was a young man, only nineteen, who had started working at Tawny Brooks about a year ago. She'd known him since he was a kid though because his father, Frank Matheson, had worked there before him. His dad had now retired. The Mathesons had always been good friends with her family and Eric was as familiar a fixture on the estate as her father's fermentation tanks. Being six years her junior, though, she had always regarded him as the shy, skinny kid who helped out his dad a lot. He'd matured of course, filled out a little, but still hadn't gained much worldly confidence. And when she stepped into the clearing he proved this by dropping his tools and reddening nervously. It was not a good colour on him given his ginger hair and freckles to match – a rather unfortunate complexion for a gardener.

'Er . . . hi, Phee.' He tipped his broad-brimmed hat at her from where he was standing in a rosebush garden bed. 'Long time no see.'

She stopped along the rocky path and smiled. 'It has been a while, hasn't it? How have you been, Eric?'

'Good, I suppose.' He hesitated. 'I hear you're getting married.'

'Yeah, the whole family's in town for it.' She jerked her thumb over her shoulder.

'We should organise a game of bung cricket sometime,' he suggested.

Her eyes widened with nostalgic pleasure. 'Man! I haven't done that for years. I remember when we used to play all the time.'

The bung was the silicon barrel cork that fitted into the side of her father's wine barrels. It made for an interesting cricket ball due to its odd shape, which made it bounce unpredictably. She remembered bung cricket had given her and her sisters many hours of fun on sunny afternoons after school or on return trips from uni. Often, any free cellar rats, vineyard workers or Eric and his father had joined in too. The memories made her sigh.

'It was good times, wasn't it?' Eric returned shyly.

'Sure was,' she said with a certain wistfulness and then added on a giggle, 'I'd love to see my future mother-in-law having a go. That would definitely be a sight. Anyway,' she sobered, 'I've come to check out the restaurant. We're going to fix it up, you know. Do you still keep the keys on your belt?'

'Yep.' He nodded. 'Here, I'll let you in myself.' He took off his gloves and joined her on the path, the keys on his belt jangling as they walked. 'I've always wondered why your father didn't fix the restaurant before now,' he said slowly. 'I mean, the kitchen is okay. He could have returned it to working order in no time at all.'

'No money, I expect,' she shrugged, making out that she had no idea. The truth was she really didn't want to talk about what had been the source of contention between Tash and Eve for over a year now. Her father's actions and the family business was quite simply *their* business, and while Eric was a valued employee and family friend, she didn't really want to share intimate family decisions with him.

'Really?' Eric cleared his throat. 'I find that hard to believe. Tawny Brooks seems to do great every year. The brand is untouchable. I have friends overseas who drink our wine.'

'Our wine, Eric?' she teased.

He laughed self-consciously, scratching the back of his neck. 'Tawny Brooks has been good to me. I consider it home almost as much as you do.'

By this stage they had reached the restaurant. It wasn't an overly large building, more quaint than auspicious, and built entirely of timber. Rectangular in shape and built on short stumps, there was an alfresco section that hung partially over the edge of 'Crazy Man's Lake', providing diners with a peaceful view of the water.

Phoebe climbed the steps to the wooden deck currently empty of tables. It was dirty and full of cobwebs – definitely in need of a good sweep and a paint. But the majority of the damage, she knew, was inside. Eric was already at the double doors and had inserted the key. He rattled the handle a bit as the keyhole appeared to be rusty and jammed. Finally the door swung open and Phoebe followed him inside.

Similar to the alfresco area, most of the furniture had been removed. There was a rustle in one corner and Phoebe jumped as a grey rabbit leapt out from behind some stacked chairs, bounded across the room and then disappeared through one of the blackened holes in the floor. There were three of these openings, at least a metre by a metre in size. The rest of the place was mostly intact. Walls and windows were grey with dirt and soot but were not unsalvageable. The floor was littered with twigs and leaves and other bits and pieces that had blown in. The gable roof was visible and she could see several birds' nests sitting on the giant wooden rafters above their heads. But otherwise, they were in good nick. Nothing a good clean-up couldn't fix.

'The new floorboards and beams are arriving tomorrow,' she told Eric. 'I ordered them myself.'

'Really?' Eric seemed surprised.

Phoebe blushed. 'I got Heath's advice first, of course. I'm no builder after all. But once I found the drawings Spider and Eve had done when they built the place, it was quite easy. We're just replacing the beams with the same timber sizes they used originally.'

'Nice.' Eric smiled.

'All right then,' she nodded, 'let's have a look at the kitchen.' She turned and walked to another set of doors on her left. They were locked as well. But Eric followed her with his keys. A second later, he'd swung the doors wide and she strode in behind him, immediately overwhelmed by memories. On her left was the wash area and on her right the pass – the stainless steel bench upon which food was delivered to waiters. She could remember busy nights when this was crowded with dishes and she'd been asked to come in to help run them out. It seemed so strange to be looking at this place now – bare, empty and silent, with a layer of dust upon every surface.

It was definitely still a modern and functional kitchen. Beyond the pass were two eight-coil stoves standing opposite each other, one with a grill on top and the other positioned between a hot plate and a deep fryer. Around the corner was a layout bench she used to be able to see her face in but which was now in need of a good scrub. The room had bench to ceiling windows on two sides, overlooking the lake or the garden. There were a few country touches here and there, such as a large timber plaque on the wall that had the words 'A family kitchen is where memories are homemade and seasoned with love' burned into its surface.

In her opinion, it would have been a wonderful place to work. It had such a large airy feel with beautiful views practically all round. With a sigh, she walked over to one of the counters and leaned across it to peer out the window. Sunshine sparkled on the lake; the branches of a large gum not far from her swayed gently with the play of the breeze.

'How could Eve not want to work here?' she wondered out loud.

'Do you want a cup of tea?' Eric enquired. 'There's a kettle here that wasn't packed away.'

She wrinkled her brow. 'Is the power on?'

He nodded. 'Since your father's new winemaker started using the back offices and storerooms for himself, your father's switched it back on.'

'Mmm,' she hesitated. 'I don't know. I should probably get back to the house. Spider is waiting for me there. All the family is due home for dinner tonight.'

'Oh,' Eric replied, running his hands over a couple of large earthenware jars sitting against the window. He hesitated. 'Your fiancé's name, Spider . . . It's such a weird name, isn't it? I mean, a spider is after all an insect, sometimes poisonous, fast on its feet, a web-spinning lurer of prey.'

The way his voice changed caught Phoebe by surprise and made her stop.

*What a strange angle to see it from.*

'Spider is called Spider,' she smiled brightly, 'because he's all arms and legs. His family has been calling him that since he was a kid.'

'Okay.' Eric seemed to accept her explanation. 'I guess that makes sense.'

But the conversation had been enough to make her pause and look out the window again. 'Actually, maybe I will have that cup of tea.'

'Sure.' He took the lid off the jar and held it out to her.

It was full of tea bags and something else.

She blinked. 'No, I . . . hang on a minute, what's that in there?' She reached in and drew out an envelope. It was unaddressed but looked like it had already been opened so she didn't feel there was any reason not to see what was inside.

She took out the typed sheet, her eyes flying over the words.

*Spider,*

*I have been meaning to tell you this for quite some time. And now that you're here at Tawny Brooks, it seems almost like a sign that I should. I love you. I want a future with you. And I know you feel the same way. We are perfect for each other, as you have shown me, in so many ways.*

Phoebe tore her eyes from the page to eyeball Eric. 'Where did this come from?'

Eric looked blankly at her. 'I don't know. I thought there was nothing but tea in there. What is it?'

She scanned down the page for the sender's name but there wasn't one. The fact that the note was typed made it even more cryptic. She folded the letter up and put it in her pocket. 'An important document. I'll take it back to the house.'

Eric closed the jar. 'Okay.'

Her thoughts in disarray, she quickly wrapped up her visit to the restaurant and left Eric to lock up. As soon as he was out of view, she whipped the note out of her pocket again and read the rest of it.

*I couldn't tell you this in person. Every time I try, I get too nervous and the words stick in my throat. So I thought*

*I'd send you this note instead. Now that I've finally come clean, will you please meet me at the Wildwood Bakery Sunday at three o'clock? We can grab your fav afternoon treat and talk about this, away from prying eyes.*

Her first instinct was to take the note to Spider and immediately demand answers. But who was to say he would have seen this before and know who it was from. In fact, it was more likely that he hadn't.

*Your husband-to-be is not a cheater.*

*Nor does he lead women on.*

Even as the thought surfaced, she glanced back at the note, chewing on her lower lip. She read the sentence 'And I know you feel the same way' at least three times.

The eternal optimist in her wanted to throw it out. But she couldn't bring herself to do it. Who had put this note in the kitchen? Had they known Spider would be working there tomorrow morning?

*And will they be at the Wildwood Bakery Sunday at three o'clock, waiting for my fiancé?*

She folded the note carefully, placed it back in its envelope and then back into her pocket. This wasn't the only secret she had now. If there was one thing keeping secrets had taught her, it was that anything was possible. And nothing should ever be taken for granted.

When she got back to the house, Spider was in the sitting room catching up with Eve.

'Eve! I'm so glad you're here.'

'Me too.' Her sister stood up to hug her. Eve looked tired and frankly just a little fed up.

Phoebe pulled back, holding her at arm's length. 'Everything all right?'

Eve nodded. 'Fine. Fine.'

Spider grinned. 'Your mum's already been on her case about eating right.'

'Really?' Phoebe winked. 'Was the theme pineapples or water?'

Before Eve could reply, the subject of their debate walked in with a tray of antipasti and a bowl of quartered fruit. 'Oranges,' she announced. 'They're the best in the South-West. All the way from Nanup. It's a long way to go to get oranges but I do it every week on principle. Once you taste these, you'll never go back.'

'That's okay, Mum,' Phoebe waved the bowl away, 'I'm all right for the minute.'

'But I drove an hour and fifteen minutes to get them,' her mother protested. 'They're the juiciest you'll ever taste.'

'I'm sure they are. I just don't feel like an orange right now.'

'Eve had one,' her mother announced waspishly.

Phoebe glanced at her sister, who shrugged helplessly. 'She insisted.'

'And what did you think?' Anita prompted.

Eve's dancing eyes met Phoebe's. 'They were the juiciest I've ever tasted.'

Phoebe grinned. *Traitor.*

'There, you see!' Anita threw up her hands as though a bill had just been passed in the senate.

'Fine, I'll have one already.' Phoebe grabbed a quarter as her mother went out again to get the drinks.

Her sister's face had lightened considerably with the exchange and so had the burden in Phoebe's pocket. Being back in the house and surrounded by her family, she began to wonder why she was making such a big deal about a forgotten scrap of paper. Who knew how long it had been sitting there? Perhaps it was years old – back from a time before she'd even come on the scene, when the kitchen was full of staff. She tried to remember the names and faces of some of their female employees. Eve would know. Maybe she'd ask her later.

In any case, the letter was not proof of infidelity. Someone had a crush on her fiancé and that wasn't a crime. It was even kind of flattering.

An hour later Spider's parents arrived and then Heath turned up a few minutes later. This provided further distraction. The family was finally coming together. Her loving fiancé was by her side. This wedding was going to happen. How could she believe that anything could possibly tear them apart now?

# Chapter 5

The scenery was gorgeous. Warmth and a feeling of well-being filled Natasha as she drove up Rickety Twigg road. It wound lovingly through the tall green forest of marri and jarrah trees from Bussell Highway to the quiet town of Yallingup – a tiny hub in this area filled with wineries. Their tall grey and white trunks stretched up to the sky but all those branches and leaves let in only a smattering of flickering sunlight, which played upon her dashboard as she wove her way through the forest. Excitedly, she wound down her window to let the fresh country air whip at her cheeks and hair. She could hear the sounds of the bush now. Birds, probably fairy wrens or New Holland honeyeaters, looking for a sweet flower or unprotected grape.

There were so many wineries in the area. Happs, Driftwood, Stormflower, Woody Nook, Rosily, Clairault. Too many to name them all. Every estate had its own history, its own methods of growing grapes and making wine, in a region so passionate about a good drop.

But amidst it all, Rickety Twigg road was the path that cut history through her life. All the properties on this road held childhood memories. She had grown up here. Driving down it now eased some of the hurt and pain she had accumulated over the past year. Coming home felt like the right thing to do.

The first winery that flashed into view was Oak Hills, with its huge wrought iron gate spread wide at the top of a red gravel track, which led into the heart of the estate. Nearly as old and well known as Tawny Brooks, it was owned by the Franklins, whom she had not seen in years. Relations between her family and theirs were mixed. In all matters of wine and business they were arch enemies, competing neck and neck for sales and James Halliday stars. Their growing and viticulture philosophies were completely different, so conversations were always too opinionated to be friendly.

Back in high school she and every other girl had been fascinated by Jack Franklin, who, from age eighteen, was the region's most notorious womaniser. She'd even had a fling with him at one stage before he'd decided to move overseas to pick up new knowledge in winemaking. She wondered where he was now. Tearing up France, no doubt. His sister, Claudia, was lovely. They'd gone to school together and always got on well. It was a shame their parents hadn't been more friendly.

She passed the entrance to the next property, which was not very big. No more than about thirty hectares. The access road was a poorly defined dirt track that came off Rickety Twigg and seemed to run straight into the bush. There was no visible sign post. So if you weren't a local, you wouldn't even notice it. The property was called Gum Leaf Grove – probably because of the huge gum trees on the road side, shielding it from view. As children, she and her sisters had dubbed it the haunted mansion. The giant rambling house on the property was falling apart and vacant. It had been for years. Whoever owned it never came to visit, but leased most of their backyard to grape growers so the vines growing around it were reasonably taken care of.

The road began to slope gently upward and her car climbed to the top of the hill. As she rolled over the peak, she took her foot off the accelerator and her breath caught in her throat. There was Tawny Brooks. Not a blemish on the land but a feature. The vines cut neat rows as they curved over the hill, interspersed by gravel tracks and the occasional tree or rosebush. The dam, or 'Crazy Man's Lake', was a prominent feature in the centre, a small gazebo and a short jetty at its shallower end. The house was not far from that. Built in the seventies but well maintained, it was made of jarrah and stone. It was only one storey and did not look that big from her vantage point but Natasha knew the floor plan like the back of her hand. The house was huge and every window had its own special view, whether it be the lake or the vines. The house had tranquillity covered from every angle.

And yet, somehow, now that she was turning onto the gravel path that led down to it, the good feelings from before receded and worry began to set in.

*You lied to Phoebe and now you're going to lie to everyone in your family.*

There would be questions. Even the most mundane one – 'How are you?' – would need to be answered. She couldn't tell them what had happened last year and that she was still jobless. Not before the wedding. What a way to dull the happiness of their moment. Her miserable news could definitely wait. Besides, what had she been chanting to herself on the way down here?

*Forgive.*

*Forget.*

*Forgive.*

*Forget.*

She had to move on. It wasn't a choice any more. She had to forgive herself and stop obsessing over Sophia. In fact, she'd been making rather good progress these last few months in the lead-up to this trip. It had been many weeks since she'd allowed the name to creep into her head. Usually at times like this she had flashes of Sophia herself. Her smile, her hair, her beautiful and enviable skin. It was sick, really, given she had never actually met Sophia in the flesh. These images were an extension of her distraught emotions sent to taunt her more than anything else. Or at least that's what her psychologist had said. This time, however, it was Heath's face that caught her mind's eye. His dark black brows drawn tightly together. His fists clenched, suppressing strong emotion. Anger or frustration, she didn't know which.

'You've got to stop talking about her,' he was saying. 'It's not helping. It doesn't get us anywhere.'

'I can't pretend she didn't exist.' Her voice arced in pain.

'I'm not asking you to,' he cried, 'but if you don't start focusing on the future, Tash, there's not going to be one. At least not for us, anyway.'

That's all he ever talked about. The future. The future.

That if she wanted to move forward, she had to stop letting past events drag them down.

'How easy for you to say,' she had flung at him. 'You speak like someone with no feelings at all.'

He'd walked out then. Not out of her life. No, that had come later. But it had definitely been the beginning of the end.

Firmly, she shut off her thoughts as cleanly as picking up the TV remote and killing the picture. She focused all of her attention on the road again. Frankly, she was sick of images like that. Bone weary of them.

Reliving the past didn't help, but a sabbatical might. Tawny Brooks was exactly what she needed. The red dirt track widened into a large car park just outside the cellar door where several wine tasters stood chatting. Next to this was the famous Tawny Brooks garden, her mother's pride and joy.

She drove on through the car park, eager to get to the house. She parked out the front beside two other cars, both Holden Barinas, just like the one she had rented.

*My sisters must be in town.*

It was strange how they were all so different, but when it came to cars, exactly the same. Her nerves hit a crescendo as she stepped under the timber arches, shading the front door of the house.

*Here goes.*

She took a deep breath and knocked.

The door swung open after a few moments and a rush of love overcame her at the sight of her mother. It was like no time had passed. Anita wore an ancient looking floral dress that Natasha was sure she had first seen as a kid. Her large coal-coloured eyes grew wet as she spread her arms.

'Tash! My darling girl.'

Natasha returned her mother's embrace, which required her to half-bend, half-stand to meet her mother's diminutive height.

'Why did you knock?' Anita scolded. 'You know it's open.'

'Sorry, Mum. City habits.'

'Where are your bags?'

'In the car. I thought I'd bring them in later.'

'All right. Come in, come in.'

She felt her mother's critical eyes on her as she stepped over the threshold. 'You haven't been eating properly, have you? You're as skinny as a leaf.'

'Am I?'

'Don't play dumb. Your sister Phoebe is exactly the same. She looks like the wind blew her in. *Well*,' she shook a stern finger as she shut the door, 'that's all about to change.'

'Really.' Natasha smiled at the direct order. Though to be honest, she was rather hungry. She hadn't brought anything to snack on in the car on the way down. She'd just driven non-stop till she got here.

Her mother grinned at her. 'People come to the South-West to eat and drink. And you girls aren't going to be the exception to the rule.'

It was true. The region had its own chocolate and cheese factories and all the pickles, jams and preserves you could possibly desire. Not to mention the liqueurs and candies, pasta sauces and every fruit and vegetable available to pick fresh off the trees should it take your fancy. It was no wonder most tourists were in town simply to drive and consume organic produce. And of course there was the added advantage of wine tasting as well. But for her, it was her mother's cooking that brought her to Yallingup. Cheesy filo tiropites, her famous chicken soup – avgolemono – and nutty, cinnamon-spiced baklava drizzled in syrup. Her mouth was watering just thinking about it.

Natasha stepped further into the house and aromas from her childhood assailed her. There was a blend of pot pourri on the hall table in a delicate glass bowl, purchased in a glass blowing house in Margaret River back when Mum and Dad had been a young married couple. The pot pourri itself was her mother's own creation. No doubt made from cuttings from the Tawny Brooks' garden. Also faint, but still discernible, was the cleaning agent Anita used on the polished wooden floorboards, a natural blend she made herself from black tea and vinegar. The floors were shiny enough to see your face in. Natasha swallowed a lump in her throat as memories flooded her mind.

'Is anybody else here?' she finally asked, snapping out of her reverie.

Her mother's lips pulled into a straight line. 'It's just your father left to arrive now.'

Natasha blinked. 'Dad? But where is he?'

'I have no idea.'

*Uh-oh.*

She didn't quite know how to respond to this. Communication had never been a problem for her parents. They had always had a very solid, loving marriage.

*Who are you to talk?*

She had seen how fast that could change.

'He left this morning,' her mother continued. 'And hasn't returned.' Anita's face clouded. 'I sent Adam to go find him, but he hasn't returned either.'

'Who's Adam?'

Anita brightened a little. 'Our new winemaker. A lovely young man. Very helpful and he loves my cooking.'

Natasha smiled wryly. Her mother loved anyone she could feed.

'You know what,' Anita placed her hand in the small of Natasha's back and gently pushed her towards the sitting room, 'you go ahead. I'm going to get some more cheese. Everyone else is in there.'

The sitting room was the biggest room in the house and the most accommodating for entertaining large groups of guests. Spacious and airy, it was lined on one side with bookshelves and on the other with two huge windows overlooking the lake. She used to sit in there and read as a kid. The four burgundy-coloured couches in the room were long and deep enough to lie on.

But she'd only taken two steps over the threshold when she stopped in shock.

The first face she registered was Heath's.

*Heath's!*

Olive skinned, with chiselled cheekbones, his large dark eyes were fringed by lashes that stared unwaveringly at her from across the room. Light flashed behind her eyes, her body went hot and then cold. She reached out and steadied herself against the doorframe, focusing all her willpower on closing her gaping mouth. His own lips were straight, neither smiling nor frowning as he regarded her with the deliberation of a cowboy before a gun draw.

*What the hell is he doing here?*

'Tash!' Phoebe materialised from nowhere, enveloping her numb body in an excited hug which didn't really form that much of a distraction considering she could still see Heath over her sister's shoulder. Sirens continued to wail in her head.

*What sort of ambush have I walked into?*

She felt bile rise up her throat as she looked around the rest of the room. Taking in the other faces. Eve's pale one on the couch. Spider, standing by the window, with a kind of half-embarrassed, half-whimsical smile. Two other people she didn't know were standing beside him and looked as nervous as she felt. A tall, white-haired couple, with similar eyes and facial features to Spider, so she assumed they must be his parents. It was almost like the scene of an intervention. But who for?

'How was your flight?' Phoebe pulled out of her arms to demand cheerfully. 'You must be exhausted driving all the way from Perth right after landing.'

'I didn't,' she responded stiffly, her eyes returning to Heath, trying to work out what angle he was playing. 'I stayed overnight at a hotel.'

'*A hotel?*' Phoebe swatted her arm. 'You should have crashed at Eve's.'

Natasha didn't know whether to be mortified or relieved as her gaze swung to the sister she hadn't seen in over a year. Eve regarded her solemnly from the couch, a self-conscious expression clouding her eyes as she said thickly, 'Of course. I mean, my couch is pretty comfortable and I have plenty of spare bedding.'

Natasha took a breath to relax but her voice still came out stilted. 'I didn't want to cause any inconvenience.'

'It wouldn't have been any trouble.' Eve shrugged but looked down at her hands as though the statement was a futile one.

Natasha completely got that. She really did. Eve's reaction to her was perfectly understandable. But Heath?

As her gaze was irrevocably drawn to his again, he walked across the room towards her. She shrunk into herself with every footfall until he was finally in front of her.

He put a hand under her chin and lifted her lips for a kiss. If they had been alone she would have resisted. His mouth burned hers with their brief contact before he said, half-smiling, 'Surprise.'

She choked. Memories. Images. Pain. That's all he brought back. She sighed in relief as he removed his hand from her chin, though in reality she felt more trapped than ever.

Phoebe slung an arm around her, nearly bowling her off her feet in her enthusiasm. 'Isn't it great, Tash! Heath's project is finishing early and he agreed to help out with the restaurant!'

'Finishing early?' She mouthed the word, wide-eyed.

'Yes.' Phoebe misinterpreted her softness as worry. 'He wanted it to be a surprise so I kept it a secret too. I mean, of course, I hope he gets more work. But for now, he can stay with us and help with the wedding. And that's a bonus, isn't it? A big family holiday.'

Heath raised an eyebrow at her, his lips curling in approval. She knew what he was doing, he was giving her the opportunity to blow the whistle, letting it be her choice.

*Wow.* Anger arced through her body. *How magnanimous of him.*

As though she would announce to her family now, in front of Spider's parents (whom she didn't even know), that their marriage was over and she didn't want him here.

She ground her teeth. How had he even known about the wedding, about coming a month early to help with the preparations? Had Phoebe gone behind her back and invited him? But why would she do that when she had specifically said he couldn't make it?

Maybe he'd just turned up by chance. Her mind raced at the possible conversation scenario. *'Hi, guys, I'm divorcing your sister and was in the neighbourhood so I just thought I'd pop by and mention it.'*

Oh yeah, that sounded completely likely.

So what was his plan? Were they supposed to pretend to be happily married? For how long? To what end? If she'd had an excuse to march him out of there immediately to demand answers, she would have. Instead, she had to play along as Phoebe introduced her future parents-in-law.

'Tash, this is Patricia and Graeme, Spider's parents.'

'Lovely to meet you.' She held out her hand to shake theirs. 'Are you staying at the house?'

Patricia nodded. 'Yes, we are and looking forward to it too. It's a beautiful home. You girls were very lucky to have grown up here.'

'Thank you.'

Anita walked in with a plate of locally produced brie and cheddar. Tash loved the smoked waxed cheddar made by the Margaret River Cheese Factory that went excellently with her father's tempranillo.

'Say cheese,' her mother joked.

Tash caught a shadow of movement and realised that Heath was positioning himself by her side. 'I'll have some,' she croaked and immediately followed her mother to the coffee table, where she extended her stay there by cutting slices for everyone else. After a while, she caught Eve studying her carefully.

Had she noticed anything particularly amiss in her behaviour?

She dusted her fingers, put the cheese knife down and retreated to the window. In her haste to get away from Eve's concerned stare, she realised she'd forgotten to cut Spider a piece of cheese. She was just about to return to the coffee table to complete the task when Heath joined her, holding out a glass of her father's semillon sauvignon blanc, which she took gingerly.

'So,' he murmured. 'Long time no see.'

Fortunately, she was saved from having to answer him by the sudden and awkward arrival of her father. The doors to the sitting room flung open and John Maxwell himself staggered in, seemingly unaware that he had company. He was thinner, browner and more weathered than she had ever seen him but he looked in fine spirits. Literally.

The smell of wine had walked in with him, along with a handsome young man. This stranger stared at the gathered group, who had stopped talking to look at them.

'Er, John . . .' He pulled Mad Maxwell's shirt from behind, causing the old man to jerk back and stop. 'Is there something you forgot to mention?'

'What?' John looked up, taking in first the startled face of Patricia Fitzwilliam and then her husband, Graeme, who happened to be standing closest to him. His eyes widened momentarily and then he cleared his throat. 'Now, Adam,' he whispered hoarsely over his shoulder, 'don't be alarmed, but I think we're at the wrong house.'

# Chapter 6

Eve covered her mouth in shock as her father began to back up towards the door. He'd always been the playful sort, but thiis was ridiculous.

'If we walk out quietly,' he was whispering to his companion, 'they may not notice we were ever here.'

This second man, in Eve's opinion, should have been named Adonis, not Adam. He had curly blond hair, startling blue eyes and creamy skin that showed every flush or heightening of emotion.

The faint pink tinge in his cheeks and twinkling eyes showed that he was enjoying her father's tipsy retreat very much. With shoulders so broad, and arms so masculine, Eve couldn't imagine a more comfortable haven than to be nestled against that very, very fine chest in front of a roaring fire. She blinked stupidly at the swift and lethal fantasy.

*Where the hell did that come from?*

She shoved the thoughts from her mind, like a bouncer pushing a drunk out of the bar.

*Greek Gods and roaring fires? You didn't get enough sleep last night.*

It was true enough. Her first day in Yallingup had been hard. Returning home was like flicking through the pages of an old diary filled with dreams that had never come to fruition. There were so many things she had tried to achieve here and failed. But transferring her unrequited love from one man to another wasn't going to help her either. She had to find balance within herself and accept the things she could not change.

Spider and Phoebe were getting married. They were very much in love.

*Look at them.*

Her eyes darted involuntarily in their direction. Her sister's hand was tucked neatly in his, her body pressed up against his side. It didn't matter what feelings Eve had had or even that she had harboured them for years. They were erased, *or should be*, by the simple and irrevocable fact that he now belonged to Phoebe and always would.

There was no room for her in this picture, except as a supportive sister.

*And you need to get a new best friend!*

She had come to this conclusion on the drive down. She simply could not continue a close relationship with Spider and move on emotionally. It was impossible. A little like her father attempting to look sober right now. It was strange to see him staggering on his feet. John Maxwell had always been a little eccentric, but he had never needed alcohol to achieve the effect before.

'Don't you dare, John,' Anita said, detaching herself from the group and coming forward. 'Where have you been?'

Her father's expression transformed from stealthy cunning to innocent surprise. 'Anita, *sweetheart.*' He spread his arms wide. 'There you are! I've been looking everywhere for you.'

Anita was not impressed. Her arms were folded and one small foot tapped menacingly. 'I've been home all day.'

Eve had been with her, helping to prepare the spare bedrooms for their guests. Eve had listened with half an ear to her mother complain for hours that their father was 'running too wild'. It was true that she had noticed a few odd things around the house, particularly the new car she'd seen parked in her parents' carport when she'd first arrived. It seemed to be one of those classic cars from the 1970s, fully restored to its former glory – a Holden Torana or something. She wasn't that into cars, let alone classic ones, but she knew her father had had a love of Holdens back in the day. She didn't think it was unreasonable if he wanted to spoil himself in retirement and so hadn't placed too much stock in her mother's worry . . . until now.

'Where have you really been, John?' Anita asked again.

'Er . . .' Her husband's face clouded in concentration. In the end the question must have got the better of him because he turned back to Adam. 'Where have we been again, son?'

'Horace Franklin's cellar,' Adam announced.

John rolled his eyes. 'My dear boy, that's a terrible cover story. I could have done better than that and I'm drunk.'

'Dad,' Phoebe came forward, her arm immediately looping through his so that she might lead him to the couch, 'I thought we agreed that you were going to take it easy from now on?'

His eyes lit with pleasure at the sight of her. 'I am taking it easy, Phee. And having a little fun as well. What are you doing here, my girl? Doing the old pop-in, drop-in.' He seemed confused. 'Or is that what I'm doing?'

'No, John,' Anita whispered hoarsely, 'everyone's here. They've all arrived to help out with the wedding.'

'Already?' He glanced apologetically around the room. 'I thought you said they were coming on Saturday.'

Anita's face reddened. 'Today is Saturday.'

'Oh! That explains it then.' He nodded as though a complication had just been sorted out. 'I'm sorry, love. I'll try to act sober.' He wobbled a little as he sat down on the couch opposite Eve's. He folded his hands neatly in his lap and buttoned his lip. The image was so indicative of a young boy deciding to behave well in class that Eve couldn't help but smile. Catching her watching him, he winked roguishly at her, immediately belying all evidence that he intended to behave.

Phoebe was not as amused by the exchange. She sat down beside him, taking one of his hands. 'Dad –'

'Stop fussing, love.' He pulled his hand away. 'I'm not an invalid.'

'Quite the contrary actually,' Anita confirmed tartly.

'Is there any water?' asked Tash, who was still standing by the coffee table. Eve noticed she had been acting rather cold and cagey since she had arrived. She had hoped that time might have mellowed the bad feeling between them but it didn't look like it.

Her older sister was dressed in a pair of well-tailored black slacks and a satin blend blue top with a scooped neckline. The average corporate executive might wear this sort of getup to work but Eve knew that for Tash, this was casual wear. Her sister would wear nothing but suits to the office. Designer label, if possible. But if you had the perfect figure, the perfect legs, the perfect hair, why wouldn't you?

Eve sighed. It was no wonder Tash could never understand where she was coming from. It must be easy to look down on lesser mortals when you had everything going for you. Good looks, great job, wonderful husband. When you couldn't imagine what life was like on the tail end of secrets and disappointment, why shouldn't you have high expectations?

Yet even as her heart squeezed with the weight of the ordeal she had irrevocably signed up for, she was not unhappy that Tash was there. Her sister had not snubbed her earlier and that, at least, was something. She was relieved to know that they could still converse on some level without creating a scene, because if there was one thing Eve hated more than anything, it was being at the centre of conflict.

Her father, on the other hand, thrived on drama.

'Water,' he scoffed. 'Where is last year's cab sav, Tash? It'll put the colour back in those pale cheeks of yours.'

'Not for me, Dad,' Tash said quietly. 'For you.'

'There's some on the desk by the bookshelf,' Eve found herself saying. Tash looked up and as their eyes met they seemed to instantly fall back into the pattern of their childhood – where Tash was the leader and she the follower. 'I'll get it if you like,' Eve automatically added.

'Thanks,' Tash nodded.

Eve got up and started to walk towards the desk by the door but found Adonis directly in her path. His proximity suddenly made her nervous. She was so busy keeping her head down that when he sidestepped out of her way she moved in the same direction, intending to walk around him. They ended up doing a rather awkward cha-cha-cha before he grabbed her by the shoulders and neatly set her aside.

'I think you mean to go that way,' he said softly.

Her ears burned as she took off again towards the water, cringing.

*Somebody kill me now.*

After getting the water, she took a different route back to the centre of the room, not willing to risk a repeat of her idiocy. She hadn't been this skittish since high school when the mere mention of the word 'boys' could make her giggle. She was a mature adult now who knew reality better than anyone. Adonis was out of her league. Men like that did not look twice at her, especially when both her sisters were invited to the same party. Besides, he was not even her type. He was far too sexy. All biceps and brawn, with a face like an angel. He belonged in a fairytale, not in her reality.

She preferred her men more real. More wholesome. More dependable and roguishly handsome – like Spider.

Men as god-like gorgeous as Adonis tended to know it, which usually made them insufferable company. Far better to steer clear.

By the time she got back to the couch, Phoebe and Natasha were already seated there on either side of her father. They had both seized the opportunity to get his attention while she had rushed off to get stuff organised. How familiar the scene was. As a young girl, she had often thought of herself as the Cinderella of the family. Only the analogy was definitely flawed – neither of her sisters were ugly and her life was still a pumpkin.

'Here, Dad, drink this.' She held out the glass of water to her father and sat down on the edge of the coffee table.

He took it rather absentmindedly as he gazed at each of his daughters in turn. 'Look at you all.' He sipped his water. 'All of you in the same room. My beautiful girls. My life is literally flashing before my eyes.'

'Dad,' Phoebe's tone was rather high-pitched, 'what were you doing in Horace Franklin's cellar?'

'Settling a bet, my darlin'.'

'A bet about what?'

'That my cabernet merlot had more vanilla. I've always thought so,' he nodded confidingly. 'So I brought a bottle of mine and he took out a bottle of his.' His thumb jerked over his shoulder. 'Adam, here, was supposed to make the deciding vote. Sadly, his palate wasn't up to scratch.'

Adonis coughed rather defensively. 'That was because –'

But her father cut him off. 'No, no, it's all right, son, I'm telling the story.'

Adonis bit his lip. He had a generous, laughing mouth. She was glad he seemed to get along with her dad. She had wondered whether her father would resent the new winemaker now that he was retired but it appeared not to be so. Adonis raised an eyebrow at her and she realised that she had been staring at him too long.

She yanked her gaze to the painting on the wall, pretending that the depiction of the ancient rock formation called Canal Rocks was what she had been studying the whole time.

*As though you don't already know that scene like the back of your hand.*

She returned her attention to her father.

'The truth is,' he was saying, 'Horace's wine just doesn't get the right oak. I've always said that French barrels are better than American.'

'Since when do you hang out with Horace Franklin?' Tash demanded.

'Since he became good company.' John grinned.

'Retirement,' Anita remarked from the sidelines, 'has finally matured them both, I think. But where are our manners? Patricia, Graeme, as you may have already guessed, this is my husband, John.'

'The Mad Maxwell of Tawny Brooks Wines,' Graeme grinned. 'To be honest, I hadn't given the local rumours much credit.'

Her father stood up rather unsteadily but managed to shake both their hands. 'My apologies. I'm not normally like this, I assure you.'

'Really?' Graeme seemed vaguely intrigued.

'Yes,' he nodded. 'Wine mellows me.'

Patricia's eyebrows jumped and her father grinned at her. 'You must be Spider's mother.' He chuckled as if reliving some private joke. 'My wife has been looking forward to your arrival for weeks.'

Anita glared at him and Patricia's lips tightened as she turned a rather interesting shade of splotchy pink.

Graeme took this moment to intervene. 'Thank you for allowing us to stay here,' he said smoothly. 'Patricia was just telling Natasha how beautiful we think the house is.'

'My wife makes it beautiful,' John murmured. 'I just live here.'

'That's not true.' Anita's voice held both protest and pain. It tripped another set of alarm bells in Eve's head. It seemed odd that her mother would take such a complimentary statement to heart unless something was going on. She was so wrapped up in herself, her sisters and Spider that she hadn't really given much thought to how her parents were doing. It was so easy to take them for granted. They were always there and, like the house, never changed . . . or so she had assumed.

Unexpectedly, Adonis spoke up next. In fact, to her absolute approval, he seemed to be making his retreat. 'Well, it was nice meeting you all.' He spread his arms as he backed towards the door. 'Hope you have a nice evening, but it's about time I got back to the lab.'

'You can't test samples now,' John disagreed. 'You've had too much to drink. Besides, it's past clock off.'

'I didn't have that much,' Adonis protested. 'And considering I was out all afternoon looking for you, I think I should put in a few extra hours.'

'Well, I'm the boss.' Her father shook his head. 'And I say you don't need to.'

'Yes, Adam,' Anita added her endorsement, 'stay and have another drink.'

'But –'

Her mother used the firm tone Eve recognised from childhood. 'Dinner will be on soon too. You might as well have it with the rest of us.'

Eve watched fascinated as Adonis's face flushed deliciously, his gaze sweeping the room in the manner of a lamb prepared for sacrifice. 'I just thought, given it's a *family* gathering, you guys might have a lot of *family* matters to discuss.' He continued to look about the room for support but found none.

Eve lowered her eyes, smiling at her hands. Was it sadistic to take pleasure in discomfort that wasn't her own?

Tash held out her hand to him, regal as a queen. 'Hi, I'm Tash. You must be Dad's new winemaker. I have to admit I've been rather curious to meet you.'

He took her hand in both of his. 'Thanks. Good to meet you, Tash.'

Eve envied Tash's confidence but also found herself vaguely jealous that he shook her hand so eagerly. She got up from the coffee table and walked to the couch opposite and took a seat there to watch the scene unfold.

'Have you been working at Tawny Brooks long?' Tash enquired.

'About six months.'

'And how are you finding it?'

He seemed amused. 'It's taking over my life.'

'He loves it,' said Anita, grabbing another bottle of the white wine out of the stainless steel bucket. 'Don't you, dear?'

'Er . . . yes.'

She held out a glass to Adonis. 'Last year's semillon sauvignon blanc?'

A kind of fatalistic resignation settled on his face. 'Er . . . all right, thanks.'

'If he gets one, so do I,' announced John.

Anita poured him some too, though only half the quantity she had given the younger man. While she was doing this, Adonis took a seat on the couch beside Eve.

*Seriously? You have to sit next to me?*

She hastily averted her eyes from his powerful-looking thighs encased in blue denim.

*Just ignore him.*

'I can see you, you know,' Adonis remarked.

'Huh?' Her eyes flicked up. And to her horror he leaned in closer. 'You're not invisible,' he whispered and she smelled the tangy, citrus sweetness of the wine on his breath. 'What's your name?'

'I – I . . .' She leaned back away from him and took a gulp of her own wine. 'I'm Eve.'

He held out his hand to her. Warm and strong, his fingers closed about hers, seeming to draw her in like the smell of chocolate chip cookies in a country kitchen. Hastily, she detached her hand and shoved it back in her lap, finishing the rest of her wine in two gulps.

Now she needed another drink. There were a few bottles in a stainless steel bucket on the coffee table.

'So how do you tell a good wine?' Graeme asked her father while she got up to refill her glass.

'It should begin and end with a smile,' John told him airily. 'Speaking of which, why haven't you both got a glass?'

'Patricia doesn't drink alcohol,' Anita announced as though her husband had hit upon the heart of the problem.

Eve watched her father blink at this shocking scandal. 'Not drink?' he demanded. 'You intend to stay in my house for a whole month and not drink?'

'I'm allergic to wine.' Patricia's hands fluttered self-consciously about her waist.

John stared at her for a full ten seconds before his features finally softened. 'Well, I guess that's all right. She can just have sparkling.'

He reached over to the wine bucket and pulled out a bottle of champagne, which he poured into a flute. He stood up unsteadily and held it out to Patricia with a wink. 'For the fainthearted, my dear.'

'I –' Patricia didn't seem to know what to say so Graeme took the glass for his wife.

Eve sipped from her own refreshed glass and glanced at Spider, who was looking at the exchange helplessly. She met his eyes and tried to smile reassuringly, understanding passing between them. As her body grew warm, she took a nervous gulp from her own glass again and cut the connection. It was too easy to forget he was no longer her private confidante and that these brief exchanges were between two close friends, nothing more. She was so busy looking at Spider that she hadn't registered the fact that his parents had taken seats on the couch and Adonis had moved over to accommodate them.

She backed up, intending to reclaim her seat and found herself rather embarrassingly in Adonis's lap instead.

'Oh!' She tried to push herself up quickly but only succeeded in sloshing her wine everywhere.

'Just a tip,' Adonis said in her ear as he removed the glass from her hand, 'I'm not invisible either.'

She leapt up as though burned by a poker. 'Oh, I'm so sorry,' she cried, spinning around to look at the man who had to be her kryptonite. His hair looked wet from her wine. So did part of his shirt. 'I thought the seat was vacant,' she groaned, grabbing a handful of napkins off the coffee table and holding them out to him.

Everyone was laughing. She had quite successfully created her worst nightmare.

'Well, I guess technically my lap is,' Adonis smiled.

Her cheeks burned so hot they were almost smoking.

Her family and Spider's seemed to laugh all the harder, making her want to crawl into herself.

She glanced helplessly at Spider, who merely gave her the thumbs up.

*What's that supposed to mean?*

While her mood didn't lighten, everyone else's certainly had.

'Oh, Eve,' Phoebe toasted her, 'we always did say that your rear-view mirrors needed adjusting.'

Eve hastily sank into a nearby red armchair – an antique that her mother had had re-upholstered.

'Your wine?' She glanced left to find Adonis holding her glass out to her. There wasn't much remaining in it but she took it anyway.

'Thanks.' She bit her lip, praying for a change in conversation. She got one too. Though not the one that she or anyone else in the room hoped for.

'All right, enough commercials,' John called the attention of the group. 'Better to get down to business.'

'What business?' Graeme asked politely.

'Do you think your son is ready for marriage?'

'*Dad*,' Phoebe protested.

'What?' John spread his hands. 'I'm entitled to know, I'm about to give you away. A man needs to be sure.'

'John,' Spider said quietly, 'I've told you that I'm ready. That I love your daughter, immensely.'

'Yes,' her father said shrewdly, 'but it's always good to have a second opinion. Particularly in this case.'

While Eve was glad to have lost the limelight she looked at Phoebe in sympathy. Her sister had stiffened, which was a flashing red light as far as Eve was concerned. Phoebe was never pessimistic or cautious. Bubbly optimism and steadfast faith were her primary characteristics. So it was surprising that she should say nothing in response.

An elbow bumped hers and a voice whispered, 'What do you see?'

She recoiled at the contact and glanced quickly to where Adonis was observing her with casual interest. 'I don't see anything.'

'Of course you do,' he nodded. 'It's written all over your face.'

'Seriously?' Her eyes widened in horror, which only seemed to make him smile all the more.

'Definitely. You have very expressive features.'

Her eyes darted to her parents and sisters. But no one was looking at her or listening to what Adonis was saying. They were all focused on her father, who seemed to be making the faux pas of the century.

'You know,' John Maxwell was nodding solemnly, 'decisions like these need to be looked at from all angles before they are set in stone.'

'What angle are you proposing we look at it from?' Patricia snapped.

'Perhaps you could enlighten them,' Adonis muttered under his breath without looking at her.

*What!*

Eve's heart jumped into her throat.

*There is no way he knows anything.*

She kept her gaze focused forward and replied through gritted teeth, 'I have no idea what you're talking about.'

'You seem to know Spider rather well.'

'He's my best friend,' she whispered hoarsely.

'I see.' He rubbed his chin languidly. 'It all makes sense now.'

This time she did not feign disinterest and looked directly at him. 'What? What makes sense now?'

His lips twitched. 'Why you think you're invisible.'

# Chapter 7

At her father's challenge, Phoebe's skin prickled defensively.

*Go on, say something. Smile. Laugh. You have a love that's built to last a lifetime.*

*There's nothing that could possibly diminish that.*

But her cheek muscles didn't quite respond. In fact, none of her faculties responded. She simply waited for someone else to say something.

In the end, it was Spider who held up his hand. He spoke to his mother reassuringly.

'It's okay, Mum. I would rather have his reservations out on the table than not.'

Phoebe released a breath she hadn't realised she'd been holding. 'Spider has nothing to hide, Dad,' she said. 'And neither do I.'

*Yes, you do. Yes, you do. And it's burning a frickin' hole in your right pocket.*

Instinctively, her hand moved there, the letter she'd found earlier in the restaurant nestled against her hip. She had almost dismissed its importance. But now, standing here with her father giving Spider the third degree, the letter's significance drew once more into sharp focus.

*Is my fiancé ready for marriage?*

If there were other unresolved relationships in his life, maybe he wasn't.

'I find your son a very difficult person to read,' her father was now remarking to Patricia and Graeme, his tone more intrigued than malicious.

'I assure you, John,' Spider tried to joke, 'what you see is what you get.'

'No, no.' Her father was not to be toyed with. 'I don't think so. I think there is a lot you keep to yourself. If you were a wine, my son, I would describe you as short.'

Given Spider was at least a foot taller than her father, this was a rather strange adjective to use. But by his frown she knew her fiancé understood, and so did she.

Spider's parents, however, were confused. 'What do you mean?' Patricia demanded.

'The finish of a wine is one of the most important elements of a tasting,' John Maxwell told her. 'It is in the aftertaste that you might discover its greatest virtues. If a wine is "short", it means it leaves the mouth quickly with little sustained flavour.'

Patricia opened her mouth to say something but her husband spoke for her. 'We trust our son's judgement and his maturity,' Graeme announced. 'He's always done very well for himself.'

'Yes, he has.' For some reason, her father looked completely dissatisfied with this assurance. He addressed Spider again. 'You started a business with my second daughter and let that go. Your commitment to her and your project together fell away after a year and a half. You got distracted by other things.'

'That's completely different. That was my career,' Spider began, and glanced at Eve, who looked positively stricken. 'You have to let your career grow and change the way it needs to. The restaurant wasn't a forever scenario. Was it, Eve?'

'No.' Eve shook her head but couldn't seem to offer much more.

Phoebe had resolved to cut her father some slack but this was ridiculous. She finally found her voice. 'Why are you bringing this up now, Dad? You gave us your blessing months ago.'

'I did.' John nodded as though he sorely regretted it. He glanced at Eve, who was keeping her head down. 'But as a father I must put all my worries on the table. Marriage is not an easy commitment to make. Is it, Tash?' He handballed the question across the room without even taking his eyes off Eve, and Tash seemed to jump where she stood as if she'd been hit by an imaginary bullet. She was standing stiffly by her husband's side and had been looking uncomfortable all evening. For the first time Phoebe wondered why. She glanced from Tash to Heath, who did not make eye contact.

'No,' Tash croaked, 'it's not easy.'

'I'm not suggesting that it is,' Spider interrupted, clearly frustrated. 'I honestly don't take this step lightly at all.' Phoebe took in his pursed lips and pale face and her heart sank.

*He's offended. As well he should be.*

Her father was being rude. She really shouldn't have let the conversation get this far, particularly in front of everyone. The whole purpose of having the wedding at home was to bring everyone together. Not drive them apart.

'Glad to hear it,' her father returned mildly, not in the least perturbed by the disturbance he had created.

*All right, this has gone on long enough.*

It was time to take the mood of the room and turn it on its head. Phoebe released her fiancé's arm and stepped forward, clasping her hands together and saying in her best, 'Boy, are you in for a treat!' voice: 'I'd like to make an announcement.'

'Announcement?' Spider's gaze flew to her. 'Did we talk about this? Should I be worried?'

'Of course not.' She flicked her hand but did not meet his eye. She knew instinctively that Spider may not appreciate his wedding being farmed out to the family but he *did* say she could do what she liked and she couldn't really see another way to repair the distance that had grown between them all. 'Now, there are a lot of jobs to be done before the 15th of March. Renovating the restaurant is just the starting point. We'll begin on that tomorrow, by the way.'

She turned to Adam, who was seated on the couch. 'Perhaps you could spare some of the men from the cellar door or the vineyard to give us a hand as well?'

Adam winced. 'It's the middle of vintage.'

'I know,' Phoebe smiled. 'I was born and raised here too, remember. But I wasn't suggesting it be a one-way street.'

Adam raised his eyebrows.

'You help us this week and we'll help you next week.'

Thankfully, her father embraced this change of subject and nodded in satisfaction. 'Behold my daughters – maiden, matron and crone, they are the triple goddesses of the vineyard.'

'I bags not being the crone,' Tash murmured.

'Dad's very spiritual about his grapes,' Eve tried to explain, reddening in embarrassment under Adam's interested gaze.

'How could anyone not be?' John scoffed. 'Every vintage is a piece of our history. A culmination of a year's sweat and tears. And I think this vintage will be one of the best we've had yet because it was so, so . . . fraught.'

'Fraught with what?' Patricia enquired.

'Love,' John said matter-of-factly. 'Desperate, hopeless, uncanny love.'

Phoebe cleared her throat and tried to get back on track. 'What Dad is trying to say, Adam, is that all of us are proficient in the ways of a winery. As a teenager I used to work part-time both at the cellar door and in the vineyard. I loved it. I can help you wherever you need help. Basically, you scratch my back and I'll scratch yours.'

'I liked the cellar door the best,' Tash revealed. 'Apart from the fact that it was a lot cleaner, you got to showcase everything we'd done for that year. And I loved watching the wine wankers trying to out-do each other with their swirling, spitting and nosing.'

'And what about you?' Adam turned to Eve, whose colour heightened again, and Phoebe couldn't help but notice how attractive she looked.

'Me? Of course I'll help out. Wherever necessary.' Eve glanced quickly at Phoebe. 'For the wedding or with harvest and winemaking.'

'No,' Adam said, 'I meant, how do you feel about the vintage?'

'How do I feel?' Eve glanced about the room as everyone turned to look at her again. Phoebe crossed her fingers behind her back.

*Go on, Eve, don't be shy.*

Her sister was always so worried about stuffing up. Granted, the restaurant had a lot to do with that but Phoebe really wanted Eve to find her feet again. Especially now.

Eve's uncertain eyes returned to Adam's. 'I think . . . I think every vintage is important and every year we need to make sure it's the best one we've ever had because . . . because every bottle tells a story about us, that someone in turn will share with their friends one day.'

The weight of her words swirled about the room like the mist of fog, shifting the air and making it thicker.

'Okay,' Adam nodded decisively and turned back to Phoebe. 'Sold. I'm in.'

Phoebe rubbed her hands together. 'But there's more. More to do than just that.'

She looked at the gathered group and put on her biggest and brightest grin before going to the bookshelves and pulling down a small box that she had placed there earlier. 'In fact, I thought we could make a game of it. You know, like a bit of an icebreaker to help bring everyone together.'

Silence.

*Okay. Tough crowd.*

She squared her shoulders. This technique had never failed her in the classroom.

*But your family isn't a bunch of six-year-olds.*

*They might as well be!*

She cleared her throat. 'This is a box of tasks that need to get done. I've written them twice on a bit of paper in here. So pick a task and the person who gets the same as you is your partner.'

She went round the room and everyone gingerly dipped into her box.

Natasha picked out a thin strip of paper that had 'Organise the music' written on it.

She held it up and Phoebe was pleased to see that by lucky chance Eve had picked the same one. Maybe these two could work out their differences by doing something together. She dipped her hand in and pulled out her own bit of paper.

'Hire a photographer,' she read out loud.

'I believe that's me.' Heath held up his hand.

Spider looked put out. 'Really? Who am I going to do mine with? I've got the linen and decorations. Isn't that something we ought to be doing together?'

'I'm not fussy about how we do up the room,' she smiled. 'It's just wrapping the chairs really, isn't it? And maybe a drape on the ceiling.'

Spider frowned. 'That's not what I meant.'

She glanced around the rest of the group and when no one owned up to this task, she looked down into the box. There was still one bit of paper left in there. Had everyone in the family taken one already? Then she realised there was an uneven number.

'Adam,' her eyes turned once more to the winemaker, 'you must be the person helping Spider.'

'But –' he and Spider both said at the same time.

'You can't have one foot in and one foot out.' She handed him the piece of paper that read 'Linens and decorations'.

'You're either in the family or not.'

'Well, actually, I was under the impression that –' Adam began but Anita interrupted him.

'Here, dear, have some more wine.' She shoved another glass in his hand.

Phoebe turned to the rest of the group to see who was paired with whom. Unfortunately, her mother and Patricia were both charged with organising the celebrant. So far they had been nothing but competitive with each other. She hoped doing a task together might make them find a way to negotiate a truce. Her father was matched to Graeme to organise the flowers. There couldn't be two more different personalities, but her father did not demure. Instead he said, 'All this talk of work is making me hungry.' He glanced at his wife. 'What's for dinner tonight, Annie?'

Anita tore her glare from Patricia. 'Why don't you all come into the dining room and find out?'

# Chapter 8

So far, Heath had been unable to engage Tash in a decent conversation. His attempt in the sitting room had been foiled by the arrival of her father and then later by Tash's high interest in Graeme's opinion on the quality of the roads between Perth and Dunsborough – a topic as bland as it was diverting.

It was hard not to be angry about this after she'd already stonewalled him for months. However, she had not been expecting him to show up today. So he decided to make a small allowance for her shock. A *very* small allowance.

As soon as Anita announced dinner and everyone began to file out, he barred her path so she was forced to fall behind with him.

'You're looking a little thin, Tash,' he said softly. 'Not eating well?'

He saw the muscles in her neck jerk but she did not respond. He sighed. 'Are you determined not to talk to me then?'

'I am determined not to let you rattle me with this little stunt of yours,' she said through her teeth.

Ah, the Tash he knew and loved. Hard as nails. Courageous to a fault. And the most obstinate woman who ever drew breath.

'Good to know,' he murmured. 'I would hate to set you on edge.'

Her lips twitched a little before her face resettled into that blank look he had grown to hate. It was the 'You are not going to get through to me today' expression – a closed and locked door to her heart. In the lead-up to their separation, he had seen it many times. No more so than the day they had finally decided to split.

'Thanks for responding to all those emails I sent you,' he commented, unable to keep the sarcasm out of his tone. 'I really appreciated hearing how you've been doing.'

She tossed her head. 'Why do you need to know how I've been doing?'

'Well, I am still paying the mortgage on that house you're living in,' he said rather bluntly.

She blanched and he was momentarily sorry for hitting back so hard. At times, Tash brought out the best in him. She also brought out the worst.

The day they had decided to separate was the perfect example. Ironically, when he'd walked into the kitchen that particular evening, he'd been on a mission to reconcile not to tear them further apart.

He'd had those tickets to Hawaii to give her and even the card he'd put them with 'Let's try again!' emblazoned across the front of it. It had been a very hard card to find. It wasn't exactly an occasion celebrated by most people. But he liked making a big deal of all the milestones – ticking all his boxes properly, so to speak. That's who he was. An engineer who liked to do things systematically. And, God help him, it had always served him well in the past. And it wasn't like he'd just sprung it on her out of the blue. He'd worked his way up to that moment.

He recalled the gifts he'd showered her with in the weeks before. Sexy lingerie, red roses, jewellery, you name it . . . he'd pulled out all the stops with the romance. Anything to cheer her up, make her forget what he couldn't face.

Sophia.

They'd lost her.

When Tash had miscarried, the grief had almost been unbearable. He hadn't wanted to dwell on it though. But it seemed like that was all Tash wanted to do. She had wanted to talk about their baby. Name her. Put a notice in the paper about her. He hadn't been able to deal with all that. It was too much like being trapped in a nightmare.

When she had finally fallen pregnant after so many years of trying, it had been the happiest point in their marriage – the moment where it had all come together for them. And he had wanted to get back to that place. Before Sophia's death, before everything had started falling apart.

In hindsight, he cringed at his own foolishness.

Presenting her with those tickets had been like a bomb exploding in his face. He'd never seen such fury in her eyes. Her voice had been so quiet when she'd finally spoken, like the white light before the big bang.

'I can't believe you've done this.'

'It's exactly what we need, Tash. We need to focus on the future and the happy things in our life. A holiday like this . . . lots of relaxing, plenty of sun. You might be pregnant again by the time we get home.'

She choked. 'Our baby was not a goldfish, Heath. You don't just go out and buy another one.'

His face had frozen. 'Hardly, Tash, it's been months. I wish you would stop harping on like that.'

Her voice shook. '*Two months* in which you have not grieved or even paused. And every time I try to talk about this with you, you brush me off like it was nothing.'

This was true. Not the nothing part, the brush-off bit.

Heath did not talk about his feelings. He never had. And, in fact, had been raised not to. His mother, the wife of a war veteran, had always steered him clear of difficult subjects.

'Don't ask Daddy about Vietnam. Don't ask him why he's crying. Don't ask him why he's having nightmares. Leave him alone. You'll just make things worse.'

He had been taught to always look to the future, focus on the positives. Don't look back because the past would only hurt you again.

'Tash, I –'

'You don't seem to feel anything.'

'Tash, I thought it was obvious how I felt. What have these last few weeks been if not a demonstration of my love for you?'

'Flowers? Jewellery? That's not the kind of love I need right now. I don't understand how you can continue to be this insensitive.'

'How am I being insensitive?'

'*I don't want to try for another baby now,*' she'd practically yelled at him. 'Do you see me, Heath? Do you see what I'm going through at all?'

And perhaps then, and only then, his head had risen above the fog of his own need to move away from the pain and he had seen her.

'I –' she placed her hand over her heart, 'I think we need a break from each other.'

His body had seized up. 'What do you mean?'

'You know that transfer your boss suggested earlier this year?' She blinked back tears. 'I think you should take it.'

'Tash, if our love for each other is to survive this, living apart is not going to help.'

She was silent for a moment and an awful premonition had caught him, making his skin tingle.

'That's the thing,' she had responded slowly, almost mechanically. 'I don't think . . . I don't think I love you any more.'

It was like a blow to the head.

'You're not the man I fell in love with,' she blurted. 'I don't recognise this new person in my life. This man who won't talk to me, won't allow me to grieve the death of my own child and who belittles my concerns.'

'You can't be serious.'

'At some point, Heath,' her voice trembled, 'a person needs to decide whether it's better to take a step back and heal or let the person you're with do more damage than what has already been done.'

He had stared back at her in shock. Her expression had not changed. She had tears in her eyes but her jaw was set. She had made up her mind. And he knew her stubborn streak better than anyone.

'Well, I guess that's it then,' he'd responded harshly and walked out of the kitchen. Pride had taken him to Melbourne and kept him silent for a couple of months. However, when all you had was time to think, it wasn't long before you began to realise that maybe the fault was not entirely someone else's. And so he'd tried to get back in touch again.

What he hadn't banked on was Tash setting up a wall around herself as thick as a hedge and as high as a prison fence. When he'd tried to re-establish contact from Melbourne, she'd cut him off at every pass. Didn't respond to emails. Didn't respond to calls, text messages or voicemail.

Then one day, she'd changed all her contact details so that his messages bounced every time. The last communication he'd had from her was an email saying that she was going on a business trip and would not be home for months. In anger, he'd cancelled the trip he'd planned home to visit her that week.

In fact, Tash had thought she'd had herself well covered until her sister had called to invite him to the wedding. He was shocked and hurt to learn that she had lost her job and had lied to him about that business trip. And then a kind of grim satisfaction had taken over. At last! Now he had a way to approach Tash where she could not run away.

It was long overdue.

They may be separated but they weren't divorced and there was a lot of water under the bridge that they needed to sort out whether she liked it or not.

As the two of them walked into the dining room, he noticed that the family had automatically left them two seats side by side. He took his next to her gratefully. At least he had their ignorance on his side. From the looks of the faces around the room, however, this was probably all that was in his favour.

Bringing their problems to Tawny Brooks might not have been such a good idea. It wasn't exactly Switzerland. His gaze flitted about the room, pausing briefly on different faces. Eve, Spider, Phoebe. He winced at the secrets he knew and had kept for so long to protect Tash – to protect their family. He didn't need to keep those secrets any more.

It was time Tash knew it all.

He paused longest on Spider, a man he had long struggled to understand. On the surface he seemed harmless, a nice enough bloke. Easy to talk to. Good for a laugh.

But Tash's dad didn't like him. With good reason too. He had wondered how his father-in-law was taking the marriage of his daughter to a man he simply did not trust. The conversation in the sitting room earlier had only confirmed John's unease.

Heath focused once more on Tash – the aching vulnerability in her face, at such odds with the way she treated him.

He had no idea whether he'd made the right choice coming here but it was done now and fingers crossed, it would serve him well.

# Chapter 9

Natasha knew as soon as Phoebe took the box off the shelf that things weren't going to go well for anyone.

*I mean, what is that girl thinking?*

*We're not a class of her students.*

She wanted to groan with the awkwardness of it all but knew there was no stopping her sister, who was trying to beat her enthusiasm into everyone else.

It was a relief to retire to the dining room until Heath fell in beside her and tried to engage her in conversation. It wasn't what he said, so much as him just being there that affected her. His energy was like a physical field that cut through her body, leaving her breathless. Or was it the fact that he looked so great that had extracted the air from her lungs?

It wasn't fair.

You would have thought by now, after everything they'd been through, that she would be immune to his good looks. She pushed the fingernails of one hand into her palm, her heart rate leaping as his arm accidentally brushed hers on the walk down the narrow hall.

He was the embodiment of tall, dark and handsome. She should be able to see through that shallow label for what it was. But instead, it conjured up good times, the early days of their marriage and the years before Sophia.

She had always been attracted to his quiet dignity. His loving consideration, unrelenting determination and crooked smile. The way he called her every day from work, no matter how busy he was, to see how her day was going. The way his head bent ever so slightly when he listened to her speak, in deference to her opinion. That wicked twinkle in his eyes when he was pulling her leg. The way he cooked her soup when she was sick.

All gone . . . There was nothing left but a stoic awkwardness between them, which sat so heavily on her heart. Right next to the memory of Sophia.

Everyone was taking their seats while her mother went to get the moussaka out of the oven. The creamy casserole baked to golden perfection had never before failed to set her mouth watering. Now, however, she seemed to have lost all appetite for it. In fact, she felt rather nauseous when Heath took his seat beside hers, his long lean fingers resting on the white tablecloth between their cutlery.

Questions were racing round her head. She was dying to get him alone, out of earshot, and yet she was afraid too. If she was feeling a pull towards him here with eight other people in the room, how was she going to cope with him all to herself?

She still needed to ask him what he was doing here. What he meant by turning up unannounced like this when he knew that she had no desire to see him.

She remembered their countless arguments in Sydney. And also the ones she'd wanted to have but he had walked away from. In the aftermath of Sophia's death, the most common feeling she'd had was loneliness. In a time of such loss, it was the worst kind of cruelty anyone could inflict upon another person. Let alone the person you were supposed to love.

Memories of her confusion and pain scalded her. Had time healed those wounds?

She remembered the day it had all gone wrong. Her pregnancy was twelve weeks along and she'd gone in for a routine check-up. Their baby had already passed away. Her heartbeat had stopped a few days before. Finding that out had been one of the worst moments in her life.

Heath had not even been there. Not that this was entirely his fault. He wasn't to know the news she would receive. But she had expected his time and his support after the D and C procedure in the hospital to remove their child from her womb.

Instead, the next day he had gone back to work and advised her to do the same.

She felt like he was angry with her. Angry and disappointed. After all, they had been trying for a child for years. All her life, she'd been able to achieve anything with hard work and perseverance.

Two degrees at uni, the career heights she aimed for, the house she'd always wanted, the suburb she'd always wanted to live in, the car she'd planned to drive when she was successful. She'd done it all by keeping her focus.

But all the smarts in the world couldn't get her pregnant.

Why hadn't anyone told her that?

Conceiving alone had taken a toll on their marriage, but losing their baby had been the death blow.

'We should name her,' she had pleaded in the weeks that followed.

'No.' Heath had refused. 'You're just torturing yourself, Tash. You're torturing us.'

'You want to pretend like she never existed.'

'But she didn't exist,' he had argued back, the words cutting her like a knife. 'She was never born.'

She had named her anyway. And whenever they spoke of her, she used the baby's name to show him that Sophia had existed. To remind him of what they had lost, so that he might grieve with her.

But he hadn't. He'd taken on more projects at work. Made plans for their future. Showered her in meaningless gifts.

'We've lost a child!' she had screamed at him.

'No, I've lost you,' he'd returned quietly before leaving her alone once more.

She stared at her plate now, unable to look up or respond to the small talk around her.

'Well,' Heath said quietly, 'since you wouldn't tell me over email, perhaps you can tell me in person. How have you been, Tash?'

'Fine,' she responded shortly, making no move to elaborate.

So he filled the silence. 'Work has been really busy for me. I was very lucky to find someone who could take over my upcoming jobs so I could get away and help here.'

Despite her earlier caution, she couldn't stop the question springing from her lips. 'Why *are* you here, Heath? Why did you come?'

'Because your sister needed my expertise. She wants me to supervise the new floor going in. She can't afford professional labour, but I can guide you guys to make sure it's done by the drawings.'

'I'm sure we could have found someone else.'

He was silent for a second. 'Do you really want to discuss this now in front of everyone?'

'Wow, so now you're pretending to be considerate of my privacy after pulling this stunt.'

Her voice had risen a little and she glanced around the table to see if anyone had heard. But no one was paying any attention.

After a moment he broke the silence again. 'I thought you might need me too. I heard you lost your job.'

*Great!* The last thing she wanted was his pity on top of everything else. 'I'll get a new one,' she shrugged. 'In the meantime, I'm happy to be having some time off.'

'If you need any help financially –' he began.

Her cheeks burned. '*I'm fine.*'

'Tash, there's no shame in leaning on someone else for help now and then.'

Her food tasted like sawdust on her lips. She shut her eyes. 'Please, I don't want to discuss this now.'

'No, you're right,' he said softly and a little too confidently as he stuck his fork back in his salad, 'we'll wait till after dinner when we go back to our room . . . to talk.'

'*Our* room?'

'Yes. We'll be able to speak there, alone.'

Of course. She swallowed hard. How could she not have seen this coming?

# Chapter 10

In her haste to move away from Adonis, Eve entered the dining room rather speedily and took a chair between her sister and mother so that he wouldn't be able to sit next to her. Had she had her head screwed on straight, she probably would have picked the seat next to Phoebe rather than Tash, who seemed hell-bent on giving her the silent treatment. Her elder sister stared steadfastly at her plate, refusing to utter a word or even look at her.

*Well, two can play at that game.*

She turned to her mother, who was busy cutting the moussaka into individual portions. She had already served a piece to Phoebe and Spider and was now holding out her hand for Eve's plate. Eve picked it up and passed it to her.

With knife and spatula poised, Anita asked, 'How much would you like, Eve?'

'Not much,' she said quietly. 'Just a little piece, please.'

'This much?' Anita poised the knife to cut a piece that was much too big.

'No.' Eve shook her head.

'This much?'

'No, still too much.'

She moved the knife further back. 'And now?'

'Er . . . yes, that's good.'

Anita huffed. 'You can't possibly only want that much.'

'I'm not that hungry.'

'Why not? You've hardly eaten anything all day.'

'Yes, I have. I had heaps of nibbles in the sitting room just now.'

'Really? I didn't see you.' Her mother frowned. 'Not to worry. I'll just give you a bit extra.'

She returned the knife to the original piece she had been about to cut, sliced it and transferred it to her plate. With a sigh, Eve accepted her giant piece of moussaka and placed her plate down in front of her.

'Bread?' She looked up to find Adonis, sitting across the table from her, holding out the bread basket, his eyes twinkling in amusement. How stupid of her to avoid sitting next to him, when being face to face was much more deadly. In any case, she didn't know why he was taking such an annoying interest in what she was doing. She liked staying under the radar and he was totally ruining that for her. Still recovering from events earlier that evening, her nerves couldn't sustain more embarrassment. Couldn't he just leave her alone?

'No, thank you,' she said firmly.

'Are you sure?' His eyes danced even more wickedly.

'Yes,' she hissed and averted her gaze to watch her mother, who had started to serve Patricia and Graeme.

'Here,' Tash spoke quietly to her, 'I don't want much either.'

While their mother was distracted, Tash cut Eve's piece evenly in two and transferred one half to her own plate.

'Quick, get some salad,' her sister whispered but Eve already knew the drill. How many times had they done this as teenagers?

They covered half their plate in leaves to disguise the actual size of their slices. By this stage, their mother had worked her way around the table and had just finished serving a slice to Heath.

'Natasha?' She held out her hand for her plate.

'You've already served me, Mum.'

Anita frowned. 'Have I?'

'Yes, see.'

'So I have.' She rested the spatula and sat down.

Eve and Tash exchanged a look.

'Thanks,' Eve whispered.

'No problem,' Tash said back with a slight smile.

A wave of nostalgia squeezed Eve's heart. In horror, she realised she was starting to tear up. *For goodness sake, Eve. Pull yourself together.*

She blinked rapidly and looked at her hands.

'Adam,' she heard her mother say, 'will you pass me the bread?'

'Sure.' The bread basket came over again and to her dismay Anita extracted two rolls, put one down on her plate and one on Eve's.

'Thank you.' Her mother nodded decisively and Adam pulled the bread back to himself, grinning mischievously as though he had personally orchestrated her downfall.

Eve couldn't help it, she laughed at the hopelessness of it all.

'Lovely,' he said appreciatively.

'Did you say something, Adam?' Anita looked up.

'I said it smells lovely.' Adam took knife and fork to his meal. 'You're a very good cook.'

'Eve is much better,' Anita smiled. 'She's a top chef in a restaurant in Perth, you know. What's it called again, darling?'

'Margareta's,' Eve responded quietly.

'That's right. Eve can cook anything and make it taste sensational. She's always had a knack with food.'

Eve felt heat crawl up her neck and wished her mother would move along to the next topic of conversation.

Luckily, Patricia decided to enter the fray at this stage. 'Yes, well, Spider has been trying for months now to get Eve onto his cooking show as a guest presenter.'

'I'm afraid,' Eve tried to stem the conversation herself now, 'that it's just not my thing.'

'But it would give you so much exposure, my dear.'

*Exactly why it's not my thing.*

'And the winery too,' Patricia addressed this comment to Anita and John.

'I don't think Tawny Brooks needs more publicity,' Anita responded. 'It's well known enough. Besides, children should be left to follow their own path.'

'Oh, I completely agree,' Patricia nodded but then went on to say, 'Spider, however, has absolutely thrived in front of the camera. His cooking is so exotic now from all the tips he's picked up trying to be different. Isn't that true, dear?'

'Cooking for TV has certainly been a very steep learning curve,' Spider acknowledged her point.

'Phoebe,' Patricia patted her future daughter-in-law's hand and said with a pointed look at John Maxwell, 'you are very lucky to be getting your own live-in Masterchef when you marry my son. Very lucky indeed.'

Surprisingly, this time her father did not interject and Phoebe began to gush, 'Oh I know, I –'

She was cut off, however, by a snort from her mother's direction. Phoebe's gaze shot to Anita, who said, while vigorously cutting her moussaka into smaller bits, 'Phoebe is quite a catch herself as a schoolteacher, you know. She'll make an excellent mother. She's absolutely brilliant with children.'

'Yes, but to be a stay-at-home mum, you need a man with a solid job and a good income.'

'Phoebe,' Anita squeezed her daughter's name out through lips that had pressed themselves together far too strongly, 'is a very independent woman who is passionate about her career. I'm sure she will find a way to do both.'

Phoebe opened her mouth to say something but Patricia got in first.

'Of course, Phoebe has ambition. But it's all about stamina, isn't it? Sometimes it's just easier to let one's partner do all the hard work.'

'O-h.' The word was pronounced so exaggeratedly as to make Anita's open mouth of surprise look rather grotesque.

Eve cringed.

Her father slapped his knee, chuckling in enormous enjoyment of the exchange as Anita began to turn a rather alarming shade of purple.

'Phoebe is not afraid of hard work.'

'Er . . . Mum –' Phoebe tried desperately to interrupt.

'She is extremely diligent with her lesson preparation after school and sinks many long hours into that. After all, she handles a classroom of thirty children daily.'

'Spider reaches a national audience daily.'

'Phoebe shapes young lives.'

'Spider shares recipes with the world.'

'Phoebe works late every night.'

'Spider never sleeps.'

'*Phoebe* –'

'Phoebe . . .' Anita's youngest daughter startled the group by rising abruptly to her feet. 'Phoebe,' she smiled, raising her glass, 'would like to make a toast.'

In relief, Eve grabbed her glass that was filled with her father's shiraz. Intense, ripe and youthful, it was the only red her mother served with moussaka as it enhanced its spicy taste.

'To family,' Phoebe raised her glass. 'Both our families, coming together, *warmly*.'

Her father chuckled again.

She fixed him with a glare before continuing, 'And openly to help celebrate our marriage.'

'Cheers!' Everyone clinked glasses.

Eve refused to make eye contact with Adonis as he clinked hers.

Phoebe sat down again as the gathering finally settled into neutral small talk. Graeme questioned John about the process of vintage and how it was all done. Her father explained how harvest was conducted in short intense bursts where they fully picked one grape variety and processed it immediately.

Phoebe and Tash both contributed and she would have thought Adonis would as well, being the winemaker and all, but he steered completely clear of it. Focusing, unfortunately, all his attention on her.

'So, do you think Spider really never sleeps?'

'Well, of course he sleeps,' she said rather impatiently, taking another sip of her wine and not meeting his eyes.

'How would you know?'

She felt her cheeks warm irrationally. 'What do you mean, how would I know?'

'Have you actually seen him sleeping?'

Chagrin gripped her. *Only once.* They'd been poring over recipe books for ideas for their restaurant till the wee hours of the morning. He'd fallen asleep on the couch and she'd covered him with a blanket. And . . .

'Are you all right?'

She looked up into those deep blue eyes and nearly had to slap herself to disconnect their gazes.

'I'm fine.' She took another gulp of shiraz and said abruptly, 'And no, I've never seen him sleeping. Maybe you should ask Phoebe, she can clarify.'

'I'd rather talk to you.'

She gritted her teeth and for once conveyed her annoyance, hoping he would get the message. '*About what?*'

He picked up his glass, sipping it and considering her as though he was trying to figure his way around a puzzling problem. 'I'm concerned that you might have the hots for me.'

She choked on her wine, spraying some out from her mouth. 'What?' She grabbed a napkin to dab at her lips.

'Don't get me wrong.' He lifted his hands to reassure her. 'I'm flattered, really.'

'How nice for you.' She glared at him, folding her arms to allow him time to hang himself.

'No, seriously.' He seemed to be at pains to spare her feelings. 'I think you're great. Interesting, quirky, maybe a little weird.'

'*Weird?*' she protested.

'In a good way. I mean, you're not like your sisters.'

Her arms tightened and her eyes narrowed. 'In what way?'

He was silent for a moment, watching her steadily until he seemed to miraculously hit upon the answer. 'You seem to be incredibly easy to annoy.'

She gasped, dropping her arms. '*That's* how you're going to differentiate me from my sisters?' What happened to quieter, shyer, even 'more retiring'? That, she could have accepted because it was the truth. 'I am not easy to annoy.'

A soft laugh vibrated in his chest. 'You're annoyed right now.'

'No, I'm not.' Her brow wrinkled in irritation.

He shook his head, grinning at her. 'What did you want me to say? That you're prettier than they are?'

Her breath hitched. 'You think I'm pretty?'

'I think you're beautiful.'

She blinked, slightly taken aback.

'But,' he sighed as one passing on a cream puff, 'you're not on my radar. Nor is any other girl in the neighbourhood. I'm here to work. So whatever you were thinking before,' he stabbed a cherry tomato with his fork and popped it in his mouth, 'it's not going to happen. I just thought you should know, before you got your hopes up.'

*Wow. This has gone on long enough.*

'O-kay.' She pronounced her words slowly, to give them time to sink into his thick conceited skull: 'I-do-not-have-the-hots-for-you. Not even slightly. In fact, right now, I think you're a narcissistic, arrogant pig.'

'Really?' He seemed genuinely surprised. 'So then why have you been sending me signals all evening?'

She was horrified. 'I have not been sending you any signals.'

'You were staring at me before.'

'In your dreams,' she hissed.

'And you did try to sit in my lap.'

'That,' she put her glass down heavily, 'was an accident!'

'And you did that whole weird thing when we first met, where you tried to bump into me on purpose.'

'You know,' she coughed as she felt blood rushing to her face, 'you have some imagination.'

'Do I?' He seemed genuinely contrite. 'Sorry, I didn't mean to jump to conclusions.'

'Good,' she said shortly, determined to end the subject. 'Apology accepted.' She picked up her fork and glanced down the table to see if she could engage someone else in conversation. Unfortunately, everyone seemed absorbed. Even her mother was talking in civilised tones to Patricia about the merits of cloth napkins over paper ones at the wedding, which, surprisingly, they seemed to be in agreement over.

'So now that we've established that you don't have the hots for me and I'm not in the market for a relationship,' Adonis addressed her again as though there had been no lull in the conversation, 'we can now have a safe conversation unfettered by sexual tension.'

'Lucky us,' she returned sardonically, now resigned to the fact that all her escape routes were blocked. 'What do you mean by "safe" exactly?'

'Well, you talk a little bit about you and I'll talk a little bit about me. And we'll just sort of get to know each other as friends.'

*Friends, of course.* All men thought she'd make a good friend.

Despite her better judgement, however, she decided to go with it. After all, she was interested to know about this man who had so easily ingratiated himself into her family.

'You first,' she declared. 'Where are you from?'

'The Barossa. I was a winemaker there for five years.'

'So why did you leave?'

He smiled a little sadly. 'Things got complicated. Your turn. Where do you live?'

'Perth. I'm a chef for a restaurant called Margareta's.'

'So I heard. But didn't you used to head up the Tawny Brooks restaurant with Spider?'

'Yes,' she snapped.

'What happened?'

'Things got complicated.' She smiled back.

He shook his finger at her. 'You're smarter than you look.'

'Much smarter,' she agreed. 'So why does my mother like you so much?'

He winked at her. 'What's not to like?'

'Please.' She rolled her eyes. 'Are you ever serious?'

'I try very hard not to be,' he admitted. 'So what do you think about this wedding?'

'I think it's great,' she said, hoping he didn't hear the squeak in her voice. 'What do you think of it?'

'I'm not a big fan of weddings,' he admitted rather cautiously. 'But that's all right. I probably won't be invited to this one.'

'Not invited!' Anita broke in on their conversation, surprising them both. 'Of course you'll be invited, Adam.'

Eve blushed. At what point had her mother started listening?

'Phoebe,' Anita shouted down the table, 'you'll be inviting Adam to the wedding, won't you?'

Phoebe smiled rather helplessly and Eve had a feeling she hadn't even thought about it.

'Don't let her put you on the spot,' Adonis assured her quietly. 'I was definitely not expecting an invitation.'

Her sister's face softened. 'Of course you should come. Especially if you're helping us redo the restaurant.'

'Face it, son, you're one of the family now,' John told him. 'Might as well just toe the line. It's not too bad. I've been doing it myself for years.'

There was laughter and as the chatter moved away from them again, Eve gazed at Adam apologetically. 'Sorry, did I just serve you up?'

He peeked up at her from the contemplation of his plate. 'Like a trussed turkey.'

'My family is not very good at the whole personal space thing.'

'Actually, I'm quite sure they don't know it exists,' he smiled. 'When I applied for this job, I didn't realise how fully integrated into the Maxwell way of life I would become.' His blue eyes took on a wistful look. There seemed to be less teasing behind his words this time. 'Honestly, I came to Yallingup to be alone. To be silent. And instead, I've never had so much noise in my life.'

'You didn't have to stay tonight,' Eve assured him. 'My mother would have understood. You could have left.'

'Really?' His eyes fairly danced at her. 'I had a choice, did I? Then put that piece of bread back now. *Go on!* I dare you.'

'All right, I take your point.' She grinned.

'You're very lucky to have them, you know. Your family.'

Her eyes widened in surprise. '*I am?*'

'As it turns out,' he said as he cut another piece of moussaka, 'quiet was not what I really needed at all.'

# Chapter 11

Natasha had a strong feeling that when dinner was finally over everyone was relieved. They'd got through it! Now they could all finally retire to their bedrooms, close their doors and not have to deal with anyone until morning.

*Lucky them.*

Not so much for her.

As far as she was concerned, she was heading off to the most stressful part of the evening – private time with Heath. Too private for her liking.

There were five bedrooms in the house. The master bedroom for her parents. The three bedrooms that she and her sisters had used as kids and a guest bedroom containing a queen bed for visitors.

Patricia and Graeme naturally got the guest bedroom. Natasha and her sisters were to sleep in their old bedrooms with their respective partners. The seven of them made the trek down the hall to the back of the house. Phoebe and Spider were at the front, all happy and holding hands. In their wake were Patricia and Graeme, who spoke in subdued but comfortable tones. And then there was Eve. Quiet, head downcast as she followed them to her room – the only person sleeping alone.

The desperation to grab Eve's arm and whisper, 'Can I bunk with you?' was almost uncontrollable. Pride stopped her in the nick of time.

Pride and common sense. After everything she had accused Eve of being, how could she beg for her help now? *Especially* on the back of her own failure. They'd had a small moment at dinner but she wouldn't say it was enough to erase the words they'd flung at each other the morning Eve had decided to leave Tawny Brooks – a day after the fire. The memory of her own contempt sliced through her. She had judged and condemned all in the one sitting.

Or should she say 'standing'? The argument had happened outside, next to Eve's car. Her sister had been packing it to leave, filling it up with her suitcases and a crate of cookbooks, when Natasha had run up to stop her.

'So you're leaving, just like that?' she'd demanded, breathless.

Eve had looked back at her blankly, her eyes red-rimmed and unseeing. 'I don't know what to say to you, Tash.'

'How about "I'm sorry for being so selfish"?'

'What?' Eve's voice had been faint as she closed the boot.

'I told you not to take Dad's money. I told you you weren't ready for a responsibility like that.'

'So what do you want me to say, Tash?' Eve looked up, already beaten. 'You were right? Fine, you were absolutely correct. I was destined to be a failure and now I am.'

'You still have a chance,' she'd argued. 'Stay and clean up your mess.'

'I can't.'

'Of course you can,' she remembered saying in disgust. 'Replace the floor and start over.'

'I don't want to.'

Natasha's mouth had dropped open. '*You don't want to?* Why not?'

'You may not have noticed but in the last couple of months we've been losing diners anyway.'

'Then fight for them. Change tactics, mix it up, I don't know. Anything but quit.'

Eve was silent for a moment, her face strangely vacant. 'I just don't think I can.'

'Don't be silly.'

'I'm not like you, Tash. I can't do it. I just need to go.' She would have turned then and climbed into her car but Natasha had grabbed her by the shoulders.

'Stop thinking about yourself. You've spent all of Mum and Dad's retirement money on that restaurant, you can't just abandon it.'

'Tash, you need to get off my case.'

'No, I should have pushed harder when I had the chance,' she swore. 'I knew they shouldn't have given you the money.'

'Really?' Eve looked stricken. 'And why is that, Tash? Because you knew it would be a dead loss?'

'No, Eve, because you run at the first sign of trouble. Look at you now.'

'I've spoken about this with Dad. He's fine with me letting the restaurant go for the moment. I may come back to it eventually, I don't know, I haven't looked that far in advance. I don't want to think about it.'

Natasha had lifted a hand to massage her temple. 'I don't believe this. How can you take advantage of him like that? You know how soft he is. Hell, you knew that from the beginning, otherwise you wouldn't have demanded he give you all his life savings.'

'I didn't demand it,' Eve protested.

'But you certainly had no guilt about asking for it,' Natasha threw at her.

'Worried about your own inheritance, Tash?'

'No,' she'd responded. 'What if there's an emergency? What if they need the money back? I wanted our parents to have choices in their old age. Choices that you've taken away from them, and for what?'

'It's none of your business.'

'Of course it's my bloody business. You don't just get to burn the restaurant down and walk out.'

'It was an accident.' Eve's voice shook ever so slightly. 'It's not like I left those candles burning on purpose.'

'It doesn't matter,' Natasha softened the accusation. 'You need to ring the insurance company. You need to fix this.'

'You can't tell me what to do, Tash.' Eve opened the door to her car.

'Come on. Don't be a fool. You're better than this.'

'I've got news for you.' Eve had cocked her head, a rather hysterical gurgle bubbling up her throat. 'I'm not.'

'I swear to God, Eve, if you drive out of here leaving our parents high and dry I'll never speak to you again.'

'Then I guess this is goodbye.'

The car door slammed. Eve started her engine and drove off.

And true to her word, that was the last time they'd spoken. In the days that followed, Natasha had tried to help their father. If Eve wouldn't stay to salvage the restaurant then she would. But her determination was stymied when her father told her the restaurant wasn't insured – a fact that made her even more angry at Eve's irresponsibility.

She asked Heath to take a look at the damage and give advice on how to rebuild. Neither of them thought it would be that costly to replace the floor even if it wasn't covered by insurance. But their father had been adamant that the restaurant was to stay as it was until Eve was ready to return. Natasha had never felt more frustrated in her life.

'But it's such a waste,' she had protested. 'You're killing your own investment, Dad. Making it worse.' All that equipment they had purchased, the furniture and the decor. Was that all to go to waste? What about the staff? Were they to be fired?

Apparently so.

She should have known that her father would choose the 'Mad Maxwell' path rather than the rational one. He'd never had a head for business. It was always their mother who had looked after the administrative side of things. For her father the vineyard was far too 'spiritual' for him to be logical about it. And she guessed the restaurant fell into the same boat. If her father's heart wasn't in it then neither was his money.

And so the Tawny Brooks restaurant became the Tawny Brooks white elephant, remarked on by tourists as 'bad luck' and by the locals as 'bad blood'. After twelve months it wasn't talked about at all. Now, in hindsight, without the anger distracting her and the benefit of her own terrible secrets, she had to wonder what she should have asked years ago.

Why couldn't Eve handle staying? Was there something she didn't know?

Natasha tore her gaze from her sister's back as it disappeared down the hall. No exchange of 'goodnight' had passed between them while she had been lost in her own thoughts.

*Damn it. I hope she didn't think I snubbed her . . . again.*

Perhaps if she had reached out, Eve would have responded like she had at dinner.

'Tash.' The unmistakeable voice, with its rich timbre, sounded behind her and her breath caught in her throat. Heath was holding the door to their room open. It was not the first time she had slept in her childhood bedroom with him. When they had been happy, they had visited her family home quite a few times. She had been on just such a visit when the fire in the restaurant occurred. All the old single beds had long since been replaced with queens. In her room the bed was in the centre, adorned with a gorgeous white doona – an intricate vine-leaf design weaved in delicate dark green thread across it. The light wooded headboard perfectly complemented the timber flooring.

Heath wheeled in her suitcase, which he had insisted on bringing in from her car earlier, to the corner next to his. She looked at the two suitcases sitting side by side next to the bed, practically a photograph from their honeymoon. Her jaw tightened.

*This is just awful. I don't want to be here.*

As if to mock her words, she heard the click of the door behind her and spun around.

'Let me out.'

'Don't be ridiculous, Tash. Where are you going to go?'

'Away from here. Away from you.'

'What will that solve?'

'It'll solve the problem I'm having right now.'

She put a hand to her dry throat as tears smarted. She held her breath like it was a lifeline.

'Tash.' He came towards her.

'Don't,' she squeaked, taking a step back. 'How could you do this to me? Humiliate me like this in front of my family, in front of my hometown.'

He tilted his head sadly. 'In what way have I humiliated you, Tash? Tell me in what way I've wronged you and I'll make amends.'

'Where should I start?'

'At the beginning,' he said. 'Or should I say . . . the end.'

Her gaze flew to his. 'You can't just waltz back into my life like this. My parents don't know anything about us, or the separation. And I don't particularly want to break their hearts right before my sister's wedding. When I do tell them I want to do it on my own terms and in private. Not while they're having a freakin' house party.'

'I didn't come here to make you tell them,' he said slowly, a muscle twitching above his jaw. 'The truth is, I haven't told anyone yet either. Not any of my friends. Not any of my work colleagues.'

She didn't know why this gave her comfort but it did. Maybe she wasn't such a coward then. It was so incredible to believe that this was where they were now.

'When Phoebe called asking for my assistance, how could I say no?'

'Very easily.'

'Not without telling her the truth,' he sighed. 'I thought you'd be pleased about this. You were so adamant after the fire that the restaurant should be restored.'

'Restoring the restaurant isn't going to do Tawny Brooks much good if it doesn't have a chef.'

'What about Eve?'

'I don't know what Eve wants,' Natasha snapped, perhaps a little too harshly. 'And I don't think she's going to listen to any advice from me. That ship has sailed.'

'So what do you want me to do?' He stood there, at least a couple of metres away, regarding her steadily. Why did she feel like all of a sudden she was being put on the spot?

'What do you mean?'

'Do you want me to go?' He folded his arms. 'In my view there are only two options here. One, I go home on some vague excuse and Phoebe finds some other engineer on short notice to supervise the restoration of the restaurant. Or, two, I stay here and pretend to be your loving husband and the dutiful brother-in-law who has offered his skills for both the betterment of the family business and the upcoming wedding.'

'That's not fair.'

He raised an eyebrow. 'What's not fair?'

'Your options. Of course I'm not going to choose to ruin my sister's wedding. She'll never find another engineer at such short notice.'

'Well, it's settled then,' he shrugged indifferently. 'I guess I'm staying.'

As if to confirm his intention to make himself completely at home, he walked over to the edge of the bed and sat down. He lifted his foot onto his knee and began to unlace his shoes.

She glared at him. 'What do you think you're doing?'

'Getting undressed.' He didn't look up. 'I was going to take a quick shower and go to bed.'

She felt the muscles in her neck tighten. 'Not in this bed you're not.'

He sighed and finally looked up at her again. 'Really, Tash? Do you honestly think I'd make a move on you or something?' He watched her impassively as he began to unbutton his shirt. 'I think I know better than that.'

After they'd lost Sophia, her lack of interest in him sexually had been another wedge between them – a circumstance that he had battled so determinedly in his campaign to win her approval. She wished he had put that energy towards healing from their loss instead of trying to seduce her back to his bed. In all honesty, intimacy had frightened her back then. It just reminded her of everything that had been taken from her. His touch had not been a source of comfort, it just made her want to run. And she did. Many times.

'I –' The words dried up at the sudden appearance of his bare torso. She looked away as a shudder rippled through her.

She wasn't aroused. Couldn't be. It was shock.

She hadn't seen him like this in nearly a year, more than that if you counted the time they were living in the same house but not sleeping together. Besides, she hadn't expected him to just whip off his shirt like she was no more than a lamp in the room.

'Do you mind?' she muttered.

'Mind what?' He stood up and she couldn't resist another peek at those washboard abs.

'Can't you . . . I don't know . . .' She pointed at the walk-in wardrobe. 'Get dressed in there?

His eyes darkened as his thumbs hooked into the waistband of his pants. For an awful moment, she thought he was going to whip them off as well. But in the last second his mouth pulled into a hard line. 'Fine.' He turned around, swiped his suitcase off the floor, walked into the walk-in robe and shut the door.

She spun away, a hand going immediately into her hair and pulling at the roots. *What's the matter with you?*

She knew the feel of that chest. Huddled close beneath an umbrella to get out of the rain. Snuggled tight after sex. She could still recall the graze of her cheek against the light smattering of hair in the centre. His heartbeat thrumming loudly in her ears.

The door to the walk-in robe swung open again and she nearly jumped as he came striding out, a towel hung low around his waist on his otherwise naked body. She avoided eye contact as he crossed the room. He opened the door and walked out of their bedroom to use the family bathroom down the hall. As soon as the door clicked shut, she began to pace the floor, wringing her hands. Honestly, this was a nightmare. Made all the worse by the fact that she didn't seem to be in complete control of her feelings any more.

Heath was the man who had abandoned her emotionally when she needed him the most; the man who hadn't stopped to grieve the passing of his own child.

She had only seen him cry once, the day after he brought her home from hospital. The day Sophia had been taken from her womb. They'd sat in the living room, looking out the window, not really saying anything as shock had dried up all their words. And then he'd teared up. Great silent sobs. He put his head in his hands to catch the tears that carved a path down a face that was normally so strong, so controlled. And she had been about to reach for him, she really had, but her hands had balled up when he said, 'If only we'd slowed down a little. If only we hadn't been working so hard. We should have just taken it easy.'

And that's when she knew that he blamed her.

He blamed her for the loss of their daughter. And really, how could she fault that, as she had come to the same conclusion herself only a few moments earlier? She shouldn't have been pushing to get her campaign program finished before the birth. She shouldn't have been taking on extra work to compensate for her upcoming maternity leave.

He'd got up abruptly from the couch and picked up the baby rocker that she had only just assembled the night before, going against his advice that it was too early to be doing this. The instructions still lay next to it on the coffee table. He'd sat down on the floor and began to take it apart, piece by piece.

'Heath?' she had asked. 'What are you doing?'

'I can't look at this thing. I'm putting it back in its box.'

For the next two weeks that had pretty much become his strategy. He removed all things baby from their house and put them in the garage.

And then he started his life again, like nothing had ever happened.

She didn't know how to deal with that, how to process such callous disregard. She wanted to talk about it. He didn't. She wanted to apologise for her part in their baby's death. He didn't want to hear it. He wanted sex though. He wanted sex a lot. Something she couldn't give.

And she couldn't understand his need. What sort of man was this? To replace grief with lust.

So she had started blocking him out. Separating her life from his, ignoring his efforts to reel her back in. As they grew distant, she could feel him growing more desperate. Maybe that's why he had suggested they try again for another baby so soon. Maybe he thought this was the way back into her heart.

It was this very tactic that had caused her to say those awful words to him. Those awful words that she couldn't take back. 'I don't love you any more.'

How cruel. And how final. But it summed up everything they had both been feeling in the lead-up to the separation. That phrase had destroyed in a few seconds what had taken years to build.

He had taken it stoically, leaning heavily against their kitchen counter, his face a mask as always. By then, she had absolutely no idea how he really felt. He hid behind his plans and his strategies, his suggestions for their future. All horrendously misplaced. Any communication between them was always misdirected. They were like two people talking to walls instead of to each other. He didn't get her.

She didn't get him.

'I guess that's it then.' He'd said it quite calmly and left the room.

He was gone the next day. Not just from their house but from the city as well. He flew out to Melbourne and she hadn't laid eyes on him again.

Till now.

She stopped pacing and glanced about the room. What was she supposed to do? How was she supposed to act? Was this really her lot for the next month? Trapped here in a marriage neither of them wanted.

*Or did they?*

Because despite the pain, and the loss, and the suffering that had come before this point, it had not prevented her heart from leaping at the sight of him. Or recalling their last kiss. She may have said she didn't love him. She may have tried to persuade herself of that fact, but she did not feel that there was no connection there.

There was *something*. Definitely something, if only she could define what that was.

Tash was all about compartments and boxes and making sure everything had its own place and a definition. And now here she was in no man's land, with nowhere to run or even hide. Her eyes swung nervously to the bed.

*Oh shit.*

Where did he intend to sleep? Surely not next to her.

She looked at the floor – polished wooden floorboards, treated with the same magic cleaning product her mother used throughout the house. The hard surface wasn't exactly comfortable, nor was there much room for Heath's tall lean frame. This room had been a single bedroom for a young girl. With a queen bed in it, there was walking space only. If someone had to lie down on the floor, the best place would be at the foot of the bed. But even then, his head was going to be hard up against the wall unless he curled into a ball, which would then have his kneecaps knocking on the plane instead. She swallowed.

*This is not the time to panic.*

To distract herself, she lifted her suitcase onto the bed, opened it and saw her nightie.

*Okay, now you can panic.*

It was a short, pink satin slip that she hadn't expected an audience for. It was very comfortable to wear, probably because there wasn't a lot to it. She had brought the dressing gown that matched it as well but this was just as short and, even with the belt tied, dived just as low at the neckline. She quickly riffled through the rest of the clothes in her suitcase. She had brought a couple of other nighties but they were very similar in style.

*Damn it!*

She clutched the lingerie to her person, wondering what her options were. Her husband chose this moment to return. The door swung open and the glory of his damp nakedness hit her like a bucket of water in the face.

He shut the door quietly behind himself, a slight smile on his lips as he took her in and what she was holding. She felt heat crawl up her neck but couldn't seem to move as he closed the slight distance and lifted a hand to finger the hem of her nightie.

'This is a surprise. I always liked you in that.'

She gasped and flung the nightie back into the suitcase, which she then zipped up and pulled off the bed.

'If you don't mind,' she said formally, 'I'm going to use the bathroom now.'

'I'm not stopping you,' he purred.

In frustration she had to step around him, their bodies brushing and her skin burning with the contact. She hoped the wheels of her suitcase ran over his toes. If they did, he neither flinched nor made comment.

Standing outside in the dark hallway – the hallway of childhood pranks and secret midnight treasure hunts – she should have felt some comfort but tears smarted in her eyes.

*What do I do? What do I do?*

She headed for the bathroom, dreading the return to her bedroom. Suddenly, another door opened and Eve came spilling out, wrapped in an oversized towel, a bag of toiletries in one hand and her nightie hanging over her shoulder – a wonderful, conservative, baggy t-shirt with a high neckline. The two of them nearly collided.

'Eve,' she said urgently.

Her sister stopped in the doorway. 'Tash?' Eve's eyes squinted at her in the dark and then opened wide in recognition.

Natasha knew she had no right, possibly no hope to ask, but she had to.

'This is going to sound really weird.'

'O-kay.'

'Can we swap nighties?'

'Huh?'

Natasha put her suitcase down, knelt on the floor, extracted her nightie and dressing gown and then stood up again.

'Here, look, it has a dressing gown to match.' She held it out, grateful that Eve could not quite make it out completely in the dim lighting of the hallway.

'But I won't fit into it,' Eve protested. 'I'm too big.'

'You're not that much bigger than me,' Natasha protested. 'Besides, it's stretchy. It'll fit all sizes. In fact, I think you'll probably look better in it than I would.'

'Not possible.' Eve's voice was slightly strained.

'It's true,' Natasha protested. 'The world knows I have no boobs to speak of. You'll fill it out much better than me. You should have it.'

'But I –'

'*Please, Eve?*' The desperation in her voice was so blatant that even she was embarrassed to hear it.

'I don't know.' Eve's voice was uncertain. 'Why can't you wear it?'

'Long story.' She shut her eyes. 'Look, I know we haven't been on the best of terms lately.'

'Try twelve months,' Eve returned levelly, making Natasha cringe with remorse and then shame at trying to sweep it under the carpet just so she could get her way.

'Okay fine. Sorry. I shouldn't have asked. You take the bathroom first.'

She started to back away, while Eve continued to watch her silently. There was a heavy sigh and her sister shut the door to her bedroom and held out her big t-shirt.

'Okay, you win. Take it.'

'Seriously?'

'I'm the girl who can't say no, remember? Now take it before I grow a brain.'

They exchanged clothes. 'Okay, I'll wait for you,' Natasha said.

'No.' Eve shook her head in the dark. 'There's no way I'm walking out of that bathroom in this getup in front of an audience. You go.'

Natasha smiled in both gratitude and affection. 'You won't know yourself, Eve.'

'That's what I'm afraid of.'

She giggled, spontaneously kissed her stunned sister on the cheek and then made a beeline for the bathroom.

It didn't take long to shower, tie her hair up and slip on Eve's t-shirt nightie that had the words 'Born to Cook' sprawled across it in big pink letters, along with a cartoon of a woman juggling pots and pans in a colourful kitchen.

A few seconds later she was wheeling her suitcase back into her bedroom and was disappointed that Heath had not gone to sleep as promised but was sitting up in bed, still shirtless, reading a book.

She shut the door and wheeled her suitcase to the wall again.

He looked up and took in her shirt. 'Wow, how much did you pay Eve to give you that?'

'I don't know what you're talking about.' She refused to look at him and made some show of trying to arrange her suitcase neatly, all the while dreading having to get into bed with him. When she finally turned around, however, he was still looking at her with that crooked smile of his, which unfortunately still had the power to set her heart beating faster.

'So I have rattled you,' he murmured.

'Hardly.' She tossed her head with all the confidence she didn't feel.

'Then why couldn't you wear your own nightie tonight?' he enquired silkily.

She rubbed her eyes. 'Heath, I can feel a fight coming on and as much as I'd like a trip down memory lane with you, I'm tired and I want to go to sleep.'

'I wasn't picking a fight.' His eyes returned to the book as she walked slowly towards the bed. 'I was just trying to talk to you.'

'Talk to me?' she scoffed. 'That'll be the day.'

His brow wrinkled. 'What do you mean?'

'I mean, you never want to talk about anything. That's why we're in this mess.'

'Talking and dwelling are two completely different things.' He looked up sadly. 'Why focus on the depressing when you can get on with rebuilding your life?'

She held up her hand. 'Okay, I'm going to stop you there. This is hard enough without opening old wounds.'

'Old wounds?' He sighed. 'This house is full of them. They're like ghosts in the walls.'

Her eyebrows twitched together. 'Why do you say that?'

He did not lift his eyes from the book he was reading – a volume ironically titled *The Art of War*.

'Go on, Heath,' she prompted. 'You obviously think you know something.'

He looked up cautiously. 'How are you and Eve getting on? Best friends again?'

'Not really.'

'Yeah, I noticed.' His mouth twisted. 'I'm surprised she gave you her nightie tonight with the tension between you two.'

Heat infused her as his gaze slid rather thoroughly over her braless chest. Baggy as her sister's nightie was, there were still some things she couldn't hide and she suddenly felt quite naked in it.

'I don't see how that's any of your concern,' she croaked, realising for the first time that being in the bed under the covers might actually be better than standing beside it, unprotected. She flicked back the doona on her side, trying not to notice the part of his body she'd briefly exposed. He was wearing a pair of boxers, exactly how he used to sleep when they'd lived together.

'Still too proud to forgive, Tash?' Heath asked, flicking to the next page in his book. He had always been a champion of Eve's when it came to the restaurant, protesting that Tash was too hard on her sister.

'That's where you're wrong.' She lifted her chin, trying to slide into the bed nonchalantly. 'I'm not angry at Eve any more. I forgave her a long time ago. Now I just want to move on.'

'Really?' His voice seemed testy. 'You just want to move on?' He closed the book with a snap and put it on the chest of drawers beside him. Then he too slid down into the bed.

'Just cut to the chase, Heath. What point are you trying to make?'

His lip curled. 'I'd rather not say. As you said, we don't want to fight tonight. But there is something else that has been bothering me since I arrived. Something, in hindsight, I think I should have told you about earlier.'

She blinked in surprise, momentarily forgetting how close he was and the warmth that was radiating from his body. 'What is it?'

'I feel like this grudge you've got against Eve is partially my fault. I thought you would have made up by now.'

She groaned. 'Heath, you were there the day of the fire and the next day when she left. You know what happened.'

'You're right, I do know what happened. I knew when I went into the restaurant to inspect the damage. I know. But you don't.'

'What?'

He sighed, finally turning his face towards hers. 'The fire was no accident, Tash.'

Her nose wrinkled. 'Yes, it was. Eve left the candles burning.'

'Tash, the fire was lit by kerosene.'

'How do you know?'

'Because it burned down through the floor instead of up through the roof. And I could still faintly smell the stuff in the ash when I went in there to examine the damage.'

Certain pieces of the puzzle began to click into place. That's why they hadn't been able to claim insurance. Not because they didn't have any but because there were suspicions of arson.

Her eyes widened. 'Why didn't you tell me this a year ago?' she asked accusingly.

'Your father asked me not to.'

She sank back onto the bed, confused. 'Why would he do that?' And then almost immediately, the answer came to her. She clutched the blanket at her chin tightly. 'He knows who lit the fire, doesn't he? Oh no. Was it Eve?'

'No, Tash.' He rolled over, propping himself up on his elbow to look down at her.

'Then who was it?' she whispered. She didn't know what to be more fearful of – his proximity or his answer.

'It was Spider.'

# Chapter 12

Eve couldn't sleep.

Apart from the fact that she was wearing Tash's indecent scrap of lingerie that was far too tight around the bust, she couldn't stop thinking about everything that had happened that day.

Phoebe trying to pull everyone together. Her father drunk on more than just life. Her mother trying to compete with Patricia. Tash acting more strangely than she ever had.

Adonis showing up and then, surprise of all surprises, trying to flirt with her.

*He wasn't flirting with you*, she corrected herself. *He was warning you off. Asking you to just be friends. He told you so explicitly.*

She cringed under the covers as she relived some of their exchanges. Why was it that men always wanted to joke around with her but not date her? Did she have 'I will make a great pal' tattooed on her forehead or something?

For once, just once, it would be nice to be treated like a . . . *like a woman*. Or was that just too much to ask?

With this wish her thoughts immediately turned to Spider and his latest text message, still left unanswered on her phone. Should I be mad about this?

He'd sent the message right after Phoebe had done her school teacher routine, by dividing up their wedding into jobs for everyone to do. Eve could certainly see why Spider would be put out by it and it wouldn't have been what she would have done. But she wasn't sure she should play best friend in this instance and take his side. Apart from the fact that her feelings for him were still on the slightly inappropriate side, Phee was her sister. She should not get involved in their spat.

She felt awkward enough as it was! At least there was one blessing that she thanked God every day for. Spider did not know how she felt about him and never would. With everything she'd lost, at least there was one thing she could still save – her face!

All Spider knew was that she was his best friend – had been for the last eight years. For about two of those years they had both been focused on the Tawny Brooks restaurant. He had rented a small two-bedroom place in the neighbouring town of Dunsborough and she had moved back in with her parents. Together, they had planned and orchestrated the design and construction of the restaurant, worked out the menu themes, developed recipes together. Then, due to an accidental fire and damage to the restaurant, they had decided to take a break from it. She had moved back to Perth to climb the ladder in a reputable upscale restaurant and he had found a new calling in the public eye. So, satisfied with their lot, neither of them had thought of coming back.

If only reality were that simple.

It was so much more complicated than that. The restaurant had been her dream, yes, but she never could have done it without Spider. He had been the catalyst for everything. Not just the love of her life but the arrow in her bow. Without him urging her on, she never would have asked her father for the money and without him she never would have had the guts to build a bloody restaurant from scratch. He had been an integral part of it all. By his side, she had felt like she could accomplish anything. Then he'd started dating her sister and had become distracted by a new career direction. Eve and the restaurant had dropped to second in his life plan and everything had fallen apart.

Yes, the fire had sealed the fate of the restaurant but it was only the final nail in an already fully built coffin.

When Spider had started focusing on other things, so had their customers. In the few months before she'd stupidly left those candles burning, they had already been steadily losing business. Left to run the restaurant mostly on her own, she hadn't been able to keep pace and an awful truth had started to dawn on her. She couldn't do it without him. Eve Maxwell, sole owner and manager, just didn't cut it.

After moving to Perth, how many times had she thought of coming back? And each time her own cowardice had stopped her. If she hadn't been able to do it on her own then, how could she possibly do it on her own now? This doubt was compounded by the fact that she was the one who had brought the restaurant to its knees with those stupid candles. She just didn't trust herself.

That sort of mettle belonged to Tash, not her. She was a cook, not a manager, and she'd proven that in spades. But along with her lack of confidence, she just couldn't face the memories. There were too many of her dreams in that restaurant, and every single one of them included Spider. When she thought back on that time they had both worked there, she wondered how she could have been so unaware that their intentions were so far apart.

She put the Eve in naive, that was for sure.

When Phoebe came home after she finished her teaching degree at university, Eve hadn't even noticed Spider taking an interest in her that was more than friendly. Phoebe had always been the bubbly over-enthusiastic type. Of course he would warm to her immediately. Everyone did.

They had both got on well when they ran into each other on the property and Eve remembered only thinking how wonderful it was that Spider enjoyed such easy relationships with her family. She'd even added this quality to the ever-growing list of reasons why she and Spider would eventually end up together.

So when Phoebe had said to her one night at dinner with the family, 'So Spider's pretty cute, isn't he?' she had thought her sister was hinting at her own crush on him, not declaring an interest in him herself. She had merely blushed and said, 'Do you think so?'

Phoebe had nodded enthusiastically. 'I do! Don't tell me you've never been tempted to cross that line, Eve?'

Given her parents were also sitting right there, she had not wanted to make any rash declarations. Unlike her sister, Eve had always worn her heart close to her chest, not on her sleeve – to protect herself against humiliation, embarrassment and rejection. She hadn't been as lucky in love as Phoebe had.

Men were never swept away by Eve's charm. She almost never got asked out and on the one or two occasions that she had been, the relationship had not lasted. Her focus was her work, and Spider. No other man compared to him. And she had thought that if she just waited patiently enough, he would realise it. Phoebe, on the other hand, dated regularly and indiscriminately. She was all about having fun and living in the moment.

So her comment about 'crossing the line' was very in character. Her father, who had, at first glance, appeared to be absorbed in his meal, looked up at that point to wink at Eve.

'Your sister is not like you, Phee. She likes to play it safe.'

Eve's face had only heated further as she wondered if her father had already guessed her feelings, though she had tried so hard not to be obvious about them.

'*I know*,' Phoebe groaned as though this quality in her had been a great source of frustration over the years. 'Sometimes I really wish you'd just live a little, Eve.'

'Not everyone is preoccupied with their love life or how best to have fun, Phoebe,' her mother had reprimanded her from across the table. This lecture was nothing new. Phoebe had been getting it her whole life but particularly recently when her only plan for the future was to take an indefinite break, bumming around down South before applying for a teaching job. This scheme did not meet with her mother's approval at all.

'Eve is very serious about her business.' Her mother had gone on to set her up as the good example. 'She doesn't want to be distracted by anything else. Do you, darling?'

What could Eve do but agree? And then aware of her sister's dubious expression and her father's smirking amusement, her defence mechanisms had made her add, 'Spider and I have been close friends for years. I think I'd know by now whether we were going to be a couple or not.'

*Stupid. Stupid. Stupid.*

In her mind, she thought she'd have plenty of time to retract that statement later. Surprise them all with a romantic story about them both finally realising the true nature of their feelings. There was no need to make any embarrassing declarations to the family right then.

In hindsight, she realised she'd basically given her sister the green light. Not that Phoebe was on the lookout for signals. She loved her sister immensely but she often wondered whether the reason Phoebe was so happy all the time was because she took no notice of what was going on around her. She literally bounced through life, never pausing to stop and smell the roses. Though, to be fair, it wasn't like Phoebe went after Spider like a femme fatale set on her prey. No, that was not her style either. It had all happened so naturally and so quickly that Eve really didn't have reason to blame anyone.

The day her eyes had been opened still played on her mind, as though if she relived the moment enough times it would somehow explain how she had missed all the hints and clues that had gone before it.

At the time, the restaurant had been open for six months and it was enjoying the tentative success of a new business. She and Spider had their evening ritual pretty much sorted. When the last customer left for the day and the other staff had all gone home, they would sit down in the kitchen and pour themselves a glass of her father's dark crimson shiraz. With wine in hand, they would perch on the stools by the window and debrief.

How close had she come to spilling her guts on those quiet nights?

Too close.

The comfortable silence, the serenity of the country air, the headiness of success – it had given her a completely unrealistic sense of intimacy.

Thank goodness for her tongue-tied shyness and her inability to get to the point, otherwise she never would have opted for the 'letter' approach over a verbal confession. She'd typed it up on her dad's computer because at the time her hand was bandaged from an accident in the kitchen. The night she had intended to give him the note ended with the usual glass of wine in the kitchen.

'Well done, Eve,' Spider had said, passing her a glass. She'd taken it and followed him to the window seats, lifting the wine to appreciate the aroma of dark cherries and different nuances of spice and anise.

'You were here too, you know,' she protested as they sat down.

'Yes,' he agreed. 'But you came up with the menu and, I gotta say, those dishes were inspired. Especially the pork belly. Heaven!'

'It's Dad's wine that really brings out the flavours.' She shook her head modestly.

'Trying to pass off credit to your father now?' He looked at her so fondly she felt her heart begin to hammer in her chest. 'Come on, Eve,' he teased, 'when are you ever going to realise your own worth?'

She didn't need to realise it, if someone like Spider did it for her. Licking her lips, she glanced nervously at the earthenware jars on the counter. She had hidden her confession there. Was now the right time to give it to him? To boost her courage, she took another sip of shiraz. The tannins were silky and seamless, leaving her marvelling once again at her father's skill.

'Eve, there's something I need to ask you.'

She looked up in surprise. So lost in her own thoughts she hadn't even noticed the way they'd lulled into silence. Now she watched him swirl the contents of his own glass, gazing into the depths of it like it was some sort of crystal ball, and she realised he too was nervous about something.

'Spider, is everything okay?'

His eyes lifted ruefully. 'Everything's fine, Eve. I'm just not quite sure how you'll react to my question. It's not about the business. It's personal.'

Her breath caught in her throat. Could it be possible? Her heart rate doubled.

'Go on . . .' She leaned forward, practically falling out of her seat.

'I was wondering if you thought it would be awkward if I asked Phoebe out.'

At first she didn't understand what she was hearing and could not respond. He peeked at her. 'I've been attracted to her for quite some weeks now.' He ran a hand through his floppy hair. 'I think she's amazing actually.'

'Amazing,' she repeated faintly.

'Well, obviously you know how wonderful she is.' He blew on his fringe. 'She's your sister.'

'My sister.'

'And that's why more than anything I thought I better get your blessing first.'

'My blessing?' Eve knew she was beginning to sound like a parrot but she couldn't help herself. Spider, luckily, didn't appear to notice her going into meltdown.

'Has she . . . has she said anything about me to you?' he asked.

Eve put her wine glass down for fear she might drop it. She didn't know how she found her voice but eventually she responded. 'She did tell me a few weeks ago that she thinks you're cute.'

His delight was unmistakeable. 'So you don't think it would be weird if we started dating? I mean, I do have a business relationship with her family and you're my best friend.'

*Weird?* Her heart struggled to beat. 'Weird' didn't even feature on her radar when 'devastating', 'heartbreaking' and 'unbearable' were all beeping wildly. She fiddled with the stem of her wine glass before making herself squeeze out the words, 'No, not at all.'

'Thanks, Eve.' He reached out and grabbed her hand. 'It means a lot to hear you say that. I mean, whatever happens with Phoebe, I don't ever want us to stop being friends.'

'Of course not.'

He had asked Phoebe out that night and the next morning she'd had almost the exact same conversation with her sister at the breakfast table, where her father also sat, eating toast and reading the paper.

'I just don't want things to be awkward for you,' Phoebe had said to her, while pouring a mug of coffee. 'I mean, he's your business partner.'

'Awkward?' Eve dolloped yoghurt on her muesli without looking up. 'Why should it be awkward?'

'You're absolutely right, I'm being completely paranoid.' Phoebe had smiled brightly. 'Thanks, Eve.'

As her sister left the room, coffee in hand, her father had looked up from his newspaper. 'What shall you do now, Eve?'

She shoved a spoonful of oats, nuts and fruit into her mouth and replied in muffled tones, 'Go to the restaurant.'

'*I mean*,' her father said, 'with regards to the fact that you lied. It *is* going to be awkward.'

She shoved more food in her mouth so she wouldn't have to speak.

Her father cleared his throat impatiently. 'I know you have feelings for that boy. Though why you haven't told him yet is beyond my comprehension.'

'I don't have feelings for him,' she protested, though she could feel tears welling in her eyes.

He sighed, folding his newspaper closed and then in half. He was one of the few people she knew who still read a physical paper daily. It wasn't a very convenient thing to do in the country given papers could not be delivered. He had to drive into Yallingup every morning to buy one.

'You know, Eve, when I first bought Tawny Brooks back in the eighties, I knew I had the land to plant at least eight varieties of grapes. I had to choose carefully what I was going to plant. Thriving of the vine was important, of course, but I also wanted uniqueness in my crop, so that I might differentiate myself from the dozens of other grape-growers in this country. Firstly, I chose chardonnay because at the time that was the most successful grape in the South-West. And I knew if all else failed, it would make me money. Then I chose cabernet, because it was strong, robust and flourished here easily. And then I settled on semillon, merlot, sauvignon blanc, shiraz and so forth and so forth. I won't go into the details of my decisions because I swear to you, Eve, it was like being given the opportunity to decide the DNA of my children. But when it came to that eighth and final variety, I was at a loss. I had no idea what to choose. I wanted it to be special. I wanted it to be different. Something that had never been grown here before. Something that had the "wow" factor. But everything in that category was risky and I was scared to invest myself so completely in something that may not turn out successfully.' He gave her a long look at that point, and she began to realise this story not only applied to him but to her as well.

'Due to my indecision and need to protect myself against failure, the land stayed vacant for many years. Compared to my other seven blocks of land, the eighth block was barren and fruitless because I was procrastinating over the risk. Eventually, your mother decided that she wanted a garden and then a cellar door. And you came along and said you wanted a restaurant. Over the years, my dream became replaced with that of everyone else's. I had waited too long.'

'I see.'

In hindsight, perhaps Eve had not fully appreciated his warning because she continued to stay quiet about her real feelings. She didn't tell Phoebe. She didn't tell Spider. Her full confession remained hidden in that jar of tea that no one ever drank. She hadn't removed it because she thought she'd get it out again one day because surely Spider would discover how unsuited he was to her flighty younger sister. Or she would tire of him. Phoebe was a free spirit, ungrounded and unfettered. She went with the flow, followed her heart and enjoyed taking chances. Spider was a homebody. Like Eve, he had been driven by the same passion since an early age – cooking. He was a planner, a steady soul with a clear compass. How could these two ever make it work?

But they did.

They had.

It was strange, almost like two lost socks coming together to make a pair. Their differences enhanced their own strengths. They really *did* bring out the best in each other and even some aspects of Spider's personality Eve had never glimpsed before. It was Phoebe who had first come up with the idea that Spider should be more involved in marketing the restaurant. He was so wonderfully fast on his feet and seemed to have a knack for engaging people, even the sternest of critics. Through a friend of a friend, she got him that first interview on regional radio, about food and wine in the South-West. That first interview had led to a permanent radio spot and eventually his own television show. The interviewer had loved the way Spider talked about his passion. Spider had thrived in the media. And while Eve was pleased for him, she was also surprised.

Spider began talking about writing his own cookbook. With all the publicity he was getting, writing a book seemed like another way to connect with people. He grew less interested in the restaurant, though he still continued to help out.

'The restaurant was always your baby, Eve,' he told her one day. 'Your father gave it to you, not to me.'

Eve began to realise that she was losing him as a business partner as well. It became particularly apparent when he drove up to Perth to do a couple of TV appearances for a breakfast show. As he became more successful in the media, the restaurant began to lose business.

Six months after Phee and Spider started dating, Eve realised the game was up. There was no turning around from this. The epiphany hit when she was standing by the window one day chopping zucchini while Spider took a break outside. She could see him chatting to her sister on the edge of the lake while Eric raked the leaves in the foreground. Phoebe was breaking the news that Eve had already heard at breakfast. She'd scored her first teaching job at a primary school in Busselton, a nearby town. They were talking and laughing excitedly, sporadically kissing as they made plans for the future. A single tear rolled down Eve's cheek.

She just wanted out. She didn't want to have to watch them every day. Kissing, holding hands. She didn't want to listen to their hopes and dreams for the future. She didn't want to work with Spider any more while she had these feelings for him and while he was in love with her sister.

She just wanted to be gone from this place. Back to the city. Away from Spider, away from them both, so that she might find the space to get over it all.

The fire in the restaurant had been the perfect excuse to pack up and leave. It released Spider from his obligations to her. And her father had let her use the excuse to leave. She hadn't had to explain herself to anyone.

*Not even Tash.*

She knew her sister had been furious at her for abandoning ship but she just wasn't in the right frame of mind to do what Tash was asking. The main thing was that nobody knew about her feelings for Spider. And nobody ever would. She'd taken the tea jar and put it in the back of the storeroom. That note she had written had never come out of the jar. It had never –

*Oh shit. The note!* The sudden thought made her bolt up in bed like a jack-in-a-box. *It's still there!*

She had never removed it. She'd forgotten all about it when she'd made her dash out of town after the fire. The kitchen wasn't damaged in the blaze, so it might still be there. Her only consolation was that nobody went in the restaurant kitchen any more. Nobody had for months.

*But people are going to be going in there a lot now*, she reminded herself. *Everybody's going to be in there tomorrow. Crap.*

She flung off the covers and turned on the light. A quick glance at the clock told her it was three am. She could go get it now while everyone was sleeping. Destroy the bloody thing before anyone was the wiser.

She jumped out of bed and grabbed Tash's dressing gown from where it lay draped over her suitcase. She knew as a modesty enhancement it was rather useless but at least it had long sleeves and was certainly better than nothing. Throwing it on, she slipped her car keys into the spacious pocket and quietly let herself out into the hall. She crept down the long passage to the laundry, hoping her mother still kept copies of all the keys in the cabinet there.

She reached under the laundry sink first and grabbed her father's torch. She shined it on the small white cupboard on the wall. Inside, still hanging on all their hooks, were keys to every nook and cranny in Tawny Brooks. Some she didn't even know about. She knew exactly, however, where the keys to the restaurant were because when she'd worked there, she'd opened up first thing every morning.

Grabbing the keys off the hook, she let herself out the laundry door. The night air was fresh and fruity but not in the least bit cold. She caught a couple of eyes glowing in the scrub behind the house, before she heard the rustle and muffled thump of large hind legs on dirt.

*Roos! Damn it.*

She'd forgotten how many of them were about at night. The night breeze whipped the flaps of her robe around her thighs as she ran towards her car, which was parked quite a distance from the house. If it wasn't pitch-black she might have considered walking down the road to where the restaurant and cellar door were. But the last thing she wanted was to run into a kangaroo. Some of the greys were as big as she was. They liked grapes almost as much as the birds did and had a similar reputation as pests around here. Some winemakers even hired snipers to cull their numbers when they got too high. But not her father. No, he loved 'all creatures great and small'. As a result, they had a bigger kangaroo problem than most. She nodded to herself. Yes, better to just hop in the car so she didn't meet one. That would also cut ten minutes off this little adventure which, to be honest, she wasn't really enjoying all that much.

In the end, she reached the restaurant quite easily with her little car, a secondhand Barina she'd had for years. As soon as she switched her headlights off, she reached for the torch on the front seat and turned it back on. The light wasn't as good as the lights on her car, but it got her to the front door and showed her where the keyhole was. A few seconds later, she was inside. She knew the electricity was back on but didn't want to flick the light switch in case someone from the house saw and wondered who was up to no good.

She nearly screamed herself silly when a crackling of leaves in the corner indicated that she had disturbed a small marsupial of some kind. Her torchlight streaked back and forth across the room but missed illuminating the animal completely. She merely caught a shadow as it disappeared into one of the holes in the floor. As her racing heart stilled, she finally had a chance to take in the rest of the room. The dull torchlight glanced off the furniture stacked in the corners, the bare walls, devoid of the artwork that had once hung there, and across the seemingly fathomless pits in the central floor, like portals to hell. The place looked terrible and quite hard to imagine full of smiling, chatty diners.

She crossed the room to the back where the doors to the kitchen lay. Surprisingly, these were unlocked, which she thought was rather irresponsible. There was a lot of expensive equipment in this kitchen. She realised her mother had been the last person here because the stainless steel counter in the centre of the room was covered in shopping bags. As her torch ran over them she could see that they appeared to contain a lot of snack food. Bags of chips, fresh fruit, a couple of boxes of biscuits. Some buns and salad items for lunch. Further inspection of the fridge showed her mother had also left a carton of beer and one of soft drink and a few other items. Obviously, she intended these for the family of renovators that were to descend upon the restaurant tomorrow.

Eve moved away from the fridge, surprised at her preoccupation with food, even in this moment. Then to her horror, she saw it – the tea jar under the windowsill again. It was right there next to the other earthenware jars as though it had never left. Someone must have found it in the storeroom and taken it out again. Her mother, perhaps?

Biting her lip, she pulled it towards her, its clay lid gritty and dusty to touch. She shone her torch inside.

Tea, nothing but tea.

She tipped all the bags out onto the counter.

Still nothing but tea.

Desperately, she pulled forward the other jars on the counter top. They were both empty. *Damn.* She sat down on the stool, slowly scooping up the tea bags and putting them back in the jar. Who had taken her note out, and when?

She tapped her fingers indecisively on the counter. Perhaps it was silly to worry about something that had probably been seen and discarded a year ago. There was no knowing how long the tea jar had been back on the counter. Thank goodness she hadn't put her name on it because she had intended to give it to him in person. If the letter hadn't caught up with her yet, then why should it catch up with her now? All the same, it was good to be sure that it wasn't lying around for someone to find. She looked across the windowsill and into the garden, lit by the reflection of the moon on the lake. Did her mother still have her vegie patch? What about the fresh herbs she'd plucked every day for use in the restaurant? Did Eric still tend them or had he replaced them with yet another bed of flowers?

A sense of longing suddenly assailed her. She hadn't even realised it but she'd missed this place, missed her sense of self here.

Being master of her own domain.

Sure, there was a lot of heartache too. But how many times had she cooked it off here, in this very kitchen? She turned around, picking up her torch, running the light over the tiled walls, over the high shelves where rows of wine glasses stood proudly next to a collection of candles still in their holders.

Suddenly, a strange desire overtook her. Half nostalgic, half rebellious. She wanted to cook in this kitchen again. Not in the morning. Not next week. But now. Right now, in the middle of the night, while no one was watching. No Spider, no Phoebe, no Tash, no Heath, no parents wondering if this was the prelude to her return to the fold.

She wanted to cook, just to enjoy the experience – to relish it. Before she changed her mind she went back to the fridge to see what was on offer. What about an early breakfast?

A cheesy omelette or some crepes laden with fruit and drizzled with raspberry jus. A feeling of naughtiness rippled through her body and a grin lit up her face. How was it that such a simple process could make her feel so wicked? She still did not want to turn on the lights. So instead she went to the shelves along the wall and brought down some candles. It was tempting fate a little as it was candles that had got her into trouble in the first place. But she would remember to put these ones out. She lit them with the gas stove lighter and set them on the island benchtop.

Her secret paradise was complete. Now it was time to cook.

# Chapter 13

The smell of eggs, bacon and brewing tea tugged insistently on his consciousness, pulling Adam out of a deep sleep and into wakefulness. There was something else there too, something fruity and tangy and utterly mouth-watering. Stubbornly, he turned on his side, rubbing his faintly throbbing head.

He'd had a few too many glasses of wine yesterday, first with John in Horace's barrel room and then with the rest of the Maxwells at dinner. It had been a little hard not to get into it – with all those fireballs being tossed across the table. Not to mention the little firecracker sitting directly opposite him. He chuckled softly as he thought of Eve. But those thoughts were interrupted by the metallic sound of a pan being laid on the counter.

He stilled. *What the?! Was there a possum in the kitchen again?*

He inhaled deeply, picking up once more the scent of delicious food. *Last time I checked, possums couldn't cook.*

And as far as he knew he was the only squatter that had been granted permission to sleep in the storeroom. The Maxwells had been very good to him. A little too good. But he just couldn't seem to turn their hospitality down. Not completely, anyway. To preserve his privacy, he'd rejected their offer to live in the house but had taken up residence in the storeroom of the restaurant. It wasn't much. A vacant room with a mattress on the floor. There was a small bathroom out the back that was perfect for his needs. He'd lived with much less as a kid so, in his view, it was very comfortable. That and the fact that Anita doted on him like the son she'd never had. It was addictive really, being so wanted – like he was one of the family.

That was something he'd never had before.

*Family.* The kind of in-your-face, overwhelming, can't-mind-their-own-business family that smothered you with love, any chance they got. It was a childhood fantasy and he couldn't help but enjoy it, any more than a pirate dancing on a mountain of gold.

He'd lost his parents before he could remember them. They'd both been killed in a car accident when he was five. He had other family who had taken him in. His maternal grandparents had been awarded official custody but looking after him all the time had been too much for them. So they'd passed him around to his aunts and uncles. As a result, he never felt like he belonged anywhere. He knew his cousins resented it when he showed up. It was like, *Oh great, I'm going to have to share my room again.*

*Oh great, he's going to expect to play with my toys.*

*Oh great, I have to let him hang out with me and my friends.*

His grandparents regarded him as work. They were getting old and didn't want a child under foot any more.

'My time for raising children is over now,' his grandfather used to say when he picked him up from school. 'I should be enjoying my twilight years.'

How many times had he wanted to run away? *Stuff them all!* he used to think. *If they don't want me, I'll just go.*

And he had too. When he was a teenager, he'd got a part-time job in a supermarket and made a bid for independence.

He had some friends who said that he could stay with them. It hadn't taken much to convince his family to let him go.

It had been nice for a while because the friends had actually been pleased to have him . . . at first. Then their parents had started to get a little weary of their house guest.

'Hasn't Adam got anywhere else to go?' they asked. 'Doesn't his family want him back?'

So he'd moved in with someone else and the musical beds had started all over again.

Eventually, of course, he'd managed to stand on his own two feet. He'd got his own place and started working fulltime in a hardware store. He'd moved from job to job, city to city, rental to rental until he ended up in the Barossa Valley, grape-picking. That's when the wine bug had bitten him, when he'd had his first glimpse of the life he could have. The life he really wanted.

He had loved that part of Australia for its beauty and its tradition. Vineyards stretched as far as the eye could see. He didn't want to be a drifter any more. He wanted to settle in that place that gave him purpose and rhythm.

Wine was all about rhythm – choosing your time and doing it right, to create something wonderful that could be enjoyed by everyone. It was as much art as it was science, and it was the first time in his life that he was truly inspired by anything.

He wanted to be a winemaker.

When fruit-picking season ended, he got work at a cellar door and started doing a viticulture degree by correspondence. It took him six years to complete and he did not regret one day of it. Wine was his passion. It was more reliable than family and more giving than friends. It was his reason for being and its influence had been surpassed by only one life event.

Falling in love.

Her name was Kathy Rixon, of Rixon Valley Estate, a fifth-generation Tanunda family whose history was steeped in wine.

He'd met her at the Barossa Valley Vintage Festival in a street parade. It had seemed like a match made in heaven.

But it wasn't. The only thing angelic about her was her face.

Fast forward a couple of years and he was back on the move. No money, nowhere to live and no desire to get close to anyone again. In fact, it had been more like going back in time, like starting over in those years when nobody had wanted him.

When he'd first come to WA, broke as a high school drop-out, accepting a job and a bed on the Tawny Brooks property had seemed like a Godsend. At least until he had enough funds to get a place of his own in Margaret River. He'd come to this region to start fresh in a town where nobody knew him, and nobody cared to know him.

Wine and surfing. That's it.

But Anita wouldn't have that. It was like she was physically incapable of keeping anyone at arm's length, and when you'd never had a mother before, her fussing was like living a fantasy he thought had long since passed him by. To be honest, he could have got his own place months earlier, but he couldn't bring himself to do it. Living at Tawny Brooks was just too easy.

After all, if Anita wanted to cook him dinner every night, who was he to complain? Sometimes he ate with them at the house, sometimes, if he was working late, she left his portion in the restaurant.

She was a fabulous cook. No sooner had he finished a bowl of her chunky chicken and vegetable stew than he was already looking forward to the next day's menu.

Her husband was a strange coot, unpredictable and uncanny. When he'd first met him he'd been starstruck. It was the great John Maxwell – founder and creator of the world renowned brand, Tawny Brooks. His reds had been described as rich and complex, his whites delicate and balanced. He didn't know what he was expecting but certainly not what he had got.

When John had interviewed him for the job, he had taken Adam on a walk through the property. They'd strolled through a block of sauvignon – the smell of dirt, sunshine and vine heavy and heady. John asked him no discerning questions nor enquired after his education. In fact, their conversation seemed rather random and John himself appeared preoccupied. He stopped constantly to check a plant, to brush the leaves fondly with his fingers, to scold birds and click back at the insects.

On first glance, Mad Maxwell was living up to his name. Like the scarecrow in *The Wizard of Oz*, he was a fixture in his own vineyard, which had miraculously come to life. He treated his business, not as a component with many parts, but as a living organism functioning as one whole. Essential to the pulse of this life was the fertility of his soil, the rhythms of the cosmos and the grace of God. His biodynamic traditions were fanatical.

No sprays. No insecticides. But specially prepared composts and emulsions made with herbs, manure and cow horns. He used the movement of the moon and the alignment of the planets to decide when to plant, when to harvest and when to pray. Wildlife and bugs lived freely amongst his vines and made Adam feel like an early settler growing his first crop.

When they came to the end of their walk, John turned to him and said, 'Adam, why do you want to be a winemaker?'

He had cleared his throat, rather dismayed because he had thought he'd made a good impression. 'John, I *am* a winemaker. Have been for a few years now.'

'All right then. Tell me why you choose it above any other profession.'

'Because I love it.'

John shook his head. 'Love, my friend, is a two-way street. Give and take. Compromise and compassion.'

Adam had scratched his head. *Where is he going with this?*

After a moment, John tried a different approach. 'What is wine?'

'Well, er . . . it's technically fermented grapes,' Adam tried to be concise. 'Water, alcohol, sugar and acid.'

'And *magic*.' John clicked his fingers as though snapping a spell. 'Without the magic part, you don't have anything. Think about it, my friend, you don't just put grapes in a tank. You put the landscape, the season, the rain and the sun in there too. The perfect balance of all is wine, good wine. To drink it is to taste the earth. Winemaking is not an occupation, my son, it is a calling. Until you realise that, you may love wine but it will not respect you and the magic will never come.'

'Are you saying you don't want to hire me, John?'

'No, I'll hire you.' John slapped him on the back. 'But on one condition.'

'What's that?'

'That you listen.'

'Of course I'll listen to you.'

'Not to me, idiot,' John grinned at him. 'To the vine.'

And then he'd walked off, leaving Adam standing there wondering whether he was supposed to ask for a contract or just report bright and early the next day. He settled on the latter and hadn't looked back since.

There was another clang in the kitchen, this time jolting him fully awake. He sat up. He wasn't dreaming, there was definitely somebody cooking in the kitchen. Had he overslept? He glanced up at the shallow windows at the top of one wall. It was still dark outside.

Rubbing his eyes, he stood up on his mattress, wrapping the blanket Anita had given him around his shoulders. There was a soft glow coming from under the door and the smell of butter melting on freshly toasted bread. He opened the door a crack and peered out.

His jaw dropped open.

What a sight!

If there was magic at Tawny Brooks, this was undoubtedly it.

In the soft glow of the candlelight stood Eve Maxwell, a vision of delectable loveliness surrounded by the flickering of tiny flames, their gentle glow providing just enough light to identify the sweet flimsiness of her attire – a short dressing gown stood open to reveal a virtually see-through pastel-pink slip. The neckline dived obligingly to reveal the swell of beautifully formed breasts. Unlike the day before at dinner, her hair was out and rioting on her shoulders, a mass of untamed glossy black curls that you just wanted to twine through your fingers. Her cheeks were flushed, her eyes wide with enjoyment. She lifted a bunch of chive stalks, which she must have picked fresh from the garden, to her nose and inhaled tenderly before sentencing them without pause to the chopping board. She was using at least three pots on the stove and one frying pan. On one side was a crepe already covered in raspberries, dusted in icing sugar. She was humming as she transferred the chives, a scoop at a time, to the frying pan on the stove, which, if Adam's nostrils were correct, contained the world's best version of scrambled eggs.

Powerless to do anything else, Adam pushed the door open further and came out.

Eve froze in the act of putting the chives into the pan. The long wide sleeves of her robe dangled low, next to the stove. For a moment, her eyes simply rounded in shock. 'You!'

She could not move, so complete was her disbelief. And then she gasped. 'I'm on fire!'

'So am I,' he agreed, most readily coming forward.

'No, you idiot,' she snapped, desperately pulling her long sleeves from the gas flames, 'I'm ON FIRE!'

She danced away from the stove, swatting and blowing on the flames, heading towards the sink, which was halfway between him and her. He acted faster. Crossing the room in two strides, he threw his blanket around her and yanked her close.

The fire on her sleeves went out.

But as he held her, looking down into those shocked brown eyes, and felt the hammer of her own heart against his, they burst to life again. Not on her sleeves, but around his heart, behind his eyes, between his legs. Hot, enticing, taunting flames that licked, tempted and burnt away the rest of the world. She fit so easily into the hard plane of his body, her fragile softness melting into his frame, making him wonder why he had sworn off women.

It seemed like such a cruel thing to do to himself, especially when gazing down at her soft kissable mouth.

'Are you sure you don't have the hots for me?' he whispered hoarsely. 'Because, frankly, this is getting beyond ridiculous.'

# Chapter 14

'Are you kidding me?' Eve demanded. 'Let me go!'

'Okay, okay. Just calm down.' Abruptly, his arms and the blanket fell away and a whoosh of cold air encircled her.

She rubbed her arms. 'You don't understand. I almost set fire to the bloody restaurant again!'

'Hardly,' he scoffed. 'I was here the whole time. It was never going to happen.'

Her eyes widened in alarm. 'You were here the *whole* time. Watching me?'

'Well, it sounds creepy when you say it like that but honestly –'

She cut him off. 'What are you even *doing* here?'

He shook his head. 'No way. I asked you a question first, which you have deliberately ignored. What is all this?'

She glared at him. 'What's all what?'

'The lingerie? The candles? The midnight feast on steroids?'

Eve realised his first accusation about having the hots for him again suddenly seemed plausible. A wave of heat rolled through her. She tried to hold up her palm calmly but her voice came out on a stammer. 'Y-you're completely getting the wrong impression here. I *do not* have the hots for you.'

He shrugged off the blanket and threw it on the empty counter behind him, and she nearly died at the sight of his completely bare chest.

*Okay, so that was my first lie.*

He was so perfectly formed that if he hadn't been standing right there in front of her, she would have sworn he was photo-shopped. Tanned, fit and muscular, he had more definition than any statue of Adonis she'd ever seen. He turned off the stove and began to walk towards her, sending alarm shooting up her spine like a shock of electricity.

'Then why are you trying to seduce me?'

'I – I . . .' She backed up as he drew closer, her bum hitting the sink behind her. 'I'm not! I wasn't trying t-to seduce you.'

He came in close, so close she had to strain back against the counter to stop her chest from touching his.

His eyes narrowed and his head cocked to one side as though he were examining a very interesting specimen. 'I have to admit, it does seem a little out of character. You strike me as the kind of girl who would want to go on a date before you cooked me breakfast.'

'This is not for you. I had no idea you were here.'

'Really? You're going to eat all this food yourself?' He reached behind her and turned on the tap. She glanced at the food on the benchtops spread around them. She had gone a little crazy. Crepes, scrambled eggs, mini quiches, breakfast bruschetta, fresh fruit. But she just couldn't seem to help herself. Once she got started, the ambience of the kitchen had just taken over. It was so easy to lose herself here. And that's exactly what she wanted to do, lose herself.

'I . . . I . . .'

He stepped back a little and was trying to grab her hand.

'Hey!' she resisted. 'What are you doing?'

'Calm down,' he said impatiently, turning her hand over so that he could put her red and blistering wrist under the tap. She hadn't even realised it was sore until the water touched the wound.

'There, you see,' he smiled down at her, 'just helping.'

He was still standing way too close for her liking, in barely nothing at all. The waist on those pyjama pants hung so low she was half afraid they were going to drop off. And then where would she be? She averted her eyes in horror at the thought.

She turned around to face the sink, pulling her wrist out of his hand. 'I can do it myself, thanks.' She hoped her voice would indicate that he should step back as well.

Thankfully, he did. She inhaled deeply again, as though she'd just come out of a tunnel. And with the fresh air came some clarity.

'So you never explained to me what you're doing here,' she reminded him tersely.

'What am *I* doing here?' He grinned. 'Now that's rich coming from you.'

She pursed her lips. 'It's a fair enough question.'

'All right,' he agreed. 'I'll answer one of yours if you answer one of mine. I'm here because I live here. Your parents let me sleep in the storeroom. It's easier because I work on the property and no one was using the restaurant before.'

'So they just thought they'd start renting rooms?' She was aghast.

'Oh, I don't pay them any money. It's not about that,' he smiled. 'I think your mother just enjoys having another man nearby who she can rely on.'

Eve gritted her teeth.

'I don't know if you've noticed,' he continued pleasantly enough, 'but your father hasn't really been himself lately.'

She glared at him. 'That isn't really any of your concern.'

'It is when I'm the one your mother sends off to look for him when he disappears.'

'Disappears?'

'Sometimes for hours on end.'

'What's he doing?'

'A bit of everything.'

'What does that mean?'

'Why don't you ask him?'

'Maybe I will.'

'Good.'

'Good.'

They fell into a very unfriendly silence. She wished he would just leave but of course he didn't. He continued to stand there, staring at her in a most intrusive fashion. She knew she should never have given Tash her nightie. If she didn't know any better she would have sworn her sister did this on purpose as an act of revenge.

'So,' he cocked his head to one side, 'back to my question. If all this food is not for me, who is it for?'

'It's not for anybody. I just felt like cooking.'

'At three in the morning?'

She lifted her chin. 'It's a free country.'

'Oh shit.' A rather unsavoury idea seemed to disturb his handsome features and his arms crossed his bare chest, making his pecs bunch attractively. 'Is it for Spider? Are you meeting him here or something?'

'What? No! Of course not. I don't know where you get your ideas from but –'

'I got them from the tea jar.'

'The what?' Her voice broke off as fear paralysed her.

He backed up towards the windowsill, picked up that fated jar that had once held all her hopes and dreams and presented it to her. 'It's all making sense to me now. You're the girl who left that note in here, aren't you?'

She turned off the tap. 'You've read it?'

'Well, of course I have,' he shrugged. 'I live here and a man needs a cup of tea from time to time.'

Her fingers fisted against her forehead. 'What have you done with it?'

'I haven't done anything with it.'

'But it's not there any more.'

'Isn't it?' He opened the jar. 'Oh, you're right. I will have a cup of tea though.'

He took a tea bag out and put the kettle on while her brain did backflips. 'This is a nightmare.'

'Well, yes,' he agreed. 'For you, I suppose it must be. But that's what you get for trying to steal your sister's fiancé.'

She laughed, almost hysterically. 'You would think that, wouldn't you? But you really don't have a clue about what's going on here.'

He poured hot water over his tea bag and drew up a stool directly opposite her, in front of the raspberry-covered crepes. 'So tell me.' He looked at her expectantly.

She stared back at him, sitting there, all broad shoulders and rippling muscles, sipping tea of all things, watching and waiting.

*Oh for Pete's sake. At this point, what do you have to lose?*

'Spider and I are very good friends,' she began earnestly. 'Have been for years. And yes, *maybe* I did at some stage develop feelings for him. Quite strong feelings *because* we were so close. But I never acted on them. I never told him about it. I was too shy. You see, I'm not very good with men and –'

'Seriously? Because you seem to know which buttons to push from where I'm sitting.' His eyes flicked meaningfully across her body and her cheeks blushed. Involuntarily, she crossed her arms over her chest, wincing as the brush of the charred fabric rubbed against her burnt wrist.

He frowned. 'You know, you could just take that dressing gown off. That sleeve is aggravating your wound.'

She reddened further. 'No, I don't think so.'

The sleeve of one arm was burnt and smelly and it was irritating her wrist but there was no way she was prancing around in just Tash's nightie in front of this guy. He'd probably ask her if she had the hots for him again.

Some of what was going through her mind must have occurred to him because he smiled mischievously as he looked down into his mug of tea.

'I wasn't trying to be a pervert. I was going to suggest before you interrupted me that you could wrap my blanket around you instead. It would provide more cover than what you're currently wearing.'

She gnawed on her upper lip. Then, while he bent his head to take another sip of tea, she ripped off the dressing gown, dropped it on the floor and grabbed the blanket from off the counter. She flung it across her shoulders and pulled it around her. It smelled of soap and man and was indeed a lot warmer and more modest than her previous attire. She sat down on a stool on the opposite side of the counter.

'Better?' he enquired.

'Much,' she agreed. 'But before *you* interrupted me, I was trying to tell you that I had to write Spider a note about my feelings because I was too shy to tell him.'

'But you never gave the letter to him,' he clarified.

'No, it stayed in the jar and I came here tonight to remove it. Unfortunately, it wasn't there, so I ended up cooking instead.'

'Like any normal person would do,' he nodded airily.

'People deal with things in different ways.'

'Of course they do.' He shrugged a little too easily. 'Some people go back to bed. Some people cook!' Putting down his tea, he indicated the plate in front of him. 'Do you mind if I have some?'

'Why not?' Sarcasm coloured her tone. 'It's not like you're going to go away and mind your own business, is it?'

'Oh no,' he agreed, 'this is all far too interesting. And that's why I'm in town, you know, for the distraction.'

'I'm glad my problems are so amusing to you,' she glared. 'Would you like some cream for your crepes?'

'Is there any?' His eyes lit up.

'No,' she said with satisfaction. 'There isn't.'

'Now that was cruel.' He pointed his fork at her. 'And for no reason at all, when I'm offering nothing but my deepest sympathy. You and I are very similar.'

'I seriously doubt that.'

'Remember that complication I left behind in the Barossa?'

'Ye-es.' She drew out the word.

His expression grew pensive. 'It was a she, not an it.'

'I figured,' she sighed. 'So what'd she do wrong, ask you to marry her?'

He had already told her he wasn't looking for a relationship so she had asked the question flippantly, intending it as a joke. She never expected him to say, 'No, I asked her.'

She sucked in a breath. 'She said no?'

He took another mouthful of crepe. 'She said yes, we planned the wedding and everything.'

'Oh.' This stumped her. 'So what happened?'

'She never showed up.'

They were silent until comprehension dawned on her and she straightened in her stool. 'So you were standing there, in front of the guests, waiting and . . .'

'Yep.' He took another sip of tea.

'Oh.' She wanted to ask more questions but felt it a little rude to do so.

She waited for him to give her more information but instead he said, 'So you see, we're not so different, you and I. Both suffering from a bout of unrequited love.'

She snorted in a rather unladylike manner. 'Oh, I think we're very different.' She reached over and grabbed the pan from the stove, tipping the scrambled eggs onto a plate in front of her.

For starters, this guy could have his pick of rebound girls. Herself included if she let him mess with her head too much. If he was looking for a 'pick-me-up' after his fleeting brush with heartbreak and he thought she was easy pluckings, he had another think coming!

'Listen, Adonis, I don't think –'

'What did you call me?'

'I – what?' She broke off in confusion. 'I didn't call you anything.'

'Yes you did. You called me "Adonis".'

'Have you tried the eggs? They're delicious.' She swapped his near empty plate for her full one.

'You know,' he said, tucking into his eggs, 'I could help you.'

'Help me with what?' she demanded, half-worried and half-relieved that her distraction with the eggs had worked.

'I could help you find out where that note went. Make a few discreet enquiries.'

'No.' She was alarmed. 'Don't say anything, to anyone. Just let it be. Please.'

Her voice was so anxious that he laughed. 'All right, all right. But what do you intend to do next, Eve?'

'Do?' she repeated, grabbing the bruschetta which was sitting at arm's length and pulling it towards her. 'I don't intend to do anything.' She cut the bruschetta in quarters. 'I just want Phoebe to be happy. I want Spider to be happy too. I'm at Tawny Brooks to be supportive.'

He chuckled. 'Really? What about Eve? Is she allowed to be happy as well?'

She rolled her eyes. 'Of course. I'm just not focused on that right now.'

'Doesn't sound like you're ever focused on it. I watched you through dinner last night and all you did was bend over backwards for everybody else.'

'That's what family is about, isn't it? Giving and sacrificing for each other. Isn't that what your family is like?'

'Er . . . no.' He scraped the last of the eggs onto his fork and put it into his mouth. 'You know, I thought your mum was a good cook but she's got nothing on you.'

Eve smiled, lifting the bruschetta to her lips. 'I do what I can.'

They fell into a companionable silence, very much like they had intended to share this meal together. Part of the pleasure of cooking was watching people enjoy what she offered. She loved the way their eyes lit up at first bite and the enthusiasm that followed as they ate the rest. Adonis was a sight for sore eyes with all that gorgeous honey skin on display. There was not a droplet of displeasure in watching a man like that eat.

'Well,' he said as he drained his mug, 'that was nice, Eve. In a weird sort of way.'

She peeked at him through her eyelashes, wondering what on earth she was going to do with him. Here was a guy who now knew all her secrets. Not exactly an ideal situation, especially given his unpredictability.

He grinned at her and, to her alarm, grabbed her hand. 'Stop worrying, Eve. I'm not going to tell anyone. Why don't we put our swords away and just be friends, huh?'

She stared down at their hands.

*My life is a broken record.* Another handsome guy on the lookout for a new friend. And who does he pick first?

He squeezed her hand. 'You can teach me how to be supportive and I'll teach you how to have fun. Seems like you bloody need it.'

Those gorgeous blue eyes were a gateway to destruction. Was she to forget Spider only to play the same game with somebody else? Spider had bled her emotionally for years without even knowing it. She'd been *so there* for him – most of the time at her own expense – and where had that got her?

'I –' Her gaze happened to stray to the window and her voice cut off as she realised how light it was outside. 'I need to go.'

She leapt up from her chair.

'Do you want me to walk you back?'

'No, that's all right,' she said quickly. 'I've got my Barina parked out the front.' She turned to go.

'Wait, Eve, you never answered my question before about being friends.'

She stopped briefly on her way to the door to look at him and, for the first time, the girl who had never said 'No' found her voice. 'Thanks, Adam.' She smiled. 'But I've got enough friends.'

# Chapter 15

Tash awoke to the slam of a door somewhere down the hall. Her first thought was who on earth was awake so early this morning? But she quickly lost interest in the answer as her body registered the arm draped casually around her waist, the breath wafting softly by her ear and the hard bare thigh resting behind her legs. Cocooned in an embrace so warm and familiar, it made tears sting the back of her eyes. She blinked rapidly as her heart rate jumped to two hundred beats per minute.

*Heath!*

She didn't dare move for fear she might wake him and be caught in this compromising situation.

'Good morning.'

*Drat.*

She cleared her throat but her voice still came out stiff. 'Good morning.'

She tried to move but the arm around her waist tightened. 'Don't go.'

'Heath,' she breathed, 'I . . . I don't think this is appropriate.'

'How are you going to convince everyone that we're happily married if you cringe every time I touch you?' he growled, but abruptly let her go, rolling over to his side of the bed and sitting up. It left her feeling both bereft and relieved. Why was she so conflicted? A year ago everything was so black and white. Now things seemed . . . murky. She had many questions that she didn't dare ask for fear his answers would hurt too much.

'Look, let's just get dressed and go have breakfast.' He ran his fingers through his hair. 'Neither of us is going to get any sleep now.'

She nodded in agreement. 'You take the bathroom first.'

'No.' He turned briefly to give her a fleeting smile that made her breath catch in her throat. 'I had it first last night.'

In the end she was grateful to dash out of there, put some safe distance between them. It wasn't like she didn't have enough on her mind without having to worry about her attraction to a man she thought she had decisively cut from her life.

What Heath had told her before they'd both fallen asleep was disturbing. She didn't know what to think and was frankly eager to get to the bottom of it. All this time she had been mad at Eve, who now looked like the victim of a terrible attack. But from *Spider*? It seemed incredible that her sister's best friend could do such a thing. And why?

The person she most wanted to talk to was her father. The man who held all the secrets in this house and guarded them behind a disguise of senility. It had always surprised her how much everyone underestimated him. But now she too had done the exact same thing. When she was dressed she didn't go back to her bedroom but went straight to the kitchen for breakfast.

The smell of coffee and toast filled her nostrils before she spied her mother behind the counter wearing a rather old-fashioned yellow nightgown. 'Hello, darling. Did you guys sleep well?'

'Yes, actually.' She was surprised to find she was telling the truth. Strangely enough, she'd had a wonderful sleep once it had claimed her. 'Is Dad up?' she asked.

'Yes.' Her mother nodded. 'He finished breakfast early and is somewhere about.' She pursed her lips. 'I hope he intends to stay around the house today but it's impossible to predict. Often when we're talking I don't really think he's listening.'

Tash popped some bread in the toaster. 'You worry too much, Mum. Dad is just being Dad.'

Her mother looked up sadly. 'Everybody keeps telling me that but I can't shake the feeling something else is up.'

'Well, I want to talk to him this morning.' Tash smiled as her toast popped. 'If you like I'll give him the third degree.'

Anita's eyes lit up. 'That would be wonderful. Where's Heath?'

Tash concentrated on buttering her toast. 'Still having a shower, I imagine. He should be coming in for breakfast any moment.'

By which time she hoped to be done with hers and off looking for her father.

'Is *that woman* up yet?' Anita whispered.

Tash grinned. It wasn't hard to work out who 'that woman' was. 'No, I don't think so. They'll have a sleep-in, no doubt.'

'Of course.' Anita's airy voice had a bit of a bite in it. 'The new beams for the restaurant are arriving in an hour. I hope they intend to be up by then.'

'I'm sure they're not going to skimp out on the work,' Tash assured her. 'Graeme and Patricia are here to help.'

'Hmph.' Her mother was unimpressed by her assurances, leading Tash to believe that this pettiness must be caused by something other than her general distrust of Spider's mother.

'All right, what's up?' She bit into her toast.

'Nothing, really.'

'Nothing?'

'All right, something. But it's not like I feel I should mention it because I don't want to cause Phoebe any distress.'

'O-kay.'

'I mean, it is her wedding. It should be a joyous occasion. And why she should be plagued with Patricia's complete inflexibility, I have absolutely no idea.'

'Of course not,' Tash agreed amicably.

'Like those invitations, for instance,' her mother flicked her hand. 'I was very upset about those. But it's not like I demanded they be retracted. No, I held my peace.'

'What was wrong with the invitations?'

'You didn't notice the order the names were mentioned?' Her mother blinked in surprise.

Tash groaned because Phoebe had already told her this story. 'Mum, no one is going to notice that.'

'You really think so?'

'Cross my fingers and hope to die,' Tash promised. 'No one will care.'

Anita sniffed doubtfully.

'So what has Patricia done now that you wish to complain about?'

Anita shook her head. 'Didn't I just say I've made up my mind to say nothing? I'm not going to upset Phoebe with this. I'm going to hold my tongue for her sake.'

Tash took another bite of toast and said wryly, 'Martyr yourself for the cause?'

'I will do anything for my children.' Anita put a hand tragically over her heart. 'Anything.'

'Yes, Mum,' Tash nodded in resignation. 'I know you would.'

'I would suffer gladly for your happiness.'

'Mum, no one is asking you to suffer.'

'But I am suffering,' Anita protested.

'Why?'

Anita ignored the direct question. 'I know this is not a Greek wedding – I'm not trying to make it one – but I think there should be a priest of some description there to bless the union. Not a Greek Orthodox priest because a garden wedding would be out of the question but at least a Christian one.'

'What do Spider and Phoebe want?'

'They don't mind. Spider is not religious. But you know Phoebe believes in God. Why should she go without? It is quite late notice, so they are happy to go with whomever is available. Why shouldn't I ask Father Christos from St Michaels in Dunsborough? He is a very nice man who I see often in town. Not at all preachy. He likes football! Which I think is quite scandalous for a priest.'

Tash sighed. 'And what does Patricia want?'

'To ruin everything!' Anita insisted. 'She's been in their ear about getting a Justice of the Peace, preferably an ex-high-court judge. She is quite determined to find one. Wants them to be as well respected as possible.'

'Well that's not bad, is it?'

'Tash,' Anita gasped. 'You are *breaking* my heart.'

'All right, all right,' Tash nodded, happy to retreat. 'I think you should get Phoebe or Spider to sort this out before you and Patricia start bringing out your cannons.'

'It is not me, I don't want to say a word. But *that woman*,' Anita's nod was brutal, 'thinks very highly of herself. I swear, she walks through Tawny Brooks garden so the roses can smell her. You mark my words.'

Just then Heath strolled into the room and goosebumps immediately broke out on Tash's flesh. He looked wonderful in that freshly showered kind of way that evoked all sorts of pleasant memories – some of which were highly inappropriate for her mother's kitchen. She turned away to grab the kettle as he approached the bench, though did not escape the subtle smell of his aftershave, which permeated the room slowly like a drop of dye in water.

'Good morning, Anita,' he said warmly as Tash poured hot water over instant coffee powder.

'Good morning, Heath,' her mother said cheerfully. 'Tash says you slept well.'

Her senses on high alert, Tash heard rather than saw him walk behind the counter to stand next to her. 'We did. Thanks.'

She'd pulled all her hair up into a neat ponytail so her neck was exposed. He put his hand there ever so casually, his thumb caressing the base like he had done so many times in the past. Her legs nearly buckled.

'What's for breakfast?' he murmured, peering over her shoulder at the condiments and boxes on the bench.

It was a good thing her mother answered because speech evaded her.

'Nothing but toast or cereal, I'm afraid,' Anita replied. 'But we'll have a big lunch. I've stocked the restaurant with heaps of goodies.'

Tash finally found her wits and moved out of Heath's reach, taking her mug of hot coffee with her. 'Speaking of the restaurant, I'll meet you guys there. I need to find Dad.'

'Okay, sweetheart,' said Heath.

'Bye, darl,' her mother added.

She waved a hand awkwardly over her shoulder. She wasn't comfortable with being called 'sweetheart' again and really had no idea how to respond. Heath was clearly taking advantage of their situation. And she was a little nervous about exactly what game he was playing. He'd said he was trapped by circumstance, that he was here for Phoebe and Spider's wedding. But at the back of her mind she knew it had to be more than that. She knew him too well.

He was an intelligent and tenacious man. Combined, these qualities made him lethal. Generally, he got what he wanted, no matter how long it took. If he had been a knight in the Middle Ages, sieges would have been his speciality. There was nothing Heath set his mind to that he didn't get.

*But what does he want this time?*

Natasha put the question out of her mind as she hurried down the hall, checking first the sitting room and then the study for her father. They were both empty, though she did pause on the threshold of the latter. Her father's study brought back so many memories from childhood, it was impossible not to feel nostalgic. Even the musty smell of the room was familiar. As she gazed upon his old leather chair she could see him sitting there, talking animatedly with some of his distributers about renewing their orders. A blue velvet box on the desk caught her eye just before she moved to close the door, and she went over to look at it. It was a strange thing for him to have in his study because it looked like a jewellery case. She wasn't wrong. Upon opening the lid, she gasped at the sight of a delicate gold bracelet studded with sapphires.

She quickly snapped the box shut, wondering if it was a present for Mum. With a smile, she placed the box back on his desk and left the room to head outside, the only other place her father could be.

She walked out the front door. The sunshine momentarily blinded her as she headed down the gravel driveway. It was a gorgeous, February morning. Warm, but not too hot. Dressed in jeans and a red t-shirt, she had no issue with walking straight into the crop. She knew her father's usual route. He'd been taking this walk up to their grand gazebo since she was a kid.

First, she had to go through a block of sauvignon. The vines were taller than her now, so entering one of the rows was like going into a roofless green tunnel that chirped with insects. The vine was heavy on its crown, the cane leaden with grape bunches, dark and bulky – barely hidden by the foliage. The grapes were ripe enough now to be very attractive to birds – in particular, the notorious silvereye, the biggest culprit for stealing fruit in the South-West. The vine was covered by nets for protection. The nets would be kept on until just before harvest. Adam would decide when this was. From what she had seen of the man, he seemed to be passionate enough. She hoped he wasn't going to let her father down.

It was a pleasant walk along this row and then through another down a block of merlot. The air was heavy with the sweet scent of fruit warmed by the sun and it lightened her mood.

Her mind had been so crammed lately with dark thoughts of the past.

Sophia. The grief she had not been able to share with her husband. The blame he put on her and the belief that he had no fault in doing so.

So many times she had wondered how he could have been so cold, so callous. But seeing him now, after so many months, left her unsettled. Because right now he was not cold. He was not vacant. God help her. He was anything but.

More like a simmering furnace. She couldn't stand far enough away from him without feeling the heat.

It made her wonder. Could it be that in her grief she had not been able to see his pain? Or that perhaps he had deliberately kept it from her. Her loss had coloured everything. For the first time, new possibilities were entering her head.

*I complained that he was never there for me, but was I there for him?*

The crunch of her feet on the gravel scared two fairy-wrens pecking on the path. They flicked their bright blue tail feathers at her before fluttering away.

Heath had never been big on talking about feelings. He was more physical than chatty – a black and white sort of man with a practical streak through him that had always been very matter of fact. He was sincere, quiet and . . . determined.

A smile tickled her lips as she remembered the first day they'd met.

It was at a bus stop in the city of all places. She was waiting for her ride home and he was working on the construction site for a new shopping mall right behind the bus shelter. The large lot had a high steel fence around it and warning signs to pedestrians – 'Danger, Do Not Enter,' and 'Authorised Personnel Only'. As she stood there in her professional black dress, shiny heels with a briefcase in hand, he was sitting on the kerb eating an apple. Dressed in khaki pants, a short-sleeve shirt and an orange high-visibility vest, he seemed to blend in with his backdrop – a kind of lone cowboy, definitely not the slick shiny type she was used to dating. She had felt his eyes on her but pointedly did not make eye contact.

Then her phone had started ringing and she'd forgotten all about him. By the time she'd fielded two calls from her assistant, one from her mother and the last one from a celebrity spokesperson who was threatening to pull out of her upcoming campaign, she had missed two buses.

At least, however, she'd saved six months of work by persuading the celebrity not to quit and allayed her mother's fears that she hadn't had the flu shot that year. She collapsed on the now vacant bench under the bus shelter both in relief and exhaustion. She barely noticed someone sitting down beside her.

'So, I know this is going to sound forward but I was wondering if I could have your phone number?'

She jumped and her gaze swung left to find the construction worker, who was really quite attractive at close quarters, now sitting beside her. She pulled her legs in and sat up straighter.

'Why?'

'I think I could use someone like you in my corner.' His eyes crinkled and his mouth stretched into a crooked grin.

'Er . . .' she began uncertainly, 'I don't know you.'

He smiled. 'Would you like to go out some time then? And get to know me?'

'Oh well, er . . .' She licked her lips. He had very strong masculine features that were easy on the eye. And if you looked past the smudge of dirt on his face and the film of white dust covering his entire outfit, his dark irises were unbelievably sensual. But, quite frankly, he could be anyone. And with the way he had been watching her just now . . .

'Thanks for the offer,' she smiled politely. 'It's very flattering. And I'm sure you're a nice man, but I don't generally go on dates or give my phone number to strangers.'

'Or serial killers?' he murmured, lacing his fingers together in a restful manner that was very attractive.

'Exactly.' She nodded and then quickly corrected herself. 'I mean, not that I think you're a serial killer, it's just that I don't know you. You're a complete stranger and –'

'And better to be safe than sorry.' He nodded back. 'I get that. You need to have all your bases covered.' He winked at her.

She blushed.

'What if,' he continued, 'we got to know each other before your bus arrives so I'm not a stranger any more. Then you can decide whether or not you should go out with me.'

'Would that be enough time?'

He shrugged. 'We'll make sure it is.'

She rolled her eyes. 'You sure are determined.'

'There, you see,' he nodded encouragingly. 'You seem to know me already.'

She laughed.

'I'm Heath Roberts.' He held out his hand to her and she shook it. His fingers were warm, strong and all encompassing.

'Natasha Maxwell,' she replied, strangely shaken by the instant zing that shot straight up her arm.

He flexed his wrists. 'So let's start at the top. What's your favourite place in the world?'

'That's the top?' She smiled in amusement.

'It's as good a place as any.' He flicked his eyes at his watch. 'But you have to be quick. We have a very limited time.'

'Okay then, the beach.'

His eyes widened. 'Same here. Do you swim, picnic or sunbathe?'

'All three.'

'Me too,' he said again, marvelling at the coincidences.

She raised a dubious eyebrow and his lips twitched.

'Okay, next question. What's your favourite food?'

'My mum's moussaka.'

'Mine is Chinese. There, you see, we have some interesting differences already. What's your favourite colour?'

'Green.'

'Yellow. Star sign?'

'Gemini.'

'Leo. First kiss?'

She choked. 'Seriously?'

'You haven't had one yet?' he enquired politely, keeping his expression completely neutral.

She groaned. 'Behind the sports shed at school with Bradley Pierce.'

'In a car with Rebecca McCarthy.'

Her bus was pulling up at the traffic lights two hundred metres away. When the lights went green it would soon be at her stop and, despite herself, she was actually feeling rather sorry about never seeing this man again.

His eyes flicked from the bus to her. 'So have you made up your mind yet? Or do I need a police clearance? If you give me your email I can have it forwarded to you by the end of the week.'

She laughed as they both stood up. Looking up into those incredible big brown eyes, saying 'no' now seemed churlish.

'Okay, you've won me over.'

'Great. What's your number?' He whipped his phone out of his pocket and she recited the digits. The bus pulled up just as they finished, choking the sidewalk with hot air and exhaust fumes. Her hair whipped about her face. 'Bye.'

'I'll call you,' he said as she turned to go.

She boarded the bus and took the first vacant seat. A smile played on her lips as she gazed out the window. The bus rolled forward, trees and buildings began to fly past. Suddenly her phone rang and she fished it out of her briefcase. It was an unknown caller.

'Hello?' she said cautiously.

'Hi, Natasha, it's Heath. Remember me? We met at the bus stop. Are you free for a drink this weekend?'

She laughed. 'That was fast.'

'I'm not good with waiting. But if you like I can call you back in a couple of days.'

'No, that's okay. I'm not good with waiting either.'

As their relationship started, so it continued. Fast and furiously – a whirlwind romance and quick engagement. They clicked right from the start and had seen no reason to ever press pause. All of a sudden, they were buying a house and trying to have kids. They didn't stop until it all started to go terribly wrong.

Perhaps if she had just taken a step back at some point, really taken a look at their marriage, she would have seen some warning signs before it was all too late. Like the fact that they had very separate lives because of their demanding jobs even before they had lived in different cities. Whenever they did come together, it was always so explosive and physical because of the limited time. She always thought that she and Heath were just too busy to sit around talking about nothing for no good reason – that it was a waste of time. They were always doing, rather than relaxing. Workaholics to the core, both of them. As a result, when crisis struck, she had to face how little they knew about dealing with each other emotionally.

This disturbing insight faded as the gazebo came into view and she saw her father sitting on a bench inside. It was a fairly large structure – the perfect stage to hold a wedding, which was exactly Phoebe's intention. Its hexagonal shape was about three metres wide, large enough for the celebrant and bridal party to gather on the pale timber deck. The guests' chairs would have to be arranged outside on the grass. But they would be able to see everything, including the magnificent view below.

'Hey, Dad.'

John Maxwell didn't turn around or even look up when she came and sat down beside him. 'I wondered how long it would take you to seek me out.'

From this vantage point they could see everything. The entire vineyard and the winery hovering on the edge – a cluster of brick and concrete buildings beside tall steel fermentation tanks winking in the sunlight. It wouldn't be long before those tanks would be full of the grape juice known as must.

'Really?' Tash raised her eyebrows. 'Did you want to talk to me about something? Mum reckons you've been acting strangely of late.'

'I'm enjoying my retirement,' he said shortly. 'I don't see what the harm is in that. You only live once. You should make the most of every moment.'

'Dad, is something bothering you?' Tash reached over and squeezed his hand. 'Where do you keep disappearing to?'

'Nowhere in particular.' Then his mouth curved into a grin. 'Last week I got a tattoo.'

'A what?' Tash gasped.

'Why is that so shocking?' he demanded. 'Aren't old men allowed to get tattoos? I've always wanted one.' He pulled up his pants and she looked down in astonishment to see a large bunch of grapes etched into his leg. Three of the grapes had names inscribed in them – Phoebe, Natasha and Eve. 'You can't take life for granted, Tash. You can sit in the same place you've always been and wonder why you're not having any fun any more.'

'It's, er . . . lovely.'

He chuckled, dropping his trouser leg back down. 'What's troubling you, Tash? You're not the same girl I saw a year ago. Nor is Heath the same man.'

Her breath caught, startled at his insight. She was reluctant to lie but the full truth was out of the question. Finally, she said, 'I lost my job, Dad. It's just been getting me down, that's all. I'll get over it sooner or later.'

'You've always been such a resourceful person. But of all my daughters you are the one who puts the most pressure on herself.'

She laughed. 'You reckon?'

'Of course.' He patted her leg. 'You don't have goals, my darling, you have missions. But I'm afraid that sometimes life is not always within your control, no matter how much you expect it to be.'

*Wasn't that the truth!*

'You know, Tash, when I first bought Tawny Brooks back in the eighties, I knew I had enough land to plant eight varieties of grapes.'

'I know, Dad, I think you've told me this story before.'

He ignored her and his voice took on a wistful note. 'I was very careful with my choices. In some ways, I was like you, my dear. I weighed up the pros and cons of every variety, researched the market potential, the likelihood of success before making my choices. I chose the varieties that were robust and that had been trialled in the South-West before. I started with chardonnay and then cabernet and then semillon and so on and so on. But when it came to that eighth and final variety, I was at a loss. I had no idea what to choose. So I thought to myself, this could be my experiment. This could be where I take my risk and just plant something that had never been tried here before and just see what happens. And it wouldn't matter if it failed because of all my contingency plans. And so I put in chenin blanc.' He gave her a long look at that point. 'Do you know what happened?'

She wrinkled her nose. 'I can't remember.'

'We had very bad weather.'

'And?'

'The chardonnay was thin, the cabernet was sour and my other varieties and blends did not live up to either my hopes or my goals. Every strategy in my arsenal was foiled by God. The chenin blanc, which I had forsaken in the mad rush to save the others, came out just fine. Of course, not my best. But definitely not the worst of my portfolio that season. Do you think this was all my fault?'

'Of course not, Dad. You can't control the weather.'

He nodded solemnly. 'Neither, my dear, can you.'

A wave of helplessness and discomfort rolled through her. She didn't know what to say but felt how closely his words pulled at the heaviness in her heart.

'But you shouldn't worry,' he nodded, 'for in every storm there is always chenin blanc.'

She laughed. 'Oh, Dad, you really are crazy, you know that?'

A toothy grin crinkled his eyes in the corners and lifted his wrinkly cheeks. 'I have my moments. But what did you come to talk to me about?'

Her gaze stretched across the vineyard to the horizon. Here, over the treetops, she could just make out a patch of dark blue sea. The enormity of the ocean sent a shiver through her. Looking out like this was like sitting on the edge of the world. And right then she felt like everything she knew was going to change. 'Dad, I want to ask you about the fire in the restaurant. The one that made Eve and Spider shut up shop and leave. Did you know that it was lit by kerosene?'

He sighed. 'I told Heath not to tell you.'

'Well, I'm glad he did,' she said a little sharply. 'Because I've been angry at Eve for months. For her recklessness, her lack of responsibility, her inability to commit. I didn't realise anyone had sabotaged her. Is she scared that they may try again?'

He was quiet for a minute before he said, 'She doesn't know that the fire was arson and I didn't have the heart to tell her.'

Her eyes widened and she realised that she hadn't truly accepted her husband's words until now.

'Heath said it was Spider,' Natasha whispered. 'But I don't believe that. Is that true?'

Her father took a while before replying. 'I've thought so,' he said finally, 'but I can't prove it.'

'It doesn't make sense,' Natasha protested. 'Why would he do such a thing to his best friend? To their business?'

'It was partially my fault.' John Maxwell sighed. 'I threatened him. I told him to resign from the business and get out of Eve's life or I'd make him regret it. I just didn't count on him having a vindictive streak.'

'Dad,' she whispered, completely at a loss, 'I don't understand. Why would you threaten him like that?'

His gaze hardened. 'He was stringing along two of my daughters at the same time.'

'What?' Her jaw dropped.

'I knew about it, you see,' John nodded. 'I found this incriminating note from Eve in the tea jar. It implied that he had led her on and encouraged feelings she had for him. I didn't tell him or her that I had discovered the note. I didn't want to embarrass Eve. Although I warned him that he had to cut one of my daughters loose. But he refused to give up his relationship with Eve. He said he wouldn't let her go.'

'Wait.' Tash's gut twisted. 'Eve was involved with Spider?'

'I don't know how far it got.' He shook his head. 'I don't want to know. But she loved him, all right. And he just used her.'

Tash was feeling sick in the stomach. 'Does Phee know about this?'

He shook his head again. 'No, God bless her. She's always been such a trusting soul. She loves him more than Eve did, I believe. And if he returns that love, which he appears to for the moment, I can't take it from her. So I have been just watching him. Watching and waiting for him to put one foot wrong.'

'Dad, this is awful.'

'Nothing for you to worry about, my dear.'

'Nothing for me to worry about!' she exclaimed. 'I can't believe all this went on under my nose. But it still doesn't completely explain why Spider would commit arson.'

'He gave me what I wanted in the worst possible way.' Her father shrugged. 'He said he'd rather burn the restaurant down than cut all ties with Eve. And then that night . . . there it was, burning.'

'It just seems a little extreme, Dad.'

'Like I said, I can't prove it. But ask Heath, he'll tell you where he found the kerosene can.'

'Heath found the kerosene can?'

'It was in the restaurant office under Spider's desk.'

'Surely he wouldn't be that dumb.'

'He was dumb enough to pursue two of my daughters under my own roof.'

'Point taken. But why did you ask Heath not to tell me any of this?'

'I didn't want Eve to suffer more than she already had. And Phoebe is determined to marry him. If he remains faithful this time, I will give my blessing . . .' He coughed. 'Reluctantly,' he added with a rueful smile.

Tash rubbed at her eyes, still trying to digest everything. She'd always thought of Spider as a rather harmless creature. Lanky and good-natured, even a tad naive. Compared to Heath, he was much less domineering and very mild-mannered. But what a 'spider' he'd turned out to be.

'I just can't believe I didn't notice. I didn't pick up on it,' she muttered half to herself, half to her father.

'It amazes me how much you girls hide from each other now. When you were younger I used to get sick of your nattering. But as it turns out, in all that chatter you had nothing to say.'

Natasha grimaced. 'Eve gets embarrassed very easily. And Phoebe is such a teaser. I'm not surprised Eve didn't tell her initially, but why didn't she say something later?'

He shook his head. 'That's a question for Eve.'

Natasha folded her arms. 'I'm going to get to the bottom of this.'

This time her father grinned at her. 'Now that is the Natasha I like to see. I would be very pleased to hear the results of this mission.'

'Do you have a staff list for the restaurant? There was more than one person in the restaurant that night, someone else could have had motive. I'm going to get an explanation for Eve. I owe her that much, at least.'

'Good.' He stood up.

'Where are you going?'

'To finish my walk.'

'Are you coming to the restaurant later?'

'Probably.' But his voice was non-committal. He seemed distracted again and she could not blame her mother for her concern.

She watched him disappear down the hill till she could see him no longer. Why was it that talking to her father always left her with more unanswered questions? Still, their exchange made her feel so much better. What she had lacked a moment ago was purpose. Goals always gave her a sense of safety.

*But you can't rely on goals, remember? There are no sure things in life.*

She rose from her seat and turned back to go the way she had come.

*No, but there are always options.*

# Chapter 16

Adam's feet scuffed the gravel as he walked through the block of chardonnay that he was in two minds about harvesting. The fruit was heavy and plump. He stopped to take another reading with his refractometer, a device that measured the sugar levels in grapes. The fruit was almost the correct balance but not quite. In frustration, he pulled one off the vine and ate it. Sometimes his tastebuds were a better gauge than a machine. Sweet, warm juice burst in his mouth. If he left it one more day, it would be perfect. Of course, he couldn't be absolutely certain until that time came, because wine was not an exact science. In these circumstances, sometimes you had to go with what your gut or, in this case, your tongue, told you.

He'd love to perform a similar taste test on Eve Maxwell. She was the kind of girl you wanted to kiss just to see what happened. He laughed as he thought about it. She was shy but fiery, reserved but sensual, quiet but passionate. She got riled up over the smallest things and he loved watching her stammer and blush before fighting back. How Spider had remained indifferent to her was a mystery. She was such a contradiction and the lure to unravel her was almost irresistible.

But with the ashes of his last relationship still smouldering, he was hardly in a position to follow up on that. He'd been hurt and used and he had no desire to do that to somebody else. And he was pretty sure Eve Maxwell was not into casual flings. The girl had seemingly remained faithful to a man who saw her only as a friend.

When they'd had breakfast together he'd felt a connection with her. A kind of common ground. She was hoping to lay low and so was he. All he'd been thinking about when he'd mentioned friendship was that it might be nice to hang out with someone who understood him, who he could be himself around. He hadn't meant to upset her.

Given her current situation, of moving from one family crisis to another, he had thought she could use a neutral friend, someone who got where she was coming from and didn't judge. But apparently that wasn't so.

Being fairly new in town himself, he didn't know that many people. He had tried to befriend some of the cellar hands and vineyard guys at Tawny Brooks, but they were all a little standoffish because, essentially, he was their boss. Some of them, he found out later, had actually applied for his position when it came up and been turned down. He knew that would suck. He understood their resentment and also their rivalry. He also noticed their lack of patience with less important staff, such as the estate gardener, Eric Matheson. The kid was only nineteen, so his opinion amongst many of the staff was not highly valued. He tended to be dismissed or sent on errands no one else wanted to do. Having himself once been the dogsbody who was always passed over, he took pity on Eric and tried to protect him a little from his peers.

The sun beat down, warming the broad brim of his hat and making him sweat. He had often wondered what it was that had made John Maxwell pick him out from the crowd. He chuckled. *Maybe I don't want to know.*

Today he was supposed to be helping out at the restaurant and he wondered how long he could put off showing up. At least a couple of hours. He would go check on his men. They were supposed to be finishing up the cleaning they'd started two weeks ago. If he was going to start pulling his first batch of grapes off the vine, all the vats had to be spotless, the de-stemmer and press had to be immaculate and the picking bins needed to be ready to go. When the chardonnay came off they'd need every hand on the estate, including those small delicate ones that had chopped chives only hours earlier.

He had every intention of putting Eve and everyone in her family to work. Somehow they'd managed to rope him into helping out with the restaurant, attending the wedding and chasing the head of the household around the countryside whenever he disappeared. Not to mention Phoebe's wedding-chore lucky dip. 'Lucky' wasn't exactly the word he'd use. He was stuck sourcing wedding chair sashes and linens for the restaurant with Spider. First, he wasn't entirely sure he liked Spider, and second, was there even an organisation out there that actually made a living from hiring out that crap? He had an awful feeling he was about to find out. In the meantime, he would be happy to dole out some of his own punishment to those Maxwell girls.

He glanced at his watch. There was something else he needed to take care of first though. It was a delicate matter which required some stealth. He grinned mischievously, surprised at how much he was enjoying this subterfuge. Early that morning, after Eve had walked out on him, he'd started cleaning up their dirty dishes, and noticed she had left her dressing gown complete with burnt sleeves on the kitchen floor. As much as he thought her penchant for leaving unprotected love letters in tea jars rather endearing, he surmised her burnt lingerie on the kitchen floor wasn't a message she'd like the whole family to receive when they turned up later that morning. So he'd picked it up, cut off the smelly burnt bits, folded it neatly and put it in the back of his ute.

He'd been considering his options on how to get it back to her. There was simply knocking on the front door of the house, meeting her discreetly in a dark barrel room or sneaking into her bedroom – all of which appealed to him a great deal but he figured wouldn't impress her overly much. Now, as he was walking back to his ute, he happened to spy a red Barina already parked outside the restaurant.

So she was there already! How convenient. The desire to go inside and tease her was palpable but he reined it in.

*Don't tempt fate, Adam.*

What an annoying thing a conscience was. With a sigh, he walked over to his ute and fished the dressing gown off the front passenger seat. There was an easy solution here that he wasn't going to pass up.

No one locked their doors in the country, so it wouldn't be a problem. He strolled over to the Barina, opened the back door and placed the dressing gown on the backseat. He was about to shut the door when a little devil on his shoulder prompted him to go one step further. Taking his notepad out of his front shirt pocket and a lead pencil from behind his ear, he wrote: 'When you're ready, I'd also like my blanket back.'

He tore the note from his pad, dropped it on top of the dressing gown and shut the door. He imagined her little gasp and cautious glance around when she found it.

*You've really got to stop pushing her buttons, Adam.*

He laughed as he hopped into his ute and drove off to the winery. *Maybe tomorrow.*

# Chapter 17

Phoebe awoke with a burst of optimism.

Spider groaned as she jumped out of bed and started rummaging around in their bedroom, looking for something to wear.

'What are you doing?' he asked. 'Surely it's not time to get up yet.'

A glance at the clock on the bedside table told her it was seven thirty-three.

'It's late enough,' she shrugged. 'I can't sleep now. I'm too excited. Aren't you excited?'

'Ecstatic.' His tone entirely contradicted the word, which hurt just a little but she brushed it off. He was just tired and cranky, not used to sleeping in this bed, which, she had to admit, was a little lumpy.

'Well, I can't sleep now.' She made her voice light as she closed her suitcase, a pair of shorts and a t-shirt over one arm. 'There's too much to be done.'

'Not really,' Spider grunted and rolled over. 'You seem to have done a pretty good job with delegation.'

She paused in the act of pulling on her shorts. 'You're not mad about that, are you?'

'What do you think, Phee?'

His voice sounded cold and instinctively she knew there was a fight brewing. It was the last thing she wanted when she was in such a hopeful mood.

'Look, can we talk about it later? I really don't want to miss the beams arriving.'

'Fine,' he murmured.

She eyed him uncertainly, not knowing whether she was risking too much by leaving him disgruntled.

'Just go, Phee,' he said without looking up. 'I know you want to. And like you said, we'll talk about it later.'

Putting off a fight did make things awkward, though – especially at breakfast. He could barely look at her when he belatedly walked into the kitchen. Or during the discussion with Eve about food at the wedding. Luckily, by that stage she was almost through her meal, so was able to make an escape alone to the restaurant without too much hassle. She arrived just in time to see a bunch of guys unloading a stack of timber from a white semitrailer.

As she waved them off, Eric strolled up. 'Hi, Phee,' he said cheerfully. He was going to help them out at the restaurant that morning.

'Oh, hi, Eric,' she greeted him warmly. 'How are you today?'

'Okay, I guess. You?'

'Ready to get started.' She nodded. 'Thanks for helping out.'

'No worries,' he replied shyly, rolling a rock under the top of his right boot. He squinted up at the sun. 'It's a good day for it.'

'Yes, it is.' She was pleased with his enthusiasm.

'So where's Spider?'

'Oh,' Phoebe waved her hand, 'he wanted to sleep in a little more.'

She tried to ignore an irritating niggle at the back of her mind. It was kind of disappointing that she was out here, game as a footballer in AFL season, and he was so uninterested.

*I mean, this is our wedding, for goodness sake.*

Even Eric was more enthusiastic than him. As if to echo her thoughts, he held up a bag. 'I've found gloves for everyone. They're just old gardening gloves from my equipment sheds but it'll save everyone getting splinters.'

'Aw, thanks, Eric.'

He blushed. 'No worries.'

As he walked off, she frowned. His thoughtfulness only highlighted further Spider's distant behaviour. But she refused to allow herself to dwell on this for too long.

The restaurant floor needed to be replaced and they didn't have a lot of time to do it. Spider's mild crankiness, if you could call it that, could be dealt with later. She could smooth his ruffled feathers over a nice glass of wine and some quality time that evening. She was sure that living with her family and his parents was taking all the romance out of this venture for him.

He just needed a bit of reassurance.

She wasn't impressed, however, when he turned up fifteen minutes later than her sisters and his own parents. What was he doing that the renovations came second? She didn't want to cause a scene so she said nothing about his tardiness and greeted him with a kiss and a hug. He responded, but very abruptly, as though something was bothering him.

Now wasn't the time to ask him about it though, so she banished the niggling worry to the back of her mind and tried to focus on the job.

After sweeping the floor, their first task was to remove the floor beams of the restaurant. It was too hard to replace just the damaged ones without the renovation looking funny so Heath had recommended they just do the lot. Once bolts were loosened, this was a lift and carry job that was done in groups. Adam turned up halfway through, bringing with him another guy from the vineyard to make the work go faster.

While they did achieve this result, Phoebe's real goal of bringing the family together was not being realised. She had thought that renovating the restaurant would make them talk, that it would become a sort of icebreaker for the various issues and hang-ups they had collected over the months and years. In her mind, all that was needed was to put her family in the same room and force them to work together.

She was wrong.

Sentences started and then stopped. Conversations turned into heavy silences quicker than cream curdles under heat. Everybody seemed to be overly anxious not to put a foot wrong.

Adam was careful with Eve. Eve was careful with Spider. Heath was careful with Tash.

And Tash was careful with her.

Spider seemed to be more focused on his parents than anything else. Not that she blamed him. They seemed to flit around nervously like tropical birds dumped on an iceberg, not knowing quite what to do. Patricia, especially, was sulking. Phoebe began to wonder at the wisdom of not having been there at breakfast with the rest of the family. Had something happened between Patricia and her mother?

There was, at least, one silver lining. Eve and Tash seemed to be getting along better. As the morning progressed their wariness around each other seemed to fade. She even saw them laughing at one point, and went over to ask them what was so funny.

'We were discussing what sort of music you and Spider might enjoy at your wedding,' Eve revealed.

Phoebe remembered that they had both drawn the task of 'Organising the music' from her lottery the day before, and congratulated herself on having at least one strategic win.

'We were reminiscing about all your old favourites,' Tash grinned.

'My old favourites?' Phoebe's eyes darted from one sister to the other. They looked entirely too mischievous.

'Backstreet Boys,' Tash said archly. 'Brian Littrell.'

Phoebe's hand covered her mouth at this blast from the past. Every generation had its dancing, singing, too-much-hair-gel boy band. And her teenage years were no exception.

'Come on, guys, you liked them too.'

'We didn't have a hundred and one pictures of Brian Littrell on our bedroom walls though.' Eve shook her head.

'Do you remember what you used to do?' Tash's eyes suddenly widened at the memory.

'Oh, please,' Phee covered her face with her hands and peeped through her fingers, 'don't remind me.'

Tash ignored her. 'She used to put on her pink cherry lip gloss, stand on her bed and kiss him on the lips all the time. Dad used to say if she didn't stop doing it she'd put a hole in his face.'

Eve gasped. 'I completely remember that.'

They laughed.

Phoebe moaned.

At this point, Spider came over. 'Should I be worried?'

Phee quickly swatted her hand at him. 'Go away, I don't want you listening to this.' She had meant it as a joke but, to her surprise, he just looked hurt.

'Fine.' With jaw set, he walked off.

*Damn it. Here we go again.* He was so sensitive about everything lately. And she was over having to deal with it. She needed Spider to step up and be strong for her now, not act like a baby. They had too much going on. The wedding, her parents, her dad . . .

'So what do you reckon?' Tash was addressing her again. 'Should we hire the local boy band? Is there one?'

'Er . . . no thanks,' Phoebe quickly informed her. 'I think I'd prefer something very classical for the wedding. Preferably no singing. And just a DJ for the reception.'

'Will do,' Tash nodded. 'I think I've got a few ideas.'

'Is that what Spider wants too?' Eve asked quietly.

'Spider said he was quite happy for me to choose whatever,' Phoebe replied airily, though her eyes strayed across the room to where her fiancé was talking to Heath.

*He did say that, right? So why is he being funny about it now?*

Eve interrupted the thought. 'I think he's just feeling a little left out, you know.' As Phoebe turned in surprise to her sister, Eve looked uncomfortable. 'I mean, I could be wrong. You know him better than I do.'

'Well, you are one of his oldest friends,' Phoebe conceded. 'I'm sure he confides in you.' She was often jealous of Spider's close relationship with Eve. Not because she believed there was anything inappropriate about it. But she did at times feel there was a piece of himself he reserved for her sister. They would always have something that she wasn't quite a part of.

'I wouldn't say he confides in me a lot.' Eve struggled under her sister's steady gaze, her hands wringing. 'Hardly at all, really. In fact, we've grown rather distant of late. I think we're in completely different places in life right now and in our careers and –'

'Eve,' Phee grabbed her hands, 'it's okay, I get it.'

Her sister gave a large sigh of relief. 'Thanks. I honestly didn't mean to intrude.'

'You weren't.'

'Okay.' Tash clapped her hands, once again taking on the role of leader. 'Recess is over. Let's get back to work.'

So they continued for another couple of hours. At one o'clock they decided to break for lunch. Everyone staggered into the kitchen, peeling off their gloves. The awkwardness between them before had slowly lessened, due in most part to exhaustion.

'I think it's Make-Your-Own,' Phoebe announced. 'Mum said she stocked the kitchen with rolls and salads and . . .' She opened the fridge. 'And apparently a stack of crepes. Eve, they look like your recipe.'

Her sister blushed. 'Yeah, I er . . . may have helped out too.'

As she finished talking, Anita breezed in. 'I thought there might not be enough food so I roasted a chicken.'

There was a groan as she put a gorgeous tray smelling of rosemary and thyme on one of the central counters. More food?

Anita put her hands on her hips. 'What? You don't want the chicken?'

'Of course we want it.' Adam immediately left his seat to come over to carve it.

'There's just so much food,' Phoebe murmured.

'With hard work you need to keep your energy up.' Anita nodded. 'Where's your father?'

'I asked him not to come.'

'Not come?' Anita demanded. 'Why not?'

Phoebe bit her lip. 'He's getting old, Mum. I didn't want him to hurt himself.'

Her mother sniffed. 'He's not so fragile. Now we have no idea where he is.'

Soon everyone was tucking into the food, chicken rolls all round, and began congratulating themselves on the progress so far. There was no doubt about it, they had made a great start on removing the restaurant floor and everyone was pretty enthused by the morning's achievement. Even Eve, who Phoebe had been worried might get a little sullen as the restaurant came back to life, was pretty happy.

*Maybe she'll start cooking in the restaurant again.*

Even as she was thinking this, she watched Spider do something very strange. He walked over to the tea jar, rummaged through it like he was looking for something, before picking out a tea bag and making himself a cup of tea.

*What the hell?*

Phoebe's heart rate quickened. Did she just see what she thought she did?

There was only one way to find out.

# Chapter 18

Spider had always prided himself on being the one everybody liked. The easygoing guy in the room, who rarely put a foot wrong. He wasn't fussy, he wasn't snobbish and, as a general rule, he had a good sense of humour.

Yet since his arrival at Tawny Brooks for their one-month stay, it felt like he had become the most hated person in the area.

First there was Heath, a guy he honestly hadn't had that much to do with and thought would be easy to befriend. After all, his future brother-in-law knew first-hand how crazy this family was. Perhaps he would have some advice to share on how to get into their good books.

But no, the guy was like a wall. Stern and mostly silent. He'd heard that he wasn't a big talker. His complete lack of engagement, however, was ridiculous – along with those long intimidating stares that seemed to indicate that he knew something that Spider might be ashamed of.

Spider couldn't think what that might be.

In turn, Phoebe's eldest sister, the lovely Natasha, was no better. She deliberately excluded him with the cheese board – must have cut a piece for everyone else in the room except him the previous evening. What she meant by that he had absolutely no idea.

Then there was Eve – his long-time friend, the one person he thought he could count on. Of all the surprises, she was *avoiding* him! Wouldn't even look him in the eye.

Why? He'd tried to discover the reason after he arrived at the restaurant that morning, only to have another run-in with his least favourite person on the team: Adam Carter.

Who the hell was this guy anyway?

He wasn't even a member of the family, for goodness sake, yet he seemed to be in on everything. He and Eve were best buddies. John had been drinking with him yesterday evening. Even Anita seemed to think the sun and the moon shone right out of his arse.

*I mean, what has he got that I haven't?*

Apart from an eighteen-inch bicep. The guy was a joker. He didn't have a serious bone in his body. And, with every interaction they had, Adam just seemed to want to make fun of him. Last night, Spider had been trying to reconnect with Anita all evening – telling her how wonderful her daughter was, how gorgeous her gardens were, how immaculately she kept her house and if she might offer him a few tips. While she accepted all his comments and answered his questions, she made no move to get to know him better.

And then she'd brought out dessert – a chocolate mousse cake beautifully covered in whipped chocolate cream and sprinkled with flakes. It looked delicious but he was too full from the main meal. So when she offered him this giant piece on a plate, he'd put his hand over his heart and said, 'No thank you, Anita. It looks lovely but I just couldn't fit another thing in.'

'But you can't go without dessert!' she gasped. 'It's a sacrilege.'

There was utter silence at the table as everyone turned to stare at him.

'The truth is, Anita,' he stammered, 'your moussaka was just so yummy that I pigged out on it. I really shouldn't have had that second helping. I honestly can't fit in cake as well.'

'Very well.' She pursed her lips and moved the plate away from him.

'I'll have it.' Adam raised his hand.

Her face immediately broke out into a huge approving smile. 'Of course you will, Adam. You love my cooking.'

'It's not that I don't love your cooking,' Spider tried to protest but his voice went unheard.

Anita was watching Adam, who was already spooning some of the cake into his mouth. 'How is it?' she demanded.

'It's sensational.' Adam closed his eyes in ecstasy.

Anita sighed. 'You're such a sweet boy. I don't know why you don't stay for dinner more often. We can always do with good company in the house.'

John chuckled.

And as Spider continued to stare in shock at the scene playing out, Adam glanced at him with wide eyes that held just a hint of satisfaction. Spider quickly looked away, desperate not to engage in a battle he obviously could not win. It seemed to be the tone of the evening really – Spider pushed aside for the needs of everybody else.

He still could not believe that Phoebe had divided up the organisation of their wedding without consulting him first. Though he shouldn't be surprised she had kept it from him – she seemed to be full of secrets these days, though she continued to deny it. He knew withdrawal when he saw it, but couldn't seem to make her open up.

All of this, however, was the least of his worries. When he had first arrived at Tawny Brooks, he had thought that his future father-in-law would be his biggest problem . . . And he definitely was.

He had never had a good relationship with John Maxwell. Since the whole fire debacle and the confrontation over his daughters, things had deteriorated even further. He had apologised as best he could for that misunderstanding and tried to prove himself a worthy son-in-law rather than getting Phee or Eve involved. He felt that this was a much less messy way of doing things and wouldn't unnecessarily upset the girls. He thought he was making progress too when John had finally given his blessing for their marriage.

If their sitting-room conversation was anything to go by, however, he was definitely wrong. To make matters even worse, prior to arriving at Tawny Brooks he had come up with a little plan to develop a better relationship with his future father-in-law.

Now that John was retired, he thought it might be a good opportunity to bond with the man in his free time.

'You know,' Phoebe had told him a few months earlier, 'there are so many golf clubs in this region. Why don't you join one with him? I think he'd be really into that. He's always expressed an interest.'

Well! Idiot that he was, he thought he'd go one step further than that. He thought he'd buy his future father-in-law an expensive gift to go with his proposal. It would be a surprise. A surprise he was sure would please Phoebe as well. Now he wished he'd told her about it first.

That morning after breakfast, he had waited for John to get back from his morning walk. Everyone else left to get started on the restaurant. He'd stayed behind in Phoebe's father's study with a very large, very expensive set of golf clubs.

'Er . . . hi, John.'

'What are you doing in here?'

'Just waiting for you.'

John's expression darkened. 'You wanted to say something to me?'

Spider cleared his throat. 'I wanted to try to assure you, again, that I have nothing but Phoebe's best interests at heart. After last night, I feel like you still don't believe me.'

'I see.'

His response was so short and vague that Spider had to fill the silence that fell between them. 'And I also wanted to say . . .'

'Go on.'

'That I'm hoping that we can be friends. Phoebe said you were interested in getting into golf. So I thought it might be a good way to spend some time together.' He tried for a smile but it was not returned. 'Anyway,' he continued quickly, 'to that end, I have bought you a gift.'

He stood back to present the clubs in their leather bag. John grunted, his eyebrows twitching together as he went over to examine them, lifting and replacing each of the shiny clubs with slow precision.

Hope grew in Spider's chest. He cleared his throat. 'Do you like them?'

John dropped the last club back into the bag. 'I'm left-handed,' he announced and walked out of the room, leaving Spider standing there with his mouth open. Not only had his gift not been appreciated, he'd completely stuffed it up. It seemed he couldn't do anything right, or should he say *left*.

Suffice it to say, by the time he arrived at the restaurant that morning, he had a severe chip on his shoulder. He did his best to ignore it, biding his time till he might have a moment alone with Phoebe. He was dying to ask her what the hell was going on and demand her support.

It was a difficult morning, but he got through it. Lunch as well, which wasn't half bad. Afterwards, he decided he needed a hot drink. He wasn't a big tea drinker but recently had got into the herbal stuff. So he'd rummaged through the tea jar in search of some camomile. He thought it might help calm his nerves. He was just lifting the steaming cup to his mouth when Phoebe finally came over and requested a moment alone with him.

'I thought you'd never ask.' He sighed in relief and indicated the back door to the restaurant. 'Shall we?'

She nodded curtly, her eyes following the cup of tea in his hands as they walked out the door. The second they were outside and out of earshot, she said, 'What do you think you're doing?'

'Huh?'

'You heard me.'

'Wait.' He paused, sensing their minds weren't in the same place. 'Don't tell me, you're mad at me?'

'Of course I'm mad at you.' She put her hands on her hips. 'What are you doing with that cup of tea?'

He looked down at the mug in his hands. 'Drinking it. What does it look like?'

'But you don't like tea.'

'Yes, I do.'

'Since when?'

'Since recently. What the hell does it matter?'

Her expression darkened. 'It just seems kinda *convenient* for a man who doesn't like tea to all of a sudden get an interest in the tea jar by the window.'

He gaped at her. 'I don't get it.'

'Next you'll be off to the Wildwood Bakery to get a sausage roll.'

He choked back a laugh. 'You're not making any sense at all.'

'Aren't I?'

Spider shut his eyes briefly before taking a deep breath. 'Phee, you haven't been making any sense for a while now. I've watched you withdraw further and further from me every day. Ever since we got engaged, in fact.'

'No, I haven't.'

'Yes, you have,' he argued, knowing how important it was that he made this point. 'I don't feel like this wedding is about us any more.'

There was a telltale hesitation. 'What are you talking about?'

'I'm talking about the fact that we're renovating your family's restaurant and dividing up wedding chores like it's a fun game to keep them all happy.'

'Weddings are about family.'

'Not to the exclusion of the bloody couple,' he cried. 'I wanted our wedding to be our day, our event and our celebration. I wanted to decide things together with you.'

'You said you were fine with whatever I decided.'

'Because I know our tastes are similar and I wanted *you* to be happy.' He rubbed his temple. 'I didn't think you were going to delegate big decisions to your family or that I'd be picking out jobs from a hat with everyone else.' He kicked a pebble with his big toe and muttered, 'Anyone but you would get this.'

She seemed to pounce on his last remark. 'What do you mean *anyone* but me?'

He looked up. 'I just mean most people would understand where I'm coming from.'

'Most people?' Her eyes narrowed. 'Like another woman, you mean?'

He threw up his hands. 'Like anyone, Phee. Don't you think we should be choosing our own music and picking our own celebrant and hiring our own decorator who understands *our* taste?'

Her voice became small and cold as ice. 'So you want me to tell everyone to stop helping when I specifically asked them to come one month early to assist with the wedding?'

'No.' Spider shook his head. 'It was to help with the restaurant, not the wedding.'

'It was both,' Phee insisted. 'Telling them to back off now will just cause a scene. My sisters will be hurt and my mother will think badly of you.'

'So?' Spider demanded. 'None of them like me anyway.'

She gasped. 'Spider, that's not true. I don't know where this is coming from.'

'No, you wouldn't know, would you?' he accused. 'You've been very happy to just ignore it.'

'Spider, you're completely overacting. You can't honestly expect me to tell my family to stop helping with the wedding when it's taking place in their own home.'

'They are interfering too much.'

She glared at him. '*So is your mother*. I don't want to put any unnecessary stress on anyone, especially my parents.'

His heart squeezed. 'But you're more than happy to do it to me.'

'That's not what I meant.' She wrung her hands. 'Look, I have my reasons for getting everyone so involved. I told you that I wanted to bring the family closer together. Especially now.'

'Closer together, yes,' he agreed. 'But it's more than that, Phee, isn't it?'

She chewed on her lower lip, watching him uncertainly like she was trying to figure out whether he was someone she could trust. *How did we get here?*

'Look,' she began desperately, 'you know having the wedding here is important to me. Please let's just do it and when the wedding is over life will go back to the way it was.'

Spider shut his eyes, gripping his cup of tea. 'Don't you see how that's not what I want? I don't want to have to *get through* my own wedding. Just tell me what's going on, Phee. If you would just confide in me then maybe I could help you. Maybe we could do this together, like we're supposed to.'

When he opened his eyes, she was staring at his mug. 'It's not like you aren't keeping secrets from me as well,' she muttered.

He slowly lowered his hands. 'What did you say?'

'I said,' she lifted her chin, 'it's not like you aren't keeping secrets from me with your sudden interest in tea, for example.'

He looked heavenward. 'You don't want me to drink tea? Fine. I won't drink the bloody tea.' He tipped the remaining contents of his mug in the dirt before shoving it back in her hands. 'But this is not how I want our wedding to be, let alone our marriage. I love you but there's gotta be some compromise. A little give and take, huh?'

'Of course.'

He waited but she said nothing. With a large sigh, he finally turned around and started walking down the gravel path to the gardens.

'Where are you going?' she cried after him.

'For a drive . . .' he called back, and then hearing her footsteps behind him on the gravel looked over his shoulder and said firmly, '*Alone*.'

'Where?'

'I don't know.' He faced forward again and kept walking. All he knew was this was not how he wanted to marry anyone.

# Chapter 19

Phoebe watched Spider disappear into her mother's garden, which was providing her with anything but tranquillity right now.

Was Spider really this hurt with her? Over what? A few wedding chores that he really wasn't that interested in, anyway?

*What am I going to tell the others?*

As if to expedite the task, Tash came striding out of the restaurant looking as upset as she was. Ironically enough, she was also holding a cup of tea. 'Oh,' she seemed to start when she saw Phoebe, 'I forgot you were out here as well.' She said the words as though she had been hoping to be alone.

*Great! Another person who doesn't want my company.*

Tash seemed to centre herself though and with trembling lips, curved her mouth into a smile. 'Where's Spider?'

'He needs a break,' Phoebe said shortly.

Tash nodded, flexing one of her wrists. 'I will admit it was pretty full-on this morning. I could do with a nap.' As she gazed across the lake, she breathed in deeply. 'Wow, I never realised how much I missed this place until I stood right here on this spot.'

'Tash,' she paused. 'Do you and Heath fight a lot?'

Tash started, a faint flush infusing her face. 'What makes you ask that?'

'Oh, no reason . . .' Phoebe bit her lip and then started again. 'Okay, there is a reason. I think I'm having a bit of a serious fight with Spider right now. And I'm feeling worried.'

Tash's shoulders seemed to relax slightly and she came closer. 'About what?'

'About the family.'

'Is it Dad's attitude? He was a little hard on Spider last night.'

'I wish it were just that. But no, he thinks everyone's too involved with the wedding. And he wants some space from us.' She walked over to a nearby park bench and sat down. It was made out of two thick logs for legs and a couple of wooden planks nailed together over the top. While simple and very rustic looking, it was an excellent vantage point for taking in the view of 'Crazy Man's Lake'.

Tash came over and sat down beside Phoebe, cradling her mug in her lap. 'Well, you know, we *are* all very involved.'

'Yes, but isn't that what happens with weddings?' Phoebe insisted defensively. 'I know Mum will take any opportunity she can get to stick her oar in but his mum is exactly the same!'

'The thing is, you didn't have to divide up the wedding planning like you did last night. Personally, I wouldn't have done that.'

How could she explain to Tash, without revealing what she knew, why it was so vital to her that everyone in the family got along? 'Tash, I feel like there's been a lot of distance in the family the last two years. Everyone's sort of drifted apart and I just want to bring everyone back together. I thought our wedding would be the perfect opportunity. And so far it's almost worked. I mean, look at you and Eve. You guys were laughing and reminiscing. And I was happy because I felt like I was partially responsible for that.'

'Phee, it's not your job to fix whatever is wrong with this family.'

'Yes, it is.' Phoebe nodded resolutely and as Tash opened her mouth to protest she put up a hand to stall her. 'I know things that you don't. I have reasons. Promises I need to keep.'

Tash's eyes narrowed. 'Is that why you're fixing up the restaurant – in order to fix up the family?'

She nodded. 'Partially. I'm also hoping Eve might come home. We used to be such good friends and . . .' Her voice trailed off. 'When you had a fight with her, it was like I had a fight with her too.'

Tash sighed, putting her arm around her. 'You know what, I've been acting like a baby for far too long. So absorbed in my own little world I had no idea what was going on anywhere else. But I do now.'

Phee smiled, her vision blurring as her eyes filled with tears. 'Are you going to do the older sister thing and take over?'

Tash slung an arm about her shoulders, pulling her close. 'Well, I'm certainly not going to let you do this whole "bringing the family together" thing on your own. Especially when half the reason we've fallen out is my fault.'

'That's not true.'

'There you go, trying to take responsibility again. Don't do it, Phee. The truth is everyone has had their part to play . . . including Spider.' Phoebe pulled away slightly and saw Tash's mouth harden into an expression she didn't like. It put her in mind again of the other reason she had allowed him to walk away from her just now.

Tash felt her sister's body tense. 'What's the matter, Phee?'

She hesitated and then her voice came out on a croak. 'There's something else I haven't told you about Spider.'

Tash, who had been rubbing her arm, stilled. 'What else is there to tell?'

'I can't be absolutely certain,' Phoebe began, 'but I think there's another woman in his life.'

To both her surprise and concern, Tash didn't seem all that shocked by this. 'All right,' her older sister sighed, dropping her arm and sitting up straighter, 'you might as well tell me everything, from the beginning.'

Slowly, Phoebe put her trembling hand into her pocket, wondering whether she was a little psychotic for carrying this note around with her constantly. She drew the creased envelope out and passed it to Tash.

'What's this?'

'I intercepted this message on its way to him two days ago.'

Tash opened the envelope and then her eye fell to the page. She whistled softly. 'Geez, Spider, you sure are popular.'

'What do you mean?' Phee pounced on this.

'Nothing.' Tash refolded the note quickly and looked up. 'But, Phee, I do know one thing. If you can't trust this man, you can't marry him. Can you trust him?'

Phoebe was silent for a minute, chewing worriedly on her lower lip. She knew her sister's words were true, she just hadn't wanted to hear them. Desperately, she searched her brain for a defence. 'Spider is a wonderful man. He's very thoughtful. If anything he's too sensitive. Just ask Eve, she –'

'That's okay,' Tash pressed her hand, 'I believe you. I know you love him. But that's not what I'm asking you, is it?'

Phee groaned. 'Like I said, I can't be certain. This is just my own conjecture. I don't want to believe it. But after today . . .'

'Well,' Tash's lips tightened, 'there is one way we can find out what game Spider is playing, if there is one.'

'How?'

'Let's go confront her.'

'Her?' Phee looked up in surprise. 'But we don't know who the note is from.'

'We do know where she's going to be though. This afternoon, three o'clock at Wildwood Bakery. Let's have a stake-out. See who shows up.'

Phee's skin prickled. 'You really think we should do that?'

'Why the hell not?' Tash smiled. 'We're taking a break on the restaurant, aren't we? And I'd love to give the bitch a piece of my mind. Who goes after an engaged man? It's despicable.'

Phoebe gasped. 'Would you say that to her?'

'Amongst other things,' Tash nodded, slapping a fist to a palm. 'And then I'd tell her to stay away from your man or she'll answer to me.'

'I think I'll do that bit, if you don't mind.' Phoebe perked up a little and sat up straighter. 'Which means I guess I'll be going with you. Let's do it.'

Tash held out her hand and they shook on it like kids, laughing as they did so.

'Okay,' Tash nodded, 'we better go in and tell everyone that work is over till tomorrow.'

*And the real job has just begun.*

# Chapter 20

Tash had been hoping that back-breaking labour might be more therapeutic than emotionally stimulating. She should have known that if Heath was in the room, she never really had a hope. That and the fact that he was completely in his element. Construction was his life. Fixing the floor of their little restaurant was peanuts compared to what he was used to. He organised them into groups and showed them how best to remove the broken beams before pitching in himself. She couldn't help but feel a little proud of him until she realised what she was doing.

*He doesn't belong to you any more. You live in different states. And as soon as this wedding is over, you're going to have to tell the family.*

The thought filled her with dread and she gritted her teeth. One thing she'd always prided herself on was her strength in the face of adversity. Like her father said, she had missions, not goals. And this would just be another one. She would get through it, and she would build a new life *better* than the one she had left behind.

*Is that what you really want, to leave Heath behind?*

She staggered slightly under the weight of the beam she was lifting. Eve, who was helping her hold up her end, glanced at her.

'Are you okay? Do you want to stop and rest?'

'No,' Tash shook her head, firmly ignoring the fact that at Eve's words Heath's head had jerked up from his task and he glanced over. 'No,' she said quickly again. 'I'm fine.'

But he was already by her side, taking the weight of the beam from her.

'I'm okay,' she protested, forced to step back and watch as he completed her task with Eve, carrying the charred and broken beam outside and dropping it onto the ever-growing pile of discarded timber. As soon as the floorboard was laid, Heath came back to her. He pulled off a glove and cupped her face.

'You look rather flushed,' he noted. 'You should have some water.'

Whilst she would like to blame her redness on the warmth of the day or her lack of fitness, she was certain it was because Heath was invading her personal space again. She wished he would stop touching her. He'd been doing it all morning. Nothing of note, of course, a caress here, a brush there. But she was powerless to stop him with all her family watching. She had to stand there like she was now, looking up into those melt-your-heart brown eyes, with his hands on her face, and take it.

*The nerve of the man!*

It was beginning to dawn on her that he was going to take every opportunity to exploit their deception to his own advantage. Whatever that advantage may be, she was sure he had an agenda that would shortly become all too clear.

'Here,' a soft voice said at her elbow and gratefully she pulled away to see that Eve was holding out a bottle of water to her.

'Thanks.' She took the water. Eve was definitely a welcome distraction. In more ways than one. She was now dying to apologise to her. After everything their father had revealed at the gazebo this morning, she felt bad about not enquiring more closely into her sister's life. She had just made all these assumptions and thought about everything from a business angle, which in hindsight was really rather cold. It was no wonder Eve had never felt she would understand.

Spider, on the other hand, was a completely different story. She realised, painfully, that she had completely misjudged the man. Now that her senses were heightened to his behaviour, she had watched him closely during the entire morning and came away feeling even more dissatisfied than before.

She was cluey enough to conclude that he was sulking. Something was bothering him, though of course she couldn't be sure what. His grumpiness was only detectable because she was looking for it. Men like Spider were always so nice. It was only now that she was realising that he covered his disappointment with a sort of passive aggression. Of all the men helping renovate the restaurant, he was the slackest, arriving late, taking frequent breaks and being easily distracted. He'd also approached Eve a couple of times, talking to her in a low voice that made her sister look decidedly uncomfortable. She didn't hear what was said, but she did watch the body language. Eve had the look of a rabbit cornered by a fox. For every step she took back, Spider took one step forward. He seemed to be frustrated by her lack of response and unwillingness to engage.

At lunchtime, when their mother turned up, he seemed to become positively frosty and stopped talking to anyone. At first glance, it didn't appear that Phoebe noticed this. Or if she did, she certainly didn't care. She was too busy talking to Eve and their mother about how good the restaurant was looking already and how pleased Dad was going to be, and so on and so on. Phoebe, in fact, was just a gush of goodwill until Spider decided to have a cup of tea. That's when the two of them had gone outside.

'See anything suspicious?'

She jumped as Heath's hand rested on the back of her neck again, his thumb caressing her nape, his breath on her ear. Her eyes darted away from Spider to the rest of the group. Her mother, Spider's parents, Eve, Adam, the vineyard worker and Eric. They were all talking and laughing around the main counter. Her mother raised a bottle of juice at her.

'Do you want some, Tash?'

'No thanks.' She smiled and then whispered between her teeth to Heath, 'Will you stop touching my neck.'

Heath's low chuckle reverberated in his chest. 'If you don't want me to touch it, you should stop tying your hair up in high ponytails.' He leaned down further so that he might murmur seductively in her ear. 'It's incredibly sexy, you know.'

She sucked in a breath as memories swamped her. He used to say that to her all the time.

His hand dropped from her neck only to catch both her hands and turn her to face him. There was nowhere to look but into his face. She couldn't even snatch her hands away for fear it might arouse suspicion.

'I noticed you've been watching Spider all morning. Did you speak to your dad about him?'

'I did,' she said coolly, with no intention of elaborating for his benefit.

'You know, Tash,' he said carefully, 'you could just as easily have asked me. I know all the answers to the questions you have.'

She remembered how her father had said it was Heath who'd found a kerosene can under Spider's desk. She was tempted to question him more closely but she hesitated. Involving him in her search for answers would only exacerbate her inability to get away from him. The problem was that she had no choice. Heath's testimony was the logical place to start.

'What's the matter, Tash?' he asked. 'Don't you trust me?'

'Well, you did keep this a secret from me for a long time. You knew I had a big fight with Eve about it. It would have helped me to know about this back then.'

'I didn't want you to focus on it any more,' he said solemnly. 'Shortly after your fight with Eve, we found out we were pregnant, remember?'

She closed her eyes at his words, but it was difficult to shut out the memories they conjured. They had been over the moon when the doctor had confirmed the result of her home pregnancy test. She remembered lying on that uncomfortable hospital examination bed listening to their baby's heartbeat through the ultrasound and feeling so full of joy her ribcage was fit to burst. How odd that a repetitive beeping and splotchy indiscernible image had the power to bring her to tears. Standing right beside her, Heath had squeezed her hand so tightly the blood had almost left her fingers. It was the moment they had been waiting for, for nearly three years. It was a glorious day that was supposed to be a turning point in their lives. They were going to be parents!

Only now, in hindsight, could she see that it was the beginning of the end.

Heath's quiet voice broke through her thoughts. 'I didn't want you to worry about Tawny Brooks. We both know that if I'd told you back then you'd just be doing exactly what you are now. Setting yourself a mission to catch an arsonist. I just wanted you to take it easy – focus on the baby.'

A knot in her belly tightened. Her own shame lashed her like a whip. 'But I didn't, did I? I didn't take it easy. And I ruined everything.'

As she averted her eyes, he released her hands and grabbed her by the shoulders. 'Hey, that's not what I meant.'

She returned her gaze squarely to his. It was time to face facts, put it out there on the table, so they were both aware of where they stood.

'Maybe that wasn't what you meant right now but I know that's how you've always felt.'

'What?' His voice rasped with pain. 'No, that's *not* true.'

'It's all right,' she tried to reassure him, 'I don't blame you. It was my fault we lost her. I accept full responsibility.'

His hands seemed to tighten on her upper arms, his fingers digging into her flesh. 'No, Tash, I won't allow you to do that.'

'You don't really have a choice,' she told him sadly. 'It's done. And now you can really let me go.'

She had meant this both emotionally and physically as he was still holding on to her. But his hands did not loosen and a muscle jerked in his jaw. There seemed to be an avalanche of emotion behind his eyes just waiting to tip him over the edge. She watched him struggle within himself, as one feeling after the other ripped across his face.

Shock. Pain. Regret.

Her eyes narrowed. *Where is the relief?*

Wasn't this what he had been waiting for? Her confession – her willingness to take responsibility for what had happened?

As they stood there staring at each other, a jovial voice sounded faintly as though coming from very far away.

'Guys!' It was Adam. 'Come and have some of Eve's crepes for dessert. They're absolutely delicious.'

Heath's hands fell from her shoulders and Tash looked across at her family as though surfacing from a dream. Adam was holding up a big plate of crepes and a jar of maple syrup. Everyone was watching them expectantly, except Eve, whose blushing gaze was on her lap.

'Er, great. Okay,' Tash muttered mechanically. She crossed the floor to the main counter where everyone was sitting, not bothering to check if Heath followed her. She had said what she needed to say and now all she wanted was to get away from him. Perhaps, since Heath had scored his absolution from all blame, he would stop trying to torment her and just leave her alone. She could live this lie for four weeks for her family's sake. But not if he was constantly playing games.

She took a seat next to Eve and a crepe already smeared with maple syrup appeared on a plate in front of her. It was indeed delicious and the first bite instantly made her feel better. Heath went to the window to make tea. She was surprised but grateful when he also brought back a steaming mug for her.

'Thanks,' she murmured.

Fortunately, he did not sit next to her. Eve, who had witnessed the exchange, leaned close and bumped her arm with Tash's.

'Sorry for interrupting your moment with Heath,' she murmured. 'I wouldn't say the crepes are that great. Adam was just trying to be annoying.'

'Your crepes are great,' she disagreed resolutely. 'And I wasn't having a moment with Heath.'

Eve's eyelashes fluttered. 'Oh, okay. I just thought . . .' Her voice trailed off sheepishly. 'But then what do I know about romance?'

Their mother, who always listened in at the moment you least wanted her to, snorted. 'For all that romance, I'm yet to see one grandchild. When are you two going to get your skates on? Tell me that.'

It was the straw that broke the camel's back. 'Trust me, Mum,' Tash said shortly, 'you'll be the first to know.' And then she stood up, her limbs stiff and shaky. 'You know, it's such a gorgeous day, I might take this tea outside.'

And so she did, hoping for a little space from everyone and everything. She had completely forgotten that Phoebe and Spider had also retreated outside and was momentarily disappointed to see her sister standing out there on the gravel until she took in the look in her eyes. She'd seen that expression before.

In the mirror.

The fearless optimist was not looking quite so fearless at that moment or very optimistic either, which immediately made her forget her own worries. 'Where's Spider?' she asked.

'Taking another break.' The heaviness in Phoebe's tone said it all.

After her complete lack of sensitivity towards Eve, she wasn't going to make the mistake of glossing over whatever was bothering Phoebe. She sat down on the park bench too and made her sister tell her everything. What a mess of a story it was, and that was without the bits Phoebe didn't know. It looked like Spider was already up to his old tricks, given Phoebe had intercepted the note recently. She didn't think Eve was devious or selfish enough to continue to pursue Spider while he was engaged to her sister.

This time, however, Spider had Natasha Maxwell to deal with as well. And nobody, nobody, was going to make a fool out of one of her sisters. The stake-out would open Phoebe's eyes. It was becoming clearer and clearer that this was exactly what she needed. The girl was too in love with him to simply be told. She wouldn't believe it.

And yes, it was all well and good for Phoebe to be a positive person and always believe the very best of people but her faith in Spider was ridiculous after everything he'd done.

Although she remembered that her dad had said he couldn't prove Spider started the fire. Not that that lessened her anger. His affair with Eve had been real enough, and it was about time his true character was revealed.

As though to sweeten the deal, Eve walked out of the restaurant just then and spied them both sitting on the park bench. Her steps slowed and her mouth formed an apologetic Oh. 'I'm sorry. I didn't realise you were talking.'

Tash stood up, expelling a breath as she turned around. Misinterpreting her frustration, Eve's face comically morphed from apologetic to stricken. 'Seriously,' she started to back away, 'I'll just go.'

'Eve, will you stop bloody apologising to me. Hell, stop apologising to everyone.'

'Sorry, I –'

'Eve!'

'S– I mean, okay. *All right*. I won't.' To Tash's satisfaction, she seemed to stand taller.

'Good,' Tash nodded. 'And come over here because you're just the person we need.'

'She is?' Phoebe stood up.

'I am?'

'Well, I think so,' Tash smiled, and for the first time since she had arrived her heart felt lighter. 'We're going on an adventure.'

'An adventure?' Eve squeaked. 'I don't know. Do we really need an adventure right now with everything else that's going on?'

Tash grinned. 'What are you? Chicken?'

Eve paused. 'Er . . . yes.'

They all laughed, including her.

'Well, I won't have it,' Tash shook her finger. 'You're a Maxwell and we're much braver than that.'

'You mean madder,' Phoebe murmured.

'Whatever,' Tash lifted her chin, 'it's all the same.'

'So what exactly are we doing?' Eve asked.

'A Maxwell sisters' stake-out, to be precise. It's at the Wildwood Bakery,' Tash informed her.

At last, a smile curved Phoebe's mouth and that sparkle of hope that had been missing a minute earlier returned. The dimple in her cheek peeped. 'It's top secret.'

'Very,' Tash nodded. 'Club members only.'

'Club members only,' Eve whispered.

'Are you in?' Phoebe enquired.

'Yes,' Eve nodded adamantly. 'Yes, I am.'

# Chapter 21

The return to sisterhood would have been an enormous boost to Eve's confidence had she not spent all morning fending off harassment from Adonis and stalking from Spider. She didn't know which was worse, Adonis's rascally advances or Spider pleading for advice about her sister.

With Spider, she had already made the decision to take a step back and had not responded to his earlier text message. When she returned to her bedroom at six am, stashing the blanket she had accidentally stolen from Adonis under her bed, it was to find three more messages added to the first.

I really need your advice.

Can I talk to you sometime this morning?

Your sister is doing my head in!

Given her eventful night, she hadn't been able to go back to sleep and so had sat on her bed for half an hour, thinking about how she should respond. It was strange how her encounter with Adonis in the wee hours had given her an insight into how she should move forward.

She had told the Greek God of the vineyard that she didn't want to be his friend.

It had been hard but symbolic. Symbolic because she didn't want to be used again. She knew that if she started hanging out with Adonis, she'd develop a crush on him. Hell! She may already have one. The man was too good-looking, too charming and he knew it. He'd end up basking in her admiration and abusing it, just the way Spider had.

Well, perhaps 'abusing' was too harsh a word. She was sure Spider hadn't intentionally strung her along. He didn't know she had feelings for him. And if someone just happened to be there for you whenever you needed them, why shouldn't you take them up on their offer? He was only human. How was he to know that encouraging her only gave her hope. No, he wouldn't have taken advantage of her like that. Spider wasn't that sort of man. It didn't change the fact, however, that she'd just spent the last five years being his prop, his fall-back and his 'fill in' when no one else was available. She just couldn't do it any more. Not for him and certainly not for anyone else.

Now sitting there, looking at his text messages, she realised it really was time to cut him loose. The same way she had cut Adonis off. She couldn't keep being 'there' for him – and she needed to tell him so. Besides the fact that even if she was still going to continue in the role of his best friend, was it appropriate for her to know intimate details of his relationship with her sister? Details that Phoebe hadn't even decided to confide in her? All these text messages seemed so underhanded. She hesitated before eventually texting.

Sorry Spider, I don't think I should get involved in your fight given Phee is also my sister. But if I were you, just be patient with her, speak your mind and you'll be fine.

*There. That should do it.*

Not a complete brush-off, but definitely a 'sort it out yourself'. He should get the message.

But he didn't. At breakfast, he'd tried to speak to her alone when the rest of the family wasn't looking. Passing her a cup of coffee with a troubled smile. 'Did you get my messages?'

'Yes,' she nodded. 'Did you get mine?'

He frowned as she walked away and sat down at the breakfast table next to Phoebe, which was just as much of a mistake.

'So I was thinking,' the youngest Maxwell child addressed the gathered group, 'about the food for the wedding.'

'An excellent point to discuss,' Anita immediately encouraged her. 'Because I have been pondering it myself.'

'It seems silly to get a caterer to supply the food when we have a whole kitchen sitting there,' Phoebe explained.

For once, Patricia seemed to agree. 'Yes, and it won't be as nice if it's prepared elsewhere and then brought in. I mean, I assume that you're not having a buffet.'

Anita frowned. 'What's wrong with a buffet?'

'*Anyway*,' Phoebe quickly interrupted, 'Spider and I were talking about this a week ago before you all arrived and we think we've hit upon a solution.' She glanced in Eve's direction.

Eve immediately felt the hairs on the back of her neck rise.

*Uh-o. What's going on here?*

'I think,' Phoebe began slowly, 'we could assemble the old restaurant team just for one night. They all still live and work locally. I'm sure they'd be willing to do us a favour. Paid, of course.'

*What?*

Eve gulped in air, for some reason feeling both pressured and violated at the same time.

'Oh, I don't mean you or Spider, Eve,' Phoebe carelessly tossed the comment in her direction. 'But if we could get some of the other chefs back in, they already know all your signature dishes. Spider and I could choose our favourites from your old menu. It would be perfect.'

The cords in Eve's neck tightened. The restaurant was her baby, her dream and her disaster gone wrong. Her father had promised her that it would remain untouched until she was ready. It wasn't for Phoebe or Spider to come in and resurrect it at the drop of a hat. Sure, she'd never had a problem with them using the actual seating area, but the kitchen . . .

'Dad promised me –'

'Eve,' Phoebe interrupted her, 'this is not about getting the restaurant going again. Of course, that's your decision.' She smiled as though the topic was a complete non-issue. 'It's just for one night. Who knows? You may feel nostalgic enough to keep it going.'

As she finished speaking, all eyes at the table turned towards Eve in hopeful anticipation.

*Great! It's a coup.*

She ground her teeth. 'I'm not ready.'

Her mother grunted. Phoebe turned back to the group. 'Well, at least it'll be like old times just for one night. Now I think I'm going to rush over to the restaurant. I really want to see those beams arrive.'

As she left, Eve stuck her spoon into her Weet-Bix, staring at her food until it swam. They just didn't get it, did they? She couldn't just pick up where she left off. There were other reasons the restaurant had closed apart from the fire. Her incompetence, to name just one. These reasons didn't get cancelled out just because Phoebe decided to get married. And pressuring her didn't help. It just made her feel more like running than ever. She didn't want to see the restaurant open again. Bringing back memories she couldn't face – not just about Spider but about herself as well.

Fortunately, Graeme changed the subject, trying rather unsuccessfully to engage her mother and his wife in conversation about the latest political scandal. Patricia ignored him and turned to her son.

'I was thinking about going into town today and having a little scout around for that Justice of the Peace. What do you think, Spider?'

He nodded without even looking at his mother. 'Sounds good,' he said, while still gazing pensively at Eve. She wished he wouldn't. There was definitely nothing more she wished to speak to him about. And in light of his complete insensitivity with reviving the restaurant for one night, she was happy to completely ignore him.

Anita, who had been pouring Patricia a cup of tea, immediately stopped at a quarter cup and put the teapot down.

'But we will need to consult with Phoebe also,' she said firmly. 'She may not want a secular minister.'

'I've already spoken to her,' Patricia said airily. 'She's fine with it. Can I have a little more tea please?'

Anita refused to pick up the teapot again. 'When? When did you speak to her?'

'Last night, before bed.' Patricia reached for the teapot and Anita pulled it out of her reach.

'Yes, well she was very tired then and quite unable to know her own mind. Let me talk to her. I'm sure I will get the true story,' Anita nodded decisively. 'In any event, today we are focusing on the restaurant, not the celebrants.'

Patricia chuckled. 'Oh, as to that, I'm certain I'll be quite useless in the restaurant. I'm a terrible handyman, aren't I, Graeme?'

Graeme smiled. 'I'd have to agree with you there.'

'Be that as it may,' Anita agreed sweetly, 'you will still want to help out, no doubt.' Then she removed the teapot completely from the table and returned it to the counter.

After that, Eve couldn't get out of there quick enough. Though, had she but known it, the breakfast table ended up being the least confrontational place for her that day.

She had hoped that Adonis would be far too busy inspecting the vines or cleaning fermentation tanks in the winery to join them that morning. But the unpredictable winemaker had showed up at ten o'clock with one of his men in tow. He looked as handsome as ever. Unshowered and bare chested had been a complete turn-on, but dressed in jeans that moulded his perfectly formed rear into a work of art was only going to keep her senses buzzing at a high frequency.

At least for the most part he seemed inclined to ignore her and she didn't know whether to be annoyed or grateful that he appeared to be taking her request 'not to be friends' rather seriously. He got straight into work after a very brief hello to everyone, and did not engage her at all.

But there was nothing more damaging to a resolution to not have a crush on this man than to watch him work. Especially when said work involved a lot of bending and lifting and stretching and reaching. If there was a muscle in his body she had not seen rippling yet, it would be a bloody miracle. Unfortunately, her secret glances in his direction mustn't have been so secret because on her fourth furtive look over he raised his eyes, gazing directly at her and gave her a wink so lecherous that she had absolutely no idea where to look.

Her heart aflutter, she quickly turned around and stumbled straight into Spider. He had been standing right behind her, in the same stalkerish fashion he had employed in the kitchen earlier that morning.

'I'm glad I caught you,' he whispered. 'We need to talk.'

She stiffened in his hands, momentarily stunned. 'Huh?'

'I got your message,' he said urgently. 'And I understand you want to stay out of it but you know her better than anyone.'

'Yes, I do,' she nodded. 'And that's why I can't be involved. Look, Spider, if you're angry about something, tell her, not me.'

She tried to wriggle out of his grasp, but he held her there, those brown eyes that were always so soft, narrowed. 'What's got into you?'

'Nothing's got into me,' she said crossly. 'Can you let me go please? I think we should get back to work.'

Spider shook his head. 'Something has definitely changed.'

'Is everything okay here?'

Adonis walked over to them and Spider dropped his hands, a rather sheepish expression on his face. 'Yeah, mate, everything's fine. Just talking.' A rather suspicious-looking blush spread across his features as he waited for Adonis to move on. But the winemaker didn't. To Eve's dismay, he continued to stand there, widening his feet and slowly folding his arms as he watched them silently. Eve tried to throw him a 'we're fine' look but he ignored her, his gaze remaining firmly on her sister's fiancé. Spider's hand snaked awkwardly into his floppy fringe, pushing it out of his eyes. He cleared his throat. 'Well, I suppose we better get back to work then.'

'Yes,' Adonis nodded with uncalled-for satisfaction as Spider awkwardly moved on. As soon as the man was out of earshot he turned back to her. 'What was *that* all about?'

She lifted her chin. 'Nothing.'

'Looked pretty hot and heavy to me.'

'Hot and heavy!' Eve gasped. '*Hardly*. He's just worried about Phoebe.'

'And you were consoling him.' He made it sound like she was half naked while she was doing it.

'Yes,' she waved her hand. 'I mean, no. I mean, how is this any of your business?'

'Since I helped you get rid of him –' he graciously inclined his head – 'no need to thank me by the way.'

'Good, because I wasn't going to,' she retorted. 'I didn't need your help. I had things well in hand.'

'Really? Because it looked more like he had you *well in hand*.' He folded his arms across his broad chest and sighed as though talking to a wayward child. 'I thought you were over the whole seducing your sister's fiancé thing.'

She gasped. 'I am. I mean, I never was into that.' She softened her tone. 'And will you please keep your voice down? Someone might hear you.'

'Relax, no one is listening.'

She glanced over his shoulder and noticed Eric watching them curiously.

'As a matter of fact they are.' She wrung her hands. 'Perhaps we should get back to work. I don't know why we need to talk about this now anyway.'

Adonis shrugged. 'I guess we don't.' His eyes twinkled. 'I'd much prefer to know when you're next cooking me breakfast. Gotta say, I really enjoyed the last one.'

'Ssssh.' She glanced at Eric again. 'You haven't lowered your voice.'

'Quite a nervous little thing, aren't you?' he murmured.

'I don't want anyone to find out what happened between us last night.'

*Especially after that conversation with Phee at breakfast.*

His lips twitched in amusement. 'Did something happen between us last night? I thought we behaved very platonically, given the temptation.'

She blushed bright red, a shot of embarrassment like whisky burning straight through her. 'No, I don't mean like that –'

He laughed as her tongue tied itself further into a knot. She took a deep breath. 'I *meant*,' she straightened, 'I don't want them to know I've been cooking in the restaurant again.'

'Why not?' He tilted his head. 'They'd love to know that.'

She steeled herself against the panic that instantly tightened her ribcage. '*Exactly*. It'll put their hopes up and they'll just increase their pressure on me.'

'Pressure? What sort of pressure?'

'Pressure to get the restaurant going again,' she said impatiently. 'I wish you would just get back to work.'

'But we haven't finished talking yet,' he protested. 'I'm finding this whole restaurant thing fascinating.'

She rolled her eyes. 'You're just saying that to annoy me. But you can't tell anyone else I was cooking in there. Promise me.'

He leaned back against the wall and studied her in a way she definitely did not like. His lips curled in a devious manner and his expression held the anticipation of one who knew delights were in store.

She glared at him. 'What?'

His eyebrows jumped. 'Only *friends* keep secrets for each

other and we're just acquaintances, remember, because you don't want to be my friend.'

She groaned, shutting her eyes.

'Just while we're on the topic,' his thumb and forefinger rubbed the stubble on his jaw, 'why exactly don't you want to be my friend again?'

She put her hands to her hips. 'Because you're an insufferable, annoying, tactless oaf of a man and I'd rather not have the work.'

'Ouch,' he nodded, straightening. 'Well, I guess that does kind of put a dampener on our relationship. But where does that leave your secret?'

'Okay, fine.' She gritted her teeth. 'You want to be my friend, be my friend.' She flicked the offer to him like stale bread to a duck. 'You're on Facebook, right?'

He laughed. 'Thanks, but I think I'll pass. Friendship is supposed to be reciprocal, you know. Perhaps I'd prefer something else as payment instead.'

'Like what?'

'Like that breakfast I mentioned.'

'You want me to cook for you again?' She blinked.

'I do like your crepes. And your eggs, too, for that matter.'

'No way.' Her nerves couldn't take another intimate meal with a half-naked Greek God.

'Are you sure?'

'Positive.'

Her eyes shot daggers at him as she mouthed the words 'Cook-your-own'.

His gaze turned innocent. 'I thought you were serious about me keeping that secret.'

'I do realise this is all one big joke to you.' Her voice trembled ever so slightly. 'But you could at least have the decency to respect my privacy without trying to blackmail me.'

'This is not blackmail,' he protested. 'I haven't said "or else" yet.'

To her great frustration, just at that moment, Eric approached them with a couple of plastic bottles of water.

'I noticed you guys were taking a break,' he said cheerfully. 'Thirsty?'

'Thanks,' Eve nodded, reaching for a bottle and taking a gulp.

'No thanks, mate,' Adonis declined politely. 'I have been meaning to get back to work for the last five minutes but this girl can talk the leg off a chair.' He patted her on the back, causing her to choke on her water.

'Go easy on him, okay?' He winked before strolling off, hands casually inserted in the pockets of his jeans.

Her eyes couldn't help but follow him, an emotion somewhere between fury and arousal making her grit her teeth.

'I know he can be hard to take sometimes,' Eric remarked with all the wisdom of a teenager, 'but he's a good guy.'

She turned to him in surprise. 'Is that so?'

'Yeah.' Eric nodded self-consciously, hesitated and then said, 'He's been great to me since he started here and all the vineyard workers love him because he's completely accepted your dad's philosophies – including the more "out there" ones. Even the cellar rats aren't giving him a hard time any more.'

'Were they doing that to start with?' she asked, curious.

'A little at first,' Eric replied. 'Jealousy, I suppose.'

'Oh,' she said, wondering how to prolong the conversation. Despite herself, all this behind-the-scenes information about Adonis was really quite interesting.

She could tell Eric worshipped the ground he walked on, which she supposed wasn't unnatural for an impressionable young man. Attention from a guy like Adonis would definitely have lifted his self-esteem. She just hadn't picked Adonis as the 'supporting the underdog' type. But maybe 'underdog' was too harsh a word.

In many ways, Eric reminded her of herself. He was a quiet achiever who blended so well into the background that he was often just part of the garden he tended so lovingly. People like that needed to know they were appreciated, otherwise they fell between the cracks. She knew what that was like.

She smiled warmly at him. 'So how have you been anyway, Eric?'

He grinned at her. 'You know me. Same old, same old. How's Margareta's?'

Her city job seemed so far away now it took her a second to answer. 'It's fine, thanks. I'm really enjoying it there.' A shard lodged in her throat. '*Can't wait* to get back.'

He seemed intrigued. 'So no plans to return to Tawny Brooks any time soon then?'

She shook her head. 'Not really.'

'Well, you never know.' He smiled. 'When the restaurant is re-done you may change your mind.'

*And there's that pressure again.*

'Maybe.' She tried to smile and moved away to re-submerge herself in work.

After that, it was an agony to get through the morning. At lunch, her chicken roll tasted like cardboard and all Adonis's high praise about her crepes didn't help matters either. She was sure he was purposely trying to rile her – make her think he was going to say something and then not. As soon as she was able to get away, she ducked outside, hoping to get some fresh air and regroup for that afternoon's game of cat and mouse, when she was waylaid by her sisters.

Not that this had turned out to be a bad thing.

They had had their first real conversation in a long time. And planned their first real outing in over a year. Although she didn't fully understand exactly what it was all about, she was definitely going along.

'I don't want to say too much in case I'm wrong,' Phoebe had tried to explain. 'I just need you there to support me.'

Her younger sister appeared quite subdued and Tash seemed to want to remain mysterious – which she supposed hiked up the adventure angle. In any event, Eve was happy to take the outing over more work at the restaurant. An afternoon with her sisters was much less stressful than another three hours shifting timber with Adonis.

'Let's go early and secure ourselves a good vantage point,' Tash suggested.

'Can I at least know the name of the person we're spying on?' Eve enquired.

Phoebe and Tash exchanged a look. Then Phoebe said, 'We don't know her name. But it's a woman. And I'll know her when I see her.'

The car ride from Yallingup to Dunsborough was accomplished fairly quickly. How many times had the three of them hit the road like this, in search of adventure? Flanked by tall trees, the road was dappled by sunshine. The signs on the red gravel shoulders were a continuous offering of treats, wineries galore, lookout points and quiet coves for an undisturbed swim. Eve couldn't decide what she liked better, the never-ending celebration of food and wine or the promise of a breezy seascape – white sand between her toes and foamy blue surf.

'What we should really do one day is have a picnic at one of the caves,' Tash suggested as they passed the sign post for Ngilgi Cave. It was one of the gorgeous, naturally occurring limestone caves in the region. Perfect if one desired both adventure and a gawk at some of Australia's most beautiful rock formations.

'It's been absolutely years since I've been there,' Phoebe agreed. 'It would be heaps of fun to make a day of it.'

'Not at all like *Picnic at Hanging Rock*,' Eve returned wryly from the backseat.

Tash laughed. 'You say that because of your experience at Mammoth.'

'I don't know what you could possibly mean,' Eve grinned, though she still shuddered at the childhood memory. Aged six, she'd been exploring Mammoth Cave and got lost in it. Not for very long. It was probably no more than half an hour before her family had found her again, but her mother had been beside herself. And for a little kid, surrounded by stalactite and stalagmite formations flickering with shadows, it had certainly made a lasting impression.

Dunsborough was a quiet coastal town – a much-loved long-weekend destination for Perth dwellers. With a small population of just over three thousand people, the widely spread town centred around a large roundabout flanked on one side by parkland. In the summer months, the small boutiques and country-style stores tended to overflow with tourists into the park. School leavers, families and wine connoisseurs alike could all be seen hanging round, eating a pie or planning their next escapade. With the beach on its doorstep and the best access to all the fresh produce in the region, Dunsborough was the likely place to stop no matter what your intention in town. With the summer school holidays over, however, the park was empty.

Eve's favourite place there was the Wildwood Bakery. They made delicious cakes but were most famous for their hot pastries. The humble sausage roll was king in town. No one could touch the recipe. Not even her – and it wasn't like she hadn't tried.

Tash parked the car and they all got out. A couple of heads turned and a few hands lifted to wave as they crossed the car park to the bakery. It was a rare occurrence these days to see all three Maxwell sisters in town together.

Mrs Alice Honey, the owner of the bakery, who was very aptly named, beamed at them when they walked through the door. She was all round and rosy, with treacle-coloured hair tucked under a net.

'Well, what do you know, it's Mad Maxwell's daughters, all together no less!'

'Alice!' Tash came behind the counter to give her a hug. 'It's been ages.'

'Hasn't it though,' she nodded, her eyes darting from one to the other. 'You girls all look incredible. You'll stop traffic walking across the park like that.'

Eve laughed. 'What traffic?'

'Well, there's me for a start.' The girls turned to find another childhood friend standing behind them. Ben Gould, a charming, friendly faced winemaker who also grew his grapes locally.

'Oh hey!'

They crowded round him, hugging him in turn. 'How's the wife? How's the kids? How's Blind Corner?' This was the name of Ben's winery.

Laugh lines creased around Ben's eyes. 'Busy. Busy. Busy. You should stop by some time. I bet you my cabernet sauvignon will give your father's a run for his money.'

Phoebe snorted. 'We'll see.'

They all placed their orders. Alice handed Ben his coffee first as he wanted to rush off to an appointment he was late for. Then she busied herself with making coffee for the girls.

As Ben said goodbye and walked off, Phoebe nudged Eve in the ribs. 'See, you should go for someone like him. Someone nice.'

It really *was* like stepping back in time. Phee and Tash, both with their steady boyfriends, urging her to put herself out there. She had always been the girl who got the 'I can't believe you're still single' speech, though she'd been shyer back then than she was now – if that was even possible.

It was funny how six years ago she'd thought Spider was the safe choice. Well, she'd been right about one thing. Unrequited love was safe. Very, *very* safe. She looked up to find Phoebe studying the emotions playing across her face.

She shouldn't have zoned out. Now her younger sister was looking all concerned.

*And you know what that means.* A lecture and a lot of unsolicited advice was coming.

'Actually,' Phoebe said as though to confirm her fears, 'I can't remember the last time you had a boyfriend, Eve. What are you waiting for?'

'Nothing.' Eve lifted her chin.

Tash laid a hand on her arm, recalling her attention. She had a weird expression on her face, like she knew more than she was letting on.

*Which is insane.*

Her elder sister had been as distant as China lately.

'I believe,' Tash said slowly, 'you need to think outside the box more, Eve. Mix it up a bit.'

Unbidden, Adonis's cheeky smile popped into her head and she groaned. 'I think I'm okay with being single for the moment,' she said firmly. 'In fact, I'm really set on the lifestyle.'

Tash's mouth twisted. 'It is true. One doesn't need a man to function.'

Eve nodded. 'I can do what I want. Go where I want. Be what I want. No anchors.' She tried a convincing head toss to punctuate her words. Unfortunately some hair whipped into her mouth, making her spit and cough rather unattractively.

*Why does that always work when Phoebe does it?*

'Er . . . Good for you.' Tash chuckled.

Phoebe wasn't as impressed. 'I don't buy it.'

Just when Eve thought that this time she wouldn't be able to save herself from her sister's all-time favourite subject – How to save Eve's love life – Alice returned to the counter with takeaway coffees and three sausage rolls.

They took their food outside to the park, about a hundred metres from Wildwood Bakery. The bakery had a lovely half-enclosed alfresco area that was completely in view from anywhere on the grass. They didn't want to be seen by their target, who was due at the bakery in half an hour.

'This way,' Tash said knowledgeably as they sat down under the shade of a gorgeous gum. 'We'll see them but they probably won't notice us.'

Opening up her paper bag, Eve pulled her sausage roll out and took a bite. Some of the delicious pastry flaked off and fell on the grass; the sausage meat inside steamed attractively. It was as delicious as she remembered. A sense of well-being overtook her as they sat there together, not talking, just eating.

When Phoebe finally opened the floor for small talk, it was easy. Maybe because they steered clear of all touchy subjects – the wedding, the family and the restaurant. It was like an unspoken agreement and she remembered how good they'd been at that. Always seeming to know what each other needed without voicing it.

They did have a good laugh about an old high school story though and shared some funny speculations on whatever happened to Melissa, the girl they'd all loved to hate.

It had been so difficult to come home, but it seemed worth it now. She had needed to see her sisters again. And Spider too. Sitting under the shade of the gum tree, the problems they were all having seemed to fade in significance. Or maybe that was just the comfort food talking.

'Do you think that's her?' Tash asked suddenly.

'Who? Where?' Phoebe sat up straighter, dusting pastry off her fingers.

'She just entered and is ordering something.' Tash sat up on her heels, shading her eyes. 'We should have brought binoculars.'

Eve giggled. 'We're not that far away. And don't you think it would have been a little obvious if we had?'

'Good point,' Tash agreed.

'I can't see her.' Phoebe shook her head. 'Why do you think it's her?'

'Well, it's nearly three. She's the only female apart from Alice in the bakery . . . *and* she's young and gorgeous.'

'Oh.' Phoebe's shoulders slumped.

'Have a look.' Tash patted her shoulder. 'See what you think. She's sitting down in the alfresco area with a takeaway coffee – short blonde hair, tall and skinny.'

Phoebe shaded her eyes to examine the scene. Eve looked over as well. The woman had short curly hair that covered her head in an elf-like style. She sat primly reading through a few pages in a slim file that she had with her, delicately sipping her coffee. Eve didn't recognise her.

'Are we supposed to recognise this person?' she asked hesitantly. As usual, Phoebe and Tash seemed to know the whole story while she was left to feel her way around in the dark.

'Yes,' Phoebe groaned, 'we are supposed to know her and we do. I mean, *I do*! She's been in town for a while. She's one of Claudia's friends and is staying at Oak Hills.'

'You've met her?' Tash raised her eyebrows.

'Yes,' Phoebe frowned. 'She's very nice. Her name is Bronwyn Eddings. I can't believe it. I won't believe it.'

'Believe what?' Eve demanded.

Phoebe looked stricken as she turned her gaze upon her. 'That Spider is having an affair with her.'

'What? That's mad.'

'Really?' Phoebe enquired. 'You really think so? Because he's been pulling away a lot lately.'

Eve's mind boggled. 'He's hurt about your behaviour, not having an affair.'

'My behaviour?' Phoebe's eyes widened.

*Damn it! You said you weren't getting involved.*

'So you know something I don't?' Phoebe glared at her.

Eve put her hands up, happy to surrender immediately. 'No, of course not. I'm just trying to say that Spider is sulking at the moment, not cheating.'

Phoebe's lips pursed and Eve added for good measure, 'He's fully dedicated to you. Always has been.' She lowered her eyes. 'Believe me, *I would know*.'

'Yes, yes.' Phoebe frowned. 'I get it. You're his best friend, he confides in you. But do you think he would tell you about an affair when you're my sister?'

Eve was growing cross. 'Why are you getting all annoyed with me? I'm trying to reassure you.'

'You just accused me of bad behaviour.' Phoebe put her hand on her hips. 'I want to know what you mean by that.'

'Nothing. I just thought maybe you could have handled the wedding preparations better.'

'Did he say that to you?'

Luckily, she was saved from answering when Phoebe's phone rang, though it seemed at first that Phoebe didn't want to answer it. She opened her mouth to say something further to Eve then shut it indecisively as her phone kept ringing. Was it possible that her younger sister was more intimidated by Eve's friendship with Spider than she let on? Finally, Phoebe yanked the phone out of her handbag to switch it off when she spotted the caller ID.

'It's Spider,' she whispered. 'Should I answer it?'

'Of course you should answer it,' Tash nodded. 'Ask him where he is.'

Phoebe put the phone to her ear cautiously. 'Hello?'

There was silence as she listened a moment to what he was saying. 'I'm in town. Where are you?' She mouthed, 'He's back home.'

Eve watched Phoebe's eyes start to mist as Spider continued talking and couldn't help but feel a lump develop in her throat. At one time she had wanted Spider for herself, but if he broke her sister's heart, she would never forgive him.

'I know.' Phoebe shut her eyes as a single tear rolled down her cheek. 'I'd like to talk too.' She covered the mouthpiece to address her sisters. 'I might just take this over here if you don't mind.'

Eve and Tash nodded and she stood up to take the call privately. Strolling over to another gum further away from the bakery, she leaned against the tree.

'Well, I gotta say,' Tash's voice sounded cynical, 'that's a relief.'

'Spider would never have an affair,' Eve announced adamantly. 'He loves her too much. What he craves more than anything is more of her attention.'

She looked over at Tash, who was eyeing her carefully, as though searching for the right words to respond.

'I just want Phoebe to marry a man she can trust,' her big sister finally said.

'Me too.'

'Then I hope those two work this out,' Tash agreed, her gaze straying back to the bakery where Bronwyn Eddings was still sipping coffee. Just at that moment someone else arrived. He sat down at Bronwyn's table, his face wrinkling briefly in an offbeat smile that seemed both casual and intimate at the same time. Bronwyn covered his hand reassuringly, holding on to it for a little too long before letting go.

Tash gasped. Eve looked in the direction of Tash's stunned gaze. 'Wha–?'

And then so many things crystallised in that one awful moment. His midlife crisis. His constant disappearing acts. Her mother feeling like he was keeping something from her.

'You've got to be kidding,' Eve cried as her eyes once again darted across the scene in front of her. 'Dad's the one having the affair?'

# Chapter 22

Tash's mind was reeling.

'Are you seeing this?' Eve whispered as Bronwyn reached over and held their father's hand again.

He was gazing at her like she was his lifeline – the answer to all his prayers. He took a blue velvet jewellery box from the inside pocket of his jacket. It was the one she had seen in his study. He passed it across the table.

'Is that . . .?' Eve gasped. 'Is that jewellery?'

'Yes,' Tash responded even before Bronwyn opened it and smiled mistily. She felt completely numb, unable to move. The hairs on the back of her neck had risen to spikes and a wave of nausea washed through her. 'I can't believe this and yet it makes perfect sense.'

Eve's eyes widened. 'I know, right? This is the secret he's been hiding.'

'He told me this morning that you can't sit in the same place you've always been and wonder why you're not having fun any more,' Tash continued.

'Mum says he's always disappearing, sometimes for hours

on end,' Eve added, glaring at the happy couple again with a shake of her head. 'Now we know where he's been. I bet you he hasn't been hanging out with Horace at all.'

'No,' Tash agreed.

They were both silent for a moment. Eve plucked at the grass beside her legs awkwardly. She glanced over at Phoebe, who was still on the other side of the park, in conversation with Spider. Her sister hadn't noticed their father rock up to the bakery yet.

'Should we tell Phoebe?'

Tash shuddered. 'No, she's having a hard enough time with Spider and the wedding. Besides the fact that it would just crush her.'

Eve nodded. 'I'm not doing so good myself.'

'Me neither.' Tash shook her head. The whole scenario was so surreal. But she could hardly deny that all the pieces of the puzzle concerning her father were finally falling into place. She felt sick. He wasn't just cheating on her mum, he was cheating on their family, on her sisters. He was going against everything he had ever taught them about loyalty.

*How could he do this?*

She must have said this out loud because Eve muttered two words, 'Midlife crisis.'

'That's not an excuse.'

'For him it is.' Eve tore her gaze from the scene at the bakery and breathed deep. Though she was putting on a brave front, Natasha could see how affected Eve was. She was as white as chalk.

'Hey,' she held out her hand, taking Eve's and squeezing it, 'we're going to figure this out.'

'How? What's our next move?'

For once, Tash did not have a plan ready. She had no idea what was correct protocol for moving forward from this point. She stared blankly into space, unable to find her voice.

Eve seemed to grow even more worried by her silence. 'Tash? Do we sit on this? Or do we confront them?'

'What do you think?'

'What do I think?' Eve swallowed. 'You're asking me?'

'Yes, I'm asking you,' Tash croaked. 'Do we sit on this? Or do we confront them?'

'I don't think we should confront them,' Eve said slowly. 'I mean, I know you're good at that sort of thing but I'm not and a public scene isn't ideal. We wouldn't want the whole town talking about this.'

Tash nodded. 'Good call. We wouldn't want Mum to find out that way either. We have to protect her.'

Eve exhaled in relief. 'For how long?'

Tash finally seemed to be getting her bearings. 'We need to talk to Dad first. See if we can set him straight.'

'Yes,' Eve agreed, 'let's do that. When?'

'Tonight, tomorrow, as soon as possible. Will you come with me?'

'Of course, and not just for moral support. I think I need to hear it from his lips.' She grimaced. 'I just can't believe that he would do this.'

'We never thought he'd retire so early from winemaking either,' Tash said quietly, 'but he did. He's changed since we last saw him, Eve. There's no doubt about that.'

Eve looked at her hands and Tash knew what she was thinking because she was thinking it too. Neither of them had seen their father in over a year because they'd been too busy fighting with each other. If they'd just been more vigilant, more like the caring daughters he'd always known, then maybe he wouldn't have had to turn to Bronwyn Eddings of all people.

'Eve –'

'Tash –'

They both spoke at the same time and grimaced at each other.

'No,' Tash held up her hand, 'let me go first. I'm the one who owes you an apology. I blew up at you way too fast after the restaurant fire. I made all sorts of judgements and assumptions. All I thought about was the money and I was completely insensitive.'

'You were just worried about our parents.'

'I was.' Tash nodded. 'But I was concerned about you too, Eve.'

Her sister seemed to clasp her hands a little too tightly in her lap. 'You were?'

'Of course. The restaurant was your dream. And you were so good at it. I didn't want to see you throw it all away.'

'I wasn't good at it,' Eve blinked. 'Spider was.'

Tash gave her the 'Are you for real?' look. And Eve tilted her head defensively.

'Well, it's the truth. After he started losing interest in the restaurant, everything went downhill. Even before the fire.'

'I think you're over-dramatising.'

'No, I'm not.' Eve folded her arms. 'I can't do it without him.'

'Yes you can.'

Eve groaned at her lack of understanding. 'I know I'm a pretty good cook but –'

'Eve,' Tash put her hand up to stop her, 'you are a *bloody fantastic* cook. It's undisputed. You should have your own TV show, not Spider. Though,' she added as Eve opened her mouth to protest, 'I know that's not your thing, the restaurant is. I was always so envious of you.'

'Me?' Eve was startled. 'Why on earth?'

'You had so much talent and you were getting to live your dream. You know, work in a job that you love with your whole heart and soul. And you can still do that.'

'You love your job too,' Eve protested.

Tash snorted. 'Hardly.'

'You excel at it. You're like a cross between a powerhouse and a bullet train. I thought you loved life in the fast lane.'

'Don't get me wrong,' Tash nodded, 'I don't hate my career, and there are some parts that I do like. But I don't *love* it. I slid into marketing.'

'I don't get it.'

Tash sighed. 'I wanted to move out of home. I wanted to go live in the city. I got good marks at school and it seemed like a good degree at university. It wasn't something I knew I was going to do from childhood. You always knew you wanted to be a chef.'

'That's true,' Eve acknowledged. 'But it doesn't mean that I haven't often had self-doubt.' She winced. 'No more so than right now and since the fire. I just didn't feel I could talk to you about that.'

'Why?' A little spark of hurt pricked.

'Because you're so perfect. I didn't think that you would understand what it means to feel like a failure. You always have it all together.'

Tash gasped. 'I *do not* have it all together. I don't even partly have it all together.'

If there was a minute in time that was perfect to open up to her sister about Heath, this was it. She wanted to and she felt safe to. Talking to Eve, she realised that she didn't need to be invincible all the time. In fact, it was better not to be. If she hadn't been so unapproachable all these years, then maybe Eve would have confided in her earlier. They certainly hadn't had that problem as teenagers. Somewhere between her moving out and getting married they'd lost that intimate connection. It wasn't until sitting across from her right now she realised how much she wanted it back.

The moment, however, was lost when Phoebe suddenly returned to them, dropping down onto the grass beside Tash in the cross-legged position. 'Spider and I had a good talk. I completely overreacted.' She smiled and added, 'Looks like Bronwyn's gone too. I can't believe I thought they were having an affair. That's so ridiculous, right? Spider's just not that kind of person.'

Eve and Tash's gazes quickly swung to the bakery. Their father and his girlfriend had indeed gone.

'Yes,' Tash agreed baldly. 'Absolutely ridiculous.'

Though the words tasted like sawdust in her mouth, she knew better than anyone how easy it was to be fooled by a person you trusted.

On their wedding day, she never would have imagined that Heath was the type of man who could forget a child of his so easily, or find her grief frustrating. It wasn't until they were actually faced with that challenge that she had seen his limitations firsthand.

It was funny how she'd always thought she was such a good judge of character – that she knew her husband through and through. Turned out, he'd never let her in his head. They weren't close like a husband and wife should be. There was an emotional barrier between them that just couldn't be breached. Whatever the case, life had to go on and she couldn't keep beating herself up about failing at the most important relationship in her life. He had not responded when she had tried to reach out. It took two to tango and he was just as much to blame as she was.

The house was fairly quiet that night when the three sisters got home. Spider and Phoebe had decided to take his parents out to another winery for dinner and Adam had not accompanied their father home that evening. So it was only the five of them around the dining table for the evening meal.

'Well, personally,' Anita commented deprecatingly, 'I find it a little insulting that they've decided to go off and eat somewhere else. What's wrong with my cooking?'

'I don't think there's anything wrong with your cooking,' Eve tried to explain to her quietly. 'They probably just wanted to explore the region a little more.'

Their father grinned and added, 'Or maybe they just wanted a little privacy.'

'Privacy?' Anita's eyes widened and Tash wanted to throw the salt shaker at him. Hadn't he done enough damage without purposely provoking their mother as well?

'Why would they need privacy?' Anita demanded, her eyes darting from one person to the next before finally resting on her husband again.

'I wouldn't know,' he responded nonchalantly.

Anita took in his indulgent smile with frustration. It stretched even further when she said, 'That Patricia woman is undoubtedly up to no good, probably trying to press her opinion on them without my knowledge.' She sniffed. 'The last thing any bride needs in her wedding preparation is an interfering third party. I don't know why she can't just keep her head down like the rest of us.'

Eve stared unwaveringly at her plate.

Tash cleared her throat. 'She means well, Mum.'

As she glanced upward, she met Heath's eyes over the salad bowl. They were dancing and that all-too-familiar warmth of intimacy streaked through her. She quickly looked away again, forcing her body to stop tingling.

Annoyingly, straight after dinner, their father left the room as they were clearing the dishes from the table. Natasha hadn't expected that he would be gone long but as they completed their team wash-up effort in the kitchen, she noticed he still hadn't returned. Apparently he had taken himself off to bed. This was highly disappointing given that Eve and Tash had intended to confront him after dinner. It looked like that was out of the question now.

'We'll have to wait until morning,' she whispered to Eve in the hall.

Her sister nodded in agreement.

After that, Tash went to the sitting room and tried to read a book, which was more or less what she expected the others to do. But her mother and Eve went off to the den to watch television instead and before she realised the trap she'd laid for herself, she was alone with Heath. He was on one couch and she on the other, both reclining, propped up with pillows. It could have been a scene from their own home a year earlier. They had always enjoyed reading together. It was almost metaphysical really. Both lost in completely different worlds, yet sharing the experience through companionship. Silence had never been a problem for them. There was comfort in just being around each other and knowing the other was there. Now as she lay there, her feelings took on a whole different form.

Never had being quiet been less easy.

She couldn't relax. In fact, she was getting pins and needles from holding her legs too still. She had read the same damn page at least three times and was about to do so for the fourth time when Heath sat up.

He swung his long legs off the couch onto the floor, throwing his book onto the coffee table so that it skated on the surface before coming to a stop. He leaned forward, lacing his hands loosely between his legs.

'I think we need to finish the conversation we were having in the restaurant this morning.'

'I thought we were finished.' She didn't look up from her book, pretending to be thoroughly engrossed.

'Come on, Tash,' he rasped. 'Put that down. I know you're not reading it.'

She finally looked up. 'What do you want from me, Heath? Another confession? I'm sorry, I'm all out of those today.'

He shook his head with a frown. 'No, of course not. I didn't want the confession you gave me this morning. Frankly, it took me completely by surprise.'

With a heavy sigh, she shut her book, hugging it to her chest and staring at the ceiling. 'Why?'

'Because I had no idea you thought I blamed you for our child's death. *Worse*, that you believed it yourself.'

After a long pause she asked, 'Well, isn't it the truth?'

'No, the loss of our child was caused by chromosomal abnormalities, which is just an unexplained problem with its DNA that basically caused it to stop growing.' It was like stepping back in time, witnessing his complete lack of compassion as he repeated to her once more the doctor's diagnosis – calling their child 'it' rather than 'she'. He had done this often, as though trying to snap her out of a trance that she knew she was not in.

'I was there, Heath. I heard what the obstetrician said. And telling me again and again and again doesn't make me feel any better.'

'Well, it should!'

She was surprised as his voice suddenly rose in volume and passion. 'Our baby's death was not your fault. It wasn't my fault either. It was just not meant to be. It was God's will.'

Her voice shook. 'Heath, chromosomal abnormalities don't just occur without reason.'

'As a matter of fact they do,' he said crossly. 'And the doctor told us that explicitly, Tash. Nobody knows how or why they occur, they just do. That's it, Tash, that's it. There was nothing you or I could have done differently that would have caused our baby to live.'

'But –'

'For goodness sake, just listen to me for once in your life and stop holding on so tightly to this belief that you can *control everything*.'

These words made her stop, blink and gasp at the sudden moisture collecting in her eyes. It was an echo of the conversation she'd had with her father only that morning. Was she really such a control freak? Did she really believe that she had power over everything? She stood up, as though doing so could help her get away from the question.

'Let it go,' he whispered, also standing. 'Set it free, for your own sake. For mine too.'

Looking up into his eyes, she was surprised to see them shining.

*Have I brought him to tears?*

As he held her gaze she was unable to look away. It was perhaps the first emotional connection they'd had in a very long time. Could it be that he was right? That she had taken too much upon herself? She felt a release so powerful it almost floored her. Her knees wobbled dangerously and suddenly Heath was there, catching her under her elbows.

'Just breathe,' he whispered.

She sucked in a deep breath and looked up into his face, alarmingly close to hers. But she didn't care. Her shoulders were lighter. Her heart seemed to expand in her chest as though it suddenly had more oxygen. Silent tears rolled down her cheeks. With the heaviness of her guilt gone, she had to wonder at the effect of that burden. Had it coloured her interactions with Heath? Regret made her legs want to buckle again.

'You're okay,' Heath said softly, lifting one hand to cradle her face. 'You're okay, Tash.'

And then he bent his head and touched her lips with his own.

There was magic in that kiss.

She put her hands up to his face, to ground herself. Guiding his mouth as much as he was guiding hers.

It had been far too long. Her skin tingled. Her hair stood on end. She felt like she was floating away.

'I'm sorry.' He lifted his head with a growl. 'This isn't going to cut it for me.'

And then suddenly they were heading for the door – her hand tucked firmly in his. He flung it open like a man possessed and tugged her down the hall. A turn right, a turn left and they were standing in front of their bedroom door.

'Heath!'

He opened the door, swung her inside and shoved it closed with his foot. His lips were reconnecting with hers before he finished doing so. He pulled her t-shirt up and over her head. She neither saw nor heard where it dropped as he backed her towards the bed. He unclipped her bra and it fell from her body. Her own hands were at the fly of her jeans, unclasping and unzipping. She pushed them down as one with her knickers over her hips. The backs of her knees hit the bed and she fell onto the soft doona. His strong hands, warm against her skin, pushed her jeans down the rest of the way and off her feet. And then suddenly there she was, naked before him as he stood at the edge of the bed taking her in. His gaze raked every curve and every hollow, making goosebumps rise on her flesh and her heart pound so madly she felt like it was in her throat, choking her. Was this the right thing to do? Doubt seized her and self-consciously she drew her legs up to cover her sex.

'Heath, I don't know about this.'

His gaze grew shuttered and his body stiffened. 'What is it, Tash? More guilt. Aren't we done with that?'

She threw up her hands helplessly, a whole host of emotions desperately fighting for attention. 'Can I trust you again? Can I trust you not to hurt me?'

He sat down on the edge of the bed. 'I don't want to hurt you, Tash. I never wanted to hurt you.'

'So why torture us with these games?'

His eyes widened. 'This is not a game.'

Her laugh was bitter. 'Heath, I know you. And I know how you operate. You're playing for something. I know you are.'

He smiled then, a crooked twist, laced with both sadness and longing. 'I'm playing for you, Tash. And I'm hoping to win.'

He leaned forward, cupping her face to kiss her again, instantly taking away the protest that rose to her lips. He rolled her naked body into his fully clothed one as he kissed her. His jeans-clad leg entwined with hers, rough against her skin but safe in their covered state. She had forgotten what it was like to be completely enveloped by this man. His hand went into her hair, caressed that place on her neck he loved so much and down her back, pausing to feather the base of her spine before his fingers curved under her bottom, hiking her further up his body so that her breasts grazed his shirt.

He lifted his head. 'You're so beautiful.' His fingers caressed the hollow above her hip. 'I've missed you so much. I want to be with you. Please don't deny us this.'

And as she looked into his eyes, warm and brown, she realised how much she had missed him too. When he'd left, a void had opened in her. And she hadn't been able to fill it with anything. Not pep-talks, or visits to her psychologist or strategic goal-setting, which made her feel like she had a handle on things but brought her no peace. She needed him. Without him, all she felt was parched.

Tentatively, she put up a hand to trace the contours of his face. The soft brush of his eyebrows, the angular jut of his cheekbone, the hard line of his mouth.

'I've missed you too.'

And there was a truth in that which she needed to face, which she hadn't wanted to look at too closely since he'd first walked back into her life. She'd made a mistake telling him that she didn't love him any more. Because however much he hurt her, however much the pain of his indifference cut, it hadn't taken away those feelings – it'd just buried them. Now, with her grief-goggles finally off, she was able to see how much she'd tried to hide from her emotions instead of facing them.

She stilled as he lowered his lips to press a kiss to her shoulder, to her collarbone and then to her breast. She gasped and arched in his arms. Liquid fire burned through her body. Her hands went into his hair, pulling at strands as she writhed beneath the gentle nuzzling of his mouth. She found his shoulders and frustratingly his shirt. Her yearning doubled as she realised that he was holding back, giving her the choice to end this now before things got out of hand.

What a joke! As though they could get further out of hand. She wanted him. She loved him. And yes, there was that risk of being hurt again. Of giving it all and getting nothing in return. Like leaping off the side of a cliff with a faulty parachute. But it was too late. Her body had already jumped.

She plucked frantically at the buttons on his shirt, moaned in relief as he helped her yank it off. His pants, too, a few seconds later. And then he lowered his body over hers.

Skin against skin.

The intimacy of first touch was so startling, she cried out with the thrill of it – wrapping herself around him in wild abandonment. He shuddered as he took her mouth, an aching vulnerability present in a kiss so tender it stole her breath away. They took their time touching and tasting each other. Exploring each other's bodies as though it was the first time . . . or the last.

It was like being granted a little slice of heaven, a moment in time, so precious because it was perfect – untouched by all the hurt and confusion they had created in the real world.

When he finally entered her, her body welcomed him, trembling with the joy of it. He pulled back on his elbows to look into her eyes, brushing the hair from her face.

'There is nothing in this world that I wouldn't do for you.'

She gasped as he began to move but the sound was lost as his mouth crushed hers again. Her arms came up over his shoulders, holding him to her, so he wouldn't stop kissing her as he pushed her to the brink.

They held on to each other tighter and more desperately until they both convulsed in pleasure.

Coming down from that high was like a feather floating from a tall tree back to earth. Tash knew the moment she hit ground again because her body stiffened and her eyes flew open, taking in the curtain gently billowing across the room. They'd left the light on so the room was starkly bright and, in her opinion, all too revealing.

His face was still pressed into her neck, her legs still wrapped firmly around his waist. She cringed in embarrassment as his mouth curved against her neck.

'You're so predictable, Tash.' He sat up, peeling himself off her carefully. 'Already worried about the consequences of your actions.'

*Shouldn't I be?*

She'd just realised she was still in love with a man who had cut her off emotionally since their daughter had died. She was worried that he may hurt her again.

Restarting physical intimacy when they were both still trying to connect mentally was a distraction from the real problem. She didn't want a closed-book marriage any more. She didn't want to be afraid to talk to him about anything.

A sheen of sweat glistened on his glorious chest. She pulled the covers from the bed over her naked body.

'Don't worry,' he sighed. 'I'm not about to suggest I move back home again because of this.'

She glanced up quickly. 'You're not?' She was strangely disappointed by his certainty.

'We've hurt each other too much already to be rushing into anything.'

She pounced on this because it had echoed her own fears so completely. 'So what's your plan then?'

He laughed and she immediately blushed. 'Tash, I haven't got a plan. Stop trying to make me the guy with the agenda. I'm just as thrown by this as you are.'

She glanced at him shyly. 'So you weren't expecting to make love tonight?'

He snorted in a manner that was actually not unattractive. Particularly the way his large shoulders jumped appealingly with self-mockery. 'The way things have been going between us? Er . . . no.'

'But you wanted to.'

He eyeballed her, making the hairs on the back of her neck stand up. 'Of course I wanted to. You're a gorgeous woman, Tash, and my wife. I've always been addicted to you. It's you who hasn't wanted me.'

'Well, that's rubbish.' She rolled her eyes.

He was silent for a moment, as though wondering whether it was safe to move into slightly dangerous waters. 'After we lost the baby, you didn't want a bar of me.'

Her eyes widened. 'That's different. Sex back then just reminded me of the baby and all that trying we went through to conceive. It just seemed wrong and futile. Making love made me uncomfortable, but it was nothing to do with my feelings for you.'

He shook his head, rubbing his temple as he did so and said on a sigh, 'I thought you didn't want me to comfort you. Because that's what it was for me, Tash. Comfort and connection. A gateway to you.'

She swallowed hard. 'I'm sorry I didn't think of that. I was hurting, Heath.'

'So was I,' he responded. 'You keep saying that I shut you out. But you shut me out just as much.'

He stood up then, reaching down and pulling on his jeans. She clutched the bedclothes to herself, eyeing him uncertainly.

'So do you blame me for the demise of our relationship?' She studied him, her own guilt warring with the anger rising in her chest. She clutched the bedclothes tighter, already trying to protect her heart from him.

He seemed defeated. 'Why is it always about blame with you?'

'Sorry,' she whispered. 'I'm still very raw from everything that's happened. I don't know what to think.'

He tugged on the hand that was holding the blankets up to her chin and drew it between his own palms. 'I don't think our separation was your fault, but I don't think it was my fault either. I think we both had our part to play in it. We were two people who had something terrible happen to them and we just got lost, Tash. We got lost.'

Her hand was cradled in his, their gazes locked.

Her breath caught. 'So what do we do now?'

He squeezed her hand before letting it go. 'We try to find each other again. That's what we do.'

# Chapter 23

In all her strategising to get her family back together, there was one person Phoebe had forgotten to take into account. Probably the most important person of all.

What she had done to Spider had been unfair to him and insensitive. This was their wedding, for goodness sake.

*What was I thinking?* Of course she knew the answer to that. She'd been thinking about her father and the terrible secret she kept for him. But was it right to continue to do so when it was causing Spider so much pain? She had tried to explain what little she could to him on the phone that afternoon outside the Wildwood Bakery. 'I'm sorry for making you feel this way. It wasn't my intention. Of course this is *our* moment, not my family's.'

'Then why do I feel like it's their moment?'

She sighed. 'Because I'm worried about my father. He's going through something right now, Spider, and I made a promise to him.'

There was a pause. 'What sort of promise?'

'That I would help him bring the family back together, to put an end to all the unpleasantness and the tension. It was wrong of me to suggest we use our wedding to do it. I didn't realise I'd let things get so out of hand.'

She heard him sigh on the other end of the line. 'Phee, you know I love you. You know I want your family to get along, right? But that's not our responsibility.'

'I get that,' she agreed. 'But if that's what you really think then why didn't you just say so earlier?'

There was a hesitant note in his voice when he spoke next. 'I thought what you really wanted was to end the tension between me and your father. And that was why you wanted a wedding at home, to get the two of us closer together.'

Her brow wrinkled. 'I don't *not* want that.'

'But it's not your number one priority, is it?' he said sadly. 'Your number one priority is your sisters and your father and your mother and whatever the hell it is they want.'

'My family is important to me.'

'And me? Am I important to you?'

'Of course you are. Would I be marrying you if you weren't? I love you, Spider, and I do want you to get along with my dad. But I think you're overestimating the tension between you both.'

Another sigh. 'Phee, he hates my guts.'

'No, he doesn't.'

'I'm telling you, he *hates* me.'

Her shoulders stiffened. 'I know sometimes he's a little rude to you. But it's just an old man being cranky. I don't think it's personal.'

'It's definitely personal.' Spider's voice came through on the phone harder than she'd ever heard it before. He'd always been such a laidback person – much like Eve in a lot of ways. It was no wonder they got along so well. He hated fighting and steered away from it when he could. Had this avoidance camouflaged something deeper that she hadn't noticed was going on until now?

His voice came through low and raspy. 'We've glossed over this issue way too many times, Phee, pretending that it's not real. But I think it's time we spoke about it.'

'But I can't fathom it,' she protested. 'Why would he hate you? He hardly ever speaks to you. Last year we didn't spend much time at my parents' place.'

'Why do you think that was, Phee?'

'I don't know,' she shrugged. 'Because I'm a bad daughter and I was too wrapped up in my own life?'

He snorted. 'Your father doesn't think the fire in the restaurant was an accident. He thinks I lit it. He thinks I'm the reason Eve left town and won't cook at Tawny Brooks any more.'

'What?' She clutched the phone tighter. 'That's insane. Why would you believe something like that?'

'Because he told me so.'

'Oh.' She could hardly refute that statement. '*Okay*. But,' she searched for a different angle, a different possibility and sighed with relief when one presented itself, 'it's a known fact that the fire started from candles. Eve blames herself.'

Spider released a breath. 'And Eve blaming herself only puts more crosses next to my name.'

'Why am I only hearing about all this now?'

'Because I didn't want you to worry. Because I wanted to try to fix the problem myself,' Spider said in a rush. 'Because I thought I could build bridges with your dad without you involved. You know, bond with him.' There was a groan in his voice. 'But he's definitely having none of it.'

She was getting cross at her father now. He could be excused for being protective of his daughters but this was beyond reasonable. 'I don't understand his logic. How could you have started the fire? It's preposterous.'

'The point is . . . you believe me, right? I didn't light any fire.'

'Of course I believe you.'

The relief on the other end of the phone was palpable. 'To be honest, I was half afraid you might side with your family again on this one.'

'Spider,' tears smarted in her eyes, 'I know it's been a rough couple of days. Just as rough for me.' She reached into her pocket and scrunched up the note she'd found in the tea jar into a ball. 'But I love you. I believe in you. And I want to marry you. We'll find a way to get through this. *You and me.*'

'Come home, will you?' His voice was gentle. 'I just want to hold you.'

'You don't need to ask twice.' She'd hung up then and returned to her sisters, who actually seemed rather subdued sitting together on the grass. In any event, they were not in the least bit dubious when she told them that she thought Spider was not having an affair and it had all been a big misunderstanding. In fact, they both encouraged her to have faith in her fiancé and everything would be okay.

But was faith enough?

There was so much she'd learned about herself and her own life recently and the secrets people covered up to protect her or to protect themselves. It seemed every time she thought she was getting somewhere, another can of worms appeared on the bench. All she ever wanted was for everyone to get along. Her father had given her such a terrible burden, and now it seemed he'd just added to it. Why on earth did he feel that Spider would do something so vindictive to Eve? They were such good friends. It was a friendship she'd often been jealous of. Eve was beautiful, smart and loyal. *And* she had so much in common with Spider. How many times had she wondered why it was herself that Spider was so attracted to and not her sister?

When she got home, her sisters disappeared to their bedrooms and she pulled the balled-up note from her pocket and gently unfolded it. There were other women out there who she needed to worry about, not Eve. This note was proof of that. How it got in the tea jar and how long it had been there still troubled her.

*Does it really matter, Phoebe?* Spider had not been meeting anyone at the Wildwood Bakery today. And if this letter was old, then it was old news and perhaps he'd never seen it.

She folded the note and put it back into her pocket, just as Spider entered the room.

'Hey, where've you been? I've been waiting for you.'

She stood there stiffly as he came over and enveloped her in a hug. Her body relaxed as she breathed in his unique scent and felt the warm pressure of his embrace.

He pulled out a little, gently kissing her lips before saying, 'I'm glad we had that talk this afternoon. I feel like we understand each other a little better.'

'Me too.' She put her hands on either side of his face. 'And I'm sorry about everything. Believe me, I don't want you to feel left out of your own wedding.'

'Thanks,' he smiled, 'and I promise I'll try to be more supportive of your family reconstruction.' He grimaced. 'Though it might help if I knew what was going on with your dad.'

'It's not my secret to tell.'

'Phee, we're going to be married pretty soon. And if you can't trust me, then who can you trust?'

He brushed her hairline with his fingertips as he voiced her concern.

Could she trust him? When she had a note from his potential lover sitting in her pocket?

'I had a terrible run-in with your father today,' he added as she was still thinking. 'I seem to be only making our relationship worse.'

'What do you mean?'

He explained in detail how he had tried to give her father a set of right-handed golf clubs. 'Why didn't you tell me he was a lefty?' he demanded in the end.

'I didn't realise it was something important you needed to know,' she protested. 'It's certainly not a big secret or anything.'

Spider's face turned pensive. 'Well, apparently everything else is.'

Of course, that was when Patricia had walked in, all smiles and suggestions, wanting them to go to Aravina's that night.

'I just feel like I haven't had you two all to myself yet,' she complained. 'With everything that's been going on, we just haven't had a chance to catch up.'

Phoebe could tell Spider wasn't entirely pleased about his mother's arrival, or the convenient way Phoebe used it to avoid the conversation he'd started.

As it turned out, dinner with the in-laws at Aravina Estate was almost as much of a nightmare as dinner with the whole family the night before. Not because Aravina didn't have one of the prettiest restaurants in the South-West. It did. Set in a stately white manor rimmed by a traditional verandah overlooking a garden to rival her mother's, the ambience was all she could have asked for. The food was great too. But honestly, it was like stepping out with a football team who knew you were supporting the other side.

Patricia seemed to be on a mission to condemn everything Phoebe's mother did. It was the positive remarks with the backhanded slap that kept Phoebe's hackles up almost the entire night.

'It's so nice to be eating dinner a little later. I just wasn't that hungry yesterday at six o'clock. Particularly with all the junk food we had beforehand.'

And, 'Your mother is such a wonderful cook, my dear. I don't know why she didn't make something of her life like your sister Eve did.'

Spider was particularly moody, no doubt because of their earlier truncated conversation. She was beginning to wonder whether she could do anything right.

When she woke up the next day, she tried to view it as a fresh start. A new beginning where everything got sorted out. After getting dressed, she entered the kitchen where her family and Spider's were all gathered to start the day. Over breakfast they decided that the men would continue with the restaurant renovations and the women would get moving on the wedding front.

Basically, her wedding-chore lottery was abandoned in favour of this simpler division of labour. She could tell some people were extremely relieved, particularly Spider and Heath, who had been tasked with organising the decorations and the photographer respectively. Spider was also glad to be letting his partner, Adam, off the hook.

'There's nothing more emasculating,' he said to her, 'than sitting around with another man and talking about chair sashes. *Especially* with a guy like Adam.'

'What's wrong with Adam?' Anita enquired tartly.

'Nothing,' Spider amended rather quickly. 'He's just not into pink satin.'

'Are we going with pink for the dining chairs?' Anita asked the gathered group at large. 'I thought you girls wanted to wear blue.'

'The chair sashes are supposed to match the bridesmaid dresses,' Phoebe informed Spider.

'Oh,' he shrugged. 'Well, I didn't know that. And I suspect neither did Adam, though I can't be positive because he's brushed me off several times when I've tried to engage him.'

Tash grinned. 'You've tried to engage him several times?'

'Call me paranoid,' Spider groaned, 'but I don't think he's interested. In fact, I don't think he likes me either.'

Phoebe scoffed. 'Now you're definitely being paranoid.'

'No,' Spider shook his head slowly. 'The guy definitely has a problem with me.'

'Eve,' Phoebe leaned across the table to try to get the attention of the sister who was keeping her head so far down it was nearly under the table, 'you talk to him the most. Does Adam have a problem with Spider?'

Eve cleared her throat. 'Not that I know of.'

'There you go,' Phoebe smiled. 'All in your imagination. Anyway, I think this division of labour is a little more sensible.'

It was also putting a smile on Spider's face again. So who was she to knock it? All she wanted was 'happy' going forward. No more drama. Tash and Eve left for town soon after breakfast. Tash, in fact, appeared very keen to get out the door that morning. She seemed nervous at breakfast, constantly glancing out the window. Heath seemed to find his wife's attitude amusing, lacing his fingers through the hand resting on the tabletop.

'Calm down, Tash,' he'd smiled. 'Rome wasn't built in a day.'

She'd glared at him as she snatched her hand away. 'You better bloody believe it.' Tash wanted to hit Busselton for dresses and also talk to a couple of DJs she and Eve had lined up who lived in the area. It seemed like a good plan to Phoebe and Eve as well. Her younger sister seemed more wedding-focused that morning too. She had asked Phoebe about the cake.

'So did you have any ideas about what you might like?'

'I don't know.' Phoebe quickly glanced at Spider, now very conscious of her obligation to be wholly inclusive. 'What do you reckon, love?'

He looked up from his bowl of Weet-Bix, a slight smile playing on his lips. 'I know for a fact that Eve makes a gorgeous fruit cake.'

Eve's cheeks coloured faintly as she dipped her head again in modesty.

A sudden undeniable flush of jealousy washed through Phoebe's body, surprising her with its potency. Although she knew she was being irrational, she couldn't help but retort somewhat irritably, 'But fruit cake is so dime-a-dozen, isn't it? A bit boring, don't you think?'

Unfortunately, that's when her mother stepped into the fray.

'But, Phee! I can't imagine you having any other type of cake but fruit cake. It's tradition.'

'Chocolate mud cake is very nice too,' Patricia put in her two cents' worth. 'I know a cake maker in Busselton, a friend of a friend I used to know in Perth, who does an absolutely marvellous one.'

'We don't need another cake maker, we've got Eve! The best chef in town.' Anita's voice brooked no denial.

'With the exception of Spider, I couldn't help but agree. However,' Patricia settled her teacup on its saucer rather coolly, 'considering most of the cake is not going to be edible anyway, I don't think we need a full-blown chef in this instance, do we?'

Phoebe watched her mother, who was blinking rapidly, with growing concern. 'Mum, it's okay.'

But Anita barely heard her. 'Not edible?' she whispered, her expression disturbingly trancelike.

'Oh yes, didn't you know?' Patricia smiled in amusement, which was possibly the worst thing she could have done. 'Most wedding cakes these days act more like centrepieces. They are completely fake apart from the top tier, which is reserved for the bride and groom to take with them on their honeymoon.'

Anita spluttered. 'But that's an outrage. What about the guests? Are they not to have any cake?'

Patricia's eyes widened. 'Anita, you mustn't concern yourself. I assure you, they won't mind. It's the done thing.'

'But I will,' her mother choked. 'I will mind very much.'

For Anita, food was synonymous with love. Mothering, hospitality, nurturing – they were all part of feeding, of giving, of loving. Without food, how was she supposed to express herself? Phoebe could see from her mother's quivering lip that she was about to have a meltdown.

'Mum –' she began, intending to reassure her that their wedding cake would definitely be entirely edible and every guest upon the Tawny Brooks property would be going home with a piece, when, to her great chagrin, Spider spoke up. In fact, he put out his hand and patted his mum's arm.

'That's a fabulous idea, Mum. Besides, Eve's got enough to do without having the cake on her plate as well. Pardon the pun.'

Eve opened her mouth to protest but Patricia got in first, smiling triumphantly. 'Perfect. Well, I'll get in touch with that wedding-cake maker I know in Busselton. We'll sort it right out – my treat.'

'Great.' Spider nodded.

Phoebe's mouth fell open. *What the?!*

As Spider returned to his breakfast, she bit her tongue. What was she supposed to do? Speak up? Go against his wishes in favour of her mother's? Put her family first again? She cringed. Hadn't she just promised to do better? She could feel her sisters' eyes on her, bringing on the guilt even more. Tash, in particular, was doing little jerky movements with her head in Anita's direction. She glanced at their mother, who was sending her a look of both pain and pleading.

Anita was expecting Phoebe to take her side, to speak up on her behalf. Gently, she shook her head, sucking in a breath as her mother pressed a hand to her chest as though she had just been stabbed in the heart.

Phoebe shut her eyes as Anita's chair scraped loudly on the kitchen tiles when she pushed it out. Standing up abruptly, her mother said, 'Excuse me,' and left the room.

A rustle sounded as her father, who was sitting at the head of the table, folded his newspaper and laid it beside his coffee. 'One–nil,' he murmured.

Silence followed as he raised his teacup to his lips, sipping delicately at the hot liquid. Everyone at the table turned and looked at him.

'What?' he shrugged. 'Somebody's got to start keeping score.'

*

The family finished the rest of the meal in relative silence before filing out to get on with their day. After a while it was just Phoebe and her father sitting there, sipping tea. He was on his third cup. The silence stretched between them and she began to grow more and more dissatisfied.

'Something bothering you, Phee?' he asked without looking up.

She choked. 'How can you ask that?'

He blinked.

'Of course something is frickin' bothering me!' She gritted her teeth. 'This is hell, Dad. And I don't mean to be insensitive, but you've put me here.'

His lips moved slightly. 'You wouldn't know what hell is, Phee.'

'Why? Because I'm your happy daughter? The one that never lets anything get her down? Well, I am down. I'm down and I'm out.'

He touched her hand. 'No, you're not. You're a rock, my dear – the strongest of my children, as hardy as the vine. That's why you always stay so positive.'

She snatched her hand away. 'Well, it's just an act because I'm not feeling positive. I'm barely holding it together. It's dreadful being the only one who knows you're leaving us. They'll need more time to adjust, Dad. Not to mention the fact that I'm desperately afraid for you.'

'I'm okay.'

'No, you're not *okay*,' she trembled, 'and I'm not either. I can't keep your secret any more.'

'So instead you'd rather rip our family apart early, three and a half weeks before your wedding? You promised me you would at least give them that. Think of your mother. Think of what this would do to her.'

She swallowed hard. 'It's not working out, Dad. There won't be a wedding if I continue to keep Spider in the dark.'

Her father's eyes darkened. And for once she saw what her fiancé might see every time he looked into the face of John Maxwell. A genuine contempt, a hard-heartedness that knew no mercy.

'Why do you hate him so much?' she demanded, the words catching in her throat. 'What did he ever do to you?'

'It's not what he did to me.' His long tanned fingers drummed upon the table. They were brown and wrinkled but they were still the hands she knew so well. Strong, capable, safe.

She remembered the feeling of her own hand tucked into his when she was no more than five years old. She'd felt as tall as a tree as he'd led her about. Nothing could touch her. Looking at those hands now though, she felt nothing but sadness and regret. There was so much she wanted to say but the words dried in her throat. They seemed so inadequate, so futile. And now, the man she wanted to marry was pitted against him. She had no idea how to deal with that. Ever since the whole wedding debacle had started, she had felt so divided. Her family on one side, her fiancé on the other. And as hard as she tried, she could not fuse them together.

'Spider told me that you think he lit the fire that chased Eve out of town,' she began, trying to keep her voice steady.

'Didn't he?' Her father's fingers abruptly stopped their drumming.

'No, Dad. Of course not. He would never do that to Eve.'

'Even to get back at me? To teach me a lesson?'

'I have no idea what you're talking about.'

'I told him I did not like his relationship with Eve. I told him that I thought he should end it or else. And he refused.'

'Well, of course he refused,' Phoebe spit out. 'You can't dictate to someone who they can or cannot be friends with. Apart from the fact that, if he's marrying me, I would hope that they continued to be friends. As I said to you a month ago, all I've ever wanted is for everyone to get along.'

He looked at her, long and hard. 'This wasn't about friendship.' His watery eyes never wavered from hers. He didn't say another word – he didn't need to. As the silence stretched between them, doubt crept through her body like dye in water.

The words of the letter, which she almost knew off by heart now, rang in her ears.

*I have been meaning to tell you this for quite some time. And now that you're here at Tawny Brooks, it seems almost like a sign that I should.*

Her brain folded upon itself.

*It can't be Eve. It can't be. She doesn't like him that way. She told me so!*

But her gut was telling her otherwise. She voiced her worst fear.

'You think they had an affair.'

She stood up abruptly and her father snatched her wrist. 'Sit down, darling. Sit down.'

'I can't.'

'Yes, you can.'

'Not until you tell me what proof you have of this.'

'A note, nothing more.'

'A note?' She pulled the crumpled piece of paper that somehow always found its way into her pocket and threw it on the table. 'Like this one?'

He slowly peeled it apart and flattened the sheet. His eyes took it in at a glance. 'I see you've found it.'

She turned away, biting hard on the fingers of one hand. 'It's not proof.'

'Nor is it innocent.'

Her mind darted all over the place, too fast to hold down one single thought. It was crazy. Utterly crazy. And sick.

Her sister and her fiancé – a double betrayal that seemed much too fanciful to be real.

'I don't believe it.'

'Please, Phee,' he pulled on her wrist again, 'sit down.'

'No.' She wrung her hands. 'You've given me these awful thoughts about the man I love and my own sister!'

'Then let me give you some good ones.'

Slowly, she sank back into her chair, gripping the table in front of her to stop her fingers from trembling. 'What else is there to know?'

'When I accused Spider of lighting the fire he denied it. And he still stands by that. He told me that he wouldn't do that to Eve and all he really wanted was to be accepted by the family. And he asked me if I could just give him a chance to prove it.'

A little ray of hope burst in her chest. 'What did you say?'

'I said no, at first, but then he told me he had asked you to marry him and that you had already said yes, though you were both keeping it a secret till you were ready to set a date.'

'So when we came to get your blessing for our engagement months later, you already knew we wanted to get married?'

'Yes,' he nodded. 'He begged me to let him demonstrate how much he loved you and how much you loved him. So I had him on trial, darling. Watching and waiting for him to slip up. He didn't. So when the two of you came over to tell me about your engagement, as though for the first time, I gave you my blessing.'

'Very reluctantly,' she sighed, wiping a stray tear from her eye as she remembered that day. Spider had been so tense. She hadn't thought there was more behind that than just nervousness at asking for her father's approval.

'I do think he loves you,' her father confirmed.

'But you don't trust him?'

'He is weak. Only time will tell whether his love for you is greater than his own weakness.'

'I really love him, Dad.'

'I know,' he sighed, his face dropping. 'That's why for your happiness's sake, I was willing to let him try.'

'Dad, what do I do? Do I turn a blind eye? Do I confront him? Do I let him go?'

She looked into her father's eyes and she was a little girl again, waiting to be told the correct answer. All she wanted was for him to take this burden away from her. To tell her what to do because she could not trust herself to make the right choice, when her own judgement had made her nothing but blind.

Suddenly her father looked older than his sixty-four years. Greyer than when she had first sat down this morning. He choked a little, picking up his tea to take a refreshing sip.

'I'm sorry.' She laid a hand over his. 'I didn't mean to tax you. It's easy to forget sometimes that . . . but I don't want to bring you lower than I already have.'

He patted her hand. 'It's all right, Phoebe. I'm old and I've had a good life.'

'Not that old, Dad,' she protested.

But he was thinking of something else. 'I remember when I first came to Yallingup, a little younger than you are. Your mother and I bought this land on the bones of our arses, mortgaged to the hilt because we had a dream.'

'Yes, I know. You were very brave.'

'I'm not talking about courage, Phee, because we weren't, you know.' He gave a self-deprecating laugh as he reminisced. 'Too young and dumb to know any better. We were bulletproof back then, invincible. Nothing could stop us. Our first big decision was what grape varieties to plant on the land.'

'That's right,' she nodded. 'You had enough land to choose eight.'

'Yes, and it was a tough call because we were so green. I chose chardonnay first because that's what the market told me to do. Same with cabernet sauvignon because it was as robust as hell. Your mother wanted chenin blanc and shiraz and I chose semillon, merlot and sauvignon blanc because they were good for blending. But then I had space for one more variety. This was going to be my show-off grape. The variety I made my name with and I already had some ideas in mind. You know how big a fan I am of the lighter reds.'

She smiled. 'Elixir for the soul.'

'Exactly. But they are more risky commercially to grow. In any event, pinot noir was number one on my list of top ten. But your mother, bless her heart, was against it.'

'Why?' Phoebe asked, unsure of why he was telling her all this.

'She said most pinot noir was grown in really cold places and I needed to think warmer. That night she cooked three of my favourite meals. Spicy lamb cutlets with pumpkin and feta, duck with pomegranate couscous, and finally salmon with artichoke puree and crisp peas. And she served them with a variety of reds she had bought that day – some local, some international brands. We ate, we drank, we laughed. And, ultimately, I chose a different variety. Tempranillo to be precise.'

'Your tempranillo is excellent.'

He inclined his head as though she'd stated a fact rather than a compliment. 'Only because I know exactly what I'm going to eat with it.'

'Dad, why are you telling me all this?'

He paused, his brow creasing. 'Sometimes what you want is not always what you need. And what you have is not actually what you think you've got. Wine tastes very different when you put it with a meal. And unless you've tasted the two together, how can you be certain exactly what wine to choose?'

She finally grasped what he was getting at. Her path was so confusing because the truth was hazy. She didn't have all the information she needed to make this call now.

'But, Dad, that's why I'm asking you what you think I should do with regards to Spider, because I honestly don't know.'

He smiled sadly. 'Darling, is it me you should be asking? Or do you really need a good chef?'

A good chef? She swallowed hard. *Spider.* He was telling her to confront Spider. He must have seen the disquiet in her eyes – the terror of asking for fear of hearing the answer.

'And now, darling,' he stood up, '*now* I'm talking about courage.'

# Chapter 24

Eve enjoyed her day out with Tash. After their deep and meaningful on Sunday, both girls seemed inclined to stick with lighter topics. It was so lovely to feel like friends again. The morning was also productive. They both ordered their bridesmaids' dresses and got the DJ sorted. It was easy to shop for gowns together because they looked good in the same colours and styles. In contrast to Phoebe, they also had the same taste in patterns – simple and elegant. Phee was the flamboyant one.

There was, of course, the situation with their father to throw a dampener on the outing. They hadn't managed to find a moment alone with him to question him about his affair. That morning, Phoebe had managed to corner him first and they supposed she had the right after his cheeky comment at breakfast.

'We'll just have to wait till tonight or tomorrow,' Tash sighed. 'I suppose no more harm can be done in the meantime.'

'No, I suppose not,' Eve agreed but she wasn't happy with the situation either. She'd always relied on her father to be the rock in the family. And, until this point, he had never let them down. She now couldn't look at him the same and it weighed on her.

Someone else who weighed on her was Adam Carter aka Adonis.

She had not made him breakfast at the restaurant that morning. Nor did she have any intention of doing so in the near future. Her secret appeared to still be safe but for how long remained a mystery. The truth was she wasn't quite sure if he really was serious about blackmailing her. She found his half-joking, half-teasing manner rather alarming.

Another problem, perhaps not as serious as the first, was the question of Tash's dressing gown. Where the hell was it? Yesterday, she had discreetly checked out the kitchen floor in the restaurant. But it was gone. She guessed Adonis must have removed it, perhaps even put it in the bin. She supposed that this was reasonable. After all, who would want to wear a dressing gown with burnt sleeves? Still, she would have liked the option of throwing it out herself. In any event, this meant she would need to find some time to purchase Tash a new dressing gown and dream up a story to explain to her how or why the first one needed to be thrown out.

When Eve and Natasha arrived home later that afternoon, Adonis was talking to Heath and her father in the sitting room. Dusty and sweaty from his work on the restaurant or in the winery that day, he still managed to look delicious. Ashamedly, it took her a little more than ten seconds to calm her heart rate at the sight of him.

'Hi, guys.' He addressed Tash as well, though his eyes rested slightly longer on her. 'I have some good news and some bad news.'

'What's the bad news?' Tash pounced – always the first to hit conflict in the face.

He grinned. 'No wedding or restaurant stuff tomorrow.'

'And the good news?' Tash lifted an eyebrow.

'I've decided to take the chardonnay off.' Adonis rubbed his hands together. 'And your father agrees.'

'Not me,' John grunted. 'The cosmos. It's a harvest moon tomorrow night. Energy will be drawn into the grapes from the soil – just as the moon pulls the tides.'

'They're also at their ripest,' Adonis added with a rush of enthusiasm. 'Great sugar, tannins and acid.'

John seemed amused. 'How do you know?'

'Refractometer and titration tests in the lab,' Adonis rattled off with a sideways glance at John. 'They're good.'

John sighed. 'Yes, but did you taste one?'

'Taste what?' Adonis raised his eyebrows.

'A grape.'

''Course I did, Max.' He grinned and cocked his head with that teasing look Eve so enjoyed.

'*And?*' Her father's brow lightened.

Adonis's eyes twinkled. 'As perfect as God meant it to be.'

'That's what I like to hear.' John's wrinkled face softened.

'Anyway,' Adonis turned back to Eve and Tash, 'we've got a heatwave coming through, starting Thursday. I'd rather get them off at first light tomorrow morning. And I'll need everyone's help to accomplish that as quickly as possible.'

There was a collective groan at the earliness of the hour. But Eve knew from childhood that it was necessary. You had to pick the grapes at their coldest because it caused better retention of the fruit flavours in the wine. Picking early morning meant the sun hadn't warmed them yet. At Tawny Brooks they only handpicked because their father thought it was better for the vine. Grape-pickers were gentler with the grapes and they wouldn't add unhealthy bunches to their tubs, so sorting was not required afterwards.

If Mad Maxwell allowed machine harvesting, it would take less manpower and they could pick the grapes through the night as not much light was required. She knew Oak Hills sometimes picked theirs at one or two in the morning, but it was not her father's way.

'What do you say?' Adonis looked around at the gathered company.

Heath glanced at Tash. 'I'm in. Tash?'

'Sure.' She nodded without returning her husband's gaze. 'I'm sure Phoebe and Spider will understand. They'll probably help too. I'm not sure about Patricia and Graeme though. They're not exactly nature lovers.'

Adonis looked directly at her then. 'What about you, Eve? Are you in?'

She lifted her chin. 'Of course.'

'Good,' he nodded and then, with another rub of his hands, headed for the door. 'I think I'll go find Phoebe and Spider now. Tell 'em the good news.'

'Tash,' Heath held out a hand to her sister, 'do you want to go for a walk? It's pretty nice out.'

'Er . . .' Tash looked uncomfortable. 'No thanks.'

He put his hand back in his pocket, a rather closed expression masking his face. Eve glanced from one to the other, feeling sorry for Heath. Why was Tash being so cold to him?

'Eve and I need to talk to Dad,' she said by way of explanation.

'Oh?' Heath raised his brows.

Their father looked up from contemplation of a family photo on the mantelpiece. His faraway look seemed to refocus. 'Really?'

'Yes,' Tash nodded firmly. 'Alone. It's a touchy subject.'

With a faint smile, Mad Maxwell shook his head. 'In that case, darling, go for a walk with your husband because I'm not ready to talk.'

Eve blinked in shock. 'You know what we're going to say?'

He sucked in a breath and released it. 'I have an inkling. And I most certainly don't want to talk about this right before Adam's harvest.'

'But –'

'It'll destroy all the positive energy in the atmosphere and sour my grapes!'

'Dad –'

'No.' He waved his hand in dismissal. 'I'm going to go play some music to my vines in preparation for harvest.' And then he headed for the door, leaving them both thoroughly dissatisfied.

Tash snorted. 'Is it just me or sometimes do you just want to shake him?'

Eve smiled. 'It's not just you.'

'Tash?' Heath looked at her questioningly again, an aching sense of vulnerability that Eve had never seen before clouding his face. She found herself wishing that Tash would just say 'yes' and not turn him down for that walk a second time, though it looked like her sister very much wanted to do so.

Tash licked her lips. 'Ah, Eve, did you want to come?'

Eve glanced from one to the other. Something was definitely up between these two. And she sure as hell wasn't going to get right in the middle of it. She'd had enough of that with Spider and Phoebe. For all their advice to her on men, her sisters really needed to sort out their own backyards before they came preaching to her.

'No.' She waved her hand airily, flopping down on the couch as though she hadn't noticed anything untoward going on at all. 'You guys go. I'm pooped. I might just sit here and read for a bit.'

Despite the early hour, it was a marvellous feeling to be out in the vineyard at dawn, enveloped by nature and refreshed by birdsong. The sun was still low on the horizon, giving the trees and the vine that gentle backlight that made their leaves look like they were outlined in gold. Eve dressed lightly, in a t-shirt, shorts and high-visibility vest. Everyone wore gumboots too because they were easy to clean sticky juice off and, of course, a hat and sunscreen.

It was a relief to be taking a break from the wedding and restaurant, if only for a day. Slow repetitive work in the crisp morning air seemed preferable to the high tension breakfast that had characterised all her mornings so far. Not that they were skipping breakfast that day.

Her mother was cooking up a big brunch to be served mid-morning when they were finished. Eve was sure by then she'd be ravenous.

The night before some of the vineyard workers had put out the ten kilo picking bins for them to fill throughout the section of vineyard they were harvesting. Adonis had pretty much worked out where he wanted everyone. That morning they dotted the fields with a pair of secateurs each, dropping grapes into the bins that had been placed there. Parked in one corner was a ute with a half tonne collection tub on a trailer hooked up to the back. A couple of vineyard guys were walking around picking up the full bins and emptying them into the larger collection tub. Adonis had given her the smallest area to take care of. So she was likely to finish first especially given she was an old hand at this. Her childhood had been full of harvest experiences. It was how she'd stumbled upon her first kiss – early morning pickings with an Italian backpacker they'd employed during one vintage, a rascally fellow with designs on most women in town. She wasn't the only person he'd kissed that season and he was gone the next. As grape-picking was required for such a select time of year, her father tended to employ students, travellers, friends and family.

Chop, drop, chop, drop. She smiled at the simplicity of the task but she was by no means bored. Not with the grasshoppers clicking around her and honeyeaters coming to say hello. She even got a look in from a fieldmouse who nonchalantly ran over her boots.

Some of the others wore gloves but she didn't. She liked the stickiness of the grapes on her fingers. The texture of the pretty three-pointed vine leaves brushing the backs of her hands.

She figured when she was done with her section she'd just help someone else with theirs. However, as if he had a sixth sense, Adonis showed up just when she was filling her last bucket.

'Hey.' He moved in close to help her with a cocky smile and her traitorous heart began to thud faster. 'The collection tub on the ute is just about full so I'm going to drive it back to the winery soon. When you're done, can you come with me?'

'Why?'

'I need your help tipping the bin into the hopper.'

She raised her eyebrows. 'You can't get one of the vineyard workers to assist you?'

He grinned. 'They're all in the field. And you're the first one to finish.'

She was getting the distinct impression he'd planned it that way and so decided to play hard to get.

'I'm not finished.'

'Why do you think I'm helping you?' She caught her breath as his arm brushed hers while he pushed some foliage out of the way to get another bunch of grapes for her bucket.

'Do you mind?'

'Not at all,' he responded unrepentantly. 'Happy to speed up your process for you.'

She groaned.

'Besides,' he murmured, 'this will give us a chance to talk.'

'About what?' she demanded nervously.

'Breakfast,' he grinned. 'We kind of never set a date.'

'That's because it's not happening.' She kept her eyes on the task. 'I can't risk being caught in that kitchen.'

He sighed, for once losing that teasing note in his voice. 'I don't get it. Why does this mean so much to you?'

'I told you,' she replied harshly, 'if my family catch me in there they'll just put a lot of pressure on me to return and I can't handle that. They are already re-opening the restaurant for one night because of the wedding. I don't want to get their hopes up.'

'Eve, you're a fabulous cook. Why do you think I want you to make me breakfast?'

'Because you like annoying me.'

He grinned. 'Yes, I do. But have you considered,' he stopped harvesting to study her thoughtfully, 'that maybe someone should be putting pressure on you to return to the restaurant?'

She glanced at him in horror. 'That's not your concern.' She turned back to the vine, snipping at a couple of stalks rather roughly.

'Okay.' He grabbed her wrist to steady her jerky movements. 'There's no need to get narky.' Her skin tingled as he released her. 'Why can't you return?'

'That restaurant was my dream since I was a little girl,' she whispered. 'And I stuffed it up.'

He folded his arms. 'So now you're just giving up? Running away from all you ever wanted?'

She smirked at him. 'Isn't that what you did when you left the Barossa?'

He clicked his tongue. 'Touché. But I can't have back what I lost, Eve. I had no choice but to start again somewhere new. You can still have your dream.'

'No, I can't.'

'Why not?'

His voice sounded so matter of fact, so clinical, that the only desire she had was to wipe that self-assurance from his expression – show him how little he really knew. As a result, she spoke before she had the wisdom to express herself less passionately.

'Because I wasn't good enough. It was all Spider's talent that kept the restaurant open, not mine. When he lost interest, so did our customers.'

'That's bollocks. The truth is, when you found out he had no interest *in you*, that's when it all went to shit.'

She shrugged. 'What's the difference?'

'A very big one, I imagine,' he nodded. 'You didn't fail at running a restaurant because you were incompetent, Eve,' he said shrewdly. 'You failed because you were nursing a broken heart. I hardly think the same thing is going to happen again. Unless you still have feelings for him.'

She blanched. 'You don't understand, we were such a great team. I relied on him for everything.'

Her words seemed to have made little or no impact on him. 'So get a new system.'

'I don't trust myself. I don't believe in my own judgement any more,' she blurted.

'Because you fell in love with the wrong man.'

'Maybe that's a part of it,' she admitted. 'But it's also because of the fire. It was my fault.'

He shook his head.

'It was!'

'What?' He spread his hands as though he were open to her argument. 'You lit a match and dropped it on the floor?'

'No.'

'You threw a mini-grenade inside when no one was looking?'

'*No*.'

He scratched his head. 'Then I'm not really following here.'

'I was distracted and preoccupied and I left the candles burning that night. They eventually set it alight. If Eric hadn't left work late and noticed what was going on, the fire brigade never would have made it on time before the entire place burnt to the ground.'

'So you made a mistake?'

'Pretty big bloody mistake,' she threw at him. 'I could have taken Mum's garden out too or our family home. I could have destroyed everything. The vineyard, the winery . . .'

'Okay, okay.' He nodded, holding up his hand for her to slow down. 'I get the picture now. You think you need to be punished.'

'You don't get *anything*,' she muttered, focusing her gaze on the ground and kicking irritably at one particularly chunky piece of gravel. The truth was, he was hitting far too close to home and she didn't like it.

'Life's not that much of a bitch, Eve,' he said softly. 'You gotta let it go. Cut yourself some slack. If you're not ready to cook in the restaurant again, fine. But you've gotta lighten up a bit. I meant what I said before when I suggested I teach you how to have some fun.'

'And I meant what I said when I responded "no thanks",' she retorted, dropping the last bunch of grapes into the bucket.

She walked off towards his ute then, leaving him to pick up her heavy bucket and bring it over. Cheekily, she hopped into the driver's seat and turned the key in the ignition, calling, 'Hurry up.'

In the side-view mirror, she watched him approach the vehicle, carrying her harvested grapes. He lifted the bucket onto his shoulder as he walked and she bit her lip at this highly arousing image. The muscles strained against his shirt. He was all man. All brawn and brass-necked presumption. How dare he ask about her personal affairs?

How dare he make judgements about the way she handled things!

*Lighten up. Teach me how to have fun. I'll teach him how to have fun!*

When he brought her bucket up to the side of the ute, she inched the car forward just beyond his reach. Frowning, he quickly corrected the gap and made as though to tip the bucket but she rolled forward again so he couldn't.

He glanced up towards the passenger door and she looked mischievously back at him via the side-view mirror.

'Eve! Are you doing that on purpose?'

'Doing what?' she called.

He lifted the bucket and she moved the ute forward again. He ran after it this time, managing to tip about half in as he jogged.

'You little rat!'

'Having fun yet, Adonis?' she asked, leaning out the window, gazing at him with eyes as wide as a baby's.

His mouth twisted, as though he were trying not to laugh. 'Eve, I appreciate that you're trying to get back at me, but this is a serious business. I don't want to accidentally throw our produce on the ground.'

'Sorry,' she said apologetically. 'Won't happen again.'

'Thank you.'

He lifted the bucket up a fourth time and approached the vehicle. Just as he was about to tip it, she inched forward again.

'Sorry, foot slipped that time,' she called.

He paused to glare at her. '*Eve*.'

'Okay, okay. This time I got it.' She waved at him with a hand out the window for him to step forward. He did so, slowly lifting the bin to tip this time.

And, at the last second, she jerked the car forward, choking in laughter as she did so. 'I'm sorry, I can't help it.'

She heard a crash as he dropped the bucket behind the ute but continued laughing, unable to stop her glee at having got the better of her nemesis. A face appeared beside her open passenger window and he reached in and turned off the engine.

'You think you're so clever, don't you?'

She was still laughing when he opened the door and pulled her from the vehicle straight into his arms.

'I want you to know,' he growled, 'that you fully asked for this.'

And then he kissed her.

It was a kiss of dominance and of fire. And a host of other things she could not name, having no more than about two brain cells to put together in that moment. He smelled of sweat and sun and man, and he felt like every fantasy she'd ever had all rolled into one. He was hard and contoured, rough but gentle – too big and unwieldy to kiss her with any sort of practised finesse. It was more raw need on both their parts.

They twisted into each other. Moulding their bodies and lips together, fusing them like two pieces of dough.

His mouth ravished hers, pulling at her lips. Her hat fell off, hitting the dust as his hands roved into her curls, down her back, curving under her bum and lifting her more securely into contact with his hard male form.

She gasped as he tore his mouth free and gazed down at her with such a startled expression on his face, for a moment she actually believed he was as shocked as she was. 'I was not expecting that.'

They heard the spitting of dirt and a horn tooted them as another ute rolled up.

Adonis immediately released her and they spun around, a deep flush washing over his otherwise perfect features.

It was Heath behind the wheel and luckily no one else with him.

He grinned at them. 'Consorting with the boss's daughter, Adam? Are you sure that's wise?'

'No,' Adonis admitted, much to her disappointment and vexation. 'What can I do you for?'

'Can I have your empty bins? The crop is much heavier on the top end of this block and we need some more up there.'

'Yeah, sure.' Adonis transferred a stack of empties including Eve's bin off the back of his ute tray and put it onto Heath's.

'Hey, Heath.' Eve quickly walked up to the vehicle also. 'How about I take these up to the top end and you help Adonis with loading the hopper.' She glanced back at the winemaker. 'I think you'd be better at it.'

Heath grinned in some amusement. 'What did you call him?'

'Huh?' Eve blinked. 'I didn't call him anything.'

'Don't worry.' Adonis swatted his hand. 'She does that sometimes.'

'I do?' Eve said, startled. 'I mean, *no I don't*.'

'*O-kay.*' Heath grinned as he stepped out of his vehicle, leaving the door open for Eve to hop inside. She did so in short order – glad to have such a conveniently placed escape route.

There was too much turmoil churning around inside her to stay and have to understand what had just happened between her and the Greek God of winemaking. In the wake of Adonis's kiss, she had discovered that she was no longer in love with Spider. And while that should have given her some comfort, it came with none of the relief she yearned for. Because the truth of the matter was, she was now in a bigger mess than she had been in a week ago.

# Chapter 25

In the end, the crop they harvested was massive and everyone was required to help after lunch with extracting the juice. Spider didn't mind. There was nothing like manual labour to burn off his frustration with Phoebe and the rest of her family.

The task was a three-step process. Firstly, they loaded the grapes into the hopper, which fed a crusher and de-stemming machine. Then they transferred the produce to a machine known as the press – a steel cylindrical unit on its side, porous with holes like a grater. This squeezed all the juice out of the grapes and dropped the skins (or marc) out the bottom after all the juice was extracted. The liquid was then pumped into stainless steel fermentation tanks, or barrels, where it would remain for at least five weeks. It was very important to get the juice out of the grapes as quickly as possible after harvest so that the grapes didn't spoil in the tubs in the heat of the day.

Everyone at the winery was involved and staff from the cellar door also left their posts to assist. Even John Maxwell dropped by to lend a hand and give Adam a few pointers, which he did generously enough. Spider watched them enviously. How was it that this other man had gained John's approval so easily? Why could he banter with John like an old friend of ten years when John had known Spider longer? He knew John blamed him for the fire but that was over a year ago now. Couldn't they move on?

Maybe he just needed to be natural. Instead of trying so hard to find something John was interested in, he should talk to his strengths and play it cool. He walked up to the pair.

'Great crop, guys. Always loved your chardonnay, John.'

John grunted. 'It's Adam's this year.'

Spider flicked his eyes briefly at his grinning competitor and tried again. 'Chardonnay goes so well with pasta. Eve and I used to recommend yours with our signature gnocchi. Slow roasted tomatoes, goats cheese, basil leaves in a tangy salty sauce. Did you ever try that dish of ours?'

'No, as a matter of fact I didn't.' John's eyes became hooded.

Spider blinked. 'I can't think why not. It was one of the bestsellers in our restaurant.'

'I'm allergic to tomatoes,' John said shortly and walked off, leaving his nerves bristling.

A chuckle sounded beside him and his rival commented, 'I can totally see what your problem is now.'

'What?' Spider demanded.

'Mate, you're not insensitive,' Adam clapped him jovially on the shoulder, 'you're just dumb.'

He was so astonished by this remark that he wasn't quick enough to respond before Adam had already strolled away to help some other person with loading. It was probably the last squeeze in his lemon of a day. He had never been so dissatisfied with his lot in life.

At least things with Phoebe had definitely improved. She was taking his side now in most things. They were making more decisions about the wedding together. However, it could not help but sting him that she still hadn't taken him into her confidence about her father. Whatever the secret was, it was bothering her. He'd seen a worried crease between her brows when she thought he wasn't looking. This wasn't like his Phoebe. She was always excited and happy about everything. She wasn't a worrier. That's what he loved about her – her optimism and her openness. Where had it gone?

It was now nearly three weeks to the wedding and he felt the secret between them was like a ticking time bomb over his head. If he was to continue the wedding preparations with any sort of peace of mind, he needed her trust. He was so glad on Friday morning when she'd suggested a day out together without anyone else in her family. They were going to hit the road and chase down everyone on the old staff chart so that they could re-open the restaurant kitchen just for one day. He was pleased to be getting away from the estate for a few hours.

'At last,' he gripped her shoulders thankfully, 'some quality time together.'

She'd nodded and smiled. 'Let's take a picnic and have breakfast in our favourite spot.'

When she looked at him like that, with such love, it was easy to remember why they were getting married. They packed some of the croissants her mother had in the kitchen, along with a flask of coffee, and sat on the beach at Canal Rocks for breakfast – their all-time favourite spot.

Canal Rocks was an ancient and unusual rock formation that extended on the coastline between Yallingup and Margaret River. The striking orange rock that lined the bank had been eroded along a straight line forming an almost perfectly cut 'canal' feature. Several smaller canals also fed into the rock perpendicular to the main one.

In wild or stormy weather, the ocean churned white and angry in the canals, smashing against its sides and spitting upwards to bless viewers standing on the manmade timber bridge crossing the canal.

It was a spectacular sight to see. But what was even nicer was a peaceful day like today. The crystal blue water contrasting against that stark orange granite was as conflicting as his own emotions. Sitting on that rock next to Phoebe, munching on her croissant, she felt so close to him and yet miles apart.

The granite was warm from the sun and strangely reassuring. A gentle breeze whipped at his face as he let his eyes stretch to the horizon of an ocean that was so immaculately calm it couldn't help but steady him a little. All he could hear was the swirl and lapping of water in the nearby rockpools and the occasional call of a seagull flying overhead. A slight movement caught the corner of his eyes and he discerned a tiny hermit crab trying to find its way home.

'You seem pretty subdued this morning,' he commented, biting into his breakfast. Perhaps in these tranquil surroundings he could get her to tell him what was bothering her.

'Did you have an affair with Eve last year?' she asked.

He choked on his pastry, spluttering and coughing as he reached for his coffee. '*No*.'

Of all the things he had expected her to say, this was not it!

'Have you ever had any feelings for her?'

'*No*.'

'Did you know she had feelings for you?'

He gave a start. 'Does she?'

'Come on, Spider.' She threw her croissant back into her lunchbox and shut the lid with a snap. 'You must know something. My father spoke to you about this last year, without my knowledge, and you never said a word. You could at least be honest about that.'

He frowned. 'He asked me to end my relationship with Eve. And by that I assumed he meant my friendship, which I thought was grossly unfair as it was innocent enough.'

'Not that innocent.' Phoebe gritted her teeth as she thought of the note. 'She was in love with you. You must have noticed.'

His heart sank as he desperately tried to pull clues from his brain. Scenes from the past flashed – little things, quiet moments that had made him wonder briefly but not for very long.

*Damn it!*

*Maybe I am just dumb.*

He searched Phoebe's face. 'You know, there were times when I was a little suspicious. But Eve is such a closed person, Phee, you know that. She never likes talking about difficult subjects.'

'Neither do you for that matter,' she accused. 'Why didn't you tell me about all this stuff earlier?'

His face crumpled. 'I didn't want to lose you. And it seemed like a one-way ticket to just that.'

He could tell her disappointment in him was palpable. 'You're going to lose me anyway if you don't tell me the full truth right now.'

He put his croissant away. 'I have told you the full truth, Phee, I swear! I have never crossed that line with Eve. I've never even spoken about it with her. And as for the fire, it wasn't arson, it was a tragic accident, the result of a few neglected candles. *That's it.* There's no conspiracy here. Unless you want to count your father's blind prejudice against me.'

'My father just wants to protect me.'

'*So do I!*'

Relief mixed with doubt flew across her face. He could tell she wanted to believe him but was afraid to.

He cupped her face in his hands. 'Phee, I love you. Please, trust me. Let's forget about all this and just get married and be happy.'

She looked up into his eyes, her own brown ones flecked with specks of green – a mirror of his emotions. She was as desperate as he was to hold on to what they had and believe in its worth. 'Okay,' she said finally.

'Okay.' He nodded in relief and bent his head to kiss her. It was a sweet caress of acceptance and forgiveness. He felt the heavy burden of the last few days lift from his shoulders. It didn't fix everything. But he could see the lightness back in her face again already. And that's what counted most.

After that, they went scouting for staff for the wedding. They planned on approaching as many of Tawny Brooks' ex-employees as possible. If they could assemble the old team together for just one night, it would be perfect. Most of their old staff had not migrated far and had, in fact, been absorbed by other local restaurants. So the balance of the day was an enjoyable roadtrip driving from winery to winery, restaurant to restaurant. It was like the ultimate scavenger hunt, surrounded by gorgeous sunshine, tall gum trees, and vineyard after splendid vineyard rolling over every hill they crested. Spider couldn't help but slip in a little wine tasting along the way and a pop in at the Margaret River Chocolate Factory for some afternoon tea indulgence. He made sure they had fun together, and forgot the worries of that morning.

By five o'clock that evening, they'd signed up almost eighty per cent of their old staff to work on their wedding day. He threw the Tawny Brooks staff chart on the backseat of the car as they got in to drive home.

'I think that'll do, don't you?' he said. 'We don't need everyone for the function. It's not going to be a full restaurant.'

'Sure.' Phoebe nodded and they drove home in companionable silence.

He was glad they'd taken this day and that he finally knew what had been going on in that head of hers. He would worry about her father later. When they pulled up in the car park at Tawny Brooks and got out of the car, he forgot to pull the manifest off the backseat.

'Tash wanted to look at it,' Phoebe said and opened the door to reach in and get it. Something on the floor of the car must have caught her eye because she reached further down for it instead. Pulling it out, horror streaked across her face.

'Phee?' He frowned. 'What is it?'

She held up a satin dressing gown trimmed with lace that he had never seen before. A note dropped out of it, which he picked up.

'Give me that.' She snatched it off him and read it out loud. 'When you're ready, I'd also like my blanket back,' she gasped. '*How could you?*'

The hair on his head stood on end. 'Phee,' he said slowly and carefully, 'I've never seen that nightgown before in my life.'

'You're a liar!' she cried, ignoring his remark. 'You lied to me about Eve.'

'No, I didn't.'

'Then what the hell is this?' She shoved it in his face.

'I don't know.'

'Stop it! Spider, stop treating me like an idiot.'

'Phee, I have no idea who that belongs to.'

'Really?' she demanded in an icy voice. 'Then perhaps I know someone who does!'

On this ominous threat, she headed straight for the house. There was nothing to do but follow her.

# Chapter 26

Eve had spent an easy day, hanging out with Tash and her mother. In the afternoon, they'd sat around the kitchen table sorting out the table arrangements for the wedding party – all one hundred and one of them, which turned out to be a more involved process than she had first supposed. In fact, if she had to liken it to anything, it was much like arranging the suspect board in a police investigation.

'Okay,' Tash held up a place setting card, 'Howard Banks, what do we know about him?'

'Wasn't he one of Dad's old friends from high school?' Eve suggested.

Tash raised her eyebrows. 'Seems like an odd person to invite.'

'He's family,' Anita revealed. 'Married my cousin Athena after I made the mistake of introducing them.' She picked an apple out of the fruit bowl and began to peel it with a knife, an art in Eve's opinion that had long since died out. She loved watching her mother create an endless curl of skin behind the blade. Sometimes she would peel the whole apple in this way without breaking the chain.

'Oh,' Eve nodded, tapping the large sheet of paper they had on the table in front of them. They'd drawn ten circles on the page, representing their ten tables of ten people, and were sorting place cards into each circle. She moved her finger across the page. 'So we put him on this table with Athena.'

'Er . . . no. They're divorced. He had an affair with my other cousin Evadine.'

'Nice guy.' Tash picked up the stack of cards on Athena's table, shuffling through them. 'So I take it Athena won't want her cousin Evadine on her table either.' She removed Evadine's card from the deck. 'Should I put her with Howard?'

'No, he dumped her.' Anita finished peeling the apple and started chopping it up into quarters.

'Okay, so we need to put Howard and Evadine on different tables. How about we put Howard with some of Spider's relatives? He can make some new friends.'

'Try to find a table without any single women on it,' Anita grunted. 'I know –' she took the card from Tash's hands – 'put him next to Patricia's brother, Alan.' She shuffled Howard in with the cards on table six. 'He's a psychiatrist,' she announced knowingly. 'Might talk some sense into him.'

'Right,' Eve's mouth twitched, 'but we've still got a problem with Evadine. Shall we put her with a different group of Spider's relatives?'

'She's such a shy woman,' Anita sighed. 'She doesn't make new friends easily.'

'Okay.' Tash picked up all the cards on Athena's table. 'How about we allow her to take some cousins with her? Who didn't take Athena's side when she and Howard broke up?'

'Well, I suppose you could move Jacinda and her husband Theodore with Evadine.'

'Hey, look,' Eve pointed, 'there're three places at Aunty Joan's table. Why not put them there?'

'Oh no,' Anita shuddered. 'Your cousin Isobel and Margaret are both pregnant. Worse than that! Isobel is having twins.'

'So?'

'Jacinda's been trying for years. I don't want to rub her nose in it.' She held out some apple to each of her daughters. 'Piece of fruit?'

'No, thanks,' Eve declined but Tash took a piece.

'Eve,' her mother said worriedly, 'are you hungry? Do you want something else to eat?'

'No thanks, Mum. I'm not hungry at all.'

'Are you sure?'

'Yes.'

'All right,' her mother nodded, 'I'll peel you an orange.' And she removed one from the fruit bowl and took to it with her knife.

Eve sighed and Tash grinned at her across the table as they continued to work the board for a spot for Evadine. In the end, they had to shuffle around three more people before finding her a suitable place that would not cause a diplomatic incident. In any event, it was a very welcome distraction from Eve's own troubles, which started with a capital 'A'.

The kiss they'd shared the day before had been playing on her mind. Or rather shaking the ground she stood on. The kiss itself had been awesome, magical even. But essentially nothing had changed. He was still a jilted man uninterested in a meaningful relationship. And she, well, she was still the kind of girl that men like him ate for breakfast. The last thing she wanted was to end up as the rebound scrap on the side of his plate. Avoiding him seemed to be the best plan for the time being.

But Adonis had other ideas. He turned up around five, waltzing into the kitchen like he was used to having free rein in the house, which he probably was.

'Can I fix you something to eat, Adam?' her mother immediately enquired.

'Sure, Anita.' He gave her his most wolfish grin. 'I'm feeling a little peckish.'

*No wonder my mother loves him. He eats anything.*

Eve looked down, hoping his visit was going to be a short one. Maybe he needed to check in with her father – ask his advice on whether they should take the cabernet off next.

'Eve, can I speak to you for a minute?'

She glanced up, startled. 'Huh?'

He pointed over his shoulder. 'Alone?'

'Er . . .' She looked from her mother to Tash. They were both staring at her with raised eyebrows.

*Great!* Just what she needed, more queries into her private life. Her chair scraped on the tiles as she stood up. Better to get this over with. 'Okay.'

She followed him to the sitting room. He gestured her in first before he cautiously shut the door behind him. She advanced as far into the room as possible, trying to keep the distance between them to a maximum.

'So I thought we should talk about what happened yesterday,' he began.

'The harvest?' she asked politely.

'No, the fact that we kissed and how bloody fantastic it was.'

'Oh that,' she said, as though she had only just remembered. 'Yeah, it wasn't bad. Did you manage to get all the grapes pressed yesterday? It was such a big crop, wasn't it? I hope you had enough space in the vats or are they all going in oak?'

'Some barrels, some tanks. But who cares?'

'Well, I'm sure my father would.' She lifted her chin. 'The oak-fermented juice tends to have a better flavour.'

'If you like that woody texture. Some people don't.'

'So you're branching out?'

'No,' he put both hands on either side of her arms, shaking her slightly, 'I'm *reaching* out . . . to you.'

She pulled herself free and took a step back. 'I don't think that would be such a good idea.'

'Why not?'

Before she could answer, the doors to the sitting room burst open and Phoebe came charging in. There was an expression on her face that Eve had never seen before and, to be honest, never wanted to see again.

'Is this yours?' Her sister thrust her hand forward.

Eve looked down in horror to see the dressing gown Adonis was supposed to have thrown in the bin in her sister's hand.

Eve put a hand to her throat. 'Where did you get that?'

'In the back of my car, along with this note!' She held up the piece of paper.

'You have a Barina?' Adonis asked Phoebe, startled.

'We all have Barinas,' Eve snapped at him.

He winced. 'Whoops.'

'This is nothing to do with you,' Phoebe shot at him. 'And I'd appreciate it if you'd just leave.'

Adonis, however, did not move and Eve didn't know whether to be relieved or annoyed. Spider came in then, shutting the door behind him. 'Eve, please explain to Phee that that dressing gown is not yours. She thinks we're having an affair.'

Eve's eyes widened. 'What?'

'Tell her she's being ridiculous,' Spider demanded.

'Quiet,' Phoebe threw over her shoulder. 'This is between me and my sister. And this time I'm going to get the truth. Eve, speak to me!' Phoebe's face was an angry red. A blood vessel pulsed on the side of her neck, making her look rather hysterical, and a sinking feeling permeated Eve's bones. This conversation was playing out exactly how she imagined it would in her nightmares.

Only worse.

The evidence of her treachery, however, was ironically off-key. Phoebe had discovered a different secret that Eve needed to keep quiet just as badly.

'Is this yours?' Phoebe's voice sounded harsh to her ears – harsh and unhinged.

'Not exactly.' She winced. That, at least, was true.

'It's mine actually.' Just at that moment, Tash stepped into the room carrying a plate with a sandwich on top. She held it up. 'Mum wanted me to give this to Adam,' she said by way of explanation as she also shut the door behind her. She passed the offering and tugged her dressing gown from Phoebe's hands. 'What are you doing with my lingerie?'

'It's yours?' Phoebe seemed floored, her eyes growing even larger than before.

'Yes,' Tash blinked. 'What are you doing with it?'

Phoebe gasped. 'What am *I* doing with it?' she repeated in disbelief. 'What is *he* doing with it?' She jabbed a finger at Spider.

'Spider?' Tash blanched. 'I didn't give it to him. I gave it to Eve. Why would I give it to him?'

'I found it in my car,' Phoebe announced, eyes still on Tash.

'I gave it to Eve on Saturday night,' her elder sister responded.

'So what you're saying is that you're in on this too?'

'In on what?'

Phoebe choked. 'Eve's affair with Spider.'

'I'm *not* having an affair with Spider,' Eve cried, losing her timidity and starting to get rather cross, especially because Phoebe thought she would do such a thing. *Especially* to her own sister. It made an absolute mockery of all the suffering she'd endured last year. All the respect she had paid her, in disregard for her own feelings. 'I can't believe you would think that.'

'I didn't want to believe it,' Phoebe said quietly. 'I haven't wanted to believe it for days. But I can't see how you can reasonably explain this.'

Eve swallowed. To be honest, neither did she. She racked her brain for a plausible lie.

'Tell me, Eve,' Phoebe's eyes glittered dangerously, 'did you go to Tash to ask for advice on how to seduce him? You've always been so incredibly gauche when it comes to men. I can see how you might have needed a few pointers.'

Eve reddened.

Adonis blinked. 'Seriously?'

Everyone ignored him.

'Seduction,' Eve gasped, 'was the last thing on my mind when I was forced to put on Tash's lingerie in place of my own nightie. *Yes!*' She raised her voice louder as Phoebe opened her mouth to protest. '*Forced!* She took my clothes.'

Adonis bit into his sandwich and watched, enthralled. 'This just gets better and better.'

'That's insane.' Phoebe threw up her hands. 'Why would Tash do that?'

'Ask her.' Eve passed the buck to Tash, who was conspicuously silent. 'She was the one acting all funny. Bringing me her clothes in the dead of night and begging me to take them.'

Both sisters turned angrily, hands on hips, to Tash, who seemed to shrink within herself. 'All right, all right,' she cried. 'You got me. I didn't want to wear it.' She hesitated, her hands ringing at her waist. 'I – I needed something more conservative. Heath and I have been having problems. We've separated, okay. Happy?'

There was a shocked silence.

Phoebe's eyes widened. 'Honey, why on earth would you think that news would make us happy?'

Tash's face seemed to collapse. 'I don't know, maybe not happy exactly, but you might think I've got my just deserts.' She looked directly at Eve. 'Don't you, Eve?'

Eve flinched as though slapped. She couldn't understand what she had ever done to leave her sisters with so little faith in her.

*Perhaps running away from the restaurant after taking all the family money to build it!*

She winced.

*Yeah, that'd do it.*

'Tash,' she implored her, 'I would never wish for your unhappiness. Ever. Why didn't you tell us about this? We could have been more understanding.'

'Oh shit.' Phoebe ran her hand down her face. 'I invited him to the wedding without you knowing, didn't I? You never wanted him here, did you?'

'It's not entirely your fault,' Tash groaned. 'I never told you what was going on. Or Mum and Dad. I was just trying to pretend everything was okay.' She rubbed her eyes.

'Tash,' Phoebe's eyes watered, 'you don't need to pretend with us.'

'Of course you don't,' Eve cried. 'All we want to do is support you. I, for one, will take any more lingerie you want to give me. I've got t-shirts galore to exchange. In fact, why don't you move into my room –'

'*Hang on*,' Phoebe busted her mid-sentence, 'stop trying to change the subject. You wore that nightgown for *my fiancé* and took one of his blankets. I want an explanation.'

Eve clenched her hands into fists. 'When on earth could I possibly have had a chance to do that? We've all been in each other's pockets since we got here.'

'I don't know.' Phoebe's face took on an uncertain look. 'But I do know how you feel about him. I found your note in the tea jar.'

Eve slumped. Her heart rate slowed right down to a languid beat that sounded uncomfortably loud in her ears. She had never been so more mortified in her life. How embarrassing, to know that Phoebe had read her private confession. And, worse, that she thought she hadn't let those feelings go. The silence stretched awkwardly. She didn't know what to say, how to explain herself.

'Oh,' Adonis interrupted cheerfully, 'so you found the note! We've been wondering where that went.'

'That note you showed me was the one from the tea jar?' Tash demanded of Phoebe. 'But that's years old. Dad told me all about it. He's read it too.'

Eve's eyes boggled and a groan erupted from her now very dry lips. '*Please tell me*, is there anyone living or working on this estate who has *not* read my letter?'

Spider raised his hand. 'Er . . . I haven't. Should I be taking a look at it?'

All three Maxwell sisters turned towards him and said, 'No!'

'Okay,' he held up both hands, 'just asking.'

Adonis stifled a chuckle with a polite cough.

'The truth is,' Eve turned to her sister Phoebe, 'like Tash said, that letter is years old. Nothing ever came of it and a lot has changed since then.'

Adonis nodded. 'A lot.'

'Will you be quiet?' she hissed at him, sick to death of his little side comments that weren't helping matters at all and were entirely distracting. She turned back to her sister. 'Do you honestly think I would do that to you? Try to seduce the man you love?'

Phoebe hesitated, her eyes filling with tears. 'I don't know. I've been in so much turmoil this week. I . . .' Her voiced trailed away.

'Phee,' Eve pleaded with her, 'the thought is abhorrent to me, sickening even. I would always sacrifice my own happiness for yours.'

Phoebe grabbed her hands. Her eyes filled with sadness and regret. 'And you did, *you have*. I can see how selfish and blind I've been.' She blinked hard. 'I should have known how you felt when Spider first came to Tawny Brooks. I should have guessed what was in that note before I read it. Instead, I blocked you out in pursuit of my own happiness.'

Eve shook her head, glancing from her to Spider. 'You did the right thing. Look at you, you're perfect together.'

'Eve –' Spider spoke up from behind his fiancé, but she held up her hand to stall him.

'Don't say anything, Spider, there's no need.'

'Honestly, if I'd known –' he began, as she winced under the embarrassment of it all.

'If you'd known,' she interrupted him, 'things would have probably played out exactly as they have. You with Phoebe, as it was meant to be.'

In truth, she didn't really want him to explain why he hadn't felt anything romantic towards her. Apart from the fact that it was humiliating, she thought that was a matter for him to talk over with Phoebe, not her.

'Er . . . Eve,' Tash interrupted. While they had been talking she had been examining her dressing gown. 'Why does my dressing gown have a sleeve missing?'

Eve turned warily towards her elder sister, who was examining the damaged gown with consternation, and she wondered how she was supposed to get out of that one.

*I burnt it on the stove in the restaurant* was out of the question when the last thing she wanted everyone to know was that she'd been cooking in there.

'And why was it in the back of Phoebe's car?' Spider asked.

'And . . .' Phoebe's eyes narrowed, 'come to think of it, whose blanket did you borrow?'

'Well, the truth is . . .' She searched wildly in her head for a plausible explanation.

'The truth is,' Adonis dusted sandwich crumbs from his fingers, as he drew her irrevocably into her side, 'Eve *is* having an affair.' He grinned broadly. 'With me.'

# Chapter 27

Maybe it had been a little high-handed of him, to have taken advantage of the situation like that. But the truth was he couldn't get that kiss in the vineyard out of his head.

When he'd arrived in Yallingup he hadn't wanted to get involved with anyone, especially in the wake of a broken engagement. In fact, what he'd promised himself was to take some time out, so that eventually he would stop asking himself why he had lost Kathy.

The truth was, since meeting Eve he had ceased to think about the past or wonder what was going on at the Rixon Valley Estate in the Barossa.

He didn't mind any more if they missed him or questioned where he'd gone.

He no longer wanted to punish Kathy or her family for the humiliation they had caused him.

He no longer questioned why she had ended it so abruptly.

He didn't care.

The information had shrunk in importance compared to his new life here at Tawny Brooks. For the first time ever, he felt like he was living at home. It was such a simple concept yet so wholly all encompassing – that feeling of belonging . . . warts and all. He wasn't trying to impress anyone and they weren't trying to intimidate him. He wasn't trying to fit in either.

But he did.

The Maxwells were a bunch of oddballs and he took to their set like salt in popcorn. In all his time engaged to Kathy, he had never been so enmeshed in her family.

But with Eve everything was different. He felt like he could be honest with her, *brutally honest*. She made him laugh and cringe at the same time. She was both fascinating and frustrating. It was true that whenever he saw her, all he wanted to do was annoy her, but that was more of a reflex action than anything else. He wanted to get under her skin, the same infuriating way she was under his. He'd never been this unsettled before or felt this crazy. She made him feel such a clash of feelings – jealousy, longing, mischief and possessiveness. It was madness.

And after that kiss . . . he no longer had the fight to resist them.

He knew Eve well enough now to know that a simple wooing wasn't going to catch her because she didn't trust herself. And fair enough too – after the way Spider had dismissed her feelings for years. How opportune that Phoebe had discovered that lingerie in her car. If this hadn't happened he never would have been able to back Eve into a corner.

'Is this true?' asked Tash.

'Are you having an affair with Adam?' Phoebe demanded.

Both sisters stared at her, open-mouthed, and he knew he had her.

She was so petrified of anyone finding out she'd been cooking in that kitchen, she would much rather they thought she was sleeping with him. She squeezed out one word between clenched teeth. 'Y-yes.'

Phoebe's expression changed slowly from shock to glee. 'Eve, you *dark horse*. How long has this been going on?'

'Ages,' said Adam.

'Barely a minute,' she responded at the same time.

Natasha looked shrewdly from one to the other. 'There does seem to be more going on here than meets the eye.'

'Not really.' Eve tried rather unsuccessfully to wriggle out of his hold but he held her tight. In resignation, she stopped struggling, turning instead to her sister. 'Now that we've sorted out the whole lingerie debacle perhaps you could give me and Adam the sitting room back.'

'Yes.' An evil devil prompted Adam to murmur suggestively against her hair. 'We were kind of in the middle of something.'

Her sisters' mouths dropped open.

'Not *that*,' Eve said crossly, finally managing to wrench herself free of his hold, perhaps because his shoulders were shaking so badly with laughter. 'But can I please have the room? I really need to talk with Adam privately.'

'Oh no,' Natasha shook her finger at her, 'you still haven't told me why there's one arm missing on my dressing gown.'

'Now that,' Adam's eyes danced, 'is a very interesting story.'

'Which we will not be sharing with *my sisters*.' Eve began to turn a rather alarming shade of red.

'Let's just say,' Adam winked at them, enjoying himself hugely, 'that your sister is a firebrand.'

Seeing her sisters' eyes almost pop out of their heads, she quickly and rather unwisely tried to explain. 'What he means is, at the time we were in the kitchen and I was standing like here and he was standing –'

'Don't give us the play by play,' Natasha gasped in mock horror.

'Ew!' Phoebe looked down at the lingerie she was holding. She threw it at Eve, who caught it against her chest. 'You can have that back.'

'Yeah,' Tash waved her hands in front of her body. 'No need for returns. That gown is yours, sister.'

'It's not what you think!' Eve choked.

'Believe me,' Phoebe rubbed her temple, 'I'm trying not to.'

'It still doesn't explain what it was doing in my car,' Spider chimed in, and then he clamped his hand over his mouth. 'You didn't –'

'Ew!' Phoebe and Tash both said at the same time, causing Eve's skin to flame all the brighter.

Adam decided to put her out of her misery. 'No,' he grinned. 'Not in your car. Eve left it on the floor at my place and I put it in your car thinking it was hers. I thought I was returning it discreetly.'

'Eve,' Phoebe shook her head, 'this is a side of you I've never seen before.'

'This is a side of me *I've never seen before*,' Eve said tightly, balling the gown in one hand and walking forward to catch both her sisters round the waist. 'Now, I really must insist you leave.'

Her sisters continued to muse on the revelations as she half-pushed, half-dragged them across the room.

'So it was *Adam's* blanket you borrowed.' Phoebe was nodding.

'I thought she was a little familiar with him on Saturday night,' Tash commented. 'I just thought she might have the hots for him.'

Adam threw up his hands. 'Thank you!'

With a grin, Spider opened the door for the girls. 'I guess we're going now,' he said to Tash and Phoebe. 'Let Eve get back to her lovers' tiff.'

'It's not –' Eve gave up. 'Fine. That's what it is. I'll talk to you guys later.'

'Make sure you do,' Tash said over her shoulder as the three of them sailed out of the room.

Eve closed the door behind them and as it gave a decisive click, she spun around to face Adam, back against the door, face set.

He winced. 'I don't suppose,' he began tentatively, 'you're going to thank me now.'

'What do you think?'

He watched her march forward, fists clenched and eyes blazing. She looked incredible, all fired up and ready for battle. It had his pulse going faster just watching her.

'*That*,' she stabbed a finger at him, 'was not funny!'

He held his palms up in surrender. 'Who said I was trying to be a comedian?'

'You're right,' she put her hands on her hips, 'more like a smart-arse.'

'Hey.' He widened his eyes to reflect his innocence. 'I did you a massive favour just then, covering for you like that.'

'You mean sinking me into a bigger lie than one of omission,' she threw at him.

'If I hadn't,' he protested, 'your little secret would be out of the bag. I went out on a limb for you, thank you very much.'

'Really?' Her voice was sarcastic. 'On a limb? *What a hero!*'

'Well,' he grinned, rather chuffed at this estimation of his character, 'if you think so.'

Her eyes narrowed. 'Have you been drinking or something?' She grabbed his face and sniffed him. In turn, he inhaled raspberries and guavas in her hair. She was so close he could see her irises dilating and those gorgeous little freckles he hadn't noticed before sprinkled across her nose. Mesmerised, he leaned in to capture her lips and she quickly released him, taking a full step back.

'Don't you dare!'

'Come on, Eve.'

'We decided,' she put her hands on her hips, 'that we weren't going to go there. And we had good reasons.' She pointed her finger at the floor. 'Valid reasons that haven't changed.'

He folded his arms. 'Well, mine have.'

'How would you know?' Her voice quivered ever so slightly. 'It's clear you're thinking with your . . . with your . . .' As words failed her, she flicked her finger at his crotch before pointing at her head. 'Not with your brain.'

He grinned. 'You know, I like this gutsy, take-no-nonsense Eve so much better than the shy, timid one I first met.'

'You bring out the worst in me, you know that?'

He shrugged. 'I think I bring out the best.'

'You forced me into a corner in front of my sisters,' she retorted. 'What are we supposed to do now? Pretend we're having an affair?'

He cocked his head. 'Or have one for real.'

'That's insane.'

'Actually,' he stuffed his hands into his pockets, 'I think it's a pretty awesome idea. We get to explore this chemistry going on between us, and you get to keep your secret.'

'I'm not having an affair with you,' she said, point-blank.

'Why not? I'm not asking for rock solid commitment if that's what you're worried about. We could take things slow. Have a little fun.'

'Have a little fun,' she repeated slowly. 'I'm going to tell you something, which apparently you don't know.' She took a deep breath. 'You are a very, very good-looking man. You could have anyone.'

'Er . . . thank you but –'

'No, seriously.' She seemed to want to drive home her point. '*Anyone*. I mean, look at you.' She shut her eyes and turned her face away from the blinding light that was, apparently, his body.

He chuckled. 'I'm glad you find me attractive but –'

She cut him off. 'You don't need to mend your broken heart on me. Invest in a supermodel or something. She'd give you a run for your money.'

He groaned. 'I don't want a supermodel.'

'And I,' she took a deep breath, 'don't want to be your rebound girl.'

He sobered. Her eyes were glistening. She was obviously very serious about this and, to be honest, he did not quite know how to respond with any degree of credibility. After all, just five days ago he'd admitted to coming to town to nurse a broken heart. He just hadn't realised how easy that would be to do with the right kind of medicine. *Shit*. Was she his rebound girl?

'Listen, Eve,' he said slowly, 'I definitely don't want to hurt you –'

'Then don't,' she responded earnestly.

'I have no intention of doing so,' he tried to say.

'You're not in a position to say that. You just came out of an *engagement*, for goodness sake. I can't compete with that. And you know what? I don't want to. I'm sick of being that girl.'

He frowned, all his humour was gone now. 'Okay,' he nodded finally. 'I hear you.'

Her lips pulled taut. 'Good, I'm glad.' With another nod she turned to go.

'So we'll have a fake affair then,' he added.

She spun back. 'A *what*?'

He blinked at her guilelessly. 'A fake affair. I assume that's what we're doing if we're not having a real one.'

'What on earth gave you that idea?'

He grinned. *Oh, Eve, did you really think you'd get rid of me that easily?*

'Well, otherwise won't you have to come clean to your sisters about what really happened in the kitchen?'

This gave her pause. She pursed her lips and her fingers curled quietly into fists.

'Won't they just ask the question again if you tell them we're not an item? I mean, it's up to you if you want to reveal the truth,' he shrugged, 'though I'm sure they'll wonder why, if you enjoy cooking in the restaurant so much, you don't just start it up again.'

'All right, all right, I take your point,' she caved. 'I'm happy to pretend. But that's it.'

'Of course,' he nodded.

She eyed him uncertainly for a moment, clearly not trusting what she saw.

And she shouldn't.

'I better go,' she said finally. 'Mum, Tash and I still have some tables to arrange.'

'Not a problem,' he said as she headed for the door. 'I'll see you around, lover.'

# Chapter 28

One week passed and the wedding preparations stepped up a notch. As far as Tash could make out, Phoebe and Spider were finally over the trouble that had been festering between them. And Eve seemed to be coming out in the open about her secret relationship.

Or rather . . . Adam was doing it for her.

He came to dinner with the family every evening now, sitting next to Eve as though he were a long-term boyfriend. Eve's embarrassed resignation to this new development had their father amused.

'Are you attempting to woo my daughter, Adam?' he asked when the winemaker showed up for the third evening in a row.

'Do you mind if I do?'

'Not at all,' John Maxwell chuckled and then flicked his fork at Eve. 'But I think she does.'

Eve turned a lovely pink hue.

'Actually, Dad,' Phoebe put in casually, 'Eve adores Adam.'

Eve squirmed in her seat.

'She calls me Adonis,' Adam informed their father.

'I do not,' Eve protested.

'Yes, you do, all the time. She thinks I look like a Greek God.'

'That's absurd,' Eve said crossly.

Their father cleared his throat. 'Might I give you some timely advice, my friend, from a man who has lived with four females? There are two great secrets to keeping a woman happy.'

Adam's eyes lit up eagerly. 'Go on.'

'The first one is, whenever you're wrong, admit it.'

'Yes, yes of course.'

'The second is, whenever you're right, shut up.'

There was a bark of laughter across the table and everyone looked up from their meals to glance at Graeme, who immediately went quiet.

'What's the matter, Graeme?' Patricia glared at him.

'Sorry, dear,' he coughed. 'Nothing at all.'

Tash hid her smile. All couples had their problems and foibles, it seemed. She and Heath weren't that special after all.

In the days following the discovery of her missing dressing gown, Heath continued to press his argument that they should try to be a couple again. He seemed to guess that their first brush with physical intimacy had been a little too much too soon and so chased her in other ways. When she overslept he woke her with coffee, like he used to do when they lived together. If he went to work at the restaurant early and she stayed at the house, he called her mid-morning to see how she was. Whilst these gestures still had the power to touch her, she could not bring herself to completely trust them without feeling some sense of panic.

Things weren't so simple that they could just go back to the way they were. If their relationship had been perfect, it wouldn't have been derailed by their loss. They would have come together, not fallen apart.

If they were going to be a married couple again, it had to be different this time. Their relationship had to be stronger and more transparent for both of them. And for that, they needed time. He couldn't just expect her to pick up where they left off.

If anything, she was a little insulted by his impatience and his 'can't you just get over it?' attitude. All it really said to her was that he'd learned nothing from their time apart.

Her sisters, now that they knew, encouraged her to lean on them and she felt the weight of her burden grow a little lighter. They made sure she was never alone with Heath or drew him into conversation when they knew she was feeling down. While this was only making her lack of communication with him worse, it was such a relief to have the pressure taken off, so she didn't tell her sisters to stop.

Phoebe gave Heath so many jobs to do, he was becoming her own personal errand boy. He seemed to take the change in their treatment with a kind of resigned acceptance. But she knew he was simply biding his time.

He told her as much in the sitting room one night after everyone had gone to bed. 'I can't throw away all our dreams, Tash. Not without a fight.'

'But what if those dreams weren't real, Heath? What if we're just two people who were never meant to be together?'

He sighed. 'Do you really believe that?'

Doubt cut through her. 'I don't know. Too much has transpired. You can't just gloss over it.'

'I'm not trying to gloss over anything.'

'Yes you are, Heath. We didn't just break up because of Sophia. We broke up because we couldn't talk to each other. You've never trusted me emotionally. And at the moment, I don't trust you.'

He gazed at her. 'Well, where does that leave us?'

'Honestly, I don't know.' She swallowed as he strode away, leaving her to chew anxiously on her fingernails. It was an awful habit from childhood that she succumbed to whenever worried. The problem was, whenever she was thinking about Heath, her fingers naturally crept to her mouth.

There was no easy answer for her because it all came down to trust. When you moved this far away from the person you loved, what was needed to return was a leap of faith. And she was not ready to do that. What she required was more of a bridge to cross back slowly.

*But how do I start building that?*

Heath had never been one to discuss his feelings much. He always kept those close to his chest. In hindsight, she realised just how much he had concealed in the wake of her miscarriage. She didn't want a marriage like that any more.

To give Heath some credit, he could see her turmoil and let her be for a couple of days. She would have been relieved if she hadn't started feeling sick.

A lasting wave of tiredness struck her. All she wanted to do in the evenings was crash. She slept so deeply that even Heath's presence in the bed beside her no longer kept her awake for hours.

And then the nausea began. At first she thought that maybe she had a stomach bug, or that she'd eaten one too many of her mother's baklava slices. They were her favourite. But after two mornings bent over a toilet bowl, the bug still hadn't cleared. On the third morning, when she left the bathroom shaky as a leaf, she began to suspect it was something else . . . though the suspicion was too impossible, too ironic – that she was pregnant after only one night with her husband. Especially after the years they'd tried and failed to conceive. It was almost like fate was conspiring against her. With everything else already going on, was it really necessary to add this to the mix?

The restaurant renovation was just about done now. The floor reconstruction was finished. All they needed to do was re-paint the walls, clean the undamaged furniture and pick up some new items to add the finishing touches to the decor. She was actually rather proud of her husband's contribution, though she hadn't told him so. He had always been a quiet achiever, beavering away in the background until he stepped back and revealed all that he had done while she wasn't watching.

On Thursday morning, everyone was finishing the painting in the restaurant. As they were nearly done, she didn't think they'd miss her if she just nipped into town for some space.

'Are you going to the doctor?' Eve asked as she was about to take off. 'I think you should see someone about that stomach bug of yours. It's gone on for far too long.'

Tash smiled, touched by her sister's concern, but shook her head. 'No, I'm feeling much better today, thanks.' She racked her brain for a different excuse. 'I wanted to check out something I intend to buy Phoebe and Spider for their wedding gift.'

Eve's eyes widened. 'Good idea. I really should get onto that as well.' She sighed. 'Too many things on my mind right now.'

She knew that feeling. Eve and Tash had not spoken recently about their father but she knew the worries were never far from her sister's mind. Eve had such a trusting relationship with their dad. Tash could tell she was heartbroken over his duplicity. They both were. The only way they knew how to deal with it was by being kinder to their mother.

They realised, with guilt, how much they had disregarded her cries for attention. She was going through so much right now: the invasion of her home and, in some respects, the dismissal of her opinion. But most of all Anita didn't understand why her husband was slowly disengaging from her. It was very difficult to watch.

After breakfast, Tash drove straight to a pharmacy to pick up a pregnancy test. She went to one in Busselton because the town was bigger, and there was a far greater likelihood that no one would know her there. If she went to a chemist in Dunsborough, her mother would receive word she was having a grandchild before she got home.

The round trip took about an hour and a half. She killed an extra hour doing some shopping, just to make her trip more authentic before returning home. Everyone was still at the restaurant, so it was easy enough to slip into the bathroom and pee on a stick.

It then took her another hour to get her head around the result.

She was still sitting in her bedroom trying to process it when there was a rap on the door. She stiffened immediately.

*Heath?*

'Tash, it's Eve. Are you okay?'

'Eve,' she breathed.

'Can I come in?' Her sister didn't wait before tentatively opening the door and sticking her head around it. 'I wanted to know –' Her voice broke off as her expression morphed into concern. 'Hey.' She opened the door more fully. 'What's wrong? You look awful.'

Tash tried, she really did. But for the life of her she could not control the dam as it burst. Tears flowed freely. Heavy sobs racked her body.

'Oh, Tash.' Eve shut the door and flew to her side, arms cradling her trembling body.

'I don't know what to do. I don't know what to do,' she chanted. 'It's all I ever wanted . . . just not right now.'

'What's happening right now?' Eve stroked her hair. 'Has Heath said something to make you upset?'

'No, not really.' She gulped in air. 'Heath thinks we should get back together.'

Eve rubbed her back. 'And you don't want to?'

'I don't know. We've been through so much. I think there's a lot we need to work through before I can trust myself with him again.'

'Is that what's upsetting you?' Eve asked gently.

'Not precisely. You see,' she paused before whispering, 'I'm pregnant.'

Eve gasped. 'But I thought you guys –'

'Don't ask.' Tash shook her head. 'It was one time, when we first arrived at Tawny Brooks. I can't explain it.'

Eve gripped her hand. 'It's okay, you don't have to. Just let me know how I can help you.'

Tash shut her eyes against the panic welling up inside her. 'This is all happening at such a difficult time. I don't know where my life is headed right now . . . and now, a baby too?'

'Does Heath know about this?'

'No.' Tash shook her head. 'I only just confirmed it myself. I don't know how to tell him. I didn't think we would have to go through this again so soon.'

Eve pulled back slightly. 'What do you mean by *again*?'

Tash gazed heavenward. 'Eve, I didn't tell you this before. Actually I didn't tell anyone, but this is my second pregnancy. Heath and I lost the first baby. That's why we started having problems. We . . .' She took a breath. 'We didn't deal with it very well.'

'Oh, Tash,' Eve said, before throwing her arms about her sister again and pressing a kiss into her hair. 'You poor thing.' She reached around her to grab some tissues by the bedside as Tash's tears began to fall in earnest.

Tash took the offered tissues, wiped her face and blew her nose.

'Why didn't you tell anyone?' Eve rubbed her leg. 'We could have supported you.'

'It was a strange in-between time. I was only twelve weeks along. We were just getting to that stage where we were going to start telling people. So when I lost the baby I guess I just completely shut down.'

'And how did Heath take it?'

'He just wanted to move on, put it behind us. He was constantly trying to take my mind off her . . . our daughter. In hindsight, I can see that he had his own way of grieving, but at the time I found his insensitivity too harsh.'

'So that's why you separated?'

Tash hiccupped. 'Basically. There were other factors too. I thought he blamed me because I was such a workaholic.

I blamed myself too. After the separation happened, I lost my job anyway and I just felt ashamed. I felt like I'd dropped the ball and let everyone down. I couldn't face it.'

'We let you down,' Eve said fiercely. 'I thought you were still giving me the silent treatment because of the restaurant. The truth was that you had bigger problems and I was so obsessed with my own issues I didn't look out for you. I feel like an idiot.'

Tash hugged her back. 'We're all guilty of a little self-obsession sometimes. Don't put that on yourself. If there's one thing this trip home has taught me, it's that blaming yourself is such a waste of energy.'

They were silent for a moment, just holding each other and drinking in the comfort the other provided. Tash knew she should be thinking about what step she should take next but couldn't find the energy to do anything more than sit.

'Where's Phee when you need her?' Eve sighed. 'She'd find the silver lining in this cloud faster than you can say . . .'

'Aunty?' Tash suggested tentatively.

'That's the spirit,' Eve nodded and then jumped off the bed, shoving Tash's shoulder in a very realistic impersonation of their younger sister. 'Really?' she gasped with Phoebe's wide-eyed enthusiasm. 'I'm going to be an aunty? But this is amazing! We can go shopping. Baby clothes are so cute. It's going to be so much fun. I can't wait.'

Tash laughed, her mood lightening. 'Phoebe would love to see you do that. You've got the tone just perfect.'

Eve grinned. 'Thanks, but seriously, Tash, you have to focus on the positives. This baby is a gift.'

'You're right.' Tash sat up a little straighter. 'I want this child more than anything. It's just . . .'

'I know,' Eve nodded. 'It's hard being pregnant like this. Listen, try to live in the moment. Just let the past go, and try to look at the future and picture what you want it to be. And then when you're ready, you'll know what to do.'

Tash already knew what she wanted it to be. It was the same gentle daydream she'd had since she and Heath had become engaged. The two of them together, with their three perfect children laughing and playing in the backyard, like a corny sitcom. But it was just a fluffy fairytale. All pink smoke and no substance. Real life was so much harder, so much meaner.

She didn't know whether she had the strength to go through it all again.

# Chapter 29

On Friday mornings, particularly at nine am, the cellar door was generally empty. If there was anyone in there at all, it was usually a hardcore wine writer or Mrs Caffrey, the local busybody, who had been doing the Yallingup winery circuit in her retirement years simply for the pleasure of collecting gossip about her neighbours.

Luckily, neither was present at the cellar door when Eve walked in that morning. She hadn't visited this part of her father's estate since she'd arrived home. Her focus had been on the restaurant and the family, not the family business, which, from the looks of things, seemed to be thriving without her attention anyway.

Everything in the Tawny Brooks cellar door was polished. Polished wooden floorboards, polished timber bar, polished tables and stools you could see your face in. As she came in, their merchandise was on her right – from hats and tea towels, to those corny silver spoons old ladies like to collect. Mrs Caffrey had a chest full of them. On her left was a group of very comfortable looking couches and a small bookshelf of wine magazines and literature. As a teenager, she had loved coming in here to do her homework, read or think. It was a quiet space that she regarded as her own.

Directly opposite the double-doored entrance, against the back wall, was a crescent-shaped timber bar, probably reflecting her father's obsession with the moon. At this magic counter, many a tourist came in to taste and comment on Tawny Brooks' finest wines. Behind it, hanging on the walls, were all the awards they'd won, and several photos of her parents at shows around Perth and interstate. There were even a couple of photos of her and her sisters up there – arms around each other, working behind the bar. They'd all done their fair share at some stage.

Memories swamped her as she moved towards the couches, her eyes glued to those photos. How could something so right become so wrong? Her father was not the man in these photos. Nor was she the girl smiling there.

And Tash . . . Tash was pregnant!

After hearing the news the day before, she was still trying to process it. It had been a wake-up call, sitting there looking at her sister's pale and washed-out face, the weight of the world on her shoulders. She was going to be a mother, and she had a decision to make that would no longer just affect her life but the life of her child.

All of Eve's insecurities seemed to pale into insignificance. She was scared of running the restaurant. In comparison, it was pathetic. People came up against challenges all the time. She could see the lines of determination on Tash's face, the strength in her heart, the depth of her love. She would get through this. With the support of her family and her sisters, she would get through this.

And then Eve saw herself, always sitting on the sidelines. Not participating and watching life pass her by. Ever since she'd arrived in Tawny Brooks all she'd done was hide. Hide from her feelings, hide from the restaurant and hide from her family, trying to be anything but herself. Being here again for just two weeks, she could feel the earth seeping back into her bones. She loved it at Tawny Brooks. She loved it at Yallingup. She didn't want to go back to Margareta's. Why did she let her fear get the better of her?

As if to back up her thoughts, her second biggest fear walked into the room just at that moment. Adonis looked deliciously virile, carrying a rather large carton of cabernet merlot, which he placed upon the bar before turning to greet her. Her heart immediately jumped in her chest as she sat there, caught in the crosshairs of his gaze. His hair was windswept and his eyes glittered dangerously. Why was it that trouble was always so bloody sexy?

'Hello, Eve.' His lips turned up in his usual facetious grin. 'Have you been lying in wait for me?'

'You wish,' she returned breathlessly, nerves and eagerness seizing her all at once. Was she actually happy to see him? Who was she kidding? Of course she was happy to see him. Her skin was already clammy.

*Damn it!* The problem with having a fake boyfriend, who held your hand in public, came to have dinner with you every night, enquired most solicitously about your life and chastely kissed you goodnight while your family waved him out the door, was that you started getting used to that sort of treatment. You started to enjoy it. You started to miss him when he wasn't around. And if he was late for dinner even by ten minutes, you grumpily began to wonder where the hell he was!

This was the first time they had been alone together since the conversation in the sitting room when it had all begun. There was no need at all for pretence in here.

'Well,' he cocked his head, 'if you're not waiting for me then why are you here?'

She shrugged. 'I just come here to think sometimes.'

'Really?' His mouth twitched as though he were about to laugh. 'You do have some strange habits, Eve.'

She could tell he was thinking about her cooking at three in the morning in her sister's lingerie, trying to recapture the dream she had lost. She blushed, hoping he wouldn't call her out again on that.

Luckily he was not looking at her but behind the bar instead. 'Where are the cellar hands?'

'I think they just stepped out for a smoke.'

He shook his head. 'I'll have to chat to them about keeping this counter manned at all times.'

'It's always slow in the morning.'

'Doesn't matter.'

There was an awkward silence.

'All right,' he nodded. 'Well, I'll get out of your hair then.'

She could not quell the disappointment inside her when he headed for the door. A kind of desperation gripped her.

'Adam, wait.'

He stopped and looked back. 'What is it, Eve?'

*I don't want you to go.*

*I want you to stay here and be with me like a real boyfriend.*

*I need someone to talk to.*

*Because I'm thinking about taking a risk, about jumping out of this skin.*

*And . . . you seem to be the only person I can truly be honest with.*

He frowned. 'What's happened?'

And because she needed some excuse to keep him around she blurted, 'Tash's pregnant and Dad's having an affair.'

'What?'

'You can't tell anyone.'

He came and sat down on the couch beside her, his eyebrows drawing together. 'Eve, your father is not having an affair. I think I would know if he was. And as for your sister, well, wow! Isn't that a good thing?'

'It's complicated.'

'Complicated how?'

She placed her hands on her face. 'I shouldn't have told you anything. It's not even my news to share.'

He sat back a little. 'More secrets you want me to keep for you. Is this all really necessary, Eve?'

As she searched his face, she realised the true reason she'd called him over wasn't just because she liked his company but because she needed his witty banter and teasing tone right now. He always knew how to make light of everything and lift her spirits. The only problem was, he wasn't playing ball.

'Sorry,' she said on a rush. 'I shouldn't have bothered you with this. I just wanted a friend to talk to.'

He looked down at her. 'So we're friends now, are we?'

She nodded with a shy smile. 'Well, yes. After everything we've been through together, I think we can call us that.'

He frowned. 'I thought you didn't want to be my friend.'

'Well, I've changed my mind.' She looked at him crossly, slightly offended by the furrow in his brow. 'I'm sorry if that upsets you.'

'Damn right it upsets me.'

'Why?' Her own brows drew together. 'Because I think you're a nice guy?'

'Eve,' he took her hands, 'you know that I'm always happy to talk to you about anything. But I haven't pretended to be your boyfriend because I'm a nice guy.' Then he grabbed her face under the chin and pressed a hard, determined kiss to her lips, causing all the breath to rush out of her body in one single blast.

He let her go. 'Just wanted to make that perfectly clear.' As soon as he stood up, she felt bereft.

'Where are you going?' she demanded.

His eyebrows jumped wickedly as he looked back. 'You want me to stay?'

She blinked in confusion. The truth was, she didn't know what she wanted. 'No, no. I'll be fine. I'll just sit here by myself and worry.'

'Eve,' he laughed, 'you know what you need to do?'

'What?'

'Cook.' He nodded decisively. 'Go to your restaurant and invite everyone to breakfast and cook.'

'What?' Her mouth went dry.

'You wouldn't do it for me,' he shrugged, 'but do it for your family. Do it for yourself. Breathe some fresh air into your life. You'll feel so much better for it. And,' he groaned, 'so will I.'

As he walked out of the cellar door, she was left to contemplate his words, and they couldn't help but ring true to her. Why was she sitting here moping, dwelling on her own fears? It was a stupid thing to do. Her own advice to Tash came back to her.

'Try to live in the moment. Just let the past go, and try to look at the future and picture what you want it to be.'

Wasn't she a hypocrite if she couldn't follow this advice herself? She remembered it was her father who had first told her to stop waiting around. She smiled. The parable of the grape varieties – he had not planted the eighth variety and time had taken the choice from him. Was that what she wanted for herself too? For all her opportunities and choices to disappear?

*Life's not that much of a bitch, Eve.* She remembered Adam's words from the vineyard and hearing his voice in her head again was like a little cut against her heart.

*You've got to let it go. Cut yourself some slack.* She stood up from the couch, determination straightening her spine. *All right, I'll do it.*

On Sunday morning, they finally completed renovating the restaurant and it was ready for use. Her sisters and their partners, Adam and a few others who had worked on the project, gathered there to admire their handiwork.

The tables were already dressed with pristine white tablecloths and flanked by high-backed, polished pine chairs.

They'd painted the walls cream to bring out the dark shininess of the boards they had laid and freshly varnished. The pictures they had hung on the walls were photos from the Tawny Brooks gardens – with camera zooms so close you could see the dew on the petals of orchids and the lines of age in the leaves of the gums. As everyone stood around congratulating themselves on how good it looked, with its freshly washed windows and modern light fittings, Eve made an announcement.

It was probably one of the first announcements she had made in her entire life. Public speaking was another fear she tended to give in to. 'To celebrate,' she lifted her voice, 'I've decided to make pancakes for you all in the restaurant kitchen.'

Faces turned towards her, nobody said a word.

'You know,' she continued, feeling like she needed to fill the awkward silence. 'Kind of like an early lunch, late breakfast. If you're keen, that is.'

Phoebe clapped her hands.

Tash gave a whoop.

'Of course we're keen,' said Heath.

Spider threw open the double-doored entrance to her old workplace. 'We'll help you.'

As they all walked through, she caught Adam looking at her, a gentle smile on his mouth. He gave her the thumbs up sign, causing her to flush. However, instead of following her in with the others, he turned around and left. She hid her disappointment by getting straight to work.

Five minutes later, however, her mother and father and Graeme and Patricia, who had not been there when she'd made the announcement, walked into the room. Anita came immediately to her side, folding her in her arms as pancakes sizzled in three different pans on the stove. Her sisters were sitting on stools teasing Eric big-sister-style and chopping fruit. Heath and Spider were whipping cream. Judging by the size of the feast in store, none of them would need lunch.

'Adam told us,' Anita whispered in her ear. 'We had to come see for ourselves.'

Her father squeezed her shoulder and kissed her cheek. 'And it was definitely worth it.'

A lump formed in Eve's throat. 'It's just pancakes, Dad.'

Mad Maxwell's eyes twinkled. 'It's a new beginning.'

She smiled. It was true and she felt lighter for having done it. The only thing that hung around her heart was that Adam had not returned with them. Of all the people in this room, he had been the one person she definitely owed breakfast to.

With the restaurant ready to go, the Maxwells and the Fitzwilliams turned their attention to the remaining wedding preparations. Eve and Natasha got together the next day to plan Phoebe's hen's night. It was also an opportunity to talk without their sister around. Ever since the bride had made up with her groom there didn't seem to be anything that could upset her. And they wanted to keep it that way.

Eve watched her sister's tired face as she focused on a computer screen. They were both sitting in front of their mother's laptop, surfing through local restaurants and reading menus.

'How are you feeling anyway?' she asked tentatively.

Tash grimaced. 'Oh, you know, nauseous, tired and totally confused.'

'Have you told Phoebe anything about you and Heath?'

'Only that we're still trying to work things out and I want it kept under wraps for now.'

'Does she know you're pregnant?'

'No,' Tash quickly shook her head, 'but let's not talk about me.' She tried to lighten the expression on her face by looking up from the screen. 'Tell me about Adam.' She leaned forward. 'You've been awfully quiet about him. Given us absolutely no details.'

Eve sighed. It was time to come clean. 'That's because there are none. It was all a ruse, we aren't having an affair.'

Tash's eyes narrowed. 'But the lingerie and the –'

'It was all just a big misunderstanding.'

'I don't know,' Tash said doubtfully. 'He looked pretty keen on you to me.'

Eve blushed. 'Maybe he is, but I don't think I should go there.'

'Why not?' Tash's eyes widened. 'You're not still hung up on . . .'

'No, no.' Eve immediately sliced her hand through the air. 'Definitely not.'

It was the truth. She was completely happy for her sister. Ecstatic in fact, that she was finally able to let go of all those fruitless feelings she'd harboured for years and realise for the first time that she and Spider would never have been good together. Not like Phoebe and Spider were. They were just too alike. Phoebe challenged him in ways that she never could.

*In exactly the same way that Adam challenges you.*

She banished the thought. Yes, in a perfect world she would love to date Adam. But she wasn't going to set herself up for a fall. And that's exactly what going out with Adam would be. She quickly outlined to Tash everything she knew about him, hoping she'd be able to confirm that she'd made the right decision.

'So let me get this straight,' Tash said as she clicked back to the search engine, 'he came to town to get over a broken heart.'

'Yes,' Eve nodded.

'And you're afraid he might be using you to do it.'

'Well, isn't he?' Eve demanded. 'I mean, look at him. Him and me together? It's just totally unrealistic.'

Tash snorted. 'I don't think so. Eve, you've got everything going for you. Looks, brains and talent. Don't sell yourself short. He'd be lucky to go out with you.'

She blinked. 'You reckon?'

'*I know*,' Tash responded adamantly. 'But that doesn't mean you should. You're right to be cautious. You need to do what's best for you.'

Eve sighed. 'Thank you. I just feel the kind of relationship I want is not the relationship that's on offer.'

Tash licked her lips. 'You think he'll hurt you.'

'I think it's more likely than not,' Eve shrugged. 'I wish there were some way to know for sure.'

'You and me both, darl,' Tash squeezed her hand and Eve wanted to cry. 'You and me both.'

After a moment's pause, Tash turned back to her screen. 'Hey, it looks like Saracen's has a new menu. I say we go with this one.'

Tash had paused on the website of the Saracen's Estate. It was a winery and brewery in one. They had a large spacious restaurant that doubled as a pub; both classy and elegant for its decking on the water and a giant fireplace for those cold winter nights.

'Okay,' Eve agreed. 'I don't have a problem with that.'

'Now for the guest list.' Tash pulled a pad and pen towards her. 'Who are we inviting?'

Eve shrugged. 'All the ladies going to the wedding?'

Tash pulled a face. 'Then we'll have all Mum's cousins there and Spider's aunties as well.'

Eve giggled. 'Not to mention Mum and Patricia. Can we really trust them not to fight?'

Tash hesitated slightly before saying, 'Nope. Let's keep it small. Just a few of Phoebe's girlfriends and us.'

'Great.'

Just at that moment, Phoebe walked in. 'There you are!' She was sunny smiles and suppressed excitement. 'I've been searching all over for you guys.'

Tash smiled back. 'We're making the guest list for your hen's night.'

'Oh,' Phoebe clasped her hands together, 'that reminds me. You know that girl we saw at the Wildwood Bakery, Bronwyn? The really nice one.'

'Y-yes,' Tash drew out the word as she caught Eve's gaze.

'I found out she's not actually staying with Claudia, she's housesitting for her. Claudia's gone to the big smoke for a holiday. So I say we invite her.' Phoebe's face lit up like it was the best idea anyone had had since they turned strawberries into jam. She leaned in confidingly. 'She's all on her lonesome there with a bunch of scruffy vineyard workers and could probably use a night out. I for one would like to get to know her better. What do you reckon?'

'Well –' Eve hunched a shoulder, darting her eyes towards Tash for guidance.

'I suppose we –' Tash searched Eve's face for clues on what to say.

'I knew you guys wouldn't mind,' Phoebe burbled on before Tash finished her sentence. 'But we can work the other guests out later. Dad's got a surprise for us in the barrel room.'

'The barrel room?' Tash repeated as Phoebe flew out into the hallway, calling over her shoulder, 'Meet you there.'

Eve groaned. 'I hate surprises.'

'And with Phoebe,' Tash agreed, 'you never know what you're going to get.'

'What are we going to do about Bronwyn?'

'Let's invite her,' Tash nodded. 'Dad won't talk to us. But there's no harm in slipping a hint in her ear to back off.'

Eve touched a hand to her temple. 'At the hen's party? I was afraid you were going to say that.'

The barrel room was a large brick and timber warehouse located in the winery. It was one of the oldest buildings on the property and in Eve's opinion the most romantic. With a tall gable roof set with muddy red tiles, it had that old barn look from the outside, until one realised that there were no windows – just two large wooden doors at the front.

This was where Tawny Brooks stored all their oak barrels, on large steel racks. With the doors closed, it was dark and cool. The perfect conditions for fermentation of must in oak. Eve loved the smell of the place, woody, sweet and heavy. The locals called the aroma 'angel's share' – the vapour of evaporated wine saved for heavenly spirits.

When she and Tash arrived, their father, Adam, Heath, Phoebe and Spider were already there, standing in the centre of the room. As vintage wasn't even halfway through yet, the barrel room was mostly empty.

'So what are we doing?' Tash folded her arms.

Eve could tell she trusted the situation almost as much as she did.

Phoebe's grin could have rivalled Willy Wonka's at the beginning of a tour. 'Dad is going to teach us all how to waltz.'

It was a well known local fact that at one point Mad Maxwell had been a ballroom champion for five years in a row. It was one of the many legends in his rather extensive and mysterious résumé that had not yet been fully disclosed.

Eve glanced into his smiling grey eyes and he nodded ever so slightly.

'Is this really necessary?' Tash sounded completely unenthusiastic.

'Come on, Tash.' Phoebe grabbed her arm and tugged her in front of Heath. 'Don't be like that. This is going to be fantastic. After Spider and I do the bridal waltz, the bridal party has to get up and dance as well. It's tradition.'

Eve glanced nervously at Adonis, who winked at her. It made her want to run for the hills and leap into his arms at the same time. He was just so beautiful. The word handsome wasn't strong enough. He was perfect. So perfect, in fact, that she had the sinking feeling that he would probably be an excellent dancer as well. The last thing she needed was to put her complete lack of coordination on display.

'Won't I be dancing with Spider's brother?' she asked quickly. 'He's the best man, right? And Heath's the other groomsman.'

'Yes,' Phoebe nodded. 'But since he's not coming till the day before the wedding, I thought you could practise with your boyfriend.'

*Of course.* Maybe she should have taken Phee into her confidence.

'Come on, sweetheart.' Adonis took her hand and twirled her in a circle. 'Surely you can put up with me for half an hour.'

She swallowed. 'It's going to take longer than half an hour to teach me how to dance.'

Phoebe nudged her. 'Oh, Eve, you're always so pessimistic.'

In the next instant she was back in Adam's arms, which played havoc with her decision to protect herself at any cost.

*Yes, but where has that ever got you, Eve?*

She had hidden from her restaurant dream too and it was only in setting herself free that she had realised how much she stood to lose.

He smelled like sunshine and man and felt so strong and dependable, it was hard to imagine him ever letting her down. Had she made the right decision to keep their relationship platonic?

'Concentrate, Eve,' her father smiled as she bumbled her way helplessly through his instructions, stepping on Adam's feet several times before he had to stop, sit down and take a 'pain' break.

She watched in embarrassment mixed with apology as he rubbed his feet. 'I told you I wasn't good at this.'

'Maybe you guys should change the dress code to include steel-capped boots,' he grinned.

Her eyes lit up. 'Can we do that?'

'No, we can't,' Phoebe said over her shoulder. She was dancing fabulously, of course. Thank goodness Tash wasn't also her usual over-achieving self. In fact, if she had to describe her elder sister's face at all, it would be to say that she looked rather green. Eve hoped she wasn't having another bout of morning sickness.

She turned back to Adam as he stood up, vowing to keep focused this time. The steps weren't actually that complex. The hard part was working out in which direction to take them.

'Eve.' Her father put his hand on her arm when she bumbled in the wrong direction yet again. 'Stop trying to work it out. That's the man's job. Just let Adam lead you.'

'Surrender,' Adam leaned down and whispered in her ear, sending a shiver straight through her body. It worked though. When she gave in, she floated around the barrel room easily enough as though they were one body instead of two. He gripped her tighter as they increased speed, pulling her in so there was no space between them at all. It was so weird dancing like that in her father's barrel room, warm and heady. They broke apart after one last circle and everybody clapped for them.

'Woohoo, guys! Well done,' said Phee.

Adam held on to her hand, his fingers laced through hers and that feeling of daring returned.

Why shouldn't she have him? Why shouldn't her fake boyfriend become real?

As he loosened his hand and walked away from her to get them both a bottle of water from the esky, she watched that long lean body, those broad dependable shoulders.

*If you want a real relationship then why don't you go after it, Eve?*

The concept was so simple it sent a jolt of electricity straight through her, rooting her feet to the floor as she wondered if she dared.

She was always the girl who waited, the one who couldn't speak her mind because that would be giving away too much. She was terrible with men, not because of the way she acted, but because of not acting at all. Her invisible dance with Spider had certainly proved that.

She watched Adam bend down and extract bottles of water from the esky and hand them out to everyone. She watched her sisters thank him with a smile, her father clap a hand on his shoulder, a joke passing between them she couldn't hear. And then Adonis turned back to her, his eyes softening perceptibly as they rested on her face.

Her hand went to her throat as a realisation paralysed her. It wasn't that she loved him, because that had been more than obvious for a while now. She was insanely in love with him.

No, it was the certain knowledge that she was going to fight for him as well. She, Eve Maxwell, was going to pursue the man of her dreams.

And she was going to get him.

Life without risk was only half a life. When she had decided to cook in the restaurant again, the fears of the past had left her. Last night, she had picked up the phone and made the call to Margareta's.

'I'm resigning,' she told May. 'I'm staying at Tawny Brooks.'

Absentmindedly, she had listened to her old boss's protests, whose outrage quickly turned to pleading. But Eve didn't care. She didn't give in. It was time to let go completely and pursue what she wanted, because she wasn't the girl who waited any more.

Of course, even as she made the decision, panic bubbled up.

Manhunting was uncharted territory for her and she wondered whether she needed some sort of plan. And if so, how was she supposed to come up with it.

'Hey,' Adonis said, crossing the room, causing her stomach to somersault, 'are you okay?'

She raised her eyes, wondering how to cover her obvious nervousness when luckily Tash took the words right out of her mouth.

'You know what, I think I'm going to be sick.'

# Chapter 30

When Tash flew from the barrel room, her hand over her mouth, Heath almost sighed in relief. At last! An excuse to get some time alone with her. He wasn't happy that she was sick, of course. However, her sisters had been working hard to keep them apart and he had a feeling that now, more than ever, they needed to talk. He looked at her family, who were staring wide-eyed at her sudden departure.

'Don't worry,' he raised his hand to reassure them, 'I've got this.'

He walked out of the barrel room, squinting slightly as his eyes adjusted to the bright light of the sun. He did not see Tash but could hear someone gagging in the scrub beyond a large green open shed in which an old tractor was parked. He hurried past the tractor and stepped into the bushes.

'Don't come any closer,' he heard Tash's weak voice warn him. 'It's not pretty.'

He frowned. 'I'll live.'

It's not like he hadn't seen her throw up before. This scenario, in fact, was pretty familiar to him – her pale face, early bedtimes and odd eating habits; the way she couldn't look at food one minute and then was ravenous the next. He'd seen all this before.

Did she honestly hope to keep this food-poisoning ruse up indefinitely? Particularly when her last pregnancy had been exactly the same with morning sickness starting earlier than the norm. Why couldn't she trust him with what was really going on?

His boots crunched on gravel and his hands pushed aside tall reeds as he found her in a small clearing, leaning against a stringy bark tree, a shaky hand passing over her moist mouth.

'I told you not to come.' Her eyes flicked towards him dispassionately.

He shrugged. 'I had to see if you were okay.'

'I'm fine,' she nodded, abruptly straightening and coming towards him.

She would have passed him too and continued to walk back but he caught her around the upper arm.

'Tash, please. Talk to me. I don't know what to do any more.'

She stopped walking but refused to look at him. Feeling like a bear, he let her go and was relieved when she didn't continue her backtrack but turned to face him.

'Neither do I,' she said at last.

'I take it your sisters know about our marriage difficulties now,' he murmured. 'They're treating me differently.'

'Well,' Tash said slowly, 'we can't pretend forever.'

His heart sank like a rock in a pond at the finality in her voice. The sound of someone who had given up. He took a breath. 'You could have told me you were ready to start telling people.'

'Why?' She looked up. 'Do you agree that we should?'

'No,' he took a breath, 'I don't. Not yet.'

He studied her face with a sense of futility. He thought he'd been reaching out to her all this time, showing her how much he wanted her back. She had seemed to respond too, to those little gestures he'd started to reintroduce into their life. Yet last week she had told him that she didn't trust him emotionally – a blow that had been very difficult to face. Or even believe. Yet now he saw the evidence of it right here in front of him.

She was pregnant and she had not told him. He had never felt more separate from her in his life.

'What's the matter, Heath?' She broke the silence that had lengthened between them. 'Upset because you can't see inside my head?' She grimaced. 'Join the club.'

Realisation hit him. This is how she must have felt, this was how she had suffered, when he hadn't opened up to her after their daughter had died. When you didn't know what your partner was thinking or feeling it was like being cast adrift on a raft to nowhere.

'Tash, I'm sorry. I'm sorry that I didn't try to open up to you more when . . .' he swallowed, 'Sophia died.' He said his daughter's name for the first time. 'I can see how much I hurt you.'

'Yeah,' she agreed. 'You did.'

He looked down into her steady glistening eyes. 'It was a stupid thing to do. Proud. Dumb,' he admitted. 'I just wanted to fix what had happened without looking too closely at it. My dad went through a lot of grief and anxiety when he came back from the war and that's how I was taught to deal with it. My family didn't talk about what he'd been through because it upset him. We avoided touchy subjects because we just wanted him to be our father again and not feel any more pain. We did everything to distract him from his past. And I guess I was trying to do the same thing with you.'

'Thank you for telling me.' She grabbed his hand and held it against her heart. 'I wish you'd told me earlier but I understand why you didn't. Really, I do.'

'If you understand,' he said quickly, 'then why are you so keen to start telling everyone our marriage is over?'

'That's not what I'm doing, Heath,' she said quickly. 'Not by any stretch. I just need some time to think, to process.'

'To talk?' he queried gently.

*Tell me you're pregnant, Tash*, he begged her in his head. *Tell me.*

If he heard it from her own lips then he would know that she trusted him again and was willing to put her life back in his hands. Not because he was pressuring her to but because she wanted to. She seemed to hesitate for a moment, searching his face. He bent his head and pressed a kiss to her trembling lips. When he raised his head, however, her eyes were cool.

'We should get back.' She nodded and began to walk out of the scrub.

He pushed his hands deep into the pockets of his jeans and watched her go.

*Too little too late, Heath.*

*Too little too late.*

# Chapter 31

There was not long now. Only three days away from the happiest moment in Phoebe's life. She knew there were still unresolved issues all around her. Tash's separation from Heath had been a huge shock, but she was optimistic that they could get back together. She had seen the looks of longing pass between them in the barrel room and hoped her 'fix up' hadn't been too obvious. She wanted a happily ever after for Tash and Heath, like she had with Spider.

After the strange confrontation with Eve about the lingerie, she had absolutely no reservations about their impending marriage. She and Spider had had a long debrief in the Tawny Brooks gardens afterwards.

'So . . . *Adam and Eve.*' Spider had slipped his hand through hers. 'It has a very fated ring to it, doesn't it?'

'And you don't mind?' She'd thrown him a sideways glance as the gravel path took them beneath the shade of a tall gum tree.

'Mind?' Spider laughed. 'I'm happy for her. And glad that she's not still holding on to feelings for me. Honestly, I had no idea, Phee. None. What can I say? Except that I'm as blind as a bat.'

She had teasingly poked him in the ribs. 'I kind of like that about you.'

'Well, will you find something your father might like about me too?' he'd pleaded with her, 'because that would really help me out.'

She'd told him everything then. Everything she had been through in the last few months, including her father's most terrible secret. She just couldn't keep it to herself any longer. The secrecy had caused too much damage.

Spider had been all that she hoped he would be. Supportive and understanding, a solid wall for her to lean on.

'I didn't want our wedding to be anything but a happy event,' she confided in him. 'That's why I put off telling you about Dad.'

'Phoebe,' he'd captured her face in his palm, 'I would never want you to shoulder burdens alone. If you're going through something then I want to go through it with you.'

How lovely that had been to hear. She had decided in that moment that she would leave it like that. She would not tell her father that Spider knew. He still distrusted him and would not understand. After all, there was still the issue of the fire that had been deliberately lit. Phoebe believed one hundred per cent that Spider had not done it. It was an accident that had been caused by Eve's candles, or it had been lit by someone else. Whatever the case, the last thing she needed right then was to get into a debate about it.

Her wedding was in three days and she wanted that to be her focus. Not a fire that had happened over a year ago. If there was an arsonist out there, he was long gone.

The final weeks before the wedding had passed in a blur of preparations. The restaurant looked fantastic and everything else was more or less finalised. From the flowers, to the music, to the cake.

That wasn't to say that there hadn't been a few hiccups along the way. Patricia and her mother were still fighting World

War Three from covert positions and her father did nothing to improve the issue by insisting on keeping score.

Patricia won the Battle of the Table Centres, getting her pick, which was the cupid statues instead of Anita's rustic flower arrangements from blooms picked in the Tawny Brooks gardens. To try to keep things fair, Phoebe had taken her mother's side over the question of the bouquets. Her argument had been for fresh flowers whereas Patricia had lobbied for fake (so that they could be a keepsake to pass on to her grandchildren).

But it wasn't just these disagreements that put Anita in a flurry. She knew her daughters were keeping things from her. Not that Phoebe could fault Eve and Tash for not wanting their mother to know about Tash's broken marriage, Eve's almost affair with Spider and new romance with Adam. All their mother would do was worry or, worse, try to wade in with advice.

How many times had she told Phoebe that Tash was thin and pale? How many times had she begged her to ask her sister what was going on? Phoebe saw the hurt expression in her eyes when Eve and Tash clammed up the second she walked into the room or began to talk rather loudly on some random subject that had been hashed out the day before.

Then, of course, there was Dad.

Phoebe's heart broke whenever her parents were together. She had never seen her mother bring a man more food than she did with her father. Whenever he was around, she was always fussing about him, trying to get past the wall he had erected around himself. Pushing tea and fruit and biscuits and the lord knew what else into his hands. 'Don't be silly, Annie,' she heard him tell her one morning, when they thought they were the only ones in the room. 'I just ate breakfast half an hour ago.'

'But you look pale.'

'I look pale because I'm tired. I wish you would leave me alone to rest.'

'Why do you shut me out?'

His voice was weary. 'I'm not shutting you out, Annie. Let's go and do something together this week. You and me. How about dancing?'

'So you can avoid my questions with loud music? I don't think so.'

His voice was edgy. 'If you don't want to spend time with me, that's fine, but enough with the incessant nagging.'

As he walked out, Phoebe walked in. Her mother was standing there in the centre, tears running silently down her face. Her face crumpled when she saw her daughter. 'He's mad at me again.'

Phoebe bit her lip as she folded her mother in her arms. 'Just leave him alone for a while, Mum. He'll come around.'

She half wished now that she hadn't agreed with her sisters' plan to make the hen's night for friends only. Her mother needed a night out, away from the house, away from her problems with Dad.

*Hang on, I'm the bride. I can have whatever I want.* 'Do you want to come with us to Saracen's tonight?'

Anita pulled back a little. 'I thought that was for the young people.'

'Tonight I think I need my mum there.'

Anita looked pleased and then her mouth pulled a little. 'Of course, this means we'll have to invite *that woman*.'

Phoebe supposed it would be impolite if they didn't, given Spider's mother was living in the same house. 'True.'

'Don't worry,' Anita patted her arm conspiratorially, 'I'll make sure she doesn't cause any trouble.'

Her sisters were strangely nervous that evening. And if she didn't know any better she would have sworn they were put out by the fact that she'd invited their mother. She knew Anita could be a pain sometimes but she thought they'd find it in their heart to remain patient with her. She tried not to get short with them and focused instead on getting ready. She didn't want anything to spoil her mother's night. Anita fussed over them as they prepared for the evening, running into their bedrooms with her perfume and her nail polish collection like she used to do when they were teenagers.

'Thanks, Mum,' she called again for the tenth time as she completed the finishing touches to her make-up.

The car ride to Saracen's was not completely unpleasant. Patricia and Anita sparred a little about the bridal corsages but otherwise they all arrived in one piece.

Eve had arranged for an alfresco table overlooking the Saracen's dam. Not much was visible at this time of night, but they could still hear the gentle lap of the water as they sat on the wooden deck, perusing their menus.

They ordered wine but made sure not to discuss it as there were so many winemakers' daughters at the table it wasn't funny. Everyone had the same opinion. Their own father's wine was the best. Phoebe knew the Maxwell sisters were no exception to this rule.

Her friend Bronwyn turned up late and she could see immediately that the pretty blonde was a little uncertain about being around so many people she didn't know. Phoebe got up to greet her right away. 'Hi,' she said, giving her a quick hug and a peck on the cheek. 'Great to see you again.'

'Thanks for inviting me,' Bronwyn smiled. 'I don't really know anyone locally so it's lovely to put names to faces.'

'No worries. I'll introduce you. Have you heard word from Claudia?'

Bronwyn blushed as she led her to their table. 'Oh, she's having a great time in Perth. I'm afraid you won't be seeing her in town for a while yet.'

Phoebe shrugged. 'That's more time to get to know you.'

She thought she'd introduce Bronwyn to her sisters first and led her over to their table. 'Hey, guys, this is Bronwyn.' She gestured at her sisters who were seated next to two other local girls. For some reason they didn't stand up. 'This is Eve and Tash.'

Her sisters looked up briefly.

'Nice to meet you,' said Tash rather coldly and then promptly turned back to her conversation with the girl beside her.

*What the?!*

Eve was also singularly unmoved, passing Bronwyn a rather stern nod before sticking her fork back into her food. Bronwyn seemed to take it rather well, happy simply to smile and move on.

'Here, come and sit next to me,' Phoebe said quickly in an effort to cover their snub. She was pretty unimpressed with her sisters' behaviour and, frankly, had been all evening.

After dessert, everyone moved inside to have drinks at the bar and she took the opportunity to pull Eve and Tash aside. Frogs croaked in the warm night air and the lights from the restaurant twinkled on the water.

'What's the matter with you two tonight?' she demanded harshly.

Eve's eyes widened and Tash blinked rapidly. 'Nothing,' they both said at the same time.

'Don't give me that.' Phoebe put her hands on her hips. 'You two have been acting strange all evening. Rude too. First with Mum, now with Bronwyn. I want to know what's going on.'

Eve looked stricken. 'We weren't rude to Mum, were we?' she asked Tash. 'I didn't think so. I've been trying extra hard with her lately.'

'Not rude precisely,' Phoebe amended, 'but impatient.'

Tash also looked upset. 'Do you think she noticed?'

'Well, I noticed and I'm not impressed. She's going through enough without you guys picking on her as well.'

'We're not picking on her,' Tash protested. 'We just didn't want her to come tonight.'

'Why not?'

Tash's lips clamped shut and Eve's eyes darted away.

Phoebe folded her arms. 'So this is how it's going to be again, is it? More secrets. I thought we were done with that.'

'Phee,' Tash grabbed her arm, 'trust me. You don't need this in your life. Especially now, right before your wedding.'

'I want to know everything. Tell me.'

'Phee,' Eve began wringing her hands, clearly looking for ways and means to stall.

'Are we best friends or are we just sisters?' Phoebe demanded. 'Whatever happened to club members only? Or am I no longer part of that club? Is it just you two?'

'No,' Eve gasped. 'We just don't want to ruin your week.'

'I think it's safe to say you're halfway there already.' Strange, how she had thought she was the only one with a secret. Yet, in all honesty, if she hadn't been able to trust them, could she really blame them for not trusting her?

Eve and Tash exchanged a glance at each other and then at the door, as though making sure no one else was going to come outside.

'Okay fine.' Tash grabbed her arm just above her elbow. 'We'll tell you.'

'Dad's having an affair,' Eve whispered. 'With Bronwyn.'

'*What!*'

'I know, it's insane. But we saw them on a date together,' Tash said urgently, holding on to her tightly as her body swayed.

'That day,' Eve finished for Tash, grabbing Phoebe's other arm, 'at the Wildwood Bakery. He turned up while you were on the phone.'

'They were holding hands,' said Tash.

'He gave her jewellery,' said Eve. 'It was undeniable.'

'*Why* was it undeniable?' She shook them both off her, furious. 'Because he's been a little distant lately, a little quiet? You idiots,' she hissed. 'He's not having an affair.'

Tash was trying to keep her voice calm and rational.

'Phee, you know Dad's been acting strange lately. Disappearing for long hours, blowing hot and cold with Mum.

He's having a midlife crisis, honey. I mean, look at that car he bought, the bungee jumping and the tattoos.'

But a blinding rage fired by months of pent-up anguish was taking over. 'I can't believe you would think this of our own *father!* That he would sell us out like that for a woman half his age? And Mum . . . after the life they've had together, after everything he's trying to spare her from, that he would just dump her like a hot brick? It's madness.'

Eve and Tash paused as tears began to cascade down Phoebe's face. She tried to dash them away but the more she wiped, the more they fell. Her sisters no longer tried to convince her as they watched her tremble and shake. Their mouths dropped open as they realised they had been wrong.

Worse than wrong.

Uninformed.

'Phee, what is it?' Eve's voice was quivering now. 'You know something, don't you?'

'I've always known,' Phoebe choked. 'I've known from the beginning, for months. Right after the doctor told him the news.'

Eve clapped a hand over her mouth.

'What news?' Tash's voice seemed to crackle.

'About the cancer,' Phoebe breathed, both relieved and guilty to finally have the news out there. 'He's got bowel cancer.'

There was silence. Stone cold silence.

Eve was the first to speak again. 'But it's treatable, right?'

Phoebe knew that exact feeling, that immediate grasp for hope in the face of this awful news. It was exactly what she had done when she had been told. Her words came out stilted in her efforts to make them gentle. But there was not an easy way to say it. 'Unfortunately, the diagnosis was late. After the colonoscopy in Bunbury, he had a CT scan and PET scan. It was all through his liver and lungs.'

'What does that mean?' Eve asked.

'The cancer is treatable but only to prolong his life rather than save it.'

'Prolong it? What do you mean?' Tash sounded angry. 'How long can they prolong it?'

'A couple of years, maybe a little more.'

'No!' Tash put her hands up against her words, blocking them out. 'This is not happening.'

Eve began to cry quietly, and Phoebe immediately moved forward to take her into her arms.

*What have I done? I've broken my promise. This is exactly what he didn't want. I'm completely useless. I've ruined everything.*

'Why didn't you tell us?' Tash whispered harshly. 'Why have you kept this to yourself? Did you think we wouldn't notice when he started getting sicker?'

'He made me promise.' Phoebe pulled back from Eve slightly, trying to get the words out quickly before they failed her. 'I found some of his medication a few months ago and so he had to tell me. He's been taking capecitabine. It's like chemotherapy in tablet form with very few side-effects.'

'Is that aggressive enough?' Tash asked.

'Not really,' Phoebe sighed. 'But he didn't want to go on the intravenous stuff till after the wedding.'

'Why?' Tash demanded.

'He wanted the family together one last time before he told you all,' Phoebe tried to explain. 'He wanted you guys to stop fighting. He wanted us to be happy and settled before he started the treatment. Intravenous chemotherapy leaves the body so weak and fragile. He just wanted a window of time with you guys while he was at his best before his health worsens.' She sucked in a breath as she moved to tell them the worst of it. 'Once he starts deteriorating,' she swallowed, 'well, let's just say, I've heard it's not much fun for anyone. He wanted this time for Mum and us, unfettered by his illness.'

'Mum isn't going to care about that,' Eve whispered.

Phoebe nodded. 'But the silly old codger is ashamed about having to put her through the pain of caring for him. He's always been the man of the house and he's really feeling this horrible sense of hopelessness.'

One of her father's biggest fears was destroying their mother's life as well as his own. When he'd asked her to keep his secret, it was the first thing he'd mentioned. 'I am going to become a burden to her. Do you think that's what I want?'

No amount of reassurance on her part had been able to take away his guilt.

Tash wiped a weary hand across her eyes. 'And here I thought he was having a midlife crisis. Really he's just been trying to cram all the stuff he wanted to do his whole life into a few weeks.'

Phoebe nodded. 'And all his doctors' appointments and blood tests too. He's been very good at keeping it all a secret.'

'And Bronwyn?' Tash prompted. 'How does she fit into all this?'

'She's a lawyer,' Phoebe told them. 'She's been helping Dad update his will.'

Eve put her head in her hands, massaging her temple. 'I can't believe how stupid we've been. How blind, and willing to jump to the worst conclusions.'

'We all make mistakes,' Phoebe relented. 'I've made the biggest of all.'

'What do you mean?'

'I've told you guys and I promised Dad I wouldn't.'

'No,' Eve hastily shook her head, 'that's not a mistake. Don't you see, Phee, that's the best thing you've done today. You shouldn't have taken this upon yourself. What are sisters for, if not to support each other?'

'Yes,' Tash reinforced her point. 'Weren't you upset when you thought we were keeping secrets from you?'

Phoebe nodded slowly.

'None of us need protection,' Tash continued. 'What we need is support and each other.'

'And so does Dad,' Eve put in. 'Though he won't admit it.'

It felt like a great burden was lifting off her shoulders. She suddenly realised how silly she'd been to keep her father's secret, and hypocritical too. Of course her sisters would want to know. They *needed* to know.

'What are we going to do?' she whispered.

They put their arms around each other, holding on tight, touching foreheads as though sharing their energy.

'The wedding is this weekend,' Tash whispered. 'Let's make it the biggest and best celebration the Maxwells have ever had.'

Phoebe smiled through her tears. 'Haven't I been saying that all along?'

# Chapter 32

Eve's alarm clock rang loudly in the room, jerking her awake, bleary-eyed and tired. The last few days had been difficult, constantly pretending that nothing was amiss – that nothing had changed. Trying to get to sleep at night was the worst. That's the time when she was finally alone and no one was watching. Thoughts of her father kept her up to the wee hours, tossing and turning and crying. How Phoebe had been able to deal with this for weeks all on her own she had no idea.

Today, however, was her sister's wedding day. The big event had finally arrived. She had to rouse herself, get the blood flowing, though it would be so easy to just lay there for another ten minutes. As long as she didn't move, time didn't tick forward and her father would not have to suffer. Life seemed so unfair. Her thoughts of the future seemed so lost without him.

Poor Tash was pregnant. The news must have been an even bigger blow to her, realising her child may never know their grandfather. She pulled herself to a sitting position, rubbing her eyes and fluffing her hair. Her elder sister was propping herself up with an iron will. They all were.

The Maxwell sisters had made a pact. No cancer today. Just love.

And that's exactly what they were going to do. It was six am and the wedding was at two. She swung her legs onto the floor. They would need every hour beforehand to get ready. She had better get a move on.

Spider had gone to his home in Dunsborough the night before, along with his parents and his brother, who had arrived that morning. So they would all be getting ready there. That left the Maxwell family and Heath at Tawny Brooks.

Her mother and father had to get ready earlier, as her mother's cousins were arriving from out of town. They would be having some pre-wedding drinks prior to the wedding.

Eve hoped her mother would be able to deal with the earlier start. She got out of bed, slipped on a dressing gown and headed for the kitchen. Anita had made coffee for everyone, including those people who were absent, and when she'd scrambled some eggs for their father she'd included some for Graeme as well. It was clear Eve's concern about her stress levels wasn't unfounded.

'I'm sorry, girls.' She glanced over at her grinning daughters. 'I don't know whether I'm on my head or my feet. It's not every day one of my beauties walks down the aisle.'

Eve looked at her father and caught his smile, tinged with a vague sadness. A lump lodged in her throat.

*Keep it together, girl.*

Heath reached out and took Tash's hand, who squeezed his hand back. She didn't look at her husband but Eve saw the relief mixed with tenderness in his eyes.

Phoebe ran her hands into her messy bedroom hair. 'Why am I so nervous? It's only what I've wanted like forever.'

'Because,' Eve threw her arm around her shoulder and squeezed, 'it's the happiest day of your life.' She threw a look at her father. 'Isn't it, Dad?'

John Maxwell glanced over at his wife. 'The day I married your mother was the day everything in my life came together. Your mother is my trellis and my wire. Without her, I can't stand up.'

'Okay, stop it,' Phoebe began rapidly fanning her face, 'I'm going to cry.'

'Well, if you're going to,' Tash said practically, 'do it now while you've got no make-up on.'

'Oh shoot, I really wanted to help you girls get ready.' Anita was frantically glancing at the clock. 'But my cousins are going to be here in a couple of hours. John, did you pick up your suit yesterday from the drycleaners?'

'Yes, dear.'

'And what about the camera? Is it fully charged?'

John blinked. 'Do we have a camera?'

Anita moaned. There was a knock on the window and they all turned to see a rather harassed looking man wearing a cap with 'Juliet's Florist' emblazoned across the top, pointing frantically towards the front door.

'Oh dear! How long has he been knocking?' Anita asked.

'I'll get it.' John rose from his seat.

'Listen, Mum,' Tash grabbed her hand, 'you just worry about yourself, Dad and your cousins. We girls can take care of Phee.'

'Are you sure?' Anita said, as John walked back in with a box full of corsages and bouquets tied with satin ribbon. Instantly, the room was filled with the fragrance of spring.

'Wow! They're gorgeous.' Phoebe jumped up from her seat and passed her nose over the box. 'Listen, you girls take the bathroom first. I'm just going to do a quick dash down the drive to unlock the restaurant so the kitchen staff can get in. I'll be back in five.'

'Is there anything I can do?' Heath asked.

'Yes!' Tash nodded. 'Could you go out and buy Mum a digital camera? She'll go nuts without one.'

'Done!'

Anita clapped her hands together. 'Oh, Heath, you're an angel.'

'Well,' his grin was lopsided, 'now that I've got competition for the top spot as favourite son-in-law, I've got to put my game face on.'

'Oh, I do like him,' Anita patted his cheek but spoke to Tash. 'I don't know why you children don't have some babies already.'

As Anita bustled out of the room, Eve got up quickly, grabbing Tash's arm and pulling her towards the bedrooms again. 'Okay, let's do this,' she said firmly. As Phoebe took off for the restaurant, Eve and Tash went to their bedrooms to lay out their dresses. Then, after taking it in turns to shower, they both sat down to trim and file their nails. Tash pored over their mother's nail polish collection, from Candy Floss to Bronze Beach, and pulled a face.

'Do you think we should have had this done professionally?'

'And take Patricia's side again?' Eve scoffed. 'We had to give Mum another win, particularly with Dad keeping score so fervently.'

Tash rolled her eyes as the hairdresser walked in – a young woman in jeans and a t-shirt. 'Hello, ladies? Who wants to go first?'

Tash slipped the nail clipper into the pocket of her dressing gown and sat down on the chair in front of Eve's mirror.

'I'll go get Phoebe,' Eve told them. 'She must be back by now and in the shower.'

Phoebe, however, was not in her bedroom or in the shower. Eve searched the rest of the house but her sister was nowhere to be found. When she walked in on her mother stepping out of the shower, Anita seemed surprised to see her.

'Everything okay, darling?'

'Perfect,' Eve nodded quickly, backing into the hall and nearly bowling Heath over. 'Have you seen Phoebe?' she whispered.

'Isn't she with you guys?' He was jingling keys, clearly about to head out to get the camera.

Eve bit her lip. 'She must be in her bedroom.'

There was no point in alarming anyone. Her mother was already like a coiled spring. So she returned to her bedroom, where the hairdresser had just finished putting curlers in Tash's hair.

'While we're waiting for those to set,' she informed Eve, 'I'll do yours.'

'Okay,' Eve agreed. But as Tash got up to vacate the seat, she whispered urgently, 'See if you can find Phee, will you? She seems to have disappeared.'

'Disappeared?'

'Is everything okay?' the hairdresser asked.

'Oh fine!' Eve quickly assured her. 'Nothing to worry about at all.'

*Just another day in the mad Maxwell household.*

Eve sat down in front of the mirror. Her hands fidgeted restlessly in her lap. Luckily, the hairdresser was not the chatty type and just seemed keen to get to work. It was insane for Phoebe to disappear just at this moment. She hoped there hadn't been another accident at the restaurant. God forbid that all their hard work should be overturned in the final hours before the wedding.

For some reason this near-miss made her think of Adam and her failed attempts to convince him that she'd changed her mind. When he came round for dinner, she went to kiss his cheek first. She took his hand and led him to the dining room. When he made his initial attempt to leave, she asked him to stay longer . . . which he did. But nothing ever came of it, especially with her sisters and her parents hanging around.

The fact was, she was just being too subtle.

*Like Spider all over again.* She swallowed hard. *You've gotta step this up, Eve. You've gotta bite the bullet and just tell him.*

Telling a man she liked him wasn't exactly her strong point. Look at the note she'd written to Spider. Wow, what a colossal disaster, and in more ways than one.

No, she was going to have to get Adonis alone and do this face to face. She chewed nervously on her lower lip. She had to make it absolutely clear that she wanted a real relationship, not a fake relationship or a rebound relationship. But a real frickin' relationship.

*Because I LOVE him.*

And then once she'd put that word out there, she had to ask him if he was still interested.

Just at that moment Tash reappeared, skidding into the room like she had a lion at her heels. The hairdresser was placing the last roller into Eve's hair so Tash quickly straightened and walked with more dignity to Eve's side.

'If you don't mind,' she said to the hairdresser, 'my mother needs you upstairs. Perhaps you can come down later and finish us and the bride when you're done?'

'Sure.' The hairdresser smiled, packing up her trolley of items and rolling out.

As soon as she was gone, Tash whipped out the hand she was holding behind her back and held up a note she'd been hiding.

'Can't find Phee anywhere,' she wailed. 'But I did find this in her room.'

Eve snatched the note out of her hand, thinking as she did so, that notes were always such terrible things and she would never ever leave one lying around again.

Dear Family,

When I woke up this morning, I realised my feelings were mixed. I can't go through with this. Please tell everyone I'm sorry.

Best wishes,

Phee

'Okay, that's bulldust!' Eve announced.

'Tell me about it,' Tash cried. 'She was ecstatic at breakfast.'

'And after everything we spoke about at her hen's night.' Eve's mouth tightened. 'There's no way she'd let Dad down. Or Spider for that matter.'

'Look at it.' Tash pointed to the page. 'Look at it carefully. This is not Phee's handwriting.'

Eve focused on the page. It was a close imitation but the letters were too close together and not as curly. And where was Phoebe's trademark signature? 'Where's the smiley face?' she demanded, flipping the note from front to back. There was nothing but a dirty smudge on the back.

'Exactly!' Tash snapped her fingers. 'Someone else wrote it.'

'Who?'

'I don't know!'

'What do we do?'

'We don't tell Mum, that's for sure.' Tash shook her head. 'She'll have a meltdown. Let's just try to find her ourselves while the hairdresser is otherwise occupied. There's no way we're cancelling this wedding.'

'Absolutely,' Eve nodded. 'Well, we haven't checked the restaurant yet and that's where she said she was going. I could go for a walk down there.'

'I'll recheck the house and the car park,' Tash nodded. 'I'll see if her car is missing. Take your phone, so we can call one another.'

'Right.'

Eve slipped on a pair of thongs, grabbed her phone and the note. She knew she looked ridiculous, with her hair done up in curlers, the nails of one hand painted and the other not. She had her pyjamas back on because they buttoned up at the front and wouldn't disturb her hair when it came time to get dressed.

She walked to the back of the house to check if the key for the restaurant had been returned to the cabinet. She opened the small cupboard and ran her eyes over the names printed above the hooks. The key was indeed missing. So Phee had not been back with it. Whatever had happened to her had happened at the restaurant or on the way.

And then she stopped focusing on the word 'Restaurant' and stared at the word 'Office' for the hook above. On the hook above that was the label 'Winery lab'. Her mouth dropped open.

No.

She looked down at the dirt-smudged note she had taken with her and compared the handwriting. There was no doubt about it. It was the same. Whoever had created the cabinet had created the note.

Then she remembered.

Hadn't Eric made this cabinet at his woodwork class in school a few years ago? He'd given it to their family as a gift . . .

Why would he want to stop Phoebe and Spider's wedding?

She pocketed the note and dashed out the back, straight for the gardens and the restaurant. Luckily, there was no one about as she half-ran, half-walked down their long driveway to the cellar-door car park.

The restaurant was unlocked. In fact, she could see a lot of movement inside. The kitchen staff had arrived and were already busy, so Phoebe must have managed to let them in.

'Eve!'

She turned around in embarrassment to see one of her old colleagues, Martin, waving at her from the alfresco area. He was laying out napkins on the white tablecloths. The chairs had all been studiously wrapped in white linen the night before as well. Gorgeous pale blue satin sashes were tied around the high backs with a loose bow. Everything looked wonderful. Not a spoon out of place.

Pity about the bride.

'Long time no see,' he smiled. 'You're looking . . . fabulous.'

'Yeah, right,' Eve groaned. 'Is Phoebe in there?'

'No.' Martin shook his head. 'Not since she opened up for us. Don't tell me you're missing the bride?'

'Not exactly, just a slight hiccup in communications.' Eve tried to infuse some lightness into her voice.

*Damn you, Eric!*

She turned around and headed straight into the Tawny Brooks gardens to find him. She hobbled over the paths, which was rather hard to do in a pair of rubber thongs.

*Ouch, ouch, ouch.*

Up ahead she could see Eric's wheelbarrow and a bag of manure under a tall red gum.

She walked over, clutching the note, looking left and right for signs of him or the direction in which he might have gone.

She was just thinking of heading over to the sheds when a hand slipped over her mouth.

'Hello, Eve? Looking for me?'

She tried to speak but he was holding her too tight. Nothing more than a groan came out. The voice, while lacking its usual deference, was unmistakeable.

Eric reached down and took the phone and the note out of her hand, chucking them both into his wheelbarrow. 'Don't worry, I'll show you where Phoebe is.'

It took her mind a moment to process that it was Eric, the shy, squeaky-clean teenager, who was half-pushing, half-dragging her through the garden, which was now starting to feel more like a haunted forest. No one could see her struggling from the house. The vegetation was too thick. She tried her hardest to wriggle out of his hold, but he held her fast. He was taller and stronger, so she never stood a chance. She just couldn't fathom why her old family friend was doing this. She tried to speak against his hand but the words came out muffled. They walked for five minutes in this close embrace through the gardens and beyond it to the back of the property. Perhaps she should have been more scared, but this was Eric pulling her along – anger and shock seemed much more appropriate.

When she saw his garden sheds at the bottom of the path, these feelings only solidified. This childish prank was getting beyond a joke. No one would hear them out here.

As if to prove the point, as soon as they drew near to one of the sheds, she could hear Phoebe yelling from within.

'Hey, is someone there? Hello! I'm locked in here! Get me out!'

With one hand wrapped around Eve's body, Eric took the keys off his belt and opened the door. Phoebe was sitting on the floor in the middle of the room. Her hands were tied behind her back and her ankles were bound together in front of her with plastic zip ties.

'Eve!' Phoebe cried.

'Phee! Thank God you're okay,' Eve cried as Eric shoved her inside. They were in even bigger trouble now that she'd been caught as well.

'Of course she's okay,' Eric snapped. 'Like I would ever hurt Phoebe.'

Phoebe's gaze flicked to him. 'I'm sorry, Eric, but your behaviour thus far doesn't really give us much confidence.'

'I wouldn't be doing any of this,' Eric retorted like a sulky schoolboy, 'if you'd come to your senses.'

Eve yelped as he pushed her to the floor.

'Hey! Easy,' Phoebe gasped. 'Are you all right, Eve?'

'I've been better.' She winced as Eric pulled her hands behind her, also securing her wrists together with the same sturdy nylon tape.

'Eric, why are you doing this?'

'There's no use talking to him,' Phoebe warned her. 'I've tried.'

'But this doesn't make any sense.' Eve turned to Eric. His face was red and sweaty from his exertions. She was sure her face must be glistening too, the shed was damn hot. She didn't know how Phoebe hadn't passed out from being in here all morning. 'Eric,' she looked at him sternly, 'this is not you.'

'What would you know?' he demanded. 'You girls are so blind, so caught up in your own little worlds. You don't notice anyone else or what they are trying to do for you.'

'What are you talking about?'

'Just be quiet,' he snapped. 'You're the worst of the lot of them. Pretending to be nice to me, but secretly stabbing me in the back.'

'Eric, calm down. If you'll just explain it all to me, maybe I would understand.'

'No, you wouldn't. Because you don't know what real action is. You're too much of a coward. Well, I'm not like that!'

Eve blanched. '*Eric.*'

'I tried to help you.' His voice wavered as he spoke to her. 'I found your note in the tea jar. I could see you were suffering. I knew how you felt because that's how I felt about Phoebe.'

*Oh shit and mushrooms.*

Eve closed her eyes and moaned at the mention of that *blasted note*. 'So,' he continued, 'for both our sakes, I set fire to the restaurant.'

Her eyes flew open. '*You what!*'

'The fire wasn't an accident, Eve. He did it,' Phoebe said crossly.

'But you were stupid.' He shot the words at her. 'You just ran away with your tail between your legs. You didn't use the opportunity I gave you at all.'

'Which was what?' she said slowly, almost too afraid to ask.

'To take Spider with you!' he ground out. 'I thought you'd carry on as business partners and go work somewhere else. Away from Phoebe, away from here. But you let me down, Eve.'

'Eric, only a simpleton would believe that a business relationship is forever. I had no power over Spider's choices.'

If anything, he'd had power over hers. All those months of self-loathing, feeling like a failure, wallowing in how much she'd let everyone down. All along it had been this guy, this over-eager teenager, who had set fire to the restaurant.

Her voice shook when she added for good measure, 'You're completely nuts.'

'No.' He shook his finger at her. 'What's insane is that everybody just continued to find excuses for Spider to hang around here, even after I put the kerosene in his office. I mean,' Eric put his hands on his head, 'how dumb can you people be?'

'What have you got against Spider?' Eve demanded.

'Nothing, particularly. Except that he stole my *girlfriend*.'

Eve glanced at Phoebe but she shook her head. 'Don't look at me like that. I don't understand it any more than you do. I was never your girlfriend, Eric. Ever.'

'We used to hang out all the time. You played bung cricket with me.'

'As a friend,' Phoebe protested. 'It was just family fun.'

He ignored this. 'You accepted all the gifts and flowers I sent you.'

'I had no idea those were from you. And I threw most of them out,' Phoebe shook her head. 'I thought all those gifts were from Jack.' Phoebe rolled her eyes. 'Or Colin . . . or Steve . . .'

'You were always very popular with the guys,' Eve smiled. 'I don't blame you for getting confused.'

'You were just as popular as me,' Phoebe snorted. 'Just more careful about giving out your address.'

'I don't think so. You were definitely the life of the party.'

Phoebe sighed. 'You mean the noisy one.'

'*Enough!*' Eric snapped. 'Remember me? The one who's holding you captive? This is not a sisters' bonding session.'

'Sorry, Eric.' Phoebe glared at him, twisting in her ropes. 'But this prank of yours is getting old. I'm getting married in a few hours. You need to let us go.'

'You're too trusting,' he said. 'When I showed you the note in the tea jar I was sure you would dump Spider and come to your senses. But you still didn't get it, did you? *Even then!*'

'Get what?' Phoebe rasped.

'That I love you.' He slapped his fist into his palm passionately. 'You just need to give me a chance to prove it.'

Phoebe chewed on her lower lip. Eve could tell she was trying to figure out a way to let Eric know this wasn't the case without incensing him further.

Eric went to the bench along the back wall where a couple of one-litre water bottles were perched. He took one and brought it back to them. 'Here, you better drink something or you'll both dehydrate.'

He gave Phoebe some first and she gulped it down. Eve frowned. It was very hot in the shed, she had to wonder whether a few sips of water would be enough.

'You know, if you tied our hands in front of us, we could help ourselves,' she suggested tentatively.

Eric squinted at her before raising the bottle to his lips. 'Not risking it,' he said shortly.

She drank quickly when he held the bottle to her lips. It was warm and not very refreshing but better than nothing.

'What happens when we need to go to the toilet?' she demanded as he pulled the bottle away.

'I don't care,' he tossed at her. 'I'll be back soon.'

He stood up then, placed the water back on the bench and headed for the door.

*Leaving already?*

'Eric, wait! This isn't going to prove anything. How long are you going to keep us in here?'

'Relax,' he held out a staying hand, 'it's just for today. I'll let you go as soon as all the wedding guests go home.' He winced slightly. 'I'm really sorry you had to get mixed up in this, Eve. You shouldn't have come looking for her like you did.'

'This is silly, Eric,' Phoebe cried. 'Holding me here for a day is not going to stop the wedding. If I don't marry Spider today, I'll just marry him tomorrow. You can't change that.'

'I'm not trying to stop you,' he smiled. 'I'm trying to stop him. How do you think he's going to feel after you jilt him,

Phee? Pretty bloody devastated, that's what. With any luck, he'll leave town.'

Eve groaned at his simple plan. 'He's been talking to Adonis.'

'Who?' asked Phoebe.

'*Adam*,' Eve quickly corrected herself, wincing at the mistake. 'I meant Adam. He left his hometown when his fiancé jilted him. Eric,' she addressed him with what she hoped was a patient tone, 'people don't always react to things the same way.'

'I'm not asking for your advice.' Eric stepped away from her. 'All you two need to do is sit tight till I get back. It's going to be a long hot day.'

On these words, he backed out of the shed and slammed the metal door behind him. Thank goodness it was a shed with windows. They heard Eric slide the door latch, securing it with the rusty old padlock.

*Great. Totally screwed.*

'You were looking for me?' Phoebe shuffled closer to her as soon as his footsteps faded on the path outside. 'Does anyone else know you're here?'

'Not really,' Eve groaned. 'I was supposed to call Tash but he chucked my phone away. She's looking for you too but she has no idea I came here.'

'So no one is coming to our rescue?' Phoebe sighed.

'Not immediately,' Eve winced. She wriggled around a bit on the floor, trying to ease the tightness of her binds. 'Geez, this is uncomfortable.'

'Try it for another hour,' Phoebe said dryly, 'then you'll really start to ache.'

'Maybe we can come up with our own plan of escape,' Eve said brightly. 'There's got to be a way out of here.'

'If you can come up with something, I'd love to hear it.' Phoebe spoke like a seasoned kidnappee. 'Struggling in these things doesn't help, it just gives you blisters. I thought maybe

I could cut the zip ties somehow. But he's more or less emptied the shed of anything sharp . . . actually, anything at all. He must have been preparing for this all week.'

Eve looked around. Her sister was right, the shed was pretty empty. There were no tools anywhere. Apart from a steel bench attached to the right wall where the water sat, there was nothing else in the room.

'Okay, we're stuffed.'

'Well,' Phoebe sighed, 'at least we've got each other.' She laid her head on Eve's shoulder. 'Nice rollers by the way. You're going to look sensational with your hair all up and perfectly curled at the wedding. *Adonis* will have his tongue hanging out.'

Eve blushed, but leaned back a little and rubbed her cheek against her sister's hair, smiling helplessly at her optimism.

'Phee, are you sure we're going to make it to the wedding? Eric seems to have all his bases covered.'

'Well, Tash is still out there looking for us. She's a smart cookie.' Phee's voice was very firm. 'She won't let anything get in her way.'

# Chapter 33

Athena Markopoulos was standing directly in Tash's way.

'*My dear*,' she cried, clasping her small chubby hands together, 'how you've grown since I last saw you! How old are you now?'

'Er . . . thirty.'

'Ah,' Athena rubbed Tash's cheek and then pinched it excitedly. 'A big girl now, yes?'

'Pretty much,' Tash said, taking a step back from the woman who was, ironically, at least a foot smaller than her. Undeterred, or perhaps unaware that Tash was trying to edge her way slowly towards the door, Athena closed the distance between them again, grabbing her hand. 'How's that husband of yours? Any children yet?'

'No, not yet.' Tash coloured, glancing rather desperately about the room for something with which to distract Athena before her mother's other cousins noticed her there as well. She had just intended to poke her head in on her search for Eve. Now it seemed Athena was not letting her go.

'Never mind,' Athena smiled knowingly and to her horror, reached out and rubbed Tash's belly. 'Very soon, my dear, very soon. But *tell me*, where are your sisters?'

Tash swallowed.

*Well, isn't that just the question of the century?*

'You know,' she waved her hand vaguely, 'getting ready in the bedrooms. Speaking of which, that's where I should be.'

'Yes, I can see you're running behind.' Athena's coal-coloured eyes ran over her hair curlers and dressing gown. At least her face was more or less done. She'd started putting on her make-up while waiting for Eve's phone call that never came.

She'd tried ringing Eve herself but her sister was not picking up either.

'You must be very excited about your sister getting married,' Athena gushed. 'I remember when I was your age I was a bridesmaid for my sister at her wedding. I was incredibly nervous.'

'I'm doing okay –' Tash tried to cut her off.

*Apart from the hyperventilating.*

'It's such a stunning venue, Tawny Brooks. Your sister is so lucky to be able to use her childhood home.'

'Yes, it's very special –'

'And so generous of Anita and John,' Athena continued. And then, to Tash's extreme discomfort, she leaned in discreetly. 'I did wonder why their names weren't mentioned first on the invitation.'

Tash blinked. 'I beg your pardon?'

Athena pressed her hand sympathetically. 'It seemed a little odd, you know, after their contribution.' She opened her eyes wide and leaned in even closer, as though expecting some sort of confession from Tash.

Suddenly a female voice shrieked from across the room, 'Well, who have we here?'

And to Tash's horror all the Greek women by the window immediately spun around.

'But it's Anita's eldest girl!'

'The one in finance, or was it marketing? Anita was so proud when she graduated.'

'Didn't we go to her wedding a few years ago?'

'Yes, but no children yet.'

There was a groan. 'What a shame! They have such a big house in Sydney, don't they?'

'Her husband is a builder,' announced the only male in the group and the women seemed to hush at the sound of his voice. 'He's very good with houses.'

This last pronouncement seemed to calm them somewhat and they all turned to her with expectant smiles on their faces, making her feel like a mouse in a trap.

'Dear,' Athena pressed her gently, 'where is your husband?'

And then, as if on cue, Heath walked into the room. His head was down, absorbed in the camera he'd just bought. Fortunately for Tash, he wasn't aware of the mousetrap he'd walked into until it was far too late.

'Heath!' she cried as though a lifeline had just been thrown to her.

'Tash?' He looked up in surprise.

With brute force, she wrenched her hand free from Athena. 'Just in time for a photo!' She snatched the camera out of his hands and pushed him towards her mother's cousins. They immediately all attached themselves to him. She snapped a photo, laughing at his shocked expression, and then lay the camera on the coffee table. 'Heath, these are my mother's family from Greece. I really must get back to getting ready.'

'Tash –' Heath called out desperately.

'You said you'd do anything for me.' She winked at him and then with a quick intake of breath, stepped out into the foyer again. The doorbell rang at that moment and with a sigh she quickly bustled over and opened it.

A small man with wizard-white hair, a priest collar and a black prayer book clutched to his chest beamed back at her.

'Father Christos,' she blinked, not recalling her mother winning The Battle of the Celebrants.

'Hello, dear, I know I'm a little early.'

'Okay,' she nodded, quickly standing aside so that he might pass over the threshold. 'I'll get my mother to help you. Could you just wait in the si– actually,' she changed tack quickly, 'would you mind waiting in my father's study?'

'Not at all.'

Shutting the front door, she swiftly ushered him further down the hall and into another room so that she could find her parents. After all, someone had to rescue poor Heath from the Greeks.

Luckily her mother was already in the hallway, with the hairdresser in tow.

'Tash, I've been looking everywhere for you and your sisters!' she exclaimed. She was dressed in green lace and white pearls, her hair pinned back with a tasteful fascinator.

'Mum, you look amazing!' Tash smiled. And she did. You could definitely see the beauty of her youth in her flushed cheeks and carefully lined dark eyes. 'Dad is going to be blown away.'

'Never mind that.' Her mother swatted her hand, though Tash could tell she was pleased. 'The hairdresser is ready to do Phee's hair.'

'I've been sitting around waiting for half an hour,' the woman by her mother's side said crossly. 'I won't have enough time to do a good job if we don't get started right away. Where is she?'

'Er . . . that's a very good question.' Tash was racking her brain for a stalling tactic.

'What do you mean, it's a good question?' Her mother's voice heightened in pitch.

'I hope it's not a case of a runaway bride,' the hairdresser said sternly. 'I do have another wedding this afternoon, so I can't stay much longer.'

Anita snorted. 'Runaway bride, indeed. That's ridiculous.'

'Too funny,' Tash agreed with a twinge.

'Where are your sisters?' Her mother turned back to her with a stern look in her eye. It was the same one from her teenage years when she got home from a party in the wee hours of the morning.

'I think they're at the restaurant,' she quickly blurted, which wasn't a complete lie.

'What are they doing *there?*' Anita demanded, but then spoke again before Tash had a chance to respond. 'Never mind, just go get them and bring them back to the bedroom.'

'Yes, I'll do that,' Tash nodded and then said to the hairdresser, 'Would you mind waiting a few minutes longer?'

The hairdresser glanced rather impatiently at her watch. 'I guess so. But please hurry.'

'Of course,' Tash agreed and grabbed her mum's arm before she could walk off. 'Mum, your cousins are here. Heath needs you in the sitting room.'

'All right, I'll just find your father first.'

On this assurance Natasha quickly trotted back to the front door to make her exit. But when she pulled it open there was someone standing on the other side, her hand poised to knock.

'Er . . . hi,' said the officious-looking lady in a white pants suit, her hair styled like Princess Diana, a pink carnation in the lapel of her jacket. 'I'm Susan Cornish. I'm here to perform the ceremony.'

Tash cringed. So her mother *hadn't* won The Battle of the Celebrants, after all.

'Er . . .' She chewed nervously on her lower lip. *Phoebe, why aren't you here when I need you?*

'Do I have the right house?' Susan tried to look behind Tash.

'Yeah, you do. Come in.' Tash stepped back, trying to think of a quick way to deal with her. 'Would you mind waiting in the . . . the . . .' She went down the list.

The sitting room: the Greeks.

The bedroom: impatient hairdresser.

The study: the priest.

'How about the dining room?' Tash suggested with a hand in the small of Susan's back. 'That appears to be safe, I mean, *free* at the moment.' She gave her a gentle shove. 'Right down the hall,' she called out. 'Last door on your left. Someone will be with you shortly.'

*I hope.*

Right now she had more pressing matters to deal with. Such as where the hell her sisters had disappeared to. There seemed to be no doubt in her mind that foul play was afoot. What with the decoy note and Eve's unanswered phone, she was starting to get rather worried. It was already half past twelve. Only one and a half hours before Phoebe was due down the aisle.

*Okay, you can do this. You can find them.*

She raced down the steps of the front porch, scanning her surroundings. All the cars were in the car park with an addition of a few extras so it didn't look like they'd driven off anywhere. She hurried down the driveway, her phone pressed to her ear with Eve's number on redial. She had already decided to search the entire estate, including the winery. But first she wanted to check the restaurant. The quickest way was through the garden. It was also less conspicuous for a woman in a dressing gown and curlers.

Ferns brushed her bare legs as she scampered past, nearly sliding on the gravel at one point. The scent of flowers filled the air and insects clicked at her as she began to sweat.

*At this rate, I'm going to need another shower.*

It was hot and sticky in the garden even under the shade of the overhanging branches of a giant red gum. And then she heard a phone ringing. Two phones ringing, in fact – one in her ear and one not too far from where she was. Her feet skidded to a halt and she dropped her hand from her ear so she could hear the other phone more clearly. She backtracked slightly until she saw a wheelbarrow in a small clearing, some gloves and a packet of manure on the ground. As she approached it, the sound of the phone got louder and louder, until she was standing over the wheelbarrow. There it was, lying on the dirt inside, the crumpled decoy note beside it.

There was a sigh behind her. 'Not you as well.' She was seized from behind, one hand over her mouth. 'All right,' he said in her ear, in a resigned voice. 'You'd better come with me.'

# Chapter 34

The door to the shed flung open and Eric pushed Tash in, hands already bound behind her back.

Phoebe's heart plummeted.

*You've got to be kidding me.*

She raised her head from Eve's shoulder. 'Tash! Not you too.'

'Are you all right?' Eve asked, sitting up straighter.

'Fine.' Tash winced as Eric pushed her down to the floor with a hand on her shoulder. 'Oh, except for the whole kidnapping thing. Why didn't you call me and tell me Eric had turned into a psycho?'

'He took my phone off me before I could,' Eve protested. 'Does anyone know where you are?'

'Unfortunately not.'

'How's Mum?' Phoebe asked. 'She's not going crazy with worry, is she?'

'I've managed to stall her but once she notices I'm missing –'

'Enough talking,' Eric barked. He knelt down in front of Tash and bound her feet with another plastic zip tie. 'You bloody Maxwell women. Can't you just stay out of each other's lives?'

'The Maxwell sisters stick together no matter what,' Phoebe informed him firmly, with a quick bolstering look at her siblings. 'Don't we, girls?'

Tash bumped Eve's shoulder as she tried to move her feet into a more comfortable position. 'Yes, we do.'

'Ow.'

'Sorry.'

Eric glared at them. His cheeks were pink and he was clearly feeling outnumbered. 'You guys aren't taking this seriously enough.' He put his hands on Phoebe's shoulder. 'I know you hate me right now, Phoebe.' His voice was low and measured. 'But one day you'll thank me for stopping you from making the biggest mistake of your life. He's not worthy of you. He doesn't appreciate you the way I do.'

As Phoebe looked into his desperate blue eyes, she couldn't help but pity him. She'd known this kid since he was twelve. He wasn't a bad guy, just a tad delusional. Perhaps if she hadn't been so preoccupied with everything else, she might have realised what a crush he had on her. Her regret, however, didn't mean she was going to allow him to ruin the happiest day of her life.

'Eric,' she said, 'I'm sorry if I've led you to believe something that's not true, but you have to face reality. The two of us will never be a couple, even with Spider out of the picture. I just don't see you that way.'

'I know.' He stood up, shaking his head. 'You see me as a silly teenage boy.'

'Well, not silly precisely.' Phoebe tried to get a certain brightness into her voice. The kind she always found herself using with him, and indeed every other child in her primary school class. 'I just think you've been a little confused this past year. And you're not really thinking straight now either.'

He frowned and she tried again.

'Do you honestly think I'm going to fall in love with you after Spider leaves town?'

'Spider's leaving town?' Tash asked in surprise.

'No, no,' Phoebe quickly reassured her. 'He's hoping Spider will do what Adonis did.'

'You mean Adam?' Tash asked, with a smirk at Eve.

'Yes, all right.' Eve said. 'Sometimes I may *accidentally* call him Adonis. It's a very similar name to Adam. So shoot me. Anyone could make that mistake.'

'Uh-huh,' Tash snorted.

'Quiet!' Eric snapped and they all turned to him expectantly.

He looked from one to the other and she could see he was starting to lose the thread of his plan. Beads of sweat were popping up on his forehead and a muscle in his upper lip twitched nervously.

'Come on, Eric,' Tash added for good measure, 'cut us loose. We promise we won't tell anyone how much you've stuffed up.'

'I haven't stuffed up,' he growled.

'I'm thirsty,' said Eve. 'Can we at least have some water? It's so hot in here.'

'And what about lunch?' Phoebe added. 'I'm starving. You're not going to torture us, are you, Eric?'

'Torture you?' Eric seemed horrified. 'You know I'm not that sort of person, Phoebe.' He wiped the back of his hand across his mouth. 'Look, I'll go get you girls some water and sandwiches.'

'Sandwiches,' Tash pulled a face. 'What about some fruit?'

'I'll bring *everything*,' Eric promised. 'And be back in twenty minutes.'

'Thanks, Eric,' Phoebe called as he backed out of the shed and closed the door behind him, bolting it once again.

'Okay, Tash,' Phoebe turned to her eagerly, 'what's the plan?'

'Why do you assume I've got a plan? I'm just as tied up as you are.'

'Really? No plan?' Phoebe glared at them both. 'Do you girls know what a rescue mission is or were you just bumbling along hoping for the best?'

Eve stuck out her tongue at her. 'Well, how were we supposed to know you were being held captive by a lovesick teen? I thought we were done with secrets around here.'

'Hey,' Phoebe retorted, 'I didn't know he had a crush on me. He's too bloody shy.'

'He is, you know,' Tash agreed with this. 'Doesn't ever speak to me unless I speak to him. So I guess it's reasonable to see how his kidnapping tendencies might have slipped under the radar.'

'Thank you!' Phoebe acknowledged her support. 'I had no idea when he approached me behind the restaurant that he was going to lock me up here. He said he had a wedding gift he wanted to give me.'

'When did he plant the note in your room?' Tash asked.

'While we were all having breakfast,' Phoebe explained.

'Well, I, for one, am over this.' Eve wriggled in her bonds, only wincing in pain for her efforts. 'And this can't be good for Tash, being in a hot shed, pregnant and everything.'

'Tash is pregnant!' Phoebe squealed, bum-shuffling across the floor to press her lips to her sister's cheek. 'Does this mean you and Heath are back together? We can go shopping for baby clothes! I know this great store where –' She stopped. 'What are you two laughing at?'

Eve choked. 'Nothing.'

'And no, Heath and I are not back together. Anyway, how is that even relevant when we're all stuck in here?'

'Of course it's relevant. It's always relevant.' Phoebe tossed her head. 'I'm so happy for you. And whatever you decide with Heath, you know I'll support you one hundred per cent.'

'I know you will.' Tash's face softened.

'And so will Eve.' Phoebe bumped her. 'Won't you, Eve?'

'Will you guys stop bumping me? These ties are really chafing my wrists.'

'Sorry,' Phoebe quickly apologised.

Eve rolled her eyes. 'And of course we'll help Tash take care of the baby. How could we not?'

Phoebe grinned excitedly. 'Oh . . . he's going to be so cute. Or she . . . whatever, we'll love her. But you'll have to move to Tawny Brooks, Tash, because Eve's going to start working at the restaurant again.'

Tash looked across at Eve with interest, wincing as she strained against her bonds. 'Are you?'

Eve raised her eyes from contemplation of her bound feet and Phoebe held her breath, hoping her prediction wasn't going to fall short.

'Yeah,' she said shyly. 'Why not?'

'Woohoo!' Phoebe's smile got bigger. 'You see, this is what I'm talking about!'

'Why is she so happy?' Tash looked heavenwards. 'Doesn't she know we're locked in a frickin' forty-degree-temperature shed and we have no means of getting out?'

Phoebe shrugged. 'I'm getting married today and I've just found out I'm going to be an aunty as well. Not to mention my sister's moving back to Tawny Brooks. It's good news all round.'

'The wedding might not be happening,' Tash reminded her softly.

Phoebe stiffened. 'Now *that* isn't an option.'

All those months of planning and organising – it wasn't going to be for nothing. She wasn't going to jilt Spider. Not because he wouldn't forgive her, but because she wasn't going to let some out-of-control teenage boy get the better of her.

They had all waited too long for this moment and so had their father. For the first time in a long time, she and her sisters were getting along again. The family was together. They needed to pull this off just as much for him as for her and Spider.

'Aren't you guys sick of bad news?' she demanded. 'We can't let this beat us. We're the Maxwell sisters, we just have to work together.'

Eve edged closer to her. 'I don't want you to miss your wedding, Phee.'

'I won't,' Phee said firmly. 'Think, guys, think! Come on, we can do this.'

'Have we got anything sharp?' Tash asked, perking up.

'Dead end already.' Eve jerked her head around the room. 'There's nothing in here but us.'

'Have you got anything sharp with you?' Phoebe asked Tash.

She started to shake her head and then paused. 'Wait, I put the nail scissors in my robe pocket.'

'Are they still there?'

'I assume so,' Tash said, brightening, before her face fell. 'Of course, I have no way of getting to them with my hands tied behind my back.'

'Well, I could try getting to them,' Phoebe suggested.

'Not if you can't see what you're doing,' Tash groaned. 'Your hands are tied behind your back too.'

'Yeah, but I can see what's going on,' Eve suggested.

Phoebe and Tash glanced at her. 'Come again?'

'We're really going to have to work as a team on this. I'll be the eyes. Phee, you be the hands and, Tash, you just try to make the pocket as accessible as you can.'

Tash nodded. 'Maybe we should stand up for this.'

'Good idea,' Phoebe agreed.

Accompanied by some groaning, they all slid along the ground towards the wall and used it to help themselves stand up. Once standing, it was a matter of hopping into a position where Eve could guide Phoebe's hands to Tash's pocket.

'Okay, higher. Now to your right and just down a bit.'

They must look absolutely ridiculous, Phoebe thought. All the same, anticipation was building in her chest as Eve guided her fingers to the pocket.

'Feeling inside the pocket now,' she announced, her fingers fumbling around against towelling. 'Got it!'

'Don't drop it,' Tash warned. 'It'll be hard to pick it up off the floor.'

Phoebe spent a few minutes carefully positioning the nail scissors in her fingers so that she could operate them with one hand. 'Okay, I think I can cut with it now but I need Eve to be my eyes.'

Tash turned around and bounced closer so that Eve could guide Phoebe through cutting the zip tie around her hands. A few seconds later, the plastic fell away.

'Amazing!' Tash cried. 'I'm free.'

'And here you were, wanting to get your nails professionally done,' smiled Eve. 'Thank goodness we all stayed on Mum's side.'

'Okay, okay,' Phoebe instructed. 'Cut mine. Eric's going to be back soon. In fact, we're lucky he's taken so much longer than he said he would.'

With Tash's hands completely free now, it was only a minute later before they all were. And not a moment too soon. Footsteps sounded on the path outside.

'He's back,' Eve hissed. 'What do we do?'

'We attack him when he unlocks the door.' Tash put her fist in her palm.

'Can we do that?' Phoebe was worried.

'There's only one of him and three of us.' Tash grabbed them bodily and positioned them both by the door. '*And* we have the element of surprise. Now, get ready.'

They waited only a couple of seconds before the door flew open.

'Now!' Tash yelled and all three girls leapt onto their captor, pushing him to the ground. Phoebe grabbed one of his arms, pinning it to the floor by kneeling on it. So did Tash. Eve straddled his chest, holding his shoulders down so that he couldn't rock about.

It was only when the dust settled that they all realised who they had overpowered.

Phoebe watched in amusement as Adam looked up into Eve's startled face, a grin stretching from ear to ear. 'You see,' his eyebrows arched at her, 'I knew deep down you wanted to jump me.'

# Chapter 35

Eve quickly scrambled off his chest, hoping the redness in her face wasn't too obvious. As usual, his comment was completely outrageous. Only this time, it was also dead on the money.

'Er . . .' She stood up, patting her hair, realising in horror that it was still in curlers.

*Damn, I must look a fright!*

'So . . . er . . .' She looked down, shy as a teenager at her first dance. 'What are you doing here?'

'Rescuing you,' he chuckled. 'What does it look like?'

Her sisters were laughing and also standing up.

'Well, as you can see, *Adonis*,' Phoebe dusted her hands, 'we don't need rescuing.'

'Damn right we don't,' Tash grinned. 'The Maxwell sisters can take care of themselves.'

They both held out their hands and helped him up. Eve wished she'd had the foresight to do so. He looked so deliciously handsome, lying there propped up on his elbows – all Knight in Shining Jeans and Flannelette Shirt, and she was dying to touch him. But every time she was even vaguely near him, she got all jumpy and chickened out.

To distract herself she pounced on the obvious question, folding her arms across her dorky pyjamas in the hope that it would somehow make them less noticeable.

'So, how did you know we were in trouble?'

'Your mother is running around like a headless chook back at the house. The hairdresser raised the alarm that you girls were nowhere to be found, causing the priest and the JP to also demand what was going on.'

'The priest and the JP?' Phoebe repeated.

'Yeah,' Adam winced apologetically. 'You've got two celebrants. But don't worry, after Heath got away from the Greeks he turned diplomat and is sorting out the mix-up.'

'The Greeks?' Phoebe squeaked.

'Mum's cousins,' Tash informed her. 'They must have wanted in on the gossip.'

'They did,' Adam assured her in a way that was not reassuring at all. 'That's when your mother rang me to look for you girls. I tend to be the one she calls when any of her family goes missing.'

'Well, I've got to say,' Phoebe patted him on the shoulder, 'you figured it out pretty quickly.'

'It was luck.' His lips twitched. 'I was walking back through the gardens on my way to the restaurant, the last place Tash was supposed to be heading to, when I spied Eric pushing a wheelbarrow.' He grinned. 'That in itself wasn't suspicious until I noticed what it contained. Three bottles of water, three sandwiches and three apples – looked like lunch for the Maxwell sisters.'

'So,' Tash prompted, 'what did you do next?'

'I took him back to the house and sicced your mother on him.'

'Oh dear.' The sisters' eyes widened.

'Was there bloodshed?' Phoebe whispered nervously.

'No, but there was a massive commotion and Heath came charging out of the dining room with the JP and the priest in tow. They got stuck into the kid too. So, you know, by the time Father Christos told him he was going to burn in hell, and the JP said he was going to rot in jail and Heath threatened to rip his freckly frickin' head off if he didn't tell him immediately where his wife was, we had ourselves some answers.'

Tash blushed but couldn't suppress a smile.

Phoebe punched his arm. 'Wow, I would have loved to have been there!'

'Well,' Adonis conceded thoughtfully, 'I was a little nervous throughout but your father enjoyed it immensely . . . sitting there on the couch watching the whole debacle – all he needed was a bowl of popcorn.'

'I bet,' Tash replied dryly.

'But where were the Greeks when all that was going on?' Eve demanded.

'They were in the kitchen,' Adonis grinned. 'Your mum hit upon an excellent way to keep them all fully occupied while we sorted it out.'

'Food,' Phoebe clapped her hands. 'But where's Eric now?'

'On his way home, most likely. Your mother called his father and he was coming over to pick him up.'

'Do you think we should report him?' Eve winced. 'Personally I'm a little reluctant to get the police involved.'

'Well, we should at least recommend he see a psychiatrist or something,' Tash suggested. 'We don't want him to think this kind of behaviour is okay.'

'True,' Phoebe agreed.

'The fire is also another issue,' Tash said firmly. 'He shouldn't be allowed to do that much damage to our property and just get off scot-free. He may be a teenager but he is legally an adult. I think we should sue him for some damages.'

Eve nodded. 'Good point.' Her eyes widened suddenly. 'Hey, Patricia's brother is a psychiatrist, maybe we can talk to him about this. He's going to be at the wedding today.'

'*The wedding!*' Phoebe exclaimed. 'Come on, we can talk about this later. I'm covered in grime and I'm getting married in an hour.'

'Oh yes, of course,' Tash grabbed her arm. 'We better get back to the house. Hopefully the hairdresser didn't leave when things started to go pear-shaped.'

'I'll be right behind you guys,' Eve called out, and then took a massive breath. 'There's, er . . . there's just something I need to tell A-Adam first.'

''Course you do.' Phoebe flicked a wink at her.

'Don't be too long,' Tash called over her shoulder as she and Phoebe made their way back up the garden path towards the house. 'And come in the back way, won't you? You don't want to get dragged into the kitchen.'

'Okay,' she yelled back, waiting till her sisters' laughs faded before turning nervously to Adonis. He was leaning on the inside of the shed, regarding her with arms folded across his bulging chest. His flannelette shirt was rolled up to the elbows revealing tanned forearms.

'Damn, it's hot in here,' she remarked. 'Should we step outside?'

'Okay.' They walked out of the shed and a warm breeze caused a few loose strands of her hair to tickle her cheek.

*Stalling again, Eve?*

She tucked them behind her ear and then clenched her trembling fingers. Why was it that whenever she needed to tell a man how she felt, her tongue tied itself in knots and she started sweating like a pig? She couldn't even raise her eyes from the ground to look at him. It was no wonder her secret unrequited love affair with Spider had been such a disaster from start to finish.

*But you're not that girl any more, remember?*

No, she was Eve Maxwell – a first class chef returning to Tawny Brooks to make her mark, one of three women to escape a kidnapping using her own survival skills and the current love interest of a Greek God.

*Girl, you're on fire. Act like it.*

'Are you okay?' Adonis smiled. 'You look like you've swallowed a frog.'

She choked. Add that to the hair curlers, the thongs and the pyjamas and this definitely wasn't perfect timing.

She looked up at Adam, who was regarding her so expectantly that she just couldn't stop.

'Sorry,' she apologised. 'I'm trying to work out how to tell you something that's been sitting with me for a while now but I just didn't have the courage to get it out there because well, you're . . .' She flicked a hand at him. '*Adonis*.'

'Okay,' he held up his palm. 'If we're going to have another conversation where you tell me to date a supermodel, I'm out.'

'No, that's not what I'm going to tell you.' She lifted her chin and straightened her shoulders. 'Though you could.' She inhaled deeply, licking her lips before slowly releasing the air. She lifted her hands helplessly. 'I like it that you're kind to my mum.'

'Huh?'

'Let's face it,' she tried to get the explanation out quickly, 'she needs to be handled with a lot of patience because she can be very high maintenance. And you're generous with people. I mean, I know Eric turned out to be a little crazy but it was so great that you took him under your wing when you first started working here and befriended a shy guy like that. It takes a certain kind of person to recognise the needs of others so easily. I know you didn't spot that he was a potential kidnapper, but then neither did we, so –'

His brows were knitting now. 'Er . . . Eve –'

'And my dad, wow!' She threw up her hands. 'He thinks you're fantastic. And he's a tough crowd to please. You're the only winemaker patient enough to have taken on board his winemaking philosophy. You're just an amazing person.'

'Okay.' He touched a hand to her forehead. 'I think you must be suffering from a little dehydration.'

'No, no.' She grabbed his hand and held on to it. 'Let me finish, I'm building up to a grand finale here and I can't be interrupted.'

'All right then.' His lips twitched as he put his other hand over both of hers and moved in closer, which was rather nerve-wracking so she sped up her talking speed again another two clicks. 'I know I told you that I don't want a rebound relationship, and that's still true. But I think in not taking that risk I've cut off the promise of something more.'

His opened his mouth to say something, but she put her finger there.

'I've realised how silly I'd been trying to protect myself from the one thing that could make me the happiest girl in the world. Because, Adam,' she stood taller, 'I love you. More than anything. You challenge me in ways that no one else ever has. I never would have decided to move back to Tawny Brooks if it weren't for your nudging. And I know this is probably coming out all disjointed because it's been a very rough morning and I'm not good at this.' She rolled her eyes heavenwards. '*Everybody* knows I'm not good at this.' Her eyes widened at her lack of foresight. 'Maybe I should have written all this down so I would sound more sophisticated.'

'No!' He released her hands and snatched her into his arms. 'No more notes.'

'Not a note,' she replied indignantly, though it was hard to keep her stern expression against the sudden pleasure of his embrace. 'More like a speech of sorts. You know, so I've really polished what I've got to say.'

'But I love it when you're all garbled.' He smiled down at her. 'I just love you.'

She stilled, her composure burnt up like coal dust in a hot flame. 'What did you say?'

'I love you, Eve. Of course I love you.' He threw back his head and laughed. 'More than anything. And okay, maybe if you do the maths, since my last relationship it hasn't been long enough. But in my heart I know that relationship was nothing like this. It can't even compare.'

'Really?' Eve whispered.

'Are you kidding me?' He grinned. 'I'm crazy about you. And if you hadn't said all that I would still be running around trying to convince you. What do you think that fake boyfriend crap was about?' He rolled his eyes. 'Apart from unmitigated torture.'

She smiled. 'Well, perhaps I should get on with the rest of what I was going to say then.'

He blinked. 'There's more?'

'Oh yes.' She nodded. 'Perhaps it's a little redundant now. But I wanted to make sure we do this right. So I was thinking . . .' He moulded her body to his while she was still talking and she lost her train of thought. 'What was I thinking again?'

'I don't know,' he growled, '. . . something.' She turned her face away to get some clarity and he took advantage of her movement by pressing his lips on her neck, then behind her ear. She shut her eyes, desperately trying to find a point of reference. 'Ah yes, the fake boyfriend thing.'

He raised his head abruptly, looking down at her with such tenderness that she forgot that she was Eve Maxwell.

*Who didn't date Greek Gods.*

*Who didn't ask men out.*

*And who certainly didn't proposition them in the garden in her pyjamas.*

'Yeah, what about it?' He raised an eyebrow.

'I was wondering,' she tossed her head, 'if you'd like to go out with me on a real date some time?'

He laughed. 'Are you asking me out?'

'Yes,' she nodded solemnly. 'This is going to be a real and proper relationship with all the trimmings and trappings.'

'So it's official then, you definitely have the hots for me?'

She flung her arms about his neck with a roll of her eyes. 'What can I say? You got me.'

'About time.' He kissed her with all the passion they'd been saving for weeks.

Brushing the stray strands of hair from her temple, he captured her face in his palms and they kissed like they were the only two people on earth.

Eve reflected on this analogy in daydreams that occurred with alarming regularity for many years to come. It was, after all, a particularly fitting sentiment given their names were Adam and Eve and her mother's garden was as glorious as Eden. The only thing that really spoiled the authenticity of the legend was their lack of nakedness. But Adam taught her not long after that that was a matter also very easily remedied.

# Chapter 36

The wedding ceremony was magical and went off, surprisingly, without another hitch. The bride was late, but only fashionably so. Phoebe looked stunning in a sheath of white satin with a lace overlay. The hairdresser had bailed on them, so Tash had done her hair. She wore it simply – half up and half down so that her veil sat nicely over the hair gathered at the back of her head. The rest had been curled and cascaded gently across her bare shoulders. In any event, there was nothing that could disguise the pure joy in her expression. Tash was supremely satisfied when she saw Spider visibly hold his breath as his bride walked to the top of the aisle to stand next to him.

The wedding took place under the shade of their father's famous gazebo – the only place on the estate fitting enough for the ceremony. The vineyard workers had put a new coat of paint on it and it gleamed almost as brightly as Phoebe's dress. Her mother had tied white roses to the columns and the chairs for the guests had been laid out on the grass behind it so everyone could also share in the gorgeous view of the entire estate.

As for the celebrant, Heath had sorted that problem out with an extraordinary amount of tact.

'Do you, Phoebe Maxwell, take Christopher Fitzwilliam to be your lawfully wedded husband, to love and to cherish, in sickness and in health, in good times and in bad, from this day forward as long as you both shall live?' Father Christos looked solemnly over his prayer book.

'I do,' Phoebe smiled through tears.

'And do you, Christopher Fitzwilliam,' Susan Cornish smiled officiously at Spider, 'take Phoebe Maxwell to be your lawfully wedded wife, to love and to cherish, in sickness and in health, in good times and in bad, from this day forward as long as you both shall live?'

'I do.' Spider's tone was firm and resonant.

Tash couldn't help but peek a glance at Heath, who was standing on the other side of the groom. She realised that he was not looking at the ceremony at all, but back at her. Those deep brown eyes were fixed upon her face, studying every nuance of her expression as though she was centre of the stage, not her sister beside her.

He looked so handsome in his tuxedo, as strong and determined as the day they first met. His waistcoat was a pale blue to match the satin of the dresses she and Eve wore. Her gown was a simple cut, sleeveless with a round neckline that gathered under the bust and then fell straight to the floor. She felt very Regency in it and almost like a debutante. This wedding wasn't just a new beginning for Phee and Spider. It was a new beginning for Eve and for her as well.

As the vows washed over her, she remembered giving them herself only five years earlier to Heath in front of a very similar crowd. She remembered how she'd felt that day, how content, how safe.

She'd lost so much since then, all because she'd lost faith in them as a couple.

It was true that he'd let her down. But she'd let him down too.

For the last month he'd been fighting like crazy for her. And what had she been doing? Still running, still afraid. When was she going to stop and fight too, addressing those vows she'd given all those years ago?

Marriage, after all, wasn't just about being there for each other when the going was good, when times were rosy and the other person made you feel great. It was for the bad times as well. She clutched her bouquet tighter as she took in his eyes. She pulled her gaze away before she burst into tears. Instead, it fell on her parents, and that only made her want to cry more.

They seemed so happy, sitting side by side. Her father was holding her mother's hand. Anita looked so proud. Delirious, in fact, as she watched Phoebe commit her life to Spider. Anita had weathered a tough month – full of both struggles and confusion – but she'd never lost faith. She just persevered, pushing through the difficult times to get to this.

Her father had withdrawn from his wife to protect her. He'd wanted to give her this moment. Tash realised that now. This moment, where she had all her family around her, celebrating love and happiness. A moment of perfection.

She knew times were only going to get harder for them from here, when her father finally told everyone the truth. He'd start getting sicker. Her mother's role would become that of carer, not just a wife.

And he knew it.

There was a sadness in his eyes as he looked not upon his daughters, but upon Anita's face, catching that shine in her eyes and holding it close to his heart. Her father had always been a strong man, a man of his own making. He was unconventional but he forged his own path – he always had. To become so vulnerable and dependent was going to be tough for him. He didn't want to go through it. He didn't want to put his wife through it either. But the choice was out of his hands.

She wasn't worried that her mother couldn't handle it. Anita would continue to give, to care and to sacrifice for her husband until he passed, which was probably why he'd held on to this time for her for so long. To see them like this pushed such a wave of pride through her heart. And the tears she had been holding back fell anyway.

She felt someone touch her elbow, and then a tissue was pushed into her hand. She glanced quickly behind her to see that it was Eve – curls piled up upon her head and tears also rolling down her cheeks.

Tash grinned sheepishly and dabbed at her own face.

'We now pronounce you husband and wife,' announced the celebrants together. 'You may kiss your bride.'

With a grin, Spider moved in before they finished talking and Phoebe returned his embrace. Everyone stood up and clapped. Her mother hugged her father. Eve slipped her hand in Tash's and squeezed it. Tash looked across at Heath, who smiled warmly at her and her heart pounded erratically against her ribcage.

A few minutes later, they were all signing the registry and the photographer's camera was having a serious workout.

'Hey.' A hand came to rest on her neck as Phoebe and Spider took off to take photos by the lake.

'Hey.' She looked up shyly. 'Great job.'

He looked down at her in surprise. 'What did I do?'

'Getting the celebrants to perform a dual ceremony,' she nodded. 'A stroke of genius.'

'Really?' he grinned. 'I thought Patricia was going to have a heart attack when she found out.'

'She'll live.'

'I guess she will.' He nodded and then Phoebe called them over for a bridal party photo. She felt strangely cheated as soon as he left her side to slot straight back into the crowd. The photos seemed to take forever, first this pose and then that in the heat of the day. Tash was glad when they were finished.

Apparently, so was Eve. She'd slipped away as soon as they hit the reception to be with Adam. It looked like those two had become a couple sometime between lunch and hors d'oeuvres.

The restaurant looked amazing, all decked out in wedding paraphernalia, flowers, hearts and bows in every nook and cranny. A little too many in her opinion, but that was Patricia's taste shining through. Not that her mother looked in the least distressed by it. If her table was overflowing with anything, it was happiness.

Shortly after entrees the speeches were announced and Tash stood up to give hers. Eve had cunningly opted out of the toast but stood valiantly next to her with a hand around her waist to show her support.

It was a short speech because there was really only one thing Natasha wanted to say.

'No one in this world deserves this fairytale ending as much as you do, Phee. You bring the sunshine to all our lives. You're the only person I know who can find a silver lining in practically anything. It doesn't matter how I'm feeling, whenever I see you, you always manage to lift my mood.' *Even when I'm being held hostage!* she thought but didn't say. 'And now you've found someone to do the same for you. Congratulations, Phee. We love you. And we love you too, Spider. Welcome to the family!'

As she sat down, her father went up to stand by the bridal table to deliver his speech. She noticed with a heavy heart the extra lines on his face and the hollows in his cheeks. He was losing weight. She'd been too caught up in her own problems to notice it.

His face wrinkled as it broke into his usual cheeky grin. 'Okay, so we all know I haven't had a soft spot for Spider. What man, with three daughters, trusts anyone who comes snooping around his property for a piece of his family? It's been a long and difficult relationship. But you know what?' He glanced at Spider, who continued to regard him cautiously. 'He persisted and he stayed there and he's still here. And I have to take my hat off to him for that because I can be a real bastard when I want to be.'

There was a collective gasp and then a giggle rippled through the room. Tash watched her father's steady gaze carefully and realised that this was his way of apologising. She hoped Spider would realise that too. Glancing his way she saw Spider grin at John and he tipped his head slightly.

'I'm sure you'll make my Phee a wonderful husband because persistence,' her father winked, 'especially where we Maxwells are concerned, always pays. However,' he lifted a solemn finger, 'that's not to say I'm not going to give you a little unsolicited advice.'

There was a groan from his audience and a few eye-rolls but he continued briskly. 'Marriage is like a vine.'

There were even more groans in the room.

'Everything's like the vine to you, Mad Max,' someone yelled from the back.

'Stay with me. Stay with me.' He raised a steadying hand. 'The wedding is the part where you're planting. There's so much to do, so much to organise. You've got to prepare the soil so it's not too rich or acidic. You've got to set up your trellises in neat rows and, when the shoots come up, twine them about the poles of the trellises so they grow in the right way. After that, you're all set. Ready for vintage. Now all you've got to do is wait for those magic grapes to appear.

'Wrong. The truth is, the work has only just begun. You don't know what's coming. You don't know whether it's going to be drought or flood, disease or insects, animals or fire that comes in to try to destroy what you've made.

'Marriage is like that too. The wedding day is always perfect. After that . . .' he shrugged, 'you don't know what the weather's going to be like. But real love is what will get you through. Today,' he raised his glass, 'I wish my daughter and her husband true and everlasting love. A bit of laughter, a bit of hard work, a bit of excitement, lots of patience, some arguments, a bit of fun, some disappointment, sharing the good times and the bad, rollercoasting up the highs and swinging through the low points, a handful of tears, a bucket of forgiveness. Journeying through life together as you promised each other on your wedding day, for always.'

By the time his speech came to an end, Tash wasn't quite sure who he was talking to. Twice he looked across at Anita, who was dabbing wet eyes and clutching her hands together in her lap as she watched him. And then he looked at her, those pale eyes seeming to see right through her, right to her very soul. As he turned his gaze to include Heath, she knew there was a message there for both of them. A message that she could not ignore any longer.

As soon as all the guests settled in for dessert, she pushed out her chair and went outside to sit on the bench that overlooked the lake. A shadow fell over her, and a smile curled her lips, though she didn't look up. 'I knew you would come.'

It was Heath, of course. One thing she'd found over the years was that he was always aware of exactly where she was in the room. She knew that because it was the same for her. He didn't say anything, simply sat down beside her and took her hand in both of his, pulling it into his lap and cradling it there as they gazed out upon the lake.

'I don't want us to end, Heath,' she whispered. 'I want to stay together.'

A sigh seemed to ripple through him.

'Not that,' her voice wavered, 'I think we should forget about what happened. If anything I think we should remember it, because I never want to lose you like that again.'

'I know.' He squeezed her hand tightly. 'Neither do I. I love you, Tash. And I'm sorry for everything I've put you through.'

'I'm sorry for everything I've put you through.' She turned to face him, pressing her legs against his, running the palm of her hand down the side of his face. Those eyes of his mesmerised her with their intensity. She licked her lips. 'I need you to forgive me, Heath, for losing faith in us. I didn't fight for us when you did. I just gave up.'

'It was worth the wait.' He put his own hand on her face, capturing it and holding it there so that he could study every nuance. As his eyes roved hungrily over her mouth, she wondered what he was waiting for and then realised that he wanted her to kiss him, just to be sure. She smiled.

*Make it count, Tash!*

'I love you, Heath. In good times and in bad. Now and for always.' She leaned in and pressed her lips to his, putting all her love and trust in that one kiss. It did not take him long to respond, wrapping his arms around her and pulling her onto his lap.

'Heath,' she cried breathlessly when they finally pulled apart, moments later. 'There's something I need to tell you.'

'Can it wait?' he asked, nuzzling her neck and making her giggle. 'You look absolutely delicious in this dress. I think you should wear it all the time.'

'I might not be able to fit into it much longer.' She grabbed his face again, so their eyes could meet. 'You see, Heath. I'm pregnant.'

His lips twitched. 'I know.'

'What?' She released his face. 'How do you know?'

'Well, it was kind of weird that you had food poisoning for three weeks straight, especially when I was eating the exact same food and no one else was sick.'

She groaned. 'I've always been such a terrible liar.'

He touched his forehead to hers. 'Just the way I like it.'

'Why didn't you tell me you knew?' She thumped his shoulder. 'Here I was trying so hard not to look green in front of you and hoping you wouldn't notice that I wasn't drinking the wine any more.'

'I didn't want you to feel pressured to be with me because of the baby. I wanted you to choose to be with me because you love me. And because we're meant to be together.'

She kissed him quick. 'Good answer.'

He smiled. 'But I am excited about having another child with you too.'

She liked that he'd said 'another'. Tracing a pattern on his suit pants with her finger, she asked tentatively, 'You're not worried?'

He squeezed her tight. 'I'm prepared and I'm ready.'

As she shared his gaze, a sense of well-being fizzed through her. 'Me too.' Her lips curved. 'Me too.'

# Chapter 37

*Three Years Later*

'Is it just me, or does this wedding seem a little quieter than the last one we had at Tawny Brooks?' asked Phoebe from her position in front of the mirror. She was putting the finishing touches to her make-up. Her hair had been stunningly styled in loose ringlets by the hairdresser about half an hour earlier.

Tash leaned over her to pick up a sprig of baby's breath on the dresser. 'Don't jinx it, Phee.' She turned around and gestured to a little girl with long dark hair and eyes so similar to her own, she could have been looking into a mirror. 'Here, Grace. Come here. Let's put this in your hair.'

'Will it look nice, Mummy?' the little girl asked tentatively.

'It'll look gorgeous,' Tash enthused. She didn't look half bad herself, Phoebe noted, in a beautiful floor-length burgundy-coloured gown.

'Sorry,' Phoebe apologised, returning her attention to the mirror and patting a stray strand of hair back into place. 'I just feel like we've had extra time to get ready.'

'Why?' Tash smiled as she dressed her daughter's hair. 'Because Eric hasn't locked us in the shed again?'

Phoebe grinned and then stood up with a groan. She pressed a hand into the small of her back, sticking out her round belly. 'This does get easier, right?' she queried. 'My back is killing me.'

'Well,' Tash winked, 'you know what they say: the only cure for pregnancy is birth.'

'Thanks,' Phoebe returned sardonically, but she was smiling as she rubbed her hand over her protruding stomach. Her gown was the same colour as Tash's but obviously not the same style, given Tash's wonderfully slim silhouette and Phoebe's ample girth.

'When are you having another?' Phoebe grumbled. 'I'm feeling terribly fat today.'

Tash's lips twitched. 'I don't know. Still trying to get used to the first one.'

As if on cue, Heath entered the room, splendid in a black tux and burgundy waistcoat. When he saw his daughter, he immediately dropped to a squat, holding his arms out wide. 'All ready, darling?'

'Daddy, I look pretty.'

'Yes, you do.' He glanced up with laughing eyes at his wife. 'Should I take her to the sitting room? The Greeks will love her! And Daddy and Uncle Spider seriously need a distraction from the conversation about Aunty Athena's varicose-vein surgery.'

'For sure,' Tash nodded. 'She's all set.'

They were just about to leave when Eve burst into the room, her heavy stride in direct contrast to the floaty gown of white satin and chiffon that swirled about her ankles.

'Eve, you look breathtaking!' Phoebe gasped.

'Forget about that.' She tossed the comment aside, panic in every line of her face. 'Has anyone seen Mum? She's missing.'

'You see,' Tash threw at Phoebe, 'you've jinxed us.'

'Ssshh,' Phoebe hushed her and came over to Eve. 'Calm down, love. I'm sure she's around somewhere. The hairdresser only just left.'

'I've searched the house.' Eve threw up her hands. 'I'm wondering whether I should run down to the restaurant.'

'Not in that, you're not.' Phoebe shook her head. 'I'll go.'

'No, I will.' Heath stopped her with a glance at her stomach. 'In your condition there's no way you'll be running anywhere very fast.'

He strode from the room and everyone turned back to Eve. 'Don't worry, honey,' Phoebe hugged her briefly. 'I'm sure she's fine.'

'You know how upset she was this morning,' Eve leaned into her. 'Thinking about Dad and how he would have loved to have been here.'

A silence fell between them as they thought of their father, who had died last year after a two-year battle with bowel cancer. He'd been cheeky to the end, even when he was completely bedridden, always trying to make light of his situation when deep down they knew how much he hated being so helpless.

All three girls had moved back to the region to help care for him – a circumstance he loved and felt guilty about at the same time. They had to assure him repeatedly that Tawny Brooks was where they wanted to be, not just because he was sick.

Spider and Phoebe lived in their house in Dunsborough, Eve moved back into the family home with their mother. And Tash and Heath had sold their house in Sydney and moved to the sticks. They'd bought a property on the beach and Heath was starting his own building company in Busselton.

When John Maxwell finally passed, it had been both a relief and a great loss. There was no doubt about it, they all missed him madly. But his deterioration, especially in his final days, had been very difficult to watch. In the end, they knew his time had come.

'Eve,' Tash came over and put her arms around her, 'he's here, watching over us. I know he is. He wouldn't miss this for the world.'

Eve hugged her back. 'It's just so hard, you know, especially today.'

'I know.' Tash rubbed her arms. 'I miss him terribly too.'

'Yes,' Phoebe sighed. 'I always used to rely on his insight. He always knew what to say when no one else did.'

'Chenin blanc,' Tash whispered.

Eve looked up. 'What do you mean?'

'The grape variety he planted when he didn't know what else to plant.'

Eve frowned. 'No, that's not the way the story goes. He didn't plant an eighth variety. He ran out of time.'

Phoebe grinned. 'He told me it was tempranillo. Mum helped him choose it over dinner.'

They looked at each other and then, with tears in their eyes, reached out and held each other's hands.

'Mummy,' Grace said, ducking under Tash's arm and pressing her little body into her mother's side. 'What's wrong?'

'Nothing.' Tash was smiling but her eyes were glassy.

They had only just realised what their father had done. He hadn't told them the story that had occurred but the story they'd needed to hear.

'Trust him to do that to us,' Eve shook her head. 'Do we even have eight grape varieties on this property?'

In that moment, their mother walked in with Heath hot on her heels. 'No, love, there are nine,' she said. She looked very stately in a pale pink lace skirt-suit, a dignified string of pearls about her neck. Her hair had been curled and stylishly framed her pale face.

'Mum!' The Maxwell sisters let go of each other to embrace her.

'Where were you?' Eve demanded. 'I couldn't find you anywhere.'

'I was in the garden, just soaking in some of your father's presence. I also got this from his study.' Her eyes glistened slightly as she held up a long box to Eve. 'Your father knew he wouldn't be here for your wedding. So he left this for you, darling. So that you would know that he's with you on this day just the same.'

Phoebe held her breath as Eve took the box and slowly opened it. On a bed of white velvet lay a delicate gold bracelet of a fine link design, studded with small sapphire stones.

'It's gorgeous.'

'Not as gorgeous as you.' Anita reached up and pulled her down to her level so she could kiss her forehead and then both her cheeks.

Tash sniffed and wiped away a stray tear.

'Are you okay?' Phoebe whispered.

'Yeah, fine,' Tash nodded quickly. 'I've just seen that bracelet before.'

As Phee looked about the room at the rest of her family, she realised that if their father was looking down right now he would be smiling because everything that he had wanted, everything that she had promised him three years ago had come to pass. Her family was no longer broken, they were stronger than ever and she could see only happiness in their futures.

'All right then,' Anita pulled away from Eve. 'I better let you girls finish up. Don't keep Adonis waiting, Eve. He's nervous as anything already, poor dear.'

'I won't,' Eve nodded, as Phoebe helped her put on her new bracelet.

Her mother, Heath and Grace disappeared out the door and she turned to her teary sisters. 'So now thanks to Dad I've got something blue and new. What about something old and borrowed?'

'Well,' Tash suggested with a wink, 'I could always lend you some of my lingerie again.'

'No way.' Eve held up her hand. 'That got me in enough trouble last time.'

'Besides, you shouldn't be lending out stuff like that to anyone who asks,' Phoebe protested. 'Lingerie is very personal.'

'Here, here,' Eve put in sternly.

'Of course,' Tash assured them, 'I wouldn't do it for just anybody. But sisters are different. Especially the Maxwell sisters.'

Phoebe and Eve smiled back at her.

'For sure,' Eve confirmed. 'Club members only.'

Tash grinned. 'Precisely.'

# Author's Note

This story is set in the South-West region of Western Australia in a quiet town called Yallingup, an Aboriginal word meaning 'place of love'. It is one of my favourite parts of Australia, to relax, to eat, to drink and to be with family.

Yallingup shares in a slice of the Margaret River wine region, an area encompassing several townships, bounded to the east by the Leeuwin–Naturaliste Ridge, between Cape Naturaliste and Cape Leeuwin, and to the west by the Indian Ocean. Some of the other towns are mentioned in this book, Dunsborough, Busselton and Margaret River to name a few. The region is most famous for its world-class wine, surfing and gorgeous natural limestone caves surrounded by beautiful jarrah-marri forest. It's a very popular holiday destination for people living in Perth or indeed anywhere around the world.

For me, setting my book here was a no-brainer. The beauty of the landscape, the romance of the winemakers and the truly Australian feel of the surrounds made it the ideal place for me to drop the mad Maxwells of Tawny Brooks Estate.

While I wanted to keep the book as real as possible for readers, I did have to invent a few places and just wanted to

clarify which areas are fictional. Rickety Twigg road, which cuts from Bussell Highway to Yallingup, is not a real road, nor are any of the estates mentioned on it, such as the Oak Hills Winery. This road and the surrounds, however, are based on Wildwood Road – the real gateway to Yallingup.

All other wineries mentioned in this novel, other than the ones on Rickety Twigg road, are real and definitely worth visiting if you're ever down this way. Similarly, Canal Rocks is a true natural landform and a gorgeous spot to enjoy Australia's beautiful coastline.

The Wildwood Bakery in Dunsborough is a fictional business – however, with a sense of the real one in mind. There has been a bakery in Dunsborough since the 1940s, famous for its pastries and delicious bread, which no tourist in town has ever been able to walk past without sampling. Ben, the young man the Maxwell sisters meet when they visit the bakery, is also a real winemaker from Cowaramup, another town in the area. He has been my 'go-to guru' for all things wine and vine. You can taste his organic label Blind Corner in many restaurants throughout Australia, including Rockpool in Perth, Sydney and Melbourne. Please do. Trust me, it's good! I relied on some of Ben's biodynamic philosophies for my character John Maxwell and his eccentric but highly successful growing techniques at Tawny Brooks. These philosophies allow for an organic, natural and sustainable wine with unique and diverse flavours to fall in love with. To learn more about Ben and his wine, or wine in general check out www.blindcorner.com.au.

Other than fabulous wine, great food and gorgeous scenery, I wasn't just aiming to give my readers somewhere to go for their next holiday. This book, at its core, is about family and about growing up and growing old. Not just that sense of becoming an adult from a teenager or retiring after many years of labour, but the idea that every time we go through a milestone in our life, it changes us. As we change, the people who love us have to grow with us, too. These people, our sisters,

our mothers, our fathers, our husbands, our children, all put their own footprint on our lives and shape us into who we are. And it's in developing and nurturing these relationships that we become stronger and, in turn, learn more about ourselves.

This is the message of my novel and I hope in all the Maxwell family drama, secrets and humour, it will shine through.

All my love to you and yours,

Loretta Hill

# Acknowledgements

There are so many people I need to thank for their contribution to *The Maxwell Sisters*, which has been a project I've been working towards for quite some time.

Firstly, I must thank my dedicated team of critique partners, Nicola E. Sheridan, Karina Coldrick and Marlena Pereira, who generously fit me around their own work and writing to give me invaluable insights into my manuscript. I am so grateful for their feedback and support. Thank you, guys.

I must thank Ben Gould, my very own winemaking expert from the Margaret River wine region, who generously provided his time and advice whenever I needed it. Without his knowledge and expertise, this book would not have the authenticity that it does. Thank you so much, Ben, for your kindness and patience, particularly with reading my manuscript and sending me notes. I cannot stress more how appreciative I am.

Similarly, to my good friend and fabulous chef, Natalie Sansom, who really helped me with the details of Eve's career, design of the Tawny Brooks restaurant and all other aspects of a chef's life. Thank you so much for answering all my questions. I know there were a lot of them!

Then, of course, there's my wonderful cousin-in-law, Dr Raphael Chee, who kindly helped me understand bowel cancer, particularly how it progresses in a patient and how to treat it. This really helped me with the timeline of the novel and I can't thank him enough for his expert knowledge and his readiness to give it in this instance. Hugs!

Thanks to everyone at Random House Australia who was involved in getting this book on the shelf, especially my publisher, Beverley Cousins, editor, Elena Gomez, and publicists, Jessica Malpass and Lucy Inglis. Your enthusiasm is such a pleasure to work with. Thank you also to my fabulous agent, Clare Forster, for her support during this time.

As a mum, with four children under seven, sometimes the most difficult thing is finding the time to write. I literally have an army of people helping me get through my week. Thank you to my mum, Aunty Moira and Uncle Richard for all the babysitting you do. Thank you to my dad, who has been picking up and dropping my kids at school every day. What a hero! To my mother-in-law, Shirley, who came to live with us (very bravely) for a week whilst I wrote non-stop for seven days to catch up on my lagging word count. To my wonderful husband, Todd, for taking time off work on several occasions to look after the kids while I retreated to the library. And finally to our nanny, Rebecca Laing, to whom the children have grown so attached. Thank you for being so flexible with your time and for bringing my children so much joy. I couldn't have found someone better than you.

As for my children, Luke, James, Beth and Michael, the brightest little stars in my life, thank you for your love, understanding and patience.